Jenny Holmes has been writing fiction for children and adults since her early twenties, having had series of children's books adapted for both the BBC and ITV.

Jenny was born and brought up in Yorkshire. After living in the Midlands and travelling widely in America, she returned to Yorkshire and brought up her two daughters with a spectacular view of the moors and a sense of belonging to the special, still undiscovered corners of the Yorkshire Dales.

One of three children brought up in Harrogate, Jenny's links with Yorkshire stretch back through many generations via a mother who served in the Land Army during the Second World War and pharmacist and shop-worker aunts, back to a maternal grandfather who worked as a village blacksmith and pub landlord. Her great-aunts worked in Edwardian times as seamstresses, milliners and upholsterers. All told stories of life lived with little material wealth but with great spirit and independence, where a sense of community and family loyalty were fierce – sometimes uncomfortable but nev~~~ ~~ ~~~ the voices that echo dow~ ope is that their strength y of the characters repres

Also by Jenny Holmes

The Mill Girls of Albion Lane
The Shop Girls of Chapel Street
The Midwives of Raglan Road

and published by Corgi Books

THE TELEPHONE GIRLS

Jenny Holmes

CORGI BOOKS

TRANSWORLD PUBLISHERS
61–63 Uxbridge Road, London W5 5SA
www.penguin.co.uk

Transworld is part of the Penguin Random House group of companies
whose addresses can be found at global.penguinrandomhouse.com

First published in Great Britain in 2017 by Corgi Books
an imprint of Transworld Publishers

A CIP catalogue record for this book
is available from the British Library.

ISBN
9780552177634

Typeset in 11.5/14pt New Baskerville ITC by Jouve (UK), Milton Keynes
Printed and bound in Great Britain by Clays Ltd, Bungay, Suffolk

Penguin Random House is committed to a sustainable
future for our business, our readers and our planet. This book is made
from Forest Stewardship Council® certified paper.

MIX
Paper from
responsible sources
FSC® C018179

1 3 5 7 9 10 8 6 4 2

For Kate and Eve

CHAPTER ONE

'*And* stretch, and twist, and relax!' Ruth Ridley ended her Friday-evening exercise class with a sing-song flourish. She clapped her hands to release fifty members of the Women's League of Health and Beauty from an hour of choreographed kicking, bending, flexing and twirling under her firm command.

The women broke ranks and split into small groups.

'Phew!' Norma Haig rested a bare, warm arm along the shoulder of her friend, Millicent Jones. 'I'm all in.'

'Yes. You'd think we'd have had enough of *mein Führer* during work hours without having her bark at us in our leisure time as well!' Millicent took a step back and slyly mimicked a *Heil Hitler* salute. Looking statuesque in her black satin knickers and sleeveless white blouse, she took hold of Norma's hand and dragged her towards the cloakroom of Overcliffe Assembly Rooms where they began to get changed into their day clothes along with the other members of their class.

'League of Health and blooming Beauty.' Norma laid it on thick. She was smaller and slighter than Millicent and felt the pace of the exercise class more keenly. 'All this leaping out of bed at six in the morning, plunging your face in cold water and exercising for half an hour each day on top of coming to this keep-fit class once a week – it can't be good for you.'

Millicent took off her blouse and slipped a lace-edged satin petticoat over her head. Then she discreetly slid the elasticated waistband of her over-knickers over her hips, letting them fall around her ankles before neatly stepping out of them. 'You know what they say: "Movement is Life"!' She quoted the League's motto with an arched eyebrow.

'Along with shaving your armpits and stuffing a clean hankie up your left knicker leg,' Norma muttered. She was new to this lark and wasn't sure she liked it – especially getting changed in public, where all and sundry caught sight of the frayed straps of her brassiere and the worn elastic of her suspender belt. She got changed shyly and quickly, aware that the striking, dark-haired girl on her right had subsided on to the bench and was dabbing her eyes with her regulation handkerchief.

'Cheer up, Clare,' Millicent advised their unhappy neighbour as she deftly pulled her printed cotton dress over her head then did up the buttons. 'The way we're going, we'll all turn into strapping Nordic specimens like the sainted Prunella Stack, leader of this great movement we've signed up to.'

'Not me. I'm not built like that, no matter how many contortions Miss Ridley puts us through.' Norma stepped in with a comment that acknowledged her own limitations. She was slender and supple – just how her young man Douglas Greenwood said he liked her. 'What's up?' she asked the crying girl.

'Nothing. Don't mind me.' Clare Bell blew her nose and sat up straight.

'That's right. Don't let Ruth Ridley upset you – she's not worth it.'

Millicent was ready to leave but she dropped a few crumbs of comfort into her old school friend's lap. 'Anyhow, she only picks on you 'cos she's jealous of the way you look – the crabby old thing.'

Norma agreed. Clare was one of those shimmeringly beautiful girls, with dark, almond-shaped eyes and creamy skin, plus a glossy cap of dark hair and a puckered, cupid's-bow mouth that looked as if it was permanently waiting to be kissed. On top of which, she could have given Prunella Stack a run for her money as 'the most physically perfect girl in the world'. 'You managed to kick your leg higher than me by a long way,' she reassured her. 'And you're a dab hand at twirling those silk ribbons in time to the music.'

Clare took a deep breath then rallied enough to get dressed, taking off her blouse and putting on a peach-coloured dress of clinging jersey knit. 'Ta. I reckon I'll keep the pledge a bit longer, then.'

3

Millicent gave a satisfied nod. 'That's the ticket – you come along next week for another dose. Norma and me, we're walking back to town over the Common. Shall we wait for you?'

'No, you go ahead.' Clare perched a cream beret on the back of her head and slipped her hands into a pair of matching lace gloves. 'I have to meet— That's to say . . . someone is waiting outside for me.'

'Ooh, a mystery man! Who can it be?' Millicent was about to plunge into a pool of delicious speculation when she noticed that Clare had coloured up and seemed on the verge of tears once more. So she brought herself up short, said goodbye and hurried Norma out of the building while Clare lingered in front of the mirror with her powder compact and puff.

'Married!' was Millicent's one-word verdict as she scanned the pavement for Clare's secret beau.

Norma laughed and held on to her straw hat in the stiff breeze that blew across the open Common. 'What makes you say that?'

'It's a racing certainty. Why else would Clare be afraid to name him?'

Norma was well aware that her worldly friend had more experience in these matters. After all, Millicent was currently 'carrying on' with Harold Buckley, a married father of two. Still, she put up an argument in Clare's defence. 'There could be a dozen reasons. We don't even know that it's a man. And if it is, it could easily be her brother or her father.'

Narrowing her eyes, Millicent shook her head and fixed her attention on a black Morris Cowley saloon – the latest model – parked on the far side of the road. The setting sun glinted on the windscreen, obscuring the driver behind the wheel, but when Clare emerged from the hall and hurriedly crossed the road, he leaned over to open the passenger door for her and Millicent and Norma caught sight of a man wearing a brown trilby hat and tan leather driving gloves. 'See!' Millicent gloated.

The door clicked shut and the car pulled away smoothly from the kerb, giving them a glimpse of the driver's handsome profile.

'Well, good luck to her,' Norma murmured with a twinge of envy. She and Douglas could hardly afford an old tandem bike to carry them from A to B, let alone a gleaming new motor car. 'Come on – let's get a move on.'

She and Millicent set off across the Common that overlooked the sloping rows of terraced houses and cramped courtyards of their grimy mill town. The identical dwellings clung to steep hillsides and formed narrow streets uninterrupted by trees or greenery of any kind. The roofs were grey slate, the walls built of millstone grit, and all were dominated by a small forest of mill chimneys that lined the canal snaking through the valley bottom. Oldroyd's, Kingsley's and Calvert's amongst others – the three-storey woollen mills stood as testament to the glory days of the British Empire when looms rattled and clacked continuously, bobbins turned and overlookers ruled over the lives of weavers, weft men and burlers with a rod of iron.

Now, in these slack years following the great slump of the 1920s, the workers in the mills were on three days a week if they were lucky – the warpers and twisters, the reaching-in people, the perchers and packers, all taking home wages that barely kept their families clothed and fed. Everyone was now forced to make ends meet, while the once smartly painted houses grew shabby and the cobbled courtyards grew weed-strewn, cluttered with broken prams, rotting planks, rusty bicycle frames and stinking, overflowing dustbins.

'Will I see you at work tomorrow?' Norma asked Millicent as they came to the top of Albion Lane where she lived with her mother and two sisters, Ethel and Ivy. Millicent had further to go to her lodgings in Heaton Yard off Ada Street.

'Yes, I'm on the early shift. I'll be at my switchboard at eight o'clock sharp.' Millicent looked at her watch and saw that she had an hour to get home and changed for her usual Friday-night rendezvous with Harold. 'I have to dash,' she added hastily. 'Cheerio, Norma, I'll see you tomorrow.'

Norma paused at the corner to watch her friend hurry on. There were lots of things about Millicent that she admired – the fact that she was confident and unfailingly cheerful, ready to laugh at herself for being an 'old maid' at the age of twenty-five; her tall, curvaceous figure, which made her stand out, and her unruly raven hair and rich, hazel-brown eyes. But Norma's strait-laced upbringing led her to take a dim view of Millicent's illicit liaison with Harold.

Maybe it's me, she said to herself as she turned down Albion Lane and felt her feet start to drag. Tonight Douglas was on duty at the police station on Canal Road so she would have an uneventful evening ahead of her, darning and mending alongside Ivy and Ethel. *Maybe I'm too narrow-minded and set in my ways.*

She was just twenty-one, the youngest of three sisters, all still living at home, whereas Millicent had branched out and led a seemingly fearless, adventurous life. *On the bright side, I do my best to keep up with fashions and so on, and I love my job – I can't deny it.*

For six days a week Norma took a tram or a bus into town, alighting eagerly in City Square and making her way through the crowds, past Marks & Spencer and Timothy White's to George Street and the brand-new telephone exchange built in the style of an Egyptian temple – all smooth lines and zig-zag decoration on the stone façade. Revolving glass doors gave access to a marble entrance hall complete with cloakroom off to the right, and from there she entered directly into the long, narrow workroom with its banks of switchboards. These high black panels featured rows of sockets and winking lights with a table in front of each operator that had

7

columns and keys, lamps and pairs of cords, front and rear for each circuit.

'Come on, girls – take the lights,' supervisors like Ruth Ridley would chide as they patrolled the central aisle – martinets in tweed skirts and prim, high-collared blouses with pork-pie frills. It was two years since Norma had passed her entry test with flying colours and come to work as a junior in the George Street exchange. She'd worked up to her Full Efficiency Test in record time and was now able to handle route and rate queries with aplomb before flicking the switch to connect the caller to their requested recipient.

I know I'm good at what I do, she told herself as she walked down Albion Lane and heard the raucous sounds drifting through the open door of the Green Cross pub. There was piano music and laughter, the chink of glasses and the sound of men greeting each other in the doorway. *I work hard and I toe the line. Isn't that good enough?*

No, she thought with a sigh as she went up three stone steps and opened the door to number 7. *Not when I set myself alongside Millicent.*

Inside the house, the wireless in the alcove next to the chimney breast was turned on and big-band music played softly in the background – an up-to-the-minute contrast with the airless, overstuffed atmosphere of the room. The black, cast-iron range was decorated with a row of polished horse brasses, the mantelpiece lined with three china shepherdesses and a lacquered tea caddy. A wall clock ticked next to a WI calendar showing Yorkshire Dales scenery – blossom trees for this month of May 1936, against a sunny background – and next to that was a small shelf stacked with dog-eared books.

'Here she comes – the body beautiful!' Sitting at the kitchen table, Ivy Haig glanced up from her darning and winked at Ethel.

Across the table, Ethel didn't bother to look up from the newspaper headlines. 'Wallis Simpson is visiting Windsor Great Park again,' she reported with a disapproving frown. 'Honestly, that woman – she's nothing but a common adventuress, painting her fingernails and drinking cocktails the way she does. Why can't the king see that?'

'Why not indeed?' their mother Hetty said from her fireside chair, arms folded and taking it easy after another long day working as a weaver at Oldroyd's. She took no notice of Norma, who put down her bag and removed her straw hat.

'He will soon,' Ivy opined, needle poised.

'Knock on wood.' Ethel rapped her knuckles against her forehead.

'He won't.' In a flat, world-weary tone Hetty struck the last contradictory note. A lifetime of observing human failings had turned Norma's mother into a thoroughgoing cynic. 'You mark my words – Wally has pulled the wool over poor King Edward's eyes good and proper.'

*

9

On her solitary way home Millicent thought through what she would wear for her tryst with Harold. She would definitely change out of her cotton frock into something that accentuated her curves – perhaps the purple satin dress with the daring halter neckline, teamed with a cultured-pearl necklace and earrings. Though tempted to add a glittering marcasite brooch in the shape of a bouquet of flowers that Harold had given her for her twenty-first birthday, she decided that this would be gilding the lily.

She came to Ada Street – a road that swept downhill even more steeply than the rest, with houses that were a cut above the basic terraced cottages of Albion Lane and Raglan Road. Here, each house sported an individually carved lintel above its doorway and there were iron railings to either side of the stone steps. Inside, there was a sitting room as well as a kitchen and two first-floor bedrooms instead of one. Still, there was neglect in the air even here. Paint peeled from doors and grass grew through cracks in the pavement. Then, when you turned off the street down a narrow alley – the locals called them ginnels – the situation became quite dire. Black slime clung to the alley walls even in summer and moss coated the paving slabs, while in Heaton Yard itself there was hardly a house without cracked or missing window panes. Doors hung off their hinges and ragged washing was draped limply from lines that criss-crossed the yard.

'Now then – how's my little ray of sunshine?'

Walter Blackburn called from his top step. His stooped, ancient figure was a fixture here, come rain or shine, and he insisted on using the hackneyed nicknames for his neighbours – 'Chalky' White the Green Cross barman at number 2, 'Dusty' Miller the unemployed joiner at number 8 and telephone girl Millicent, his 'little ray of sunshine', at number 10.

'I'm tickety-boo, thanks, Walter.' She hurried on past the dustbins and the outbuilding that housed a privy shared by the twenty-odd inhabitants of the yard. She forgot her rule of not breathing in as she passed its open door and got the full stench in her nostrils.

'What's the rush?' the old man called after her. A worn tweed jacket hung off his scarecrow frame and baggy grey trousers concealed rickety legs. 'Don't tell me. Who's the lucky man, I'd like to know?'

'Wouldn't you just?' Millicent threw him a smile and was about to disappear through her door when she heard her name being called and she turned to see Cynthia Ambler emerge from the ginnel. Her heart sank.

'I'm glad I caught you,' a breathless Cynthia began as she approached. Though nineteen years old, her wavy fair hair and slight figure made her look younger, as did the girlish belted mac and dark beret that she wore, whatever the weather. Her voice was light and her movements conveyed schoolgirl apprehension. 'I'm afraid it's that time of the week again.'

'Rent day,' Millicent groaned. Grudgingly she fished

in her purse for the three shillings and sixpence that Cynthia wanted. 'Did you ever see a less likely-looking rent collector?' she remarked to Walter as she handed over the money. 'It's as if a Girl Guide has come bob-a-jobbing and puts her hand out for payment after she's cleaned your windows for you.'

'Aye, and I've already told her she'll have a long wait to get her pound of flesh out of me,' Walter growled. 'I'm not paying another penny until William Brooks stumps up the cash to mend my leaking downpipe. If I've told him once I've told him a hundred times.'

'Uncle William is poorly.' Cynthia explained away their landlord's failings, her face flushed with embarrassment. 'Ta, Millicent. Anyway, Mr Blackburn, my cousin Bert will be taking over from me, starting at the beginning of next week. I'll get him to pass on the message about your leak.'

Millicent was intrigued by this piece of news. It was common knowledge that their miserly landlord had taken in his niece straight after she left school – when was that, about five years ago now? An only child, Cynthia had left home and gone over to Hadley to work without pay as live-in housemaid to the ailing skinflint. Soon after she'd moved in, he'd landed the job of rent collecting on her unlikely shoulders – again without financial reward. 'Is old man Brooks finally letting you off the hook?'

Cynthia blushed again then managed an awkward smile. 'I've got myself a new job,' she explained. 'It follows on from me learning bookkeeping and shorthand at the Workers' Education Institute.'

'Does it indeed?' Millicent decided there was more to this little slip of a thing than met the eye. 'What does your Uncle William have to say about that?'

'He doesn't know yet. I'm building up to telling him. Anyway, it just so happens that Bert is coming up to fourteen now.' Cynthia let a silence develop – there was no need to say that the old man obviously saw advantages in the boy's muscular strength and cocky air when set against Cynthia's innocent appearance. 'I'll carry on living in and cleaning the house for him, though, even after I start my job.'

'Which is what?' Millicent asked quickly. She was running late now but Cynthia's story interested her.

'I answered an advert to train as a telephonist. Then I took the entry test.'

The awkward reply amazed Millicent. 'Whereabouts will you work – at George Street?'

Cynthia nodded. 'I reckon it's a big step up for me.'

'You're telling me!' From unpaid skivvy and reluctant rent collector to telephone girl in one mighty bound – Millicent was impressed. 'And talk about coincidence – that's where I work too.'

'I know. I saw you there when the supervisor showed me round.'

Ah yes, the supes. Millicent secretly wondered how Cynthia would cope with Ruth Ridley in particular and the relentless speech training that would go into rounding out the girl's flat Yorkshire vowels and force her to put proper 't's and 'g's on the ends of her words. Moreover, how would she cope with 'Adolf's' military-style commands? 'Take the lights. Come on, girls. Chop-chop!' She pictured the supervisor marching up and down, ready to take aim and fire at the rookie operator's smallest faults.

'You were busy at your switchboard – you didn't notice me,' Cynthia added.

'Well, you'll see me again on Monday.' Making an instant decision to take the new girl under her wing, Millicent gave her a broad smile. 'Don't worry – you won't be let loose on our customers to start with. They'll put you to work as a home and address clerk – bringing the list of subscribers up to date.'

Cynthia seemed relieved. 'Is that what they do with beginners?'

'That and making the tea, being at everyone's beck and call, running after the supes whenever they click their fingers.'

'I'm used to that, at any rate.' A wry smile flickered across Cynthia's face.

Another glance at her watch told Millicent that she was really cutting it fine. 'As for Ruth Ridley, our senior supe – I hope you've got a thick hide.'

Cynthia laughed uneasily. In fact, as an only child brought up by chapel-going older parents, she was unusually sensitive to criticism and had spent her school life and young adulthood working hard to avoid it.

'In Ruth's case, her bite is definitely as bad as her

14

bark,' Millicent quipped. *Best for Cynthia to be prepared*, she thought.

Walter cackled from his doorstep. 'She's a card, is Millicent. Don't you believe a word of what she says.'

Nevertheless, a knot formed in Cynthia's stomach at the prospect. 'I'd better keep my head down, then.'

'You'll be all right. I'll keep a weather eye out. So will Norma – Norma Haig. She was trained by the dragon a couple of years back, so she'll be able to give you a few tips.'

'Ta,' Cynthia said with a weak smile that didn't disguise an air of panic as she slipped Millicent's rent money into the leather satchel slung from her shoulder.

'And now I really do have to dash,' Millicent said, disappearing indoors.

Back on Albion Lane, Norma endured her sisters' carping and her mother's nagging for as long as she could.

'How much do you pay for those so-called Health and Beauty classes of yours?' Ethel wanted to know as Norma settled into a bout of mending at the kitchen table. At twenty-six Ethel was considered well and truly on the shelf – and all because she'd let herself go, according to Ivy, who was trimmer and smarter. Ethel had never cared about her appearance, preferring to wear her long, straight hair in an old-fashioned bun and eating whatever she fancied regardless of the inches slowly but surely being added to her waist and hips.

'It's sixpence a go,' Norma told her. Her task tonight was to turn the collar on her mother's white blouse, putting the frayed side out of sight. She unpicked the seam with care then turned it and reached for pins to fix it back in place.

'And how many are there in the class?' Ivy wanted to know. Trained as a bookkeeper, she prided herself on having a head for figures.

'Fifty.'

'That's one pound five shillings going straight into Ruth Ridley's pocket,' Ivy said with a low, envious whistle. Unlike Ethel, twenty-four-year-old Ivy was ambitious to better herself, though her current wage as a shorthand typist at the Yorkshire Bank wasn't high enough to allow her to leave home just yet. She and Norma both took after their late father, Edward Haig, who had been small and upright, with a thick head of dark hair that had made him look young for his age.

'No, that's not right,' Norma objected. 'A lot of that money goes to the League. Then there's the hire of the hall. I'd be surprised if Ruth gets more than five shillings out of it.'

'Still,' Ivy noted. Five shillings for an hour's work was not bad.

The three sisters went on sewing while their mother complained about her aching feet and her failure to get to Clifton Market in time to scoop up the end-of-the-day bargains. 'I missed the cheap sausages from Maynard's stall,' she complained. 'He'd shut up shop by the time I got there. That's why we had to use up the leftover ham from yesterday for our tea.'

I wish I'd stopped in at the Green Cross on my way home, Norma thought. The company here left a lot to be desired. She stopped sewing and glanced up, first at Ivy with her hair in curlers and wearing a flowery, cross-over apron over her dark green work dress of dull crêpe de chine, then at Ethel whose broad, homely features were done no favours by the horn-rimmed glasses she wore for close work. 'Friday night, and aren't we having fun,' she said with a resentful sigh.

Douglas was walking his beat and she was stuck at home listening to this. Others were out on the town, taking in a flick at the Victory or dancing the night away at one of the new jazz clubs. Take Millicent, for instance: this very minute she'd be dolling herself up for an evening out with Harold. Illicit thrills or not, that had to be a darned sight better than sitting here with needle and thread, blocking her ears to her mother's grumbles with only the prospect of another busy day at the switchboard to cheer her up.

CHAPTER TWO

Millicent liked the choosing-what-to-wear and getting-ready part of her regular assignations with Harold. She loved the perfumed smell of her powder compact as she flipped it open to dab her nose with the cool, flat puff then approve of the gleam of her jet-black hair in the small, round mirror.

What she didn't like was the hanging around on street corners – a different one each time – wondering whether or not Harold would show up. Standing in the shadows clutching her handbag in front of her for protection while various men eyed her up and down was a kind of self-inflicted torture. Would he keep his promise and turn up bearing a small gift of chocolates or nylons, or would something have happened at home to prevent him? His wife, Doris, might fancy going out for a change. There would be a babysitter already arranged and no getting out of it for Harold, who would play the dutiful husband and take Doris off to the pictures to see the latest Fred Astaire musical, or perhaps to the working men's club on Westgate Road, where rules were occasionally relaxed and ladies were allowed to join their husbands for a drink.

Which will it be tonight? she wondered as she hovered in the entrance to the corporation baths on Canal Road. After a few changes of mind, she'd settled on the purple dress and matching pearl necklace and earrings, teamed up with a loose cream jacket, sling-back sandals and jaunty pill-box hat. This smart appearance drew favourable comments and wolf whistles from passers-by.

'Hello, Millicent.' Dusty Miller, her lanky neighbour from Heaton Yard, broke free from a group of friends on their way into town. 'My, you're a sight for sore eyes.'

So much for the anonymity of meeting Harold close to the town centre, she thought. 'Hello, Dusty.' She gave a frosty smile then glanced up the road as if on the lookout for a tram.

'You're not going swimming in that get-up, are you?' His quip drew guffaws and lewd comments from his gang.

'The swimming baths are closed for the night, in case you hadn't noticed.' Her heart beat faster as she saw Harold alight from a bus across the street. He'd been able to come after all. But he'd better wait a while before he approached her, otherwise their secret would be out. Luckily he spotted Dusty and wisely hung back until Millicent's neighbour left off teasing her and his down-at-heel pals dragged him away.

'There you are!' Millicent greeted Harold with a petulant pout.

'What? I'm bang on time, aren't I?' He gave her a peck on the cheek. Smart as usual in blazer and twill trousers, with his dark brown hair parted down one side and slicked back with brilliantine, he pretended not to notice her bad mood, taking her by the elbow and steering her down the steps on to the pavement. 'I thought we'd go for a drink in town – somewhere nice and quiet.'

That goes without saying, Millicent thought, for some reason struggling to regain her usual happy-go-lucky air. 'How about the King's Head off City Square?'

'Yes, that won't be busy on a Friday night,' he agreed. He too was on edge, his lean, clean-shaven face looking gaunt and drawn, his grey eyes avoiding contact with Millicent's.

The King's Head was tucked away behind the new Woolworths building, down a side street, next to a Lyons' Corner House. Thronged on weekday evenings with dispirited bank clerks and shopworkers, weekends saw the pub's regulars drift off to watering holes on the outskirts of town, leaving only a smattering of customers at the cramped bar.

Millicent and Harold walked side by side along Canal Road, talking about their weeks. Always the gentleman, which was one of the things that had attracted her to him in the first place, he stayed closest to the busy road, shielding her from the traffic. 'Oldroyd has laid off twenty-five workers this week,' he told her. 'Mainly from the spinning shed. Everyone's wondering who's going to be next for the chop.'

'Your head's not on the line, is it?'

'Not yet,' he said through gritted teeth. As mill manager, he was Joseph Oldroyd's right-hand man. The job came with an end-of-terrace house – three storeys, with a patch of garden that was tended by Oldroyd's own gardener. The house overlooked a small park laid out by old Josiah Oldroyd in that patrician way that the Victorians had – *mens sana in corpore sano* – a space for recreation, with its bandstand and artificial pond for sailing toy boats. 'They say things will be on the up if the country has to gear up for another war and the government comes to us for cloth for the extra uniforms.'

'Don't wish that upon us.' In spite of the warm evening, Millicent shivered then grew determined to change the subject. They crossed City Square, past the bright entrance to the Odeon, then the imposing entrance to the Spiritualist church where a billboard at the foot of broad stone steps advertised a forthcoming talk by the famous medium Estelle Roberts. 'How about getting us tickets for that?' she suggested brightly. 'Shouldn't you like to know what the future holds for us?'

'It's not the future that lot are interested in,' he pointed out with a sardonic wink. Now aged thirty-eight, Harold had caught the end of the Great War. He'd been enlisted into the army aged eighteen and sent out to Belgium in the winter of 1916 where he'd witnessed the aftermath of the bloodbath they called the Battle of the Somme. Thousands of young lives had been wasted in that sea of mud – and still, twenty years later, their mothers and sweethearts visited these mediums in their thousands in the desperate hope of contacting their poor, lost boys.

But still, the future . . . Millicent lingered by the billboard, wondering what it would hold. Would she and Harold still be going on like this in five years' time, say, or ten – meeting in secret each week, once in a while risking a weekend away if Doris took it into her head to scoop up the children and take them to her sister's place in the seaside town of Saltburn? Might he actually keep his promise to leave his wife once the kids were grown up? That was looking a long way ahead, she knew. Meanwhile, they snatched their pleasure where they could.

Harold paused at the entrance to the King's Head. 'A penny for them,' he said when she joined him and they went in together.

'They're not worth it,' she replied. The pub, unchanged for decades, was gaslit, with engraved mirrors lining the walls and a row of brass pump handles along the mahogany bar. Around the room were small, private booths where customers sat playing games of dominoes or chatting over pints of beer, their faces illuminated by the softly hissing, flickering mantels.

'What'll it be?' Harold asked Millicent as they approached the bar.

'Dubonnet and lemonade,' she decided. She caught the back view of a slender, dark-haired girl she thought she recognized but for a few seconds she couldn't place her. Then she noticed the good-looking man in a trilby hat sitting opposite her, who stared directly at Millicent and blatantly ignored whatever it was his earnest companion was telling him.

The girl glanced round and Millicent saw it was Clare Bell. Their eyes met fleetingly to acknowledge a shared, guilty secret then Clare turned away.

'Come on, let's sit over there,' Harold suggested as he handed Millicent her drink and led her towards a dimly lit corner. 'Tell me more about your week. I'm all ears.'

With the heavy satchel of rent money slung across her shoulder, Cynthia made her slow way home. She walked up the long hill out of town on to the moor road, leaning against a drystone wall on the summit and taking in the grand sight of Brimstone Rock in the far distance. There was no hurry, she told herself. Her Uncle William wouldn't be back yet from his Friday-teatime billiards session at the Village Institute, which gave her this precious time to herself and a chance to enjoy the view.

And what a view it was. Banks of heather rolled away on all sides, broken by outcrops of dark rock. Scattered sheep grazed on the windswept slopes, while speckled, long-beaked curlews rose into the air and soared, along with a clumsy pheasant that clattered its wings and rattled away at the sound of an approaching motorbike.

The motorbike slowed and stopped. Cynthia recognized the flat-capped rider as Leonard Andrews, an out-of-work gamekeeper who was rumoured to have turned his hand to poaching a few rabbits and pheasants from the Oldroyd estate where he'd once worked. That, and taking up odd jobs as a gardener, plus scratting for coal during the winter months, now filled up most of his time.

'Hop on,' he invited Cynthia with an affable smile.

She smiled back. 'Why not?' she said and took up position on the pillion seat.

'Hold tight,' he warned.

So Cynthia wrapped her arms around Leonard's waist and felt the bike begin to pick up speed. Soon they were swooping down into dips and rising again, the engine at full throttle, leaning into bends with the wind driving into their faces until at last they came to the village of Hadley with its straight main street backed by grey slag heaps and old mine workings, silent reminders of a once thriving community.

On the outskirts of the village, Cynthia tapped Leonard on the shoulder. 'You can drop me off here, thanks.'

He nodded and stopped next to the cricket club with its green and white pavilion and manicured pitch, putting both feet on the ground to steady the bike.

From here it was a short walk to a fork in the road

and the house where she lived so she slid nimbly to the ground. 'Ta very much, Leonard. That saved me a long walk.'

'Any time.' He nodded, opened the throttle and chugged on down the street.

Cynthia was exhilarated by the ride, but the spring in her step gradually faded as she drew closer to home – a detached Victorian villa named Moor View, set back from the road and shielded by iron railings atop a sturdy stone wall. The house itself had a central gabled porch with living rooms to either side, a kitchen to the back and three spacious bedrooms above, with an attic storey lit only by small skylights. This was Cynthia's cramped refuge from her uncle's seemingly endless demands. It was where she had until recently supposed that she would serve out her sentence until the point when the sickly old man, her mother's brother, eventually passed away.

She knew it was far from ideal – living in an attic and acting as a live-in maid without even the benefit of a proper wage. It was a lifestyle that most girls of her age had already rejected – the before-dawn cleaning of hearths and laying of new fires in kitchen and living rooms, followed by work with floor polish and duster ('Plenty of elbow grease,' the old man would bark), dustpan and brush ('Now then, Missy, you missed that bit of fluff under my bed') and back-breaking labour with washboard and mangle on a Monday ('Put some oomph into it, for pity's sake!').

Until January of that year it had seemed to Cynthia that she had no choice.

'Your uncle has been good to us,' her mother Beryl would remind Cynthia during visits home on her Sunday afternoons off. 'We couldn't have managed if William hadn't stepped in when he did.'

In his chair in the corner of the kitchen on Raglan Road, Cynthia's father Ellis would grow evermore silent. His empty pipe now rested in the hearth next to a tub of pipe cleaners and wooden spills – he went without smoking these days due to the cost of tobacco and the fact that he was no longer entitled to the dole money of seventeen shillings per week.

The empty pipe came to represent an empty life, Cynthia realized with a pang of pity. Ellis Ambler was a grey shadow next to the fireplace who had not 'been right' for years, unable to hold down his job as a letterpress printer due to poor timekeeping and absentmindedness. He'd tried his hand as a joiner but his unreliability had put paid to that too. A short spell as a loom cleaner at Kingsley's had ended the same way. Drifting, saying nothing, retreating from the world save for a weekly outing to the Wesleyan Chapel on Albion Lane, he'd grown thinner, greyer and evermore ghostly.

For her part, prim, trim Beryl had soldiered on. She kept everything to herself – the fact that Ellis was 'under the doctor' for his nerves, that she too suffered from bouts of gloom which even her faith in the teachings of John Wesley couldn't shift. Poverty ground her down in private, but in public she managed to put on a good face along with the cloche hat and coat with its fox-fur collar that she'd worn since 1925. She was very well, thank you, and yes, Ellis was very well too. Cynthia was still living out in Hadley, a lucky girl to have the protection and guidance of her uncle, William Brooks – such a grand house he had, with a proper garden and a view of the moors. Cynthia was doing well – very well. And she was a kind, clever girl to boot, thank goodness. Beryl didn't know what they would do without her.

It had all felt like a trap that Cynthia couldn't break out of. She loved her mother and father but not her uncle – she would never call the feelings that she had for him affection, let alone love. It wasn't the opposite, though – not hatred. The emotion was too dull and dreary for that, like the drip-drip-drip of petrifying water on the hats and gloves left in Old Mother Shipton's Wishing Well in Knaresborough that slowly turned objects to stone.

Uncle William had that effect without knowing it. Demands dripped from his mouth and they had to be met. He must have porridge for breakfast every morning at seven o'clock on the dot, except on Sunday when he would have bacon and eggs. Cynthia must go down to the newsagent in person to collect his newspaper because the delivery boy insisted on wrinkling and tearing it as he forced it through the narrow letterbox. And she must religiously keep accounts of every penny spent at Clifton Street Market on meat and vegetables.

Proving to be good with figures and trustworthy from the start, she was soon put in charge of collecting the rents from Heaton Yard – all without a word of praise or thanks.

'Walter Blackburn will be out on his ear if he's not careful,' he would grumble if the old man's rent didn't come in on time. Or, 'That Miller fellow at number eight is pushing his luck, expecting me to fettle the upstairs window frame for him. Isn't he a joiner when he's at home?'

Thickset and badly overweight, William's jowly face and plodding, gouty gait set Cynthia's nerves on edge on a daily basis. She escaped from the house whenever she could – to evening classes in bookkeeping for a start.

'What are you wasting your time on that for?' Uncle William had complained. 'A girl like you doesn't need to bother her head with the ins and outs of things.'

'It'll help me keep track of the rents,' she'd replied defensively. 'Who owes what and how far behind they are, and so on.'

Grudgingly he'd let her attend the Wednesday-evening class. He'd noticed a difference in his niece, a growing confidence, and he'd done his best to snuff it out. 'Don't forget – the stair rods still need polishing when you get back,' he'd call as she donned mac and beret in time to catch the half-past-six bus into town.

'I won't forget,' she'd reply on her way out. Fresh air filled her lungs, the seeds of secret ideas germinated in her brain.

The bookkeeping classes were held in town, in the Workers' Education building close to the telephone exchange on George Street. One night she spotted in its modern, brightly lit entrance a billboard advertising for telephonists. In the gloom of a late-March evening she'd crossed the road to read the details – no prior experience necessary, full training would be offered to successful applicants.

A telephone girl! Someone whose job it was to take incoming calls and flick mysterious switches, to plug jacks into sockets and connect two trunk lines. And woe betide you if you pressed the wrong talk key or lit up a lamp connecting the caller to the wrong end of the country. After all, these days telephone lines ran the length of the land from John O'Groats to Land's End, even under the Atlantic to America, for goodness' sake! A smartly dressed girl who was trained to talk clearly and politely, sitting in front of the switchboard with headset and speaking-horn. 'Hello, London. Hello, Manchester. Hello, Southampton.' A world away from floor polish and dustpans, from Hadley and Uncle William's drip-drip-drip.

Can I really do it? she asked herself on this Friday evening as she waited for her uncle to arrive home.

She had gone into the dining room, opened her satchel and spread out the week's rent money across the crimson chenille tablecloth when she heard the click of the front door and William's shuffling footsteps in the hallway.

He came into the room without saying a word, pushed her to one side and began to separate shillings from sixpences then three-penny bits from coppers, making small piles then clearing his throat before counting aloud and reaching a total. 'Seventeen shillings and sixpence.' He looked up enquiringly at Cynthia. 'Where's the rest?'

She felt her stomach lurch. 'Mr Blackburn said to tell you he wouldn't pay any more rent until you mended his downpipe.'

'We'll see about that.' Her uncle gave a scornful laugh then gathered the money together in a heap. 'You'll have to go back tomorrow and get him to stump up. Tell him there's a queue of people as long as my arm waiting to take his place in number four if he doesn't.'

Cynthia nodded but said nothing.

'You hear me?'

'Yes, Uncle.' A jolt of dislike passed through her, giving her the courage she needed to go on. 'By the way, there's something I've been meaning to mention.'

'Come on, then – spit it out.' He swept the rent money into a black metal cash box then turned the key in the lock.

Cynthia breathed in deeply and looked him in the eye. 'I've filled in an application form for a job.'

A look of alarm flickered across the old man's fleshy features, soon turning to distrust then irritation. 'What kind of a job?'

'As a trainee telephone girl.' She had to swallow hard but she held her own. 'In the George Street exchange. They accepted me. I start on Monday.'

He knitted his brows and stared angrily at her, the veins in his forehead bulging. 'Who put you up to that? Was it Beryl?'

'No. Mum doesn't know. You're the first person I've told.' Actually, the third if you counted Millicent Jones and old Walter Blackburn. 'Don't worry, I'll still find time to cook and keep house for you. And you'll have Bert to collect the rent in future.'

'A telephone girl?' The words tumbled around his mouth and emerged in a rising tone of mockery. 'What's that when it's at home?'

'It's someone who connects—'

'No, don't bother – I couldn't give a monkey's. They've seen you, have they – the people who'll pay your wages?'

'Yes, Uncle. I went for an interview.'

'And they liked you?' Mockery turned to disbelief and a shake of the head as he took in his niece's defiant stare.

Cynthia felt herself shrink. She was ten years old again, a fair-haired child with wide grey eyes who looked as if she would be blown over by a breath of wind, walking all the way from Raglan Road out to Hadley with a message from her mother. Could William please give Cynthia the money to pay for a pair of school shoes? Beryl didn't like to ask but the old ones were worn out beyond repair. It was a one-off. It wouldn't happen again. *Until the next time*, Cynthia had thought even back then.

Ten years old and painfully ashamed, wearing white socks that rode down out of sight and exposed her bony ankles, her pale face flushed with embarrassment as her uncle took out the black money box from his bureau and turned the key. For as long as she could remember she'd been beholden to a man she didn't like and for whom she had no respect.

'The worm has turned, eh?' Back in the here and now, he blinked then looked away to conceal his surprise before changing his tone back to his usual, low-level mockery. 'Well, Missy – let's hope the lad has his head screwed on when he takes over from you next week,' he muttered. 'But then, let's face it – it won't take a genius to fill your shoes.'

'Hold your horses!' It was Monday morning and Millicent shouted after Norma as they both crossed a crowded City Square, heading for work.

Norma dodged a bus that set off jerkily from its stop, hopping on to the kerb to wait for Millicent. A light drizzle felt cold on her face and she was glad that she'd decided to wear a coat over her flimsy Tricolene dress – a man-made material that tended to cling and turn see-through in the rain. 'Lovely weather for ducks,' she commented as Millicent joined her.

'Don't I know it?' Millicent wailed. 'Just look at my hair.'

'There's nothing wrong with your hair.' Norma was openly envious of her friend's raven mane. 'If you carry on moaning, I'll drag you into Sam Bower's at dinner time and make you have it all chopped off.'

As they passed the barber's shop with its red and white striped pole, Norma gave Millicent a dig with her elbow. She kept things light-hearted, avoiding the subject of Harold Buckley and indeed of men in general. After all, they'd had time during work on Saturday morning to gossip about Millicent and Harold's low-key night at the King's Head and Norma's boring evening in. Harold had gone on and on about problems at work, Millicent had reported. Then he'd moved on to the fact that both of his kids had bad cases of chickenpox and were off school, which put a strain on things at home that he could well do without. On top of which his football team had lost two–nil to Sheffield Wednesday the previous week and were now in danger of being relegated.

'I don't know what you see in him,' Norma had commented, in between connecting a local caller to a number in the capital – 'Hello, London – I have a new ticket, wanted as soon as possible' – and having to explain to another that their party line was busy.

'Hmm.' Millicent had apparently given the comment serious thought. 'What I see in Harold is something others can't see – not with his clothes on, at any rate.'

'Millicent!' A scandalized Norma's high-pitched squeak had attracted the attention of the weekend supervisor, Agnes Mercer – a small, brisk and darting woman who had gained the nickname 'Miss Mouse' because of her dull hair, brown eyes and dowdy clothes.

'Come on, girls!' Agnes's sharp glance as she swept down the central aisle had dampened their mirth. 'There are lights to take – chop-chop!'

So the weekend had come and gone without further events and now Millicent was grabbing Norma's arm and pulling her into the barber shop's doorway out of the rain.

'What are you doing? Who are we waiting for?' Norma demanded.

'For our new girl.' Millicent pointed to the figure of Cynthia Ambler alighting from a number 65 bus outside Marks & Spencer. 'I had a word with her on Friday and she told me that she was starting work at our place today. I just caught a glimpse of her face through the bus window. She looked scared to death, poor thing.'

Norma saw that it was true – the girl approaching the exchange seemed to be gathering her courage by taking deep breaths and looking fixedly at the revolving doors into the building. She was smaller than either Millicent or Norma and looked a good deal younger, easy to mistake for a shy schoolgirl in beret and mac, though her features were pretty enough and her head and neck had a graceful turn.

'I said we'd keep an eye on her.' Explaining how she came to know Cynthia, Millicent stepped out of the doorway and accosted her with a broad, welcoming smile. 'Hello there. Into the lions' den, eh?'

The newcomer smiled nervously and nodded, allowing Millicent to slip an arm through hers and lead her up the wide steps.

'This is Norma Haig. I mentioned her to you.'

Norma came up on Cynthia's other side and all three shuffled through the revolving door together. 'Hello, Cynthia. Don't worry – you'll soon get the hang of things. Here's the cloakroom where we all put our coats. You can hang your hat here as well, but don't risk leaving anything valuable in your pockets. There's a ladies' toilet through here and a washbasin and mirror if ever you want to run a comb through your hair or touch up your face.'

Behind Cynthia's back Millicent gave Norma a poke in the ribs. Clearly Cynthia wasn't one for rouge and lipstick. Cynthia caught the sly move in the mirror, realized its meaning and blushed. This was certainly a new and alien world she was entering into.

'Well, well – who have we here?' Bright as a button, fellow telephonist Molly Scaife breezed into work. Eyeing Cynthia as she took off her coat then went briskly to her switchboard, she summed up the newcomer to Brenda Locke as someone who wouldn't say boo to a goose.

'Who wouldn't say boo?' Brenda took off her headset so that she could tune in to the latest gossip.

'The new girl. Hush – here she comes now.'

All eyes turned as Cynthia entered the room, flanked by Millicent and Norma. Millicent directed her towards Ruth Ridley who was sitting at her desk in the small office at the far end of the long central aisle.

Cynthia felt her heart jump within her chest. It was the moment she'd been building up to ever since the offer of a job had landed on the doormat. Recovering from the shock in the privacy of her own room, she'd begun to plan for her first day at work. She would wear her favourite dress – the blue one with a white daisy pattern – and she would style her hair to make herself look more grown up. This had entailed fifteen minutes experimenting in front of the mirror, teasing the front locks back from her forehead, twisting them and pinning them in place to give a fashionable upswept effect. A natural wave meant that she could leave the rest of her shoulder-length hair untouched. She would team the daisy dress with a thin white belt but would have to make do with a pair of sensible, flat brown shoes that didn't go with the rest of her outfit.

Anyway, for all her planning and imagining, she hadn't been prepared for the scrutiny that Brenda,

Molly and a dozen others inflicted on her as she walked unsteadily down the aisle.

'You were right.' Brenda leaned towards Molly and whispered in her ear. 'I never saw such a little mouse.' Brenda herself rested secure in the knowledge that her tailored linen jacket, pinched in at the waist, and her straight, calf-length skirt with a back vent that allowed everyone a good view of her seamed nylon stockings gave her the air of a mannequin stepping out of the pages of *Woman's Weekly* magazine.

'Poor little thing,' Molly intoned. 'Ruth will make mincemeat of her.'

Breaking away from Cynthia to take their seats at their stations, Millicent and Norma glared in their direction.

'Don't you dare!' Millicent hissed at Brenda as she sat in the swivel chair next to her.

'Dare do what?' Brenda lived up to the redheads' reputation for being quick-tempered and it was often only Millicent who was brave enough to challenge her.

'Say a word!' Millicent warned. 'Let poor Cynthia settle in before you have a go at her.'

'Oh, so you've taken her under your wing already, have you?' Settling her headset into a position that didn't flatten her hair against the top of her head, Brenda noticed that a light had begun to flash on her back panel and swiftly pressed the corresponding front key on her desk. This allowed her to talk to the person on the other end. 'Hello, caller. Go ahead, please.'

A voice crackled down the line. 'This is Mrs Padmore on 970.'

'Ah yes. Good morning, Mrs Padmore. How can I help?'

'I'd like to speak to Mrs Gardiner on 548. Is the line free?'

'Let me check for you. Hold the line, please.'

Millicent pursed her lips and took up her pencil, which she tapped impatiently against the desk. She stole a glance at Cynthia who had by this time made her way to the door of the office where Ruth Ridley stood waiting.

Cynthia would never know, when she reflected on it later, what had kept her upright instead of letting her sink to the floor. Her heart had continued to jump and skip every step of the way. Her knees felt weak and her mouth was dry as the supervisor scanned the newcomer's appearance from head to toe and plainly found it wanting.

'I take it you're Cynthia Ambler?' were her first words, delivered quietly but forcefully.

'That's me, Miss,' Cynthia mumbled.

'Speak up. Good Lord above – they're sending them to me straight from school now, are they?'

'I aren't straight from—' Cynthia began, all grammar lessons clean forgotten.

'*I'm not*,' Ruth corrected. 'Say, "I'm not straight from school." In that case, how old are you?'

'Nineteen, Miss.'

'"Nineteen, Miss Ridley."' The supervisor's expression intimated that the new recruit was a lost cause even before she'd begun. 'And tell me, Cynthia – have you ever used a telephone before?'

'Only from a public kiosk,' Cynthia admitted. 'Where you put coins into a slot then press button A.' Her stuttering reply made her cringe – even to her own ears she sounded hopelessly naive.

The grilling continued. 'And what do you know about party lines and such like? Do you realize, for instance, that in our area up to four parties may share a single line?'

'No, Miss Ridley.' To Cynthia, the business of laying electric cables and connecting them to telephones inside people's homes was a mystery.

'Very well, we'll overlook the technical aspects for now and start from scratch, which in your case will take us back to the basic principles of elocution. You must learn to speak properly and not miss the beginnings and ends off words, which is a very sloppy way to go on.'

'I'm sorry, Miss Ridley,' Cynthia breathed, blushing to the roots of her fair hair. It was hard not to feel like a squashed cabbage leaf cast aside on the floor of Clifton Market and she saw that Millicent had been right to warn her that the supervisor was a dragon in disguise.

'Don't be sorry – be correct. Accuracy, efficiency and courtesy – those are our three watchwords.

Remember this and strive to improve on a daily basis. In that way we'll learn to get along.' Ending her lecture, Ruth turned to scan the rows of switchboards to either side of the room and saw that for the moment Norma was free. She beckoned her across.

One look at a wilting Cynthia told Norma that rescue was needed so she rushed to join them. 'Yes, Miss Ridley?'

'Norma, I'd like you to show our new junior here how to perform the duties of a name and address clerk. Demonstrate how you can use the telephone number to gather the necessary information. But this doesn't mean you should neglect your columns. Remember – only break off to show Cynthia the ropes when you have no light to take.'

'Of course. Follow me, Cynthia.' Turning on her heel, Norma led the way. ('She was white as a ghost and shaking like a leaf,' she reported to Millicent later. 'Cross my heart, I expected her to fall down in a dead faint.')

With the supervisor's words still ringing in her ears, Cynthia sat in the chair that Norma drew up for her. *Accuracy. Efficiency. Courtesy.* All around her lights winked and flashed, fingers flew over keyboards, cords were pushed into jacks, connections were made. The minute hand on the giant clock above the door jerked forward at a snail's pace.

'Hello, Hull – I have a new ticket.'

'Calling London 5492. Hello, Mr Turner – I have Mr Simpson on the line.'

On and on Cynthia heard the cacophony of female voices accepting and directing calls and above them all was the sound of their supervisor chiding and chivvying, correcting and criticizing.

This is too much for me to learn, she thought, fighting back the tears. *I'll never do it, not with Miss Ridley breathing down my neck.*

CHAPTER THREE

'The main thing is to take no notice of Ruth Ridley,' Millicent insisted. She and Norma had scooped Cynthia up the second they got the go-ahead for their dinner break and marched her out of the exchange, along the street and straight into Marks & Spencer where acres of gleaming counters, stained wooden floors and shining glass pendant lights beckoned. 'By which I mean, take on board the things you need to know about keys, lamps and cords and such like, but don't let her upset you in other ways.'

Norma picked through the packets of nylons on display at the hosiery counter. 'Millicent is right. I had to learn to do that when I first started. Now I've got the hide of a rhinoceros, thank you very much.'

'Ruth is like this with everyone,' Millicent explained.

'Why?' Cynthia's first morning had left her feeling as if she'd been put through the mangle and it was all she could do to frame the one-word question.

'She'll make a mug out of you just to test you out and see how you react.'

Norma agreed and laughed mischievously as she pointed out to the shop assistant the nylons she wanted. 'Anyway, that's the big, unanswered question! Why is Ruth Ridley the way she is? Could it have something to do with a dark past, I wonder?'

Millicent brushed aside Norma's suggestion and whisked Cynthia back out on to the pavement where they stood in the late-spring sunshine waiting for their workmate to pay for her purchase and join them. 'Seriously, Cynthia, you have to stand up to all the supes, but Ruth Ridley in particular. You'll never get into her good books unless you do.'

'I'll try,' Cynthia resolved out loud, though privately she wasn't able to shake off the paralysing fear of her strict new boss who had spent the morning patrolling the aisle, reminding the girls to keep their elbows tucked in and giving grudging permission for 'urgents', which allowed an operator to leave her chair for five minutes to go to the toilet.

The worst moment had come when Miss Ridley had caught Molly Scaife listening in to a conversation on a party line. With a face like thunder she'd leaned over Molly's shoulder to flick off the front key then marched her into her small office at the far end of the room. Two minutes later Molly had emerged, red-faced and dabbing her eyes with her handkerchief, to take up position at her switchboard.

'I'm on my last warning,' she'd confessed to Brenda. 'One more slip-up and I'll be out on my ear.'

It had created a bad atmosphere in the workplace

and all the girls remained edgy and resentful for a while.

'Where's the new girl got to?' Ruth had snapped at Norma ten minutes later as she swept past her station and saw the vacant chair.

'Cynthia took the updated name and address list upstairs to the general office,' Norma had replied evenly.

'As soon as she comes back, give her this RRQ booklet to study. Tell her there'll be a test on pages one to ten first thing tomorrow.'

Norma had taken the closely printed leaflet without comment and passed it on to Cynthia when she came back. 'Here – you've to set to and learn all the routes and rates up to page ten.'

Cynthia had settled down to studying the names and numbers – a task she felt she could accomplish, even if it meant burning the midnight oil. After all, her memory was good and columns of figures didn't throw her. It was when it came to opening her mouth and running the risk of mispronouncing her words that her courage failed. Now, though, standing with Millicent next to the department store, she was boosted a little by her and Norma's friendliness.

'We've got time for a quick cup of tea and a ham sandwich in Lyons' café if Norma gets a move on.' As Millicent checked her wristwatch, a burly lad on a bike mounted the pavement and screeched to a halt. He propped the bike hurriedly against a lamp-post, stuffed his cap into his jacket pocket and jostled against her as he rushed by. 'Hey, watch where you're going!' she yelled after him.

He took no notice but Cynthia gave a sharp intake of breath as she recognized her cousin, Bert Brooks, who since leaving school had worked part time as a lather boy in Sam Bower's.

Put out by Bert's rudeness, Millicent stormed after him into the barber's shop which adjoined a plush, newly opened ladies' hairdresser's called Sylvia's Salon. Sam Bower's establishment, by way of con-trast, was devoted to the old-fashioned business of male shaving and hair clipping, which involved a row of men of all ages sitting reading newspapers while Sam and his boy worked with shaving cream, brushes, razors and scissors. An adjustable swivel chair took up half the space in the dark, cramped room with its brown, cracked lino on the floor and a mottled mirror above a chipped sink.

'Your lad there nearly did me an injury,' Millicent told the barber in an accusatory tone. 'There I was, minding my own business, when he barged by and practically up-skittled me.'

Sam wrinkled his nose and twitched his heavy grey moustache without looking up. 'Did he, by Jove?'

Already busily applying shaving foam to the next customer's chin, the ill-mannered Bert was unabashed. 'I never,' he claimed.

'Yes, you did!' Millicent in full flow in the crowded male domain was a sight to behold. Sparks flew from her hazel eyes and she swished her beautiful black hair in a shining wave from right to left as she addressed the barber and his boy. 'And look at that bike – the way it's flung against that lamp-post, ready to tip over and trip someone up.'

Sam's scissors went on snipping. The row of men smiled broadly over their copies of the *Mirror* and the *Express*, clearly enjoying the sideshow.

'Right,' Millicent decided. 'If you're not going to make the little so-and-so say sorry, I'll go outside and take that bike, wheel it down to the canal then chuck it straight in. That'll show him.'

'Hey-up, Sam – she means it,' one of the men observed with a chuckle.

'Best move the bike, Bert,' the stooping, elderly barber said in an undertone, again without looking up.

Cynthia's cousin glowered at Millicent but did as he was told. He barged out of the shop, past Cynthia who had been joined by Norma, swearing under his breath as he took the bike and wheeled it down an alleyway next to the ladies' hairdresser's.

'Charming!' Norma noted before Millicent emerged grinning and brushing the palms of her hands together.

'Now for that cup of tea,' Millicent reminded them. She led the way past Sylvia's Salon, pausing only to arch one eyebrow and nudge Norma with her elbow to point out that it was none other than Clare Bell, immaculately dressed and coiffed, who sat behind the reception desk of the posh establishment. '"You too can look as beautiful as me if you come in here for a haircut!"' she cooed teasingly as she gave Clare a small wave then sailed on.

'Except we can't because we don't have her natural advantages, do we, Cynthia?' Norma said with a sigh.

'You speak for yourselves,' Millicent declared. 'I'm happy with the way I look, ta very much!'

That afternoon, Ruth loaded Cynthia down with more printed material – this time a heavy tome describing the history of the telephone since 1876 and a lighter one containing phonetic examples of the correct pronunciation of commonly used words.

'Good luck, old thing. If you can get to grips with carbon transmitters and induction coils in under a week, you're a whole lot brainier than I am,' Norma joked as Cynthia began to leaf through the well-thumbed pages. 'As for electromagnetic receivers – well, they still have me beat.'

Daunted by the complex science, Cynthia felt her vision blur and her head begin to spin. She turned to the book of pronunciations but struggled again with some unfamiliar symbols.

'Remember – "bath" and "path" rhyme with "hearth", which has to have an "h" at the start of it, by the way, and don't forget the "g" at the end of "something", which is never under any circumstances to be pronounced "summat".' Cheerfully Norma ran through some ground rules in between taking lights.

'"I am not, you are not, he is not,"' Millicent enunciated. '"We are not, you are not, they are not." Get it? As for the history part, remember Alexander Graham Bell brought out the first patent in 1876 and his model 102 telephone has been in use for over thirty years now. That's the sort of thing you'll need to know for your Full Efficiency Test.'

So Cynthia turned back earnestly to the weightier of the two books and read up about Giles Gilbert Scott's design of the first bright-red public kiosk and the launch of the coin box in 1925, together with the other recent invention of the Strowger system. This had introduced automatic exchange calls in the larger centres, leaving smaller ones still to be operated manually by the insertion of cords into jacks. Growing fascinated by the details, Cynthia kept her head down and read on, surprised when Norma tapped her on the shoulder to tell her it was time to clock off.

'That's it – your first day done and dusted,' she informed her as they exchanged places with the gang of girls who had come in to take the evening shift. 'How do you feel?'

'Worn out.' Cynthia admitted that the frenetic pace of placing calls in response to constantly flashing lights had wearied her, even though she wasn't yet actively involved.

'Don't worry, you'll soon get used to it.' In a hurry to get away and meet up with Douglas, Norma fetched her coat and hat, leaving Millicent to linger with Cynthia on the steps of the building.

'You've not been too put off, I hope?' Millicent checked with her.

Cynthia looked out on to the bustling square and smiled weakly. 'No. Thanks to you and Norma, I haven't.'

'We're not a bad bunch, once you get to know us. And, you have to admit, operating a switchboard beats loom-cleaning into a cocked hat.'

The picture of more than a dozen smartly dressed girls sitting at their stations and speaking into mouthpieces as lamps lit up and switches were flicked was still fresh in Cynthia's mind. Smart and confident, fashionable and up to the minute – that was how she wanted to be. Not like the girls trailing into the mills each morning, shawls around their heads, feet shod in wooden clogs as they had been for a hundred years or more. She wanted to turn out like Brenda with the flame-coloured hair and wear a bright, multicoloured, narrow-waisted dress. She would save up and buy high-heeled, sling-back shoes like Molly's and show off her seamed stockings. 'It certainly does,' she answered with her chin up and her shoulders back, stepping out on to the pavement with fresh determination in her gait.

Millicent kept up with her, one hand holding on to the crown of her saucer-shaped straw hat in case the strong wind caught it and blew it away.

49

'I've just thought of a sure-fire way for you to get into Ruth Ridley's good books.'

Cynthia spotted a number 65 pull up at the bus stop and joined the end of the short queue. 'Don't tell me – I have to learn the routes and rates off by heart.'

'Besides that.' As Cynthia stepped on to the back platform of the bus and it drew away from the kerb, Millicent started to trot alongside it. 'This is it, Cynthia – I think you should join our League of Health and Beauty class on a Friday evening. Pay your sixpence to stretch and bend and twirl a few ribbons under Ruth Ridley's command – that's certain to put a smile on the crabby old thing's face.'

Douglas Greenwood was still in police uniform when he met up with Norma straight out of work. He wheeled his bicycle up George Street and his heart skipped a beat when he saw his sweetheart hurrying towards him, hat in hand and coat flapping open, a broad smile lighting up her face.

'Am I glad to see you,' he told her, planting a firm kiss on her cheek as she leaned in towards him. The day's tawdry routine of attending scenes of petty crime and arresting burglars slipped away as he breathed in her eau de cologne and felt her smooth skin against his lips.

'Likewise,' she replied, her heart lifting with pride and not caring that people were staring at a police officer openly canoodling with his girl. They were a handsome couple and worth looking at.

Take Douglas, for a start. He was above average height and every inch of him was trim and upright. He glowed with health and confidence and his clean-shaven face, strong, even features and neatly parted brown hair gave him the air of someone in whom you would place absolute trust.

She smiled on as they crossed the square and headed for his lodgings on Canal Road. 'What do you fancy doing? Shall it be a game of dominoes in the King's Head or a bike ride out into the country?'

'Whatever you like,' Douglas said, quickly putting aside the thought of the physical things he would most like to do with Norma. Nice girls like her didn't agree to do anything like that until after they were married, which was one of the reasons he planned to propose to her before the summer was out. The other was that he was simply head over heels in love with a girl too good to be true. Bright and breezy, lush as a spring meadow – that was his dimpled, dark-haired Norma.

'A bike ride, then.'

'A bike ride it is.' Arriving at his lodgings, he wheeled his bike down a side ginnel and Norma followed. 'Come in and wait while I get changed. Will we need to call in at your place on our way?'

'No – I've already told Mum I'd be meeting you after work.' She followed him from the small yard at the back of the house, up some steps and along a narrow corridor into Douglas's ground-floor room, which overlooked the busy main street. It was big and light, with a wide bay window, faded flowered wallpaper and fancy plaster cornices that suggested a grander past. There was a single bed down one side, a small brown sofa in the bay and a mahogany chest of drawers against the wall opposite. The only table was a baize-topped card table rescued from Napier's rag and bone yard and the only chair a tubular steel and canvas one – the sort you saw in doctors' and dentists' waiting rooms.

As Douglas got changed, he chatted on about this and that. 'Face away from me – don't turn around until I tell you. Did you see this morning's headline about the *Queen Mary*? They're all set to launch her later this month, all 81,000 tons of her. That'll be a sight to see.'

Tempted as she was to sneak a look, Norma stood at the window and stared out on to the street at buses and trams and the steady flow of workers making their way home. She heard Douglas unbutton his dark blue tunic and hang it on the door hook, feeling herself blush as he shrugged his braces from his shoulders then stepped out of his trousers into his flannel slacks. 'Imagine sailing all the way across the Atlantic on her,' she said wistfully.

'Yes, the closest we'll get to water this year is a swim in Beckwith Lido, and that's if we're lucky.'

'I'd like to go there as soon as the weather gets warmer.'

'All right – you can look now,' he told her.

Norma turned around to find him in Fair Isle sweater and slacks, bicycle clips and flat cap already in place. She glanced down at her lightweight cotton coat and full-skirted dress. 'I'm not really dressed for this, am I?'

'It doesn't matter – I'll do most of the work,' he promised, taking her hand and leading her back into the yard where they took their tandem from the shed and prepared to set off. 'Where to?' he asked after he'd wheeled it out on to the street.

'Let's follow the towpath out towards Beckwith.' Mention of the lido had put the idea into her head. Sticking by the canal meant there would be no steep hills to cycle up and they would soon find themselves out beyond the scruffy town section that was littered with old car tyres, beer barrels and broken mangles, and instead amongst fresh green fields and hawthorn trees laden with white blossom.

'We'll go down the steps by the side of the Victory,' he decided.

No sooner said than they were down on the towpath and sitting astride the bike – Douglas in front and Norma behind, both pedalling steadily. He started to whistle the tune to 'Daisy, Daisy' and she joined in with the words,

'Give me your answer do'.

The sounds of the song echoed down the tunnel that took them under Bridge Street and they were still whistling and singing when they emerged on the far side.

'I'm half crazy, all for the love of you,' she trilled.

Douglas whistled and smiled to himself. Life was champion, here under a blue sky, heading out beyond the grime. He cycled on, feeling that he could do anything as long as Norma was riding pillion – he could reach sergeant by the time he was thirty in five years' time and he and his sweetheart would be married and living together in a house on Chapel Street or maybe Ada Street if they could afford the rent there, with a lovely little family of a girl and a boy thriving and about to start at Lowtown Junior School.

Norma's skirt lifted in the breeze and she had to hold it down with one hand. 'It won't be a stylish marriage,' she sang and hummed along. 'Tra-la, tra-la, tra-la-la.'

'But you'll look sweet,' he joined in as they bumped over potholes and rode steadily on. 'Upon the seat . . .'

'Of a bicycle made for two!'

Arriving home from work after a long wait for a bus and a detour up Albion Lane to buy a loaf of bread, Millicent stooped to pick up a letter from the doormat. Recognizing Harold's neat handwriting, she opened it quickly and with an uneasy sense that all was not well. Harold never wrote to her unless it was bad news, and sure enough her heart sank as she read through the short contents to discover that he would be tied up this weekend – Friday at a pal's birthday party in the working men's club, Saturday at a darts match at the King's Head. 'Tied up!' she said in disgust, tearing the letter in two. She felt like marching round to his precious mill manager's house and knocking on his smartly painted door, just to enjoy the look of shock on his face.

Instead, she threw the letter in the wastepaper bin then made herself a tea of cheese on toast, washed down with a strong, hot brew. *He might at least have the good grace to say sorry*, she thought. *It wasn't like this at the beginning. Once upon a time he swore I meant the world to him. Now he just keeps me dangling on the end of a string. But what's to stop me putting on my glad rags and going out by myself for a change? Or nipping down to the Green Cross with Norma after Health and Beauty if she's free?*

Such questions circled in her brain all that evening, even though she busied herself by ironing then hanging up a fresh set of net curtains. Still, she thought of Harold ensconced with his wife and kids – Doris doling out the fish pie for supper and the two boys, Freddie and Derek, who sat at the well-laid table with their spotty chickenpox faces; Harold with sleeves rolled up, looking gaunt and brooding about the latest lay-offs at Oldroyd's and reaching for his umpteenth cigarette of the day.

Why? she asked herself as she made her way upstairs to bed. *Why do we carry on this way – me at home on my ownio, him grinding on in a loveless mar-riage?* Or at least, that's what Harold was fond of telling her. Life at home was hollow – there was no affection between man and wife any more, only the shell of respectability and a sense of duty.

Millicent took off her clothes and put on her nightdress, caught sight of her reflection in the dressing-table mirror and for a second didn't recog-nize herself. The face staring back at her was sad beyond words – the full mouth turned down at the corners, the eyes dull and shadowed.

What am I doing? she asked herself.

Living in a fool's paradise. The answer flew at her with the force of a sharp stone hitting her forehead. *Kidding yourself that the man you love will one day have the courage to leave his wife and family. Telling yourself that his feelings for you are as strong as yours for him. They're not, you know. Otherwise he'd have given up his old life to be with you a long time ago.*

Dazed, Millicent took up a brush and ran it through her thick hair. She delayed turning out the light and getting into bed because she knew the darkness would crowd in and turn her in on herself. There would be more questions she couldn't answer, more home truths that were too much for her to face.

So instead she read the latest Mills & Boon romance and tried to lose herself in that. The gas-light on the wall flickered on well past midnight, long after Chalky White had returned to the yard after locking up the doors at the Green Cross and

56

Walter Blackburn had fallen asleep in his fireside rocking chair.

Cynthia's new job at the telephone exchange meant that she had to plan her domestic duties well ahead of time. Arriving home at six o'clock, she lit the gas oven and heated up a Lancashire hotpot that she'd prepared the night before. While her uncle ate, she checked the larder and made a list of the groceries she would need to buy the next day. There was plenty of oatmeal for his porridge and the milkman would deliver more milk first thing. But they were short of eggs and sugar, and the loaf of bread was almost finished.

'Well?' William demanded as she took away his plate and offered him rice pudding. 'Have they given you the sack yet?'

Cynthia shook her head. She ought to be used to his humourless teasing, but still the mockery found its target and she struggled to change the subject. 'The other girls were a big help – Millicent Jones and Norma Haig especially. Oh, and I saw Bert working in the barber's. It's just up the road from the exchange.'

'Well then, you can pop in there tomorrow and ask him to pay me a visit. Tell him Wednesday teatime, six o'clock sharp.'

'I will, Uncle.'

'It's to talk to him about collecting the rents, so I want you to be here as well.'

Anxious to go up to her room to study for her RRQ test, Cynthia rushed the washing-up and knocked the handle off a teacup – a crime which her uncle would take at least a week to forget. Then he chided her about a small stain on the best linen tablecloth. It was half-past seven before she could finally settle down to her homework, aware that at any time he could call up the stairs for her to fill his hot-water bottle even though the nights were growing warmer, or to stand on a stool to lift the tin of biscuits down from the high shelf in the pantry where he kept them out of temptation's way. 'Two rich tea biscuits with a nice cuppa to round off the day,' he would say, regular as clockwork. 'Where's the harm in that?'

Determined to impress Ruth Ridley, Cynthia carried on with her studying until her eyelids drooped. She imprinted list after list on her memory, closing her eyes to repeat them to herself, pacing the floor until her uncle knocked on his bedroom ceiling with his stout walking stick.

'Stop that racket!' he yelled up at her.

So she undressed and crept into bed, still rehearsing facts and figures. Her dress for tomorrow was hanging from the door – a striped green and white one that she'd updated with a floppy silk bow at the collar. She would team it with a darker green, hand-knitted bolero top, and though she wouldn't look anywhere near as smart and sophisticated as the others, it would have to do. Rain was forecast so she would be forced to wear her dowdy old mac, but she would whip it off as soon as she got through the revolving doors. She resolved to put part of her first week's wages to one side in order to save up for some summer shoes. And the beret had to go. Better be bare headed than carry on wearing that old thing. Millicent and Norma would never be seen dead in it, and goodness only knew what Brenda and Molly would think.

CHAPTER FOUR

At the end of her first week working as a telephone girl at the George Street exchange, Cynthia went along with Norma and Millicent to their keep-fit class as planned.

'I only wish it wasn't so far out of town,' Norma complained as the three young women waited for the bus that would take them up to Overcliffe Common and from there to the edge of town where the Edwardian Assembly Rooms overlooked the wide moors and the distant, craggy horizon.

'At least it's in the right direction for you, Cynthia.' Millicent knew she had to cajole and encourage their new young friend, who had survived her first few days by the skin of her teeth, no thanks to Ruth's sharp tongue and piercing eye. 'You can pick up the number 65 again outside the Assembly Rooms and go straight from there back to Hadley.'

Norma too sensed Cynthia's reluctance and did her best to include her in the conversation. 'You did tell your uncle that you'd be late home?'

Cynthia nodded and waited anxiously. As if learning the ropes of a new job hadn't been bad enough, here she was, putting herself through fresh torment by 'prancing about in your underwear', as William had put it when he'd learned where she wanted to go.

'League of Health and what?' he'd quizzed on the Wednesday evening, with Bert sitting at their dining-room table, laughing out loud.

Bert had come to Moor View, as arranged, to pick up the rent book and satchel and to hear from Cynthia the best order for collecting the rents.

'Beauty,' she'd repeated for her uncle's benefit through gritted teeth.

'Oh, blimey!' Bert's laughter had developed into side-splitting guffaws. 'Is that the silly business where you strip down to your vest and knickers?'

'What if it is?' she'd said stiffly.

'And they play music and you canter around the room like circus ponies?'

'That's the one,' Cynthia had replied, scarcely able to refrain from giving Bert's cheek a hard slap. Just to look at her cousin made her mad – he was so cock-sure, grinning and bursting out of his old schoolboy jacket, his tow-coloured hair slicked down with brilliantine. 'If you must know, it's called callisthenics. Why – would you like to join us?'

'Me? Not on your nelly. Anyway, it's only for women.'

'That's right.' Cynthia had fixed him with an angry stare. 'You'd fit right in.'

Bert had risen to the clumsy insult, saying she of all people was wasting her time in the pursuit of beauty, or words to that effect.

Cynthia couldn't remember precisely how the row had developed, only that their uncle had stepped in and said she could go to the class, if only to avoid Bert and Cynthia running into each other again when Bert brought the rent money back.

But now she seriously regretted agreeing to come. She wasn't the 'prancing around' sort, for a start. And she wasn't very good at joining groups – at the age of seven, for instance, she'd left the Brownies after only a few weeks, without a single badge to her name.

'I don't like going,' she'd told her mother quietly after the fourth or fifth week of holding hands to form a circle then dancing around the toadstool, promising to do her duty and learning to tie knots with trembling, nervous fingers.

Relieved to not have the expense of buying the uniform, her mother hadn't insisted and Cynthia had stayed at home on Tuesdays from then on.

'Cheer up, Cynthia – this isn't a visit to the dentist's. It's meant to be fun.' Millicent bundled her on to the bus without giving her the chance to back out.

It was jam-packed with mechanics and mill work-ers, seamstresses and shop girls returning from work, so Cynthia stood in the aisle squashed between Millicent and Norma as it chugged along.

'By the way, just in case I miss Bert later on, here's

my week's rent money.' Millicent slipped some silver coins and coppers into Cynthia's mac pocket. 'That'll help swell the old man's coffers to bursting point.' Then she turned to Norma. 'Are you and Douglas going out later?'

'Yes, to the flicks, all being well. What about you and Harold?'

'Don't ask.' Millicent pulled a face. She paid her fare and allowed the conductor to squeeze by. 'Harold's not in my good books, if you must know.'

As the bus swayed and rattled on up the hill, Norma veered away from the touchy subject. 'What about you, Cynthia? Do you have a nice young man to walk out with?'

'Not at the moment.' Not ever, in fact. Cynthia hid another of the reasons why she felt gauche and naive next to everyone else at the exchange. All the girls there had so much more experience of the world than her. It went along with their fashionable clothes and hairstyles and brought with it a confidence that she sorely lacked.

The conductor – a fair-haired chap in his early twenties – picked up the gist of their conversation. 'This must be my lucky night,' he quipped as he took Cynthia's fare. 'I finish my shift in half an hour. What do you say to you and me meeting up outside the Victory?'

'And you a man engaged to be married, Wilf Evans!' Pretending to be shocked, Millicent gave Norma and Cynthia an exaggerated wink.

'Spoilsport.' The conductor laughed and handed Cynthia her ticket. 'I hope you get wet,' he kidded as rainclouds descended from the moor top.

'Come on, this is our stop.' All too soon for Cynthia's liking, Norma alighted from the bus.

Heads down against the wind, the three women felt the first drops of rain as they ran for the entrance to the Assembly Rooms and made for the cloakroom where they changed into their keep-fit uniforms alongside six or seven other late arrivals, including Clare Bell.

'Here you are, Cynthia.' Millicent dug deep into her bag to pull out a neatly folded white satin top and some black knickers. 'Lucky for you I have a spare set.' She turned to the new receptionist at Sylvia's Salon. 'Clare, meet Cynthia. Cynthia – Clare. This is only Clare's third time so you two can learn the routines together if you like.'

Daunted by the creamy, smooth-skinned vision of loveliness, Cynthia smiled shyly at Clare then the four of them dashed into the hall, catching Ruth's eye as they entered. Music blared from a phonograph positioned at the edge of the stage, competing with the chatter of the large group of women gathered for their weekly session.

Looking at her watch and seeing that it was time to begin, Ruth lifted the needle from the spinning record and clapped her hands. 'Take your positions. Beginners, stay at the back for our warm-up. No more talking, Millicent. Pay attention, everyone, please.'

Cynthia glanced at Clare, who shot her an anxious look. Ignored by the other women, they rallied and did their best to mirror Ruth's twists and bends and to keep time to the music that had begun again – a jaunty brass band tune with a military air that got them all stepping and kicking in unison as they kept to their rows and began their routine.

Thank heavens I can hide at the back with Clare, was Cynthia's main thought, surrounded as they were by pale, bare limbs, twisting torsos and faces full of concentration. But it turned out that she had a good sense of rhythm and could quickly pick up the steps so she soon relaxed and began to take in her surroundings. She glanced up at the high, beamed ceiling and at the heavy crimson curtains then down at the polished wooden floor marked out with white lines for games of badminton. She noticed that Clare also seemed to have found her feet and was swinging her arms with gusto. Here they were, beginners together, fitting in well and starting to enjoy themselves until the music ended and Ruth found fault with everyone's timing and execution.

'Knees higher,' she instructed. 'Everyone, point your toes. Cynthia at the back – swing those arms as if you mean it. Clare – chest out, shoulders back. Once more – from the beginning.'

As Ruth set the needle down on the record a second time, Cynthia tugged at the hem of her satin top then adjusted the skimpy bloomers that Millicent had lent her.

'It's all right – you're decent,' Clare assured her – the first words she'd spoken since Millicent had introduced them.

'Ta.' Cynthia nodded back at her.

It was all there was time for before they launched into a repeat of the marching routine but Cynthia was grateful. She wondered why she hadn't run into Clare before now, or at least got wind of her reputation as an outstanding beauty. Looks like that got you noticed then whisked away to places like London or Paris to become a fashion model or even to Hollywood and a starring role on the silver screen. Cynthia resolved to find out more from Millicent and Norma soon.

'Not good enough! Again, please . . . Dorothy, you're out of step . . . Clare, those toes are not pointed. Your feet are like fillets of haddock on a fishmonger's slab.'

Commands and insults poured from Ruth's lips until the session ended and the class was dismissed.

'That's it!' Clare declared from the safety of the changing rooms, where she sank on to a bench and half disappeared under her lilac-coloured dress hanging from its hook. 'You won't see me here again, not for all the tea in China.'

'Ruth does seem to have it in for you,' Norma acknowledged, while Millicent as usual advised her to let it wash over her.

'Here's my opinion, for what it's worth,' she went on. 'Ruth Ridley wasn't always an old sourpuss. From what I hear, she once had a husband – not here, but in a town over Manchester way. The marriage didn't last. The story goes that Ruth's old man went off with a girl who was no better than she should have been, if you know what I mean. He was never heard of again.'

'But why does that make Ruth pick on poor Clare especially?' Norma wanted to know.

'Here's what I think . . .' Millicent's air of intrigue drew curious looks from half a dozen women who were getting changed nearby. 'Just suppose that Clare Bell happens to remind Ruth of the girl who stole her husband's heart – the same milky-white skin, those dark eyes, a figure that most women would die for.'

'Never!' commented one of the women. 'There can't be two like Clare in the whole of England. Just look at her.'

'I know – lucky her,' another remarked.

'I *am* here, you know,' Clare reminded them as she stood up with a resigned air and took her dress from the hook.

'Oh, but we are all green with envy, aren't we, girls?' Millicent declared. 'And the thing about you, Clare, is that you go around in a little world of your own, not knowing or caring about the effect you have.'

'I don't mean to.' Clare's humble remark was genuine. In fact, she saw herself as the opposite of lucky, having been driven from home at the age

67

of fifteen by a tyrannical father and a mother too sickly to stand up for her or her two younger brothers.

Out on her own and living from hand to mouth as low-paid jobs in mills and factories came and went, she had gradually established herself in cramped lodgings above a bookmaker's shop on George Street. She'd been spotted a few weeks earlier by a woman called Mrs Parr who was busy setting up the ladies' hairdresser's further down the street. Phyllis Parr had liked what she'd seen and immediately offered Clare not only a bigger room above the salon but also a job as the receptionist – the first stroke of good luck that had ever come Clare's way. It still seemed too good to be true – the job was temporary and could end any time, she reminded herself. Meanwhile, she would work slavishly and do every-thing possible to stay in Mrs Parr's good books.

'Anyway, tell us more about Ruth.' Norma dragged Millicent back to her original topic. 'What do you sup-pose happened after her husband upped and left?'

'It seems she licked her wounds for a while then gave up on men for good and came to live over this side of the Pennines. Now it's all work, work, work with Ruth, apart from joining the ramblers' club and teaching keep-fit with the League, that is. She's made her mark on the local committee and has all sorts of ideas about callisthenics and the good it does you. Exercise is her religion, you might say.'

'Well, good luck to her.' Norma found a flicker of

new respect for their switchboard supervisor and tried to draw Cynthia and Clare into the conversation. 'What about you two – don't you think there's something to be said for giving up men and devoting yourself to your career?'

'Maybe,' they answered hesitantly.

'Says the girl who's about to get engaged!' Millicent reminded Norma, who blushed.

'What do you mean? Douglas hasn't even popped the question yet.'

'Ah, but he will.' One look at the two young lovers, hands entwined, billing and cooing as they walked along, told Millicent as much. 'Come this time next year, you'll have that wedding ring firmly on your finger and you'll be well and truly up the duff.'

'Millicent!' Norma's reaction drew giggles from the other women. 'Wash your mouth out with soap and water.'

'Who was that lady in *Hamlet* who protested too much?' Dredging up a half-remembered quotation from her schooldays, Millicent continued to tease. 'Methinks it's true – Norma and Douglas will soon tie the knot. What about you, Clare? When will that handsome chap in the trilby hat go down on one knee?'

The cheeky question made Clare give a sudden start then let her hair swing forward to cover her burning cheeks. Hastily gathering her belongings, she almost ran from the room. 'Can someone tell Miss Ridley I shan't be back?' she said.

As Millicent and Norma tried to intervene, Cynthia stepped forward. 'Leave it to me. I'll mention it at work tomorrow if I get the chance.'

'Ta.' With a quick nod and in obvious distress, Clare was gone.

Norma shook her head and tutted at Millicent. 'Trust you,' she muttered.

'Why – what did I do?'

'You're like a bull in a china shop, mentioning the chap in the trilby to her. Didn't you see how red she went?'

'I was right first time – Clare has a bad case of guilty conscience.' Millicent raised her eyebrow in a worldly way.

'You would know all about that,' Norma retorted, upset on Clare's behalf as she took her comb from her bag and stood in front of a mirror. Honestly and truly, there were times when she could fall out with Millicent Jones and this was most definitely one of them.

As Millicent returned undaunted to Heaton Yard for an enforced night in and Norma rushed home to get changed for her meeting with Douglas, Cynthia boarded the bus out to Hadley. She had plenty to think about as she travelled the moor road, not least Millicent's revelations about their sharp-tongued supe. She tried hard to imagine what it must be like to be married and then divorced – the shock of discovering that your husband had broken his wedding vows and the shame of being left in the lurch, with everyone knowing the reason behind it. And it wasn't that Ruth Ridley wouldn't have been considered attractive in her younger days. She was still slim and stylish, carrying herself well and making sure that she made the best of herself. Perhaps, though, she'd always had a hard edge to her voice and impatient mannerisms, which in themselves might have been off-putting to most men. Cynthia gave up the puzzle and agreed with Norma – it was impossible to fathom the ins and outs of Miss Ridley's past.

'A penny for them.' A man's voice broke into Cynthia's thoughts as the bus sailed across the moor buffeted by the wind and cresting one hill only to plunge down into a dip then rise again like a ship on an ocean of heather. The man leaned forward and tapped her on the shoulder, making her turn. 'Wilf Evans,' he reminded her. 'I saw you earlier.'

It was the cheeky conductor, without his brown uniform and peaked cap. Cynthia registered the boyish face – smooth and smiling, with light blue eyes and fair hair swept back from a high forehead – and didn't have time to object as he quickly switched seats to sit down beside her.

'You turned me down,' he reminded her. 'But no hard feelings, eh?'

'Course not.' Struggling to find her tongue, she suspected that she was still being teased and kept up her guard.

'Anyway, here I am, off duty – ready and willing if you are.'

'To do what?'

'To take you out. What's your name, by the way? And where have you been hiding all my life?'

The cheek of it! Cynthia clutched the handbag resting on her knees more tightly and felt her heartbeat quicken.

'I mean it – why haven't I run into you before now? Are you a pal of Millicent's?'

She nodded. 'I work with her and Norma at the telephone exchange. I started there on Monday.'

Wilf gave a low whistle. 'Then you're far too brainy for me. I'm only a lowly conductor on the corporation buses.'

And engaged to be married, Cynthia remembered. 'I can't come out with you in any case. What would your fiancée say?'

'I don't have one of those any more,' he said in a more serious tone, picking a stray thread from his trouser leg. 'That was Adelaide Williams. She gave me the old heave-ho a few months back.'

'Oh, I'm sorry.'

'I'm not. Not now. To tell you the truth, I wasn't really looking forward to our little trot down the aisle.'

Glancing out through the window, Cynthia saw they were approaching the village cricket ground and her fork in the road. She stood awkwardly, ducking her head to avoid the luggage rack above. 'This is my stop.'

Wilf leaped up to let her out then followed her. He got off the bus with her. 'You still haven't told me your name.'

She looked at him, unable to ignore her rapid heartbeat and somehow drawn in by the teasing light in his eyes. 'Cynthia Ambler,' she said quietly.

Hands in pockets and leaning back, he tilted his head to one side. 'Well, Cynthia Ambler, are you going to let me take you out or not?'

'When?'

'Tomorrow night.'

'Where to?'

'Wherever you like. There's a dance on in the Institute. I can meet you here at six and we can walk along.'

'All right,' she said without stopping to think, her heart fluttering madly. 'I'm working tomorrow, though. I'll need time to get home and changed.'

'Let's make it seven, then.' His head was up and he was already walking away, looking over his shoulder as he went. 'I'll see you at seven o'clock on the dot. Wear your dancing shoes and get ready to foxtrot the night away.'

The new month had arrived with a rush of sunshine, blue skies and burgeoning green.

'This is what they mean by flaming June.' As planned the night before, Douglas rode up to Albion Lane on the tandem to collect Norma. They both had Saturday off for once and the good weather forecast had made them decide to take a jaunt out to Beckwith Lido, setting off early to beat the crowds.

She'd been ready and waiting at the door, ignoring Ivy's well-meaning advice to stay out of the sun and taking on the chin Ethel's strong reminder that she'd promised to be back in time to go with their mother up to Clifton Market to scoop up the last of the day's bargains.

'Don't forget!' Ethel had called after her. 'I'll be busy with Ivy, manning the Scouts' jumble sale at the chapel. You're the only one who's free.'

'I won't forget,' Norma had promised, slamming the door after her. Here was Douglas, greeting her with a kiss and an upbeat remark about the weather. She stowed her swimming costume and towel in the pannier bag and hopped on the bike. 'Come on – let's make the most of it.'

They set off gaily, once more choosing the towpath to take them out of town then on along country lanes to the neighbouring spa town of Beckwith, nestled under a rocky promontory and famous for its sulphur well. Taking the water was now going out of fashion but it had been responsible for the large and splendid hotel built in the town's Victorian heyday and for the posh shops and cafés along its main street, complete with wrought-iron canopies.

'I don't know about you, but I'm sweltering.' Douglas steered the tandem towards the lido in the valley bottom. The sun beat down and there was scarcely a breeze. 'I can't wait to dive head first into that pool.'

'Me neither.' Norma smiled as they followed the signs. She saw the tall beech hedges surrounding the lido, heard the splash of the fountain beyond.

'I'll race you,' she said as Douglas parked the bike and she dashed ahead, through the turnstile and into the changing rooms. Within five minutes she was out of her dress and into her costume and cap, running to meet him at the side of the pool.

'I beat you.' He slid his arm around her waist and she did likewise. 'This is the life, eh?'

She took a look around. The sparkling pool was circular, with a large fountain in the centre, and surrounded by smooth lawns. A low white café building stood to one side. There were already a few families here, complete with canvas windbreaks and deckchairs, and a dozen or so children splashing in the shallow end or sitting under the fountain, shrieking with laughter.

Norma gave Douglas's waist a squeeze. The water was clear and tempting. Sliding her arm free, she took up position, legs bent at the knee, toes feeling for the edge of the pool, ready to dive in.

He watched her, hair completely hidden beneath the white rubber cap, her lithe body crouching over the water, arms outstretched. He loved the curve of her spine, the tilt of her slim hips – everything about her.

She plunged in and he followed. Two splashes and

they were under the water, swimming like fishes, emerging glistening and laughing into the sunshine.

Accuracy, efficiency, courtesy. Cynthia repeated the three key words to herself in an effort to concentrate on her work rather than on the prospect of walking out with Wilf Evans. To either side of her, jack lamps winked, cords were connected and operators spoke into their mouthpieces.

'Good morning, Olive. How are you this morning and how can I help?' Recognizing a local number that wasn't shared by other parties, Millicent adopted a friendlier tone than usual. 'Let me try to make that Manchester connection for you . . .' Leaving both cords up and listening hard, she waited a while, closely observed by Cynthia who sat next to her.

Cynthia saw Millicent's eyebrows shoot up in surprise as she listened through her headset to a conversation on the requested party line.

'I'm sorry, Olive. That line is busy.' Millicent returned to her caller, more formally than before. 'Please try later.' She quickly flicked her rear key to cut off the caller then took off her headset and sat back in her chair.

'What's the matter?' Cynthia tried not to laugh at the exaggerated expression of surprise on Millicent's face.

'Never you mind.' Millicent glanced to the end of the aisle where today's supe, Agnes Mercer, gave instructions to Molly who was having difficulty making an international connection via London to Berlin. Though Agnes was nowhere near as strict as Ruth, Millicent decided to save her salacious scrap of gossip until later. Cynthia, meanwhile, went back to swotting up on more routes and rates.

Having dealt with the Berlin call, Agnes walked down the aisle and stopped behind Cynthia. 'Come with me,' she told her quietly.

Cynthia followed obediently to the supes' office then waited at the door.

'Come in.'

She entered the small room lined with shelves stacked high with telephone directories, maps and large grey files. The clutter dwarfed Agnes, who was under five feet tall. Unmarried at twenty-eight, strait-laced and ambitious, she nevertheless had a kindly air.

'Sit down,' she told Cynthia, who had to remove two files from the chair being offered and find space for them beside the black typewriter on the desk. 'I have a few minutes before dinner time to teach you some basic switchboard rules. Let's start with the most important. It may seem obvious, but first and foremost in this job is to be a good listener. *Listen* to your caller, obtain all the facts. Second – be patient. If the caller gives you unclear information, tease it out until you understand where to direct the call. Third – be polite at all times.'

Cynthia nodded eagerly, absorbing information as

if her mind were a piece of blotting paper soaking up ink.

Agnes paused to take in Cynthia's earnest expression. The new girl was certainly pretty and presentable in her striped green dress and bolero jacket, if a little unpolished. But my goodness, she was quick to learn facts and figures, as her RRQ test earlier in the week had proved. 'I'm teaching you how to deal with customers because I believe you'll soon be ready to take your test and man a switchboard,' she told her. 'Remember – listen patiently, be polite, connect the cords. That's all there is to it.'

'Yes. Thank you.' A tongue-tied Cynthia was thrilled to be on the brink of starting her new job in earnest.

'Of course, you'll still have to work your way up to the Full Efficiency Test before we can increase your wages from trainee to fully fledged operator.'

Cynthia nodded and tried to keep her excitement in check.

'And before we let you loose on customers, you must practise your pronunciation. Do you have a gramophone at home?' Agnes delved under the paperwork on the desk to slide out a black record in a buff-coloured paper sleeve.

Cynthia found her voice. 'Yes, Miss Mercer. My uncle keeps a wind-up one in the corner of the sitting room.' It stood next to the bureau, rarely played, in its shiny mahogany case, its trumpet turned towards the wall.

'Very well then – take this. It's a recording of the correct pronunciation of words we use a lot here in the telephone exchange – phrases such as "Hello, London", "Go ahead, please", and so on. You play the recording then copy what is being said – do you get the idea?'

'Yes, Miss Mercer.' 'Hello' with an 'h', 'London' said with two 'o's rather than the blunt, back of the throat 'u's she would normally employ. Cynthia's sensitive ear picked up the differences and she rehearsed them to herself.

'You know what they say – practice makes perfect.' Agnes drew the teaching session to a close. 'You must listen to this every night.'

'I will.' She could hardly wait for the quiet times during the week after her uncle had gone to bed when she could play the precious recording without interruption.

Dismissed by the supe, she rushed to join Millicent, on her way out of the building for her dinner break.

'Someone looks like the cat who got the cream,' Millicent observed as she linked arms with Cynthia and headed for the Lyons' café where a waitress in a smart black dress and white apron and cap sat them at a window table. She then took a pencil from behind her ear and wrote down their order for egg and cress sandwiches and a pot of tea.

'Miss Mercer says I'll soon be ready to take the switchboard!' Excitement bubbled up into a broad, brilliant smile.

'Fancy that.' Millicent didn't show it, but she envied Cynthia's enthusiasm for the job. She herself had been at it for four years now and the shine had gone off it, especially when Ruth was on patrol, pacing up and down the aisle, refusing you an urgent or looking over your shoulder to pick up on tiny errors of pronunciation. 'What else?' she asked as the nippy brought their order.

'What do you mean?'

'It can't be just that. There has to be something else behind the Cheshire cat grin.'

Cynthia realized there was no point trying to fob Millicent off. 'If you must know, I've agreed to walk out with your friend Wilf. We rode home on the bus together after Health and Beauty and he asked me to go dancing with him tonight.'

'Cheeky blighter!' Millicent took a big gulp of tea then swallowed hard. For once, she was genuinely taken aback. 'Let me get this straight – you're going to get your glad rags on and meet up with Wilf Evans?'

'Yes. Why not? Oh, if you're thinking he still has a fiancée, you're wrong. The engagement has been broken off. He's a free agent.'

'Oh, so Adelaide gave him his marching orders, did she?' Millicent assumed that this had been the case. 'Did Wilf give a reason?'

'We didn't go into it. Why – there's nothing wrong, is there?'

Apart from the fact that he considers himself a man of

*the world and you, Cynthia, are still wet behind the ears –
no.* Keeping this thought to herself for now, Millicent
veered off in a new direction. 'I hear he's just this
week moved with his mother. She's the new housekeeper at North Park, the Oldroyd estate. That's out
your way, isn't it?'

'Yes – at the far end of the village. That explains
why he was taking the same bus home.'

'So what will you wear?'

'It's between my blue dress with the white daisies
and this striped one,' Cynthia admitted. 'They're the
only summer dresses I own.'

Millicent tutted and eyed her companion up and
down. 'Then there's nothing else for it – I'll have to
lend you one of mine.'

'No, I couldn't . . .'

'Don't be daft, of course you could. I have a pale
green dress in a nice soft material that should fit
you. It's cut on the bias to show off your figure – not
too daring, but not drab either.'

'Are you sure?'

'Certain. What size shoes do you take?'

'Size five.'

'Perfect – you can have the shoes to match. Come
home with me after we've finished at work and get
changed at my house. What with the dress and the
shoes, plus a touch of rouge and lipstick, we'll make
a new woman of you.' *Cinderella, you shall go to the
ball!* Millicent's envy deepened. Oh, to be young,
pretty and innocent, with doors opening ahead of

you instead of slamming shut behind you. She thought of the prison she'd made for herself in her liaison with Harold – the secrets and lies, the heady delusions.

'Millicent?'

Cynthia's voice sounded far off and Millicent had to force herself back into the present, delving into her purse as the waitress waited impatiently for payment. 'Rightio, roll up your sleeves, ready for more routes and rates,' she said briskly as they paid up and left the café. 'Blimey, it's hot out here! Come along, Cynthia, chop-chop. We need to get out of this sun double quick.'

CHAPTER FIVE

'Do you see what I see?' With a sharp dig in Cynthia's ribs, Millicent pointed to a man and a woman coming out of Sylvia's Salon.

At five o'clock on the Saturday afternoon, after a busy shift at the switchboards, the two telephone girls emerged from the exchange to find that the street was still blisteringly hot and there was not a cloud in the sky. Long, deep shadows had begun to creep across the road, but the new hairdresser's shop still caught the full glare of the sun.

Shading her eyes with one hand, Cynthia made out a small woman in a tailored, pearl-grey two-piece and matching toque hat, finished off with white gloves and shoes. She was arm in arm with a younger man, equally smart in a broad-shouldered, navy blue blazer with wide lapels, his face hidden by the rim of his rakishly tilted straw hat. 'What are we meant to be looking at?' she asked.

'It's him!' Millicent hissed as she rushed Cynthia on down George Street.

'Who?'

'Clare Bell's mystery man – this time with a mystery woman.'

Crossing the street to negotiate City Square, Cynthia had to concentrate on not getting run over by taxis, cars and buses whose drivers seemed to have grown careless and bad tempered in the sultry heat. 'Are you sure it was him?' she gasped, once they'd battled the traffic and started the long walk out of the town centre towards Ada Street.

'Certain.' There had been no mistaking the up-to-the-minute outfit and shoulders-back swagger.

'Was Clare with them?'

Millicent shook her head and frowned.

'Couldn't that have been his mother?' The glimpse Cynthia had caught showed a big enough age difference, though the woman's slim figure, dyed blonde hair and upright carriage disguised it well.

'Lord, no!' Instinct told Millicent otherwise. 'If that was mystery man's mama, I'll eat my hat. They were too cosy for that. No – that was more likely to be the owner of the hairdresser's, if you ask me.'

They hurried on in silence, letting their thoughts run off in different directions.

Cynthia's heart was beating fast. In two hours' time she would meet up with Wilf beside Hadley cricket pitch – a scarcely credible notion for this novice in the romance stakes. What should she say? What should she do? Wouldn't it be better just to turn tail and run?

Millicent, meanwhile, continued to feel a festering resentment at always coming a poor second to Harold's wife and children. *It's not fair*, she told herself as she and Cynthia approached Heaton Yard. *If his lordship thinks he can hide me away in a corner for ever and for me not to mind, then he has another think coming.*

Distracted by her thoughts, she led the way across the yard, hardly bothering to reply to Walter's friendly greeting, then went inside without inviting Cynthia to follow her.

Cynthia hovered on the doorstep and did her best to rise to the challenge of the old man's banter.

'What's that lad of yours called again?' he yelled across the yard.

'Which lad?'

'The one your uncle has set on to us for the rent money – built like a bull terrier, with manners to match.'

'That's my cousin, Bert.' Cynthia heard Millicent go upstairs. Within seconds she was back down with the promised pale green dress and shoes.

'Pop upstairs and put them on while I make us a cuppa,' Millicent ordered briskly as she drew Cynthia into the house. 'There's a handy zip down the side. Let me know if you need any help.'

So Cynthia did as she was told. Once dressed, her reflection in Millicent's bedroom mirror came as a pleasant surprise – the fit of both shoes and dress was perfect, showing off her slim ankles and giving a glimpse of her knees when the skirt swung out as she turned to study herself from various angles. The wrap-over style made the best of her figure, though she felt self-conscious about some visible cleavage and the fact that the material was carefully shaped with darts and tucks to make the most of her bust.

'Perfect,' was Millicent's verdict when Cynthia appeared downstairs. 'Pretty as a picture – that's what you are.'

'I'm not overdoing it, am I?'

'Take it from me, you're not. One look at you and Wilf will fall head over heels.'

Is that what I really want? Cynthia wondered as she accepted a cup of tea from Millicent and took special care not to spill the contents. It was her first visit to Millicent's house and she took in the modern touches that her new friend had tried to impose on the ageing building. The silver clock on the mantelpiece was in the sleek, streamlined style named art deco and the wireless on the alcove shelf was similarly up-to-date. But there was no disguising the cracks in the ceiling or the creak of the sagging floorboards hidden beneath the bright green and orange rug.

'I'm green with envy.' Millicent's sigh lay heavy in the room. 'I'm telling you, if I had my time over again, I'd do things differently.'

'Why – how old are you?' Until now, Cynthia hadn't thought to ask.

'Twenty-five going on forty. That's what it feels like, anyhow.'

'Twenty-five isn't exactly over the hill.' Somehow Cynthia had imagined the age gap between them to be wider.

'Ta very much.' The remark drew a hollow laugh from Millicent. 'Seriously though, Cynthia, I'd advise you to go carefully with Wilf Evans.'

'Oh yes, don't worry, I will.'

'No – don't brush me off like that. I mean it. The truth is, Wilf had a bit of a bad name with women both before and after he got engaged to Adelaide. And you know what they say – a leopard can't change his spots.'

Cynthia swallowed hard. If she'd been nervous before, Millicent's warning made it ten times worse. 'What sort of a bad name?'

'Nothing to be too worried about. Let's just say he fancied himself as the local lothario.'

'Right you are.' Without really knowing what the word meant, Cynthia put down her cup with a trembling hand. 'Perhaps I ought to give backword. Do you think I should?'

'By no means,' Millicent declared as she bundled Cynthia out of the door in her borrowed dress and shoes. 'You walk out with Wilf as planned and knock him down dead, as the Americans say. Just don't stand any nonsense from him, that's all.'

After Cynthia rushed away from Heaton Yard in a flurry of mounting nerves, the minutes on Millicent's mantel clock ticked by at a snail's pace. She stared at the square black face marked only with lines on the quarter hours and watched the silver hand jerk forward. Tick – tick – tick. Where would Harold be now, right this minute? At the King's Head, playing in his precious darts match – that's where. He'd be wearing his weekend outfit of open-necked sports shirt and yellow cravat, together with his checked sports jacket and flannel trousers, his brown brogues brushed and polished.

She pictured him leaning forward and taking aim, releasing the dart and hearing it slam into the board, going back to his table and taking a drink from his pint glass, drawing the back of his hand across his mouth.

'That's it!' she said out loud. 'I'm going to have it out with him once and for all.'

So she put on her blue summer coat and hat and marched from the house, across the yard and down the hill on to Ghyll Road where she caught a bus into town. She didn't notice the queue that snaked along the pavement outside the Victory or the police cars parked close to the station, but stared straight ahead as she embarked on her single-minded mission.

'Where to?' The stout conductor had to stoop over her and ask for her fare.

'George Street,' she told him and received her ticket without offering a thank-you.

The bus approached City Square then drew up outside Marks & Spencer.

'George Street!' the conductor reminded her sharply.

Millicent got off, making her way past the Spiritualist church before cutting off down a side street and finding a back way to the King's Head. It was only when she got there that she paused to work out exactly what she should do next.

Both she and Harold would lose face if she walked in and demanded a conversation, she realized, and it would give his fellow darts players open season for ribald remarks. Worse still, the interruption would be sure to get back to Doris.

Millicent sighed impatiently and retreated to the steps of the Spiritualist church from where she could keep careful watch on the entrance to the pub. Sooner or later the darts match would finish and the players would emerge.

Determined to stay where she was, she watched a trickle of men come out in various states – one staggering aimlessly on to the pavement and stumbling into the gutter, followed by two pals who picked him up and walked him to the nearest bus stop before two more came whistling jauntily in her direction.

The taller one – a tidily dressed man in his fifties, with a trim moustache and an upright military air – noticed her on the church steps. 'I wouldn't hang around here if I was you, love,' he advised. 'People might get the wrong idea.'

'Thank you,' Millicent replied stiffly. 'I'm waiting for someone.'

The men walked on and she retreated further into the shadows until at last she saw Harold emerge, head bowed and hands cupped to his mouth as he lit a cigarette.

With her heart in her mouth, she ran down the steps and called his name.

'Millicent!' Fixed to the spot, he flicked the spent match on to the pavement and waited for her to draw near.

The look in his eyes reminded her of a cornered animal – cowering yet ready to launch an attack. She saw him afresh. Yes, he was familiar in his sports jacket and slacks, but his face was leaner than she'd realized and his hunched shoulders suggested deep suspicion.

'We have to talk,' she insisted.

'Not here.' A glance over his shoulder confirmed that no other members of the darts team had followed him out, so he took her by the shoulder and quickly marched her down the alley, out of the glare of the street lamps. He stopped outside the delivery entrance to Marks & Spencer and pushed her roughly against the padlocked door. 'What the devil?' he demanded, one hand gripping her shoulder.

She let out a short gasp and tried to push him away. 'Harold, there's no need—'

'There's every bloody need. What are you up to, Millicent? Do you want to ruin everything? Because if you do, this is the way to go about it.'

'Let go – you're hurting me!' She could smell the brilliantine on his hair and the smoke on his breath, see the spittle on his thin top lip as he recovered from the shock of seeing her. This was not the man she'd fallen for. At the start of their affair, Harold had stood out because of his ready wit and a penchant for natty sports jackets and brown brogues – shallow enough reasons to be drawn in, she now realized to her cost.

Still glaring, he eventually stepped back. 'I'm sorry,' he muttered. 'But what was I supposed to do – let everyone see us?'

She straightened the collar of her coat. 'Yes!' she declared. 'Why not?'

'You know why not.' He drew deeply on his cigarette.

'That's just it – that's exactly why I'm here.' Gathering herself, she made him walk on down the alley until they emerged on to a wider, better lit street. 'I'm fed up of being stuck away in a corner, Harold. That's the long and the short of it.'

'You want to break off?' A deep frown stayed etched on his face and he avoided looking at her as he spoke.

'No, that's not what I want. I just want some . . . acknowledgement.'

'How?' he shot back.

'I don't know. I just don't want to carry on as we are, that's all.'

They came to another corner and stopped at the

kerb. Harold finished his cigarette, threw it down then ground it with the ball of his foot. 'What do you want me to do? Come out into the open and let everyone know we're carrying on behind Doris's back? Is that it?'

'No.' The reality of the situation, the baldness with which he confronted her, made her shake her head and start to walk away. Then she stopped, went back and tried again to put her point of view. 'You don't know what it's like, being hidden away out of sight, having to keep our secret. Sometimes I feel as if I'll burst.'

The suspicious look returned. 'You haven't told anyone about us, have you?'

'No.'

'I don't believe you.'

'All right then – only Norma at work. She's my best friend. And Cynthia too. Don't worry – they won't spread it around.'

Harold clicked his tongue against his teeth in disbelief. Why couldn't women keep quiet the way men could? Why did secrets always have to worm their way out? He lit another cigarette and inhaled deeply. 'We should break off,' he said quietly. 'It would be for the best.'

'Best for who, Harold? For you and your precious family, that's who.' He always, always put himself first, never her. And yet he still claimed he loved her, bringing back to mind those first wonderful days they'd spent together. Her anger turned quickly to bitter resignation. 'Very well, then. If that's what you want.'

A single-decker bus turned the corner and came to a halt. Passengers alighted and dispersed. The bus drew away. Keeping their distance, Millicent and Harold walked on along the street between pools of yellow light.

'I don't *want* to,' he argued, head bowed and still not meeting her gaze. 'But you're not leaving me any choice.' On they walked, out on to Canal Road, scarcely noticing where they were going.

'It's not as if I've rushed you,' Millicent pointed out. 'It's been five long years, Harold, and I've got to the point where enough is enough.'

'So what?' he demanded. 'I'll ask you again. What do you want me to do – leave Doris and the kids and set up home with you?'

'Why not? You've said you would often enough.' The first time had been on Boxing Day three years back. Then after that it had been during a weekend away in Blackpool, and again in January this year – each time he'd raised her hopes and then dashed them. Tears of exasperation rose as she remembered the broken promises.

'If it was just Doris, it would be easy,' he confessed, though he knew in his heart that it wasn't that straightforward. There would still be the scandal of leaving his wife to contend with – the disapproval of his straight-laced boss, Joseph Oldroyd, then the possible loss of his job and house. 'But it isn't just her – it's Freddie and Derek.' *True, true!* His heart was squeezed at the thought of losing them and he realized with a sharp pang that his tie to his children was stronger than anything else.

'Yes.' *Here we are, back at the same old sticking point. Freddie and Derek.*

'If it wasn't for them . . .'

'Yes.'

They stumbled into a silence that lasted until they reached the corner of Brewery Road and stopped at the entrance to the vast wool-carding shed of Oldroyd's mill where sacks of shorn raw fleece arrived daily and were put on to conveyor belts ready for combing.

'You do know how I feel about you.' Speaking in an altered, softened tone, Harold took Millicent's hand and raised it. There was no one like her for looks and spirit – that mane of black hair, the shining hazel colour of her eyes.

She shuddered as she felt the brush of his lips on the back of her hand.

'Can't we go on as we are?' he begged. 'It's better than nothing, isn't it?'

'I don't know. Maybe.' *Oh, these familiar phrases, these sad, pleading looks – they tear my heart in two.* But perhaps he was right – what they had was better than nothing. In the other direction, loneliness beckoned – a sickening void of absence and loss.

'I'll be free next Friday,' he promised in a low

whisper, resting her hand against his cheek. 'We can go anywhere you like – you decide.'

In spite of all her so-called spirit, Millicent was easily beaten. It proved too hard to break the habit of their secret meetings and lovemaking, to turn her back on the tenderness she'd once felt. 'Very well,' she murmured. 'Let's take a bus out of town – to Beckwith.'

Harold led her under the shadowy arched entrance of the carding shed and drew her to him. He kissed her on the lips for a long time. 'I do love you,' he whispered into her ear. 'You know I do.'

'You want to go *where*?' Cynthia's Uncle William stood between her and the front door.

'To the dance at the Institute,' she repeated in a quavering voice. She'd decided to call in at Moor View to drop off her work things but now she regretted it. At this rate she wouldn't be in time to meet Wilf.

'And why are you all done up, pray?'

'I'm not,' she replied, the treacherous colour mounting to her cheeks.

'Yes you are – done up like a dog's dinner.'

It was a silly phrase and she disliked him for it, accompanied as it was by a sneering smile. Her irritation came to the fore and she had half a mind to push past him in the narrow hallway and slam the door after her.

'I thought you had to do your homework – your routes and rates, or whatever it is you call it.'

'Not tonight, Uncle William. It's Saturday.'

'Yes, and your mother's visiting us tomorrow, don't forget.' He breathed heavily and refused to budge. 'So I'd get your work done tonight if I were you.'

'Mum won't be here until the afternoon. I'll have plenty of chance in the morning.' Time was ticking by and her nerves were in shreds. 'Please, may I go?'

'Wait. You can do something for me while you're at it.' William delved into his pocket and produced a shilling piece. 'Give this to Leonard Andrews, and tell him I want him here again, same time next week.'

'Where is he?' Plucking up the courage to squeeze past, Cynthia opened the door and stepped out.

'Right there in front of your nose, sowing seeds in the veg patch.'

Sure enough, Leonard was at work in a corner of the garden with his back turned to them, crouched down and showing his eleven-year-old son, also called Leonard, how to lay down radish seeds in narrow drills. 'Cover them up carefully,' he advised. 'Not too deep, mind.'

Cynthia hurried across the lawn, her cheeks aflame with exasperation.

'My, don't you look nice,' the odd-job man commented with a friendly wink. He wiped his hands on his corduroy trousers then took the shilling. 'I take it you're off somewhere special?'

'Just to the village dance,' she said, almost running down the path and out of the gate and feeling more and more certain that agreeing to meet Wilf had been a big mistake. It would be all around the village for a start – Cynthia Ambler arriving at the Institute with Wilf Evans, the chap who worked as a conductor on the buses, who no one knew much about, other than that he and his mother had recently moved into North Park lodge on the Oldroyd estate. A lot would be read into Cynthia and Wilf walking in together, she was sure.

I wish I'd said no, she thought to herself as she hurried towards the cricket pitch and the fork in the road. No to Wilf's cheeky invitation, no to Millicent's loan of the dress and shoes, no to everything.

Yet the moment she caught sight of Wilf's tall, long-limbed figure leaning against the signpost, hands in pockets and smiling as she approached, she had a sudden change of heart.

'Hello, Cynthia!' he said, launching himself free of the post and coming to meet her. His smile was warm and welcoming, his manner easy, as if they'd bumped into each other by chance and it was a pleasant surprise. He was smartly dressed in collar and striped blue and red tie, blazer and slacks, his chin freshly shaven and hair combed back with a neat side parting.

'Hello.' *Here I am – I've done it!* she thought, instantly feeling more at ease with the situation. She felt she did look 'nice', as Leonard had said – Millicent's dress suited her and the heeled shoes brought a sway to her hips as she walked.

Wilf looked her up and down then whistled admiringly, offering her his arm to cross the road and walk down the straight main street. The Institute was a quarter of a mile down the road, opposite the village pub and next to the church.

'How was work?' he asked, as if he'd known her a long time. 'Were you run off your feet?'

'No, I'm still learning the job,' she answered honestly. 'Miss Mercer taught me some of the basics today – accuracy, efficiency and courtesy, that's what being a telephone girl is all about. Oh, and learning the right way of speaking. That's the hard part.'

'Why? There's nothing wrong with the way you speak.' *Or the way you look, the way you walk, the way you smile* – that's what he thought but didn't say. Normally he would have pitched right in, but something cautioned him not to go over the top with compliments as far as Cynthia was concerned. 'And what about your dancing – how are you with that?'

'I'm all right on the waltz and country dances like the Gay Gordons. We learned them at school. Not so good on the foxtrot, though.'

'The foxtrot has you foxed, eh?'

'Hah! Yes, but I can give it a go. How about you?'

'You mean, do I have two left feet?' Wilf pulled a face then laughed. 'You'll have to wait and see.'

They'd reached a row of terraced cottages backed by the rusty framework of old mine workings, including the tall steel tower topped by a giant wheel once used to crank the conveyor belt that brought coal up from deep underground. Beyond that lay grey slag heaps, ugly and bare of grass, which always reminded Cynthia of sleeping prehistoric beasts.

'So, Miss Ambler, what else did you learn at school, besides the waltz and the Gay Gordons?'

'Plenty,' she said archly, intending to break free of the trap of being teased. 'What about you?'

'Not much,' he laughed. 'I was the bad lad at the back of the class, firing ink pellets at the teacher. They couldn't wait to get rid of me.'

Cynthia deftly turned the tables. 'Then it must be a case of opposites attract, supposing of course . . .'

He winked. 'I asked you to walk out with me and you said yes. I reckon it's an open and shut case,' he said with a confident grin.

By this time they'd reached the high iron railings of the Institute building and could hear strains of music drifting out through the open doors. They crossed the gravelled yard and went in to find a group of five musicians sitting on a small stage at the far end of a long hall. The room had seen better days – the old radiators were dusty and the greyish-green walls in need of a fresh coat of paint – but the band was smartly dressed in dark pinstripe suits and polished black shoes and they attacked a polka score with gusto, led by two violins and a tinkling upright piano. Only a smattering of couples were attempting the energetic dance, with everyone else lining the walls, either talking or watching warily in case one of the couples spun out of control. When Cynthia and Wilf walked in, all heads turned.

Leonard's wife, Mary, was the first to recognize Cynthia and recover from the surprise of seeing her teamed up with the new lad from North Park lodge. 'Squeeze in over here,' she mouthed, beckoning them across. 'There's room for two littl'uns.'

'That was fast work,' Dick Richards, a long-time Hadley resident, complained to his cousin, Ron Black. The two young men stood stolidly sipping beer and leaning against the radiator furthest from the door. 'Wilf Evans hasn't been in Hadley for five minutes and he lands the best-looking catch for miles around.'

'You should have made your move sooner.' Ron knew that Dick had been like a lovesick calf around Cynthia for months but had been too shy to act. She was too butter-wouldn't-melt for Ron's taste, but he could see she would have suited Dick down to the ground.

'Mary, this is Wilf Evans.' Across on the other side of the room and speaking as the polka came to an end, Cynthia made the introductions. 'Wilf, this is Mary Andrews.'

'Pleased to meet you.' Mary's smile carried a great deal of curiosity and she used the gap between dances to prise as much information as she could out of the newcomer. 'How are you and your mother settling in at the lodge?'

'We're champion, ta.' Wilf didn't plan to pay much attention to the homely, dumpy woman with crimped hair and work-worn hands, but he underestimated her terrier-like tenacity.

'Where was home before you came here?'

'We lived in town – alongside the canal, on Bridge Street.'

'And how long were you there?'

'Four or five years.'

'Just the two of you?'

'Yes, just me and Mum.' He wished the band would start playing again, to drown out any further questions, but the musicians were fiddling with their sheet music and there was a long lull between numbers.

'Which end of Bridge Street?'

'The far end, close to the gasworks.'

'Then I'm not surprised your mother would jump at the chance to move out to North Park, where you can breathe the air, even if Mr Oldroyd does keep a tight rein on his domestic staff.' Mary had known Cynthia ever since she came to live with her uncle and her motherly tendency was coming to the fore. She was looking Wilf up and down when the band at last struck up a new tune and she carried on watching him as he swept Cynthia on to the dance floor for a Viennese waltz. 'There's something about him,' she muttered to Tilly Baker, who ran the branch library and had volunteered to do the interval tea and biscuits with her.

'In what way?'

'I don't know. He's just not my cup of tea.'

Tilly, who was in her twenties and ever on the lookout for a suitable beau, disagreed. 'I think he's a good catch.' She studied Wilf, who was handsome and smiling, a nifty mover on the floor, able to guide Cynthia between other couples and keep a smooth rhythm as he whirled her around.

1-2-3, 1-2-3 – Cynthia felt light-headed. 1-2-3 into the furthest corner of the room then back across the polished floor, weaving in and out, twirling and tilting in unison. She felt her skirt flare and feared that others would catch a glimpse of her stocking tops if she wasn't careful but she was enjoying herself too much to really mind, her left hand resting lightly on Wilf's shoulder while he kept a firm hold of her waist.

All too soon the waltz ended but he didn't relax his hold. They waited in the middle of the room as other couples milled around them, breaking up and re-forming, chatting and laughing.

'Let's hope the band livens things up a bit with this next one.' Without taking his eyes off Cynthia, Wilf tilted his head towards the stage. 'I fancy a rumba or a cha-cha-cha.'

'You'd have to teach me,' she warned. The Latin American dances were too racy to have been taught at school, involving as they did a lot of motion with the hips.

'My pleasure,' he said with a wink. He was disappointed at first to hear a number from *I Live for*

Love, the latest Busby Berkeley musical, then quickly made the most of the romantic tune by drawing Cynthia in even closer for a slow waltz.

Chest to chest, with his arm around her waist, she found that she had to tilt her head back to see his face – so close that it was out of focus, the grey eyes flecked with blue and green, his skin soft and unlined, smelling of shaving soap.

'All right?' he checked with her as the floor grew crowded and their movement more restricted. 'Not too warm?'

'No – just right,' she whispered back, as if there was nobody else in the room, nobody looking, nobody judging – just her and Wilf in a world of their own.

CHAPTER SIX

On the following day, Sunday, Douglas arrested a tramp for causing a nuisance on the steps of the corporation baths. After that he nabbed two fourteen-year-old lads for breaking the plate-glass window of George Green's tripe shop on Ghyll Road, then a bicycle thief collared by the quick-thinking owner who had scattered a handy box of tacks on the road to puncture the front tyre and bring the bloke crashing down.

'All in a day's work,' he explained to Hetty and Ethel at Albion Lane as he waited for Norma to get ready for a late-afternoon stroll. 'It was the early shift, so there wasn't a lot going on.'

'Why the tripe shop?' Ethel asked. Her Sunday had consisted of chapel in the morning, followed by a big roast dinner then a chit-chat with her friend, Bunty Knight, on a bench outside the Green Cross. Now, listening to Douglas's account of his day at the police station, she picked up scraps of local gossip, ready for her next session with Bunty.

'They had a grudge against the owner. George Green is known for finding any old excuse to sack his delivery boys without paying them. These lads thought it was time to teach the old skinflint a lesson, but it's my job to show them you can't go taking the law into your own hands.' Douglas was uncomfortable in the stultifying atmosphere of the Haigs' living room. Hetty never had the window open, even on sunny days, and the smell of roast beef hung in the still air. There were pots and pans left to dry on the draining board and Ethel's out-of-shape shoes lying on the rug where she'd stepped out of them.

'Tell Norma to get a move on,' Hetty told Ethel. In her opinion, her youngest daughter spent far too long getting ready for these outings with Douglas, faffing over her lipstick and generally fiddle-faddling over what to wear. She was copying those photos of film stars she had pinned to the wall in her corner of the attic room she shared with Ethel and Ivy. They gave her ideas above her station and made her forget that she came from a family of mill workers and tinkers, stall holders and labourers.

'Norma!' Ethel yelled from the bottom of the stairs. 'Mum says to hurry up.'

With one last look in the mirror, Norma hurried down. She was wearing a short-sleeved, cream blouse with rosebuds embroidered into the collar and a gored jade-green skirt. 'Do I need my coat?' she asked Douglas, who came forward to greet her with a respectable peck on the cheek.

'No, it's still warm out there.' There was always a moment whenever he saw Norma when he wanted to sweep her into his arms and carry her away like a knight on a white charger, to breathe her in and soak her up like a sunny day. 'Ready?'

She nodded and they escaped from the house, heading up the hill towards the Common.

'Phew!' Norma showed that she'd rushed her preparations for his sake and fanned her face with her hand.

'Yes – phew.' He was glad to be out, breathing the fresh air and taking in the vista at the top of the hill. The Common was a large area of unfenced grassland criss-crossed by cinder tracks and grazed by half a dozen dray horses from nearby Thornley's Brewery. In the centre there was a pretty pavilion where bands played on special occasions such as the Whitsuntide Gala. Beyond it, open moorland stretched on towards the jagged horizon.

Norma and Douglas headed for the pavilion. They sat there for a long time holding hands in contented silence, their backs to the town, facing the wide-open space and basking in the sun's last rays. A swallow had made its nest under the canopy. They watched her fly in and out with food for the noisy chicks, swooping down from a great height and scarcely pausing at the nest before turning and soaring off again. In and out, in and out, with midges and daddy-long-legs in her beak – never enough food for the greedy chicks with their gaping yellow mouths.

'Shall we walk on?' Douglas asked. 'We can get most of the way to Brimstone Rock and back before the sun sets.'

Norma nodded. Beyond the pavilion, the cinder tracks turned to grassy paths with meadow flowers to either side – at this time of year a riot of buttercups, clover, pale milkmaids and low purple vetch. White clouds drifted overhead, moving from east to west towards the setting sun.

'I must be the luckiest man in the world,' Douglas declared as they left the town far behind. He almost strutted with pride to have Norma on his arm, nodding hello to fellow walkers and standing to one side for a passing cyclist. 'Tell me – what did I do to deserve you, Norma Haig?'

Her eyes shone with pleasure. 'Stop, or you'll make me even more big-headed than I already am.'

'Who says you're big-headed?'

'Mum. "Don't go getting ideas above your station" is what she says.'

Norma's accurate imitation of her mother's narrow, world-weary voice made Douglas smile.

'It started when I got my job at the exchange. Since then, she and Ethel have made it their mission to take me down a peg or two.'

'Don't listen to them.' He gave her hand a comforting pat. 'They're only jealous.'

'Maybe. But Mum doesn't realize that times are changing. She's well and truly stuck in the past.'

'What age is she – sixty?'

'Sixty-three and still slaving away at Kingsley's four days a week. She and Dad had no savings – not even enough to pay for his funeral after he had a heart attack and died. Ethel chipped in with what she could, but Ivy and I were too young to help. Since then we've started earning our own money but we still struggle to make ends meet – like everyone else, I suppose.'

Douglas said nothing for a while. He looked ahead at the horizon, not down at the heather that encroached on the grass underfoot. It was high time he screwed his courage to the sticking point, he decided. He'd been thinking about it long enough. So, with a rapidly beating heart, he let go of Norma's hand and dropped down on to one knee. Startled, she took a step back.

'Douglas, what are you doing?'

He spread his arms wide in a gesture that he'd pictured and planned for. Kneeling, spreading his arms – that's how a man made a proposal to the woman he loved. 'Norma Haig, will you marry me?'

She gasped. He was doing what they did in books and on the silver screen – Rudolph Valentino in a military jacket and white trousers, with lovelorn expression and trim dark moustache. Except that Douglas was here in the flesh and her heart was racing. He was really doing it – he was asking her to marry him. 'I . . . I don't know,' she answered in a whisper.

Doubt flickered across his features. He caught hold of her hand. 'Say yes!'

Norma shook her head. Panic shot through her. Her words came out in a jumble. 'I'm not saying "no". I don't want you to think . . .'

The moment that should have changed their lives for ever had come and gone. Here he was, kneeling and looking up at her – making the grand gesture – but it had somehow gone wrong. Awkwardly he got to his feet and sought an answer in her flushed cheeks and downcast eyes. 'I love you. I thought you loved me.'

'I do,' she murmured. 'Honestly, I do. But—'

'But what?'

'I wasn't expecting it.' Swallows swept across the clear sky with dizzying speed. Her head reeled. *Say yes*, she told herself. *Don't make the poor man suffer.*

It had all gone wrong and his dreams had come crashing down – the wedding ring and the little rented house, the satisfaction of coming home and finding Norma there at the end of each working day. 'I'm sorry – I rushed into it,' he said in a choked voice. 'I should have built up to it, chosen a better time.'

'No . . . Yes. Don't say sorry.' Norma struggled to breathe. 'I really am not saying "no", Douglas.'

'But you're not saying "yes" either.' Her first words – 'I don't know' – were already etched in his memory. They were three short words that would colour their lives for ever, whatever she decided in the end.

'I'm not sure of my answer,' she confessed. 'I can't picture what it would be like, getting married and leaving my job to be a full-time housewife . . .'

'Living together.' Douglas held this out as part of the cherished dream – he and Norma eating their meals and keeping house, climbing the stairs to bed.

She looked at him in fresh confusion. 'We would be engaged first?'

'Yes – however long you like. You can choose your ring – a ruby, a sapphire – anything you want.'

'Oh, Douglas!' It was what girls wanted – a glittering ring, a handsome fiancé. And Douglas was wonderful to look at, with his light brown eyes and straight brows, a small cleft in his chin that just now bore a dark shadow because he hadn't stopped to shave when he got changed out of his uniform but instead had dashed up to Albion Lane to meet her. More importantly, he was known as the friendliest bobby on the beat. He saw good in everyone, even in the petty criminals that he arrested every day of the week. Everyone deserves a second chance, he would say, believing that a short spell in Armley prison would set wrongdoers back on the straight and narrow. Upbeat, affable, ambitious, a pillar of the community – what more could she ask?

'What's wrong?' he murmured, reaching out to cradle the back of her head in his hand. Her hair was soft and perfumed. He adored her, would lay down his life for her.

'It's too much for me,' she said weakly. *Say yes*, the voice inside her head repeated. But her heart was doubtful.

'I'm sorry.' He withdrew his hand and stepped

back to try to get his feelings under control, turned away towards the Crag then looked back at her.

'Give me a while to think it over,' she pleaded humbly.

He swallowed hard then nodded to show that he would respect her wishes. 'I won't mention it again until you're ready. Come on. I'll walk you back home.'

Gratefully she slid her hand into his and they walked back the way they'd come. They parted at the pavilion with a sad, hopeful kiss.

'I'll meet you out of work on Wednesday, then?' he asked, still searching her face for the answer he really wanted. 'I'm on mornings this week, so I'll finish early.'

'Yes.' She nodded, her heart beating fast, her head in a whirl. 'Outside the exchange. I'll see you then.'

Sunday wasn't treated as a day of rest by Millicent. She liked to be out and about, exercising by taking a bike ride into the country or joining her rambling group for a day's walking in the Dales, which is what she chose to do on the day after she'd confronted Harold outside the King's Head.

The company will do me good, she'd told herself. Out early, she met up at the corner of Ghyll Road and Albion Lane with regulars Herbert Carney, the two Janets – Holtby and Jenkins – Ruth Ridley and Agnes Mercer from work and a new member called Sam Altham. They were all outdoorsy, energetic types equipped with stout shoes and binoculars, carrying small canvas rucksacks containing sandwiches and thermos flasks. The women wore jumpers and pleated skirts that allowed freedom of movement, the men were in khaki shorts, long socks and open-necked shirts. Everyone wore hats – berets, cloches or flat caps.

A bus journey out of town took them through Hadley and far beyond, heading north through quaint villages that hadn't moved with the times – not much sign of the twentieth century here, with farmers out in the steeply sloping fields scything grass or loading milk churns on to horse-drawn carts. The houses were low with stone slate roofs and mullioned windows, set around village greens complete with church, pub and post office.

Millicent's group alighted at a remote village called Shawcross and spent the day walking over high escarpments into the neighbouring dale. It was a steep climb over shale and rock into a green valley then down and along a riverside track, stopping for a picnic by an ancient packhorse bridge then covering another eight miles before they reached Saxby and the one bus of the afternoon that would carry them home.

After a ten-minute wait, the bus hove into view and the men hung back to let the women on board first, which put Millicent behind Agnes and Ruth for the homeward journey, with Herbert Carney next to her and the rest of the group spread around.

Herbert, a confirmed bachelor with horn-rimmed

glasses and thinning hair, wasn't much of a talker, so Millicent settled in for a quiet ride, taking in more of the countryside and slowly tuning in to the conversation between the two supes from work.

'Brenda and Molly are talking about setting up a record club for the switchboard girls,' Agnes told Ruth. 'They propose to club together and buy a phonograph for the restroom.'

'Whatever for? We have a wireless, don't we?' Ruth's response was predictably unenthusiastic.

'They say they want to listen to more up-to-date music during their dinner breaks.'

'I might have known Molly and Brenda would be behind something like that.'

On they went, with Millicent lending an idle ear, until the supes' conversation drifted away from work on to acquaintances they had in common.

'You know about George Green's window getting broken overnight?' Agnes mentioned.

'Yes. I bumped into his wife first thing – she told me all about it.'

'Done by a pair of his delivery lads, apparently.'

'That's what I heard, too.' Again, Ruth couldn't summon up much interest and she quickly moved on. 'But what about Joseph Oldroyd's plan to lay off more people in the weaving shed? That's going to come as a big blow.'

'That's news to me,' Agnes admitted.

Able only to see the backs of Ruth and Agnes's heads, Millicent pricked up her ears for more details.

'I heard it from Doris Buckley, who's a chum of mine from our badminton club. If it's true, this time it's not just the learners who are in for the chop – the reaching-in people and the loom cleaners – it's the weavers themselves and the weft men.'

'Doris must know what she's talking about,' Agnes conceded. 'She'll have heard it straight from Harold, after all.'

Ruth leaned her head closer to Agnes and spoke more softly. 'Don't spread this around, but she dropped a hint that Harold is worried about his own job.'

'No – Oldroyd would never sack his manager!'

Millicent frowned and leaned back in her seat. She stared steadfastly out of the window, now trying to block out what she was hearing.

'I wouldn't waste much sympathy on Harold Buckley.' Ruth's caustic remark turned the talk in yet another direction.

'Why is that?'

'Rumour has it that he follows interests outside of his wife and family, if you pick up my meaning.'

'Never! Does Doris know?'

'She's not daft. I'm sure she suspects. A wife does, when something like that is going on.'

In the seat behind, Millicent's face flushed deep red. Try as she might, she couldn't avoid being plunged into the purgatory of hearing Harold's name dragged through the mud.

'He's the type,' Ruth insisted with the certainty that came out of bitter experience.

'Really? I can't say I've noticed.'

'Believe me – I know when a man is carrying that kind of secret around with him. You just have to take one look – Harold is shifty through and through.'

'But it's not right.' Agnes struggled to comprehend. 'He has two kiddies to think about.'

'That's just it – they don't *think*,' Ruth said sourly. 'Just like the "other woman" in these situations – they don't think of anything or anyone except themselves.'

Millicent felt her throat constrict and she clenched her fists until her knuckles turned white.

'Are you all right?' Herbert asked. 'You've gone white as a sheet.'

'I'm a bit queasy, that's all,' she confessed. 'It's the motion of the bus when it goes round the bends.'

Herbert took a bag of peppermints from his pocket. 'Suck one of these,' he suggested.

'Ta.' She took a mint and clumsily undid the wrapper.

'Selfish through and through,' Ruth concluded with unconcealed venom. 'If what I've heard is true, Harold Buckley deserves to lose everything – wife, kiddies, house, job – the lot.'

Cynthia's head was full of Wilf Evans – Wilf had said this, said that, turned his head in a certain way, had a rising inflexion in his voice when he wished her goodnight.

115

'Goodnight?' he'd said as they'd parted at the fork in the road the night before.

'Yes, goodnight.' Her heart had raced at what else he might expect.

She hadn't leaned in to kiss him, which was answer enough. This was a young chick teetering on the edge of the nest, he reminded himself. Slowly, slowly she would prepare to take flight. 'Have you had a nice time?'

'Very nice, ta.' She had thrilled to every single moment, danced every dance with him, held his hand as they left the Institute and walked towards Moor View.

'Will you walk out with me again?'

Her breath had caught in her throat as she'd nodded.

'How about next Friday?'

Another wide-eyed nod. Six whole days to wait before she felt his arm around her again, felt his cheek against hers – the unexpected sandpapery roughness and dryness, the smell of Imperial Leather soap.

'Shall we go to the flicks?'

'Yes please. I'd like that.'

'Champion. Where shall we meet?'

'In town, next to the cenotaph in City Square?'

'Rightio. Goodnight, then.'

He'd let her go and she'd walked on along the narrow path under the moon and stars, past the cricket pitch, through the gate and up to the house

116

where she'd turned her key in the lock and entered quiet as a church mouse so as not to wake her uncle.

She'd crept upstairs and got undressed then lay awake as the church bell struck midnight, one o'clock, two o'clock. Wilf was still there in her imagination, smiling at her, tilting his head, whisking her off her feet. At last she dropped off to sleep and woke to hear her uncle's stick thumping the ceiling below her.

'Missy, wake up!' he called. 'It's ten past eight. Where's my cup of tea?' And so she began the routine of the day – take the old man his tea and then clear out the grates in the kitchen and living room. After that, she cooked a breakfast of bacon and eggs, swept the floors, made the beds then sat down to study more routes and rates in the front room overlooking the garden.

Once her head was stuffed with names and numbers, she put the booklet aside and placed the training record on the turntable of the wind-up gramophone. She reread the printed instructions on the brown paper sleeve.

'This record provides correct pronunciations of words commonly used by telephone operators throughout the United Kingdom. Regional variations are discouraged. Listen carefully and proceed slowly. Remember – practice makes perfect.'

Cynthia wound the handle then set the turntable spinning before gently lowering the needle on to the record, which produced a static hiss. Then a woman began to speak – slow, high and nasal like the voices you heard on the radio. 'Hello, caller.'

'Hello, caller,' Cynthia repeated with a self-conscious grimace.

'I have a connection.'

'I have a connection.' *Pronounce the 'h' distinctly, don't slur the last word.*

'Go ahead, please.'

'Go ahead, please.'

'Well, well.' The door opened and Beryl entered the room in her brown cloche hat and fox-fur collar, straight off the bus from chapel, bemused by what she saw. 'What have we here?'

Hastily Cynthia lifted the needle and rested the arm back in its cradle, then she flicked the switch to its off position. 'Hello, Mum. I'm practising for work.'

'So I see. William told me all about it over a cup of tea.'

'I didn't know you were here.'

'I slipped in the back way.'

Cynthia invited her mother to inspect the gramophone. 'The record tells you the right way to say things. What do you think of that?'

Beryl eyed the machine with sniffy disdain. 'I'm happy with the way I talk, ta very much.'

'That's not the point. This is for switchboard girls only.'

'And why can't you use your normal voices? That's what I'd like to know.'

'Because.' There was no point in entering into explanations, Cynthia realized as she sat her mother down in the chesterfield by the window. 'Anyway, how are you? How's Dad?'

'Your dad's caught a cold. He risked going up on to his allotment – when was it? – on Wednesday and got caught in a shower. He came home soaking wet and took straight to his bed.'

'Did you call Dr Bell?'

Beryl shook her head and eased off her threadbare gloves. 'We can't afford to bother the doctor with a common cold, can we?' Beryl's hard-done-by expression deepened. 'I was telling William – I honestly don't know what we'd have done without him. It's bad enough trying to feed two mouths on what your father earns from odd jobs here and there – whenever he feels up to it. If your uncle hadn't stepped in when you left school, we'd never have managed.'

Cynthia tried to shrug off the burdensome responsibility that her mother regularly placed on her shoulders. 'How's Bert getting along with the rent collecting – did Uncle William say?'

The lame attempt to change the subject quickly backfired. 'If you want to know what I think – you never should have handed that job over to Bert.' Beryl shook her head wearily. 'It gives him a foot in the door.'

'But I couldn't carry on – not with the hours they expect me to work at the telephone exchange.'

Her mother raised her eyebrows but said nothing.

'It's a good job, Mum, and the supes say I'm a quick learner.'

'Supes?'

'Supervisors – Miss Mercer and Miss Ridley. I'll soon be put on the actual switchboards – once I've learned the proper pronunciations.'

'Oh yes, you're a right little Eliza Doolittle, I'm sure.' Beryl's flash of sarcasm contained a lifetime of thwarted ambition. Like Cynthia, she'd been a bright spark at school, always top of the class in reading, writing and arithmetic. Her aim had been to study hard and become a pharmacist and she'd travelled a fair way down that road as an apprentice until she'd made the big mistake of meeting and marrying Ellis Ambler.

That had been in the build-up to the Great War, when he'd been young and full of life, apprenticed to a picture framer on Westgate Road. Then the war took him to the trenches in Belgium where the mud and the blood, the hiss of gas and the choking cries of comrades had extinguished any flame of hope that may once have flickered in the young man's breast. He'd been invalided out at the start of 1917 and returned home with stooping shoulders, a glazed expression and an aversion to mixing with his old friends and family that he never succeeded in shaking off.

Cynthia winced but she was used to her mother's criticism – if not outright then always inferred. Her mind flashed back over the efforts she'd made as a small child to please her parents – to be polite at all times, to sit on the window sill and learn her ABC while other little girls ran up and down the street, plaited hair flying, bare knees scraped and muddy, screeching each other's names.

It had been enough to win the occasional pained smile from her mother; there had never been any flicker of a response from her father.

Beryl stared at her now with an anxious expression. 'As a matter of fact, William isn't in the best of moods. He says he had to knock on the ceiling to get his cup of tea this morning, and that's because you went out gadding last night.'

'I didn't go far – just to the Institute.' Cynthia grew hot under the collar as she tried to cover her tracks.

'Who with? No, don't tell me. Let me guess – it was one of the women from the telephone exchange. I'm sure they're very modern – just the type to lead you astray.'

'Not at all,' she protested. 'They're very kind to me.'

Beryl ploughed on regardless. 'William caught sight of you done up to the nines in an outfit he'd never seen before.'

'I borrowed a dress from Millicent – yes. And some shoes.' *Let Mother get side-tracked away from Wilf* was the thought at the forefront of Cynthia's mind.

'You see – I was right. Those girls will turn your head in the wrong direction if you're not careful.' The weight of the world was evident in Beryl's lined face as she sat with her hat on, her coat undone and her darned gloves laid neatly across her lap. 'I've said it to your father a dozen times and I'll say it to your face – new job or not, your first duty is still to your uncle. That must come before every-thing else.'

'Yes,' Cynthia acquiesced, for there was no point arguing.

'And don't let Bert step in and make himself too useful, do you hear?'

'Yes, Mum.' She smiled to herself at the idea of crash-bang-wallop Bert cleaning grates, polishing stair rods and doing the laundry. 'I can't see him being that handy with an iron, can you?'

'It's no joke, Cynthia. We're relying on you to mind your Ps and Qs with your uncle and not to upset him.' It had been a long waiting game as far as Beryl was concerned, with Moor View as the prize. Though she never expressed this outright, it was the natural order of things. An ailing bachelor brother had to make a will and it ought to be in favour of those who had helped him most – which was her and not their estranged younger brother, Gilbert – Bert's dad. 'Promise me you won't do any-thing to upset him.'

'I promise.' In secret, Cynthia clung on to the sun-shine world that was just opening out, that contained

Wilf Evans and laughter, dances, embraces, kisses and who knew what else.

Beryl stood up and buttoned her coat with an air of finality. 'Good. Let's leave it at that then. The bus into town is due in ten minutes. Walk me to the stop, there's a good girl.'

CHAPTER SEVEN

'Listen, you two – I need your advice.' Norma collared Millicent and Cynthia at the start of their dinner break next day. They came off duty in shifts and had had to wait until Molly, Brenda and some others had returned at one o'clock before they were free to leave their switchboards. 'Out of the blue Douglas has asked me to marry him!'

Millicent responded with a shrill peal of laughter. 'Come off it, Norma. Don't tell me you weren't expecting it!'

'I really wasn't,' she protested as all three collected their coats then crowded together in one section of the revolving door. 'Honestly, Millicent – whenever you teased me about it, I let it in through one ear and out the other. I truly thought Douglas and I were jogging along nicely from week to week, not looking to the future.'

'Well, believe me – you were the only one who was in the dark about Douglas's intentions.' Emerging on to a street where the pavements were wet and a steady drizzle descended from thick grey clouds, Millicent put up her umbrella and shared it with the others. 'Wasn't she, Cynthia?'

'I couldn't really say.' Cynthia hugged her own secret about Wilf close to her chest and held back from expressing an opinion on matters of the heart. 'I haven't met Douglas.'

'You mean, PC Perfect.' Millicent herded them down the steps, past Sam Bower's and into the new hairdressing salon where the smart, older woman they'd seen previously sat at the reception desk, talking on the telephone. In the background, two customers sat draped in pink nylon capes while their young stylists snipped and curled away. A strong smell of permanent-wave solution struck the back of their throats as Millicent, Norma and Cynthia walked in. 'To be honest, I'm surprised it's taken him this long.'

'Did you say yes?' Cynthia was eager to know as Millicent closed her umbrella and placed it in the stand by the door.

'That's the thing. I didn't – not straight away,' Norma confessed.

Millicent pulled a sad face. 'Poor Douglas – don't tell me you're making him wait.' Norma's situation was so much in contrast to her own that she grew determined to press her point home. 'For goodness' sake, what's stopping you? Once upon a time, if a certain someone had been free to go down on one knee and propose marriage to me, I'd have jumped at the chance.'

'I know you would. But I didn't know what to say. I was lost for words.'

They'd come to Sylvia's to make three appointments for later in the week – Millicent and Norma for a trim and Cynthia for a consultation and a complete change of style, which was what the other two insisted she needed.

'We'll turn you into a woman of the world before you know it,' Millicent had promised as they made their plan to call in at the hairdresser's before they ate their sandwiches back in the restroom. She'd dismissed Cynthia's protestations and now here they were, waiting for the salon owner to come off the telephone.

'Boo-hoo, poor Douglas,' Millicent said again. 'Why have you left him on tenterhooks? Don't you love him?'

Cynthia could see their reflection in a large mirror on the wall facing them – she was dressed in her beige mac, standing between Millicent in a short, cherry-red jacket, her black hair swept up and held in place by a pair of silver combs, and Norma in a pale blue coat with a stand-up collar teamed with a royal blue dress. Yes, it was high time to change her style, Cynthia concluded with an upward tilt of her chin.

'I do love him.' Norma was in no doubt about that. 'But?'

'But think about it, Millicent. If I say yes and rush into marriage, that'll be the end of my days at the switchboard.'

'Ah, I see.' Millicent thought this through for a while. 'Not necessarily. It's not like teaching or nursing. The GPO doesn't have a law against employing married women.'

Norma shook her head. 'No, but how many of them do we have here in George Street?'

'All right – none. Oh yes, one – Ruth Ridley.'

'She's divorced so that doesn't count. Anyway, it might not be against the rules as such, but we all know what happens when a woman gets married.'

'She has babies.' Millicent grasped the point at last. 'Then she stays at home and looks after them.'

'And I don't think I'm ready for that yet.' Norma had lain awake most of the night trying to understand her feelings for Douglas, listing them like ingredients in a cake. There was a big dollop of love and longing plus a good spoonful of spicy desire – she recognized this as she pictured him high on the diving platform during their recent visit to the lido. He'd been by far the most handsome man there as he stretched his arms forward and plunged into the water, straight as an arrow. Her heart had lurched as he hit the water with scarcely a splash and only beat steadily again once he'd resurfaced. Yes, she loved and desired him, but was it the right mixture – her and him blended and baked together till death did them part?

The woman behind the desk put down the phone then spoke to them in stiff but apologetic tones. 'I'm sorry to have kept you waiting.'

As usual Millicent took the lead. 'That's all right. We'd like to make three appointments for Saturday, please.'

'By all means.' Instead of welcoming new business, the woman seemed irritated and unsure as she glanced around the room then opened a large diary and unscrewed the top of a pen. She was interrupted by one of the stylists who cleared her throat as she approached the desk. 'Excuse me, Mrs Parr – Clare wasn't feeling very well. She had to go upstairs and lie down. You were busy on the telephone so she asked me to tell you.'

'Did she say what was the matter?'

'She was feeling light-headed, I think.' The young hairdresser spoke with downcast eyes, clasping her hands in front of her.

'Thank you, Barbara.' In the absence of her receptionist, the shop owner prepared to note their details, giving Cynthia, Norma and Millicent time to take in her appearance – not a blonde hair out of place, of course, and wearing a loose-fitting cream jacket over an apricot-coloured dress with two strings of pearls around her long neck. Her carefully powdered face had arched eyebrows and thin lips, plumped out by a lipstick in a darker tone than her dress. The whole effect was superior and in the vein of Wallis Simpson or of a royal lady-in-waiting, Norma decided, though the clipped voice contained flat, short vowels, giving away less than aristocratic origins.

'I've made two appointments for one o'clock and

one for half past with Barbara and Margaret,' Mrs Parr said, pressing white blotting paper over their names.

'Ta very much.' Breezily casting a final glance around the room at the revolving leather chairs, polished parquet floor and shiny mirrors, Millicent seemed satisfied. 'Come along, girls – dinner time!'

They were on their way out when they were rapidly overtaken by a man who had appeared as if from nowhere – in fact, from a rear door that gave access to the upstairs rooms. He seemed to be in a hurry but he remembered his manners in time to hold open the door for them and they got a close view of his face – fair skinned, with small, straight features and deep-set grey eyes – the man in the Morris Cowley who Millicent had seen with Clare in the King's Head, who had popped up a few days later emerging from the hairdresser's with the salon owner on his arm.

'Ta very much,' Millicent said as she slid easily by.

'Thank you,' Norma and Cynthia added more shyly.

They were out on the pavement, considering this set of coincidences and passing snap judgements on the natty dresser as he headed towards City Square.

'Those gloves and that hat must have cost a pretty penny,' Millicent remarked.

'What was he doing behind the scenes of a ladies' hairdresser's?' Norma wondered. 'Unless he is what's-her-name's son, after all.'

'Mrs Parr's? You're way off the mark.' Millicent was still adamant on that score. 'He's Clare's secret beau, I'll bet my bottom dollar. I know for a fact she has lodgings above the salon.'

'It looks as though they were up there together,' Norma realized with an air of scandalized surprise. 'Alone!'

Millicent made a show of covering Cynthia's ears. 'Hush – not when there are children present!'

It wasn't so funny a few minutes later, when they sat in the restroom at work, eating sandwiches and still reflecting on what they'd seen.

'That chap's like a bad penny, turning up when you least expect him,' Norma said with a sigh. 'Close up, I'd say he's far too cocky by half.' She recalled the way he held open the door for them with one eyebrow raised and a smile that could easily have been a smirk, thin lips tilted up at one corner. 'If I were Clare, I wouldn't want anything to do with him.'

'Well, you're not her,' was Millicent's only comment. Her mind had gone off at a tangent on to Harold and the times when she, Millicent, had skulked in corners with him – though never quite so blatantly. She liked to think their trysts were more discreet and more tasteful, but after what she'd overheard on the rambler group's bus ride home from Saxby she was no longer so sure.

'It's coming up to two o'clock,' Cynthia alerted them, one eye on the clock above the door.

'Yes, indeed.' Norma stood up and brushed crumbs from her skirt. 'Come along, girls, it's time to take the lights.'

Norma's afternoon of tapping front and rear keys to complete hundreds of cord circuits went without incident. Daylight filtered into the long room through high windows and Cynthia sat next to her, quietly observing every move.

'Remember, these jacks on the back panel are all female sockets,' Norma instructed. 'Each one is wired as a local extension, or else as an incoming or outgoing trunk line. And when a jack lamp lights up, you place the rear cord into the jack and that automatically throws the front key forward.'

Norma went through the procedure as she spoke. 'Then my caller tells me the number he would like to connect with . . . Hello, Mr Brown. Go ahead, please . . . Hello, London, I have a new ticket, wanted as soon as possible.'

Keeping her eye on the switchboard and pressing keys and speaking with accustomed ease, Norma pushed her headset back and spoke again to Cynthia. 'Once I connect the two lines, both cords are left in the up position.'

Cynthia took in every scrap of information. 'How do you know when to end the call?'

'Simple – there's no need to listen in. In fact, it's against the rules. This supervision lamp on the back panel lights up to alert us that it's time to remove the jacks from the sockets.' Norma removed the cords as she spoke. 'See – it's as easy as pie.'

'Elbows in, Millicent. Take that light, Brenda. Come along, girls – chop-chop!' Ruth Ridley patrolled the central aisle, keeping everyone on their toes. Up and down she went, vigilant as a sergeant major, ready to find fault with everyone and everything. 'Cynthia, don't lean in so close – you're getting in Norma's way.'

'Ignore the crabby old thing,' Millicent murmured as she swept by, having managed to get permission for an urgent and taking her handbag with her in order to touch up her powder and lipstick.

'Sshh!' Norma warned as Ruth kept an eagle eye.

As soon as Millicent left for the cloakroom, the supe made a beeline for Molly at the far end of the row. She stopped, leaned over Molly's shoulder and wrenched two cords from their jacks then told Molly to follow her into the office. The door closed firmly behind them.

'Uh-oh,' Norma murmured to Brenda, who manned the switchboard to her right. 'Is it what I think it is? Has Molly been caught listening in again?'

Brenda shrugged and carried on taking lights.

'I'll bet she has,' Norma said darkly.

Knowing that their fellow telephonist was on her last warning, everyone held their breath and kept their headsets clamped to their ears, so that it was only Cynthia who heard raised voices from the office then saw Molly emerge, pale-faced and trembling.

She went straight to her switchboard and picked up her handbag from beneath her seat then hurried, head down, along the aisle and out of the door across the foyer and into the cloakroom.

'Whatever's the matter?' Millicent asked as she emerged from one of the cubicles to find the usually unflappable Molly leaning against the green-tiled wall with her eyes closed.

'Ruth's only gone and given me my marching orders for listening in.' Molly turned her head towards Millicent and spoke bitterly.

'Don't worry – we've all done it at one time or another. They can't give us all the sack.'

'But she means it this time – I'm out on my ear.'

'Poor you. She's had it in for you for weeks,' Millicent sympathized.

Molly nodded. 'She wouldn't let me get a word in edgeways.' As her defiance crumbled and tears welled up, she spilled out her side of the story. 'All I did was pick up a call from someone calling himself Sidney Hall. He asked to speak to Clare Bell at the salon next door but one. So I connected them and I could tell straight away that Clare was upset. It made me stay on the line a few seconds longer than I should have.'

'And Frau Hitler pounced?'

'That's right. I tried to explain – the poor girl was sobbing and saying no, she didn't want to go with him.'

'Where to?'

'He called it a "soirée". He shouted at her and said she would go if she knew what was good for her. That's when Ruth snatched the cords from the jacks and hauled me into the office.'

Millicent was upset by Molly's account – partly because Ruth Ridley's actions could ruin Molly's future prospects and partly on behalf of Clare. She had no doubt that this Sidney Hall was the suave man they'd seen her with, who now seemed to be bullying her into doing something she didn't want to do. 'Would it make any difference if the rest of us put in a word for you once Ruth has calmed down?'

'I doubt it.' Molly dabbed at her eyes with a handkerchief.

'Well then – do you belong to a trade union?'

'No, I never got round to joining. Perhaps I will now.' Molly too suspected that her future lay in ruins, all for the sake of eavesdropping for a few moments too long. 'Just you watch – they'll put Cynthia at my switchboard first thing tomorrow and there's not a thing I can do. Anyway, you'd better get back in there – otherwise the dragon will come down on you like a ton of bricks as well.'

Molly was right so Millicent patted her shoulder and left her to pull herself together then hurried back to work. Nothing more was said before the end of their shift, when Millicent shepherded Cynthia and Norma into the restroom to bring them up to date with what she'd heard. She waited until the room was empty then gave them a full account of what Molly had told her.

'"Soirée" is what this chap Sidney Hall called it,' she said scornfully. 'You can just picture it – his lordship issuing orders and Clare crying her eyes out. He sounds like a downright bully, if you ask me.'

'Never mind that – what will happen to Molly?' Norma's first reaction was to try to help their workmate. 'Is what she did today enough to get her the sack?'

'It depends if she's already had a written warning or not.' Like Norma, Millicent would be sad to see Molly go. 'I hope not. She helps liven this place up.'

As they put on their coats and hats, Norma and Millicent tried to think of ways both to help Molly to keep her job and to keep Clare out of Sidney Hall's clutches.

'Could what he said be seen as an actual threat?' Norma wondered out loud.

Millicent considered this. 'Maybe. We don't know exactly what it was about.'

'But we know that Clare was upset and that he has some kind of hold over her.'

'Aren't we guessing that last bit?' Millicent paused to run through what Molly had told her. 'No, you're right – he was definitely forcing her to go to this soirée whether she liked it or not. And when I saw her with him at the King's Head, she did look frightened.'

135

'Goodness knows what they were doing upstairs at the hairdresser's earlier today then,' Norma said with a shudder. The more she thought about it, the worse the picture looked. 'Let me talk to Douglas,' she decided, 'on the off-chance that he's come across this Sidney Hall character.'

Millicent gave a nod of approval. 'Yes, do. The thing is – if there really are threats involved, it might be in Molly's favour.'

Norma didn't see the connection. 'How do you work that out?'

'I mean, she'd have had a good reason for listening in if she said she was gathering information in order to help Clare.'

'Why don't we just ask Clare?' Cynthia spoke for the first time to give what seemed the most obvious course of action. 'Instead of jumping to conclusions.'

'We wouldn't get the truth out of her – that's why not.' Millicent was sure on this point. 'We've seen with our own eyes that Sidney is friendly with Mrs Parr. Now, Phyllis Parr pays Clare's wages, so Clare's not likely to queer her pitch by complaining about Sidney's bullying, is she?'

'Bullying, or worse,' Norma added. Though it might seem to be stretching things, she'd heard enough from Douglas about men ill-treating their girlfriends to realize what sometimes happened when relationships turned sour.

'I don't know – maybe we're making mountains out of molehills.'

Exhausting the subject for now, Millicent led the way out of the exchange on to the street. The earlier drizzle had turned to heavy rain so they put up their umbrellas and prepared to set off for home through heavy traffic. Cynthia split off first to join a long queue for the Hadley bus, while Norma and Millicent stepped over puddles and crossed City Square together.

'In any case,' Norma said, stopping beside the tall cenotaph – the soot-stained memorial to those who fell in the Great War, 'I will ask Douglas what he knows about Mr Sidney Hall.'

'When will you next see him?' Millicent tilted her umbrella to shield herself from a strong gust of rain-drenched wind.

'On Wednesday after work,' Norma told her. 'I don't know Clare as well as you do, but it's nattering me. I get the feeling that she isn't very good at looking out for herself, if you know what I mean.'

'I do.' Millicent nodded, struggling again with her umbrella as the wind suddenly changed direction. 'For all her advantages – her looks, her figure, and so on – I've always thought of her as a babe in the woods.'

'Leave it with me,' Norma decided, watching the wind turn Millicent's umbrella inside out.

'Drat this weather!' Millicent fought to straighten the spokes the right way out. 'If this is summer, I'll eat my hat.'

*

'Dear Harold,' Millicent wrote. 'I've been thinking it through and have decided not to meet you on Friday after all.'

She paused and looked at her neat, forward-sloping handwriting, at the royal blue ink still wet on the page and at her trembling hand.

'I'll try to explain,' she went on, bending over the kitchen table and shutting out the sounds of dustbin lids being lifted then clattered shut and Chalky White on his top step calling out to Walter at number 4. 'Going on as we are is no good for either of us. On your side, you have too much to lose if ever we were to be found out. For my part, even though I do love you and believe you when you say you love me, I can see in my heart of hearts that we're going nowhere.'

Pausing again, she thought with a sharp pang of envy of Douglas proposing marriage to Norma. She frowned then shook her head and wrote on.

'It's not right and we both know it. I can say this in a letter in a way I never can do when we're face to face because something makes me break my resolution each time I try. I mean it when I say it's over between us. I'm sending this letter to your office address and hope you won't be too upset. Goodbye, Harold. I won't forget our time together. Love from Millicent.'

Carefully she blotted the paper and folded it. She reached for an envelope, ready to write the address, but instead she opened up the letter and read it through one last time. 'Goodbye, Harold. I won't forget our time together. Love from Millicent.'

She glanced up and out of the window to see Chalky heading off for his evening shift at the Green Cross and old Walter leaning against his doorpost. She sighed as she took up the letter and tore it in half then into quarters and threw the scraps into the empty grate. She took a match and struck it, set light to the torn pieces and watched them flare orange and yellow then curl and turn to grey ash.

'Fares, please!'

Sitting on the lower deck of the bus into town two mornings later, Cynthia heard the familiar voice with a shiver of anticipation.

Wilf came down the spiral metal staircase and spotted her sitting near to the front. 'Look who it isn't!' he said with the broadest of smiles as he made his way down the aisle, his peaked hat tilted back and collector's satchel and ticket machine slung casually from one shoulder.

'Hello, Wilf.' She aimed for a demure smile in front of the other passengers but couldn't hide her pleasure at seeing him. She was glad that the day was warm enough for her to have left off her drab raincoat and to have dressed instead in her blue, flowered dress and white cardigan with little pearl buttons and that she'd chosen a pretty blue Alice band to take her hair back from her face. She looked up at him with wide grey eyes. 'A ticket to George Street, please.'

He adjusted a dial on his machine then pressed a lever to produce the ticket. As he handed it to her, he brushed her palm with his fingertips. 'How's work going?'

'Very well, ta. I'm gradually getting to grips with the jacks and cords on the switchboards. How's your mother?' she added, just to keep him talking.

'Settling in nicely at the lodge, ta.' His smile told her that he too wanted to go on chatting, even though other passengers were giving them knowing looks. 'She says it's miles better than the house we lived in on Bridge Street, what with the view of the moors from her kitchen window.'

The bus stopped at the top of the steep hill down into town and more passengers got on. It set off again with a sudden lurch that made Wilf grab hold of the strap hanging above Cynthia's head. He ducked down and spoke in a lower voice. 'Are we still on for the flicks on Friday?'

Cynthia nodded and smiled up at his boyish, eager face.

'Champion!' he said with a wink as he turned away. 'Any more fares?' he called. 'Fares, please. Any more fares?'

At work that day, the switchboard at the far end of the room remained vacant. Agnes was on duty, refusing to answer questions about Molly's fate.

'There's no point asking – Miss Mouse won't give anything away,' Millicent surmised. She was quieter than usual during a dinner break that she shared with Norma and Brenda, still thinking about the ashes of the unsent letter lying in her grate in Heaton Yard.

'No, but she and Ruth are thick as thieves,' Brenda pointed out, shoes off and her feet resting on the low table in the middle of the restroom. A thin spiral of blue smoke drifted up from the cigarette she held between her slim fingers. 'I wouldn't mind betting that Ruth went straight round to Agnes's house on Monday and told her everything, word for word.'

'Did you manage to see Molly yesterday?' Norma asked.

Brenda shook her head as she leaned forward and stubbed out her cigarette. 'I tried, but there was no one in when I called. It seems she's gone to ground.'

'What'll happen if she loses her job?' Norma knew that Molly lived with her widowed mother in a smart new semi-detached council house on the outskirts of town and that it was Molly's wage that kept things ticking over.

'Lord knows.' Brenda slipped her feet back into her shoes then patted her hair into place, ready to start her afternoon stint. 'I suppose she should have thought of that before she listened in to a caller's private conversation.'

Her lack of sympathy made Norma and Millicent frown. 'Don't worry,' Norma murmured, letting

Brenda go ahead of them. 'I haven't forgotten about talking to Douglas later on, to see if he can cast any light on Sidney Hall.'

'It's a long shot and it might not help Molly, even if he turns out to be a rum sort,' Millicent pointed out.

'Don't tell me you're getting cold feet.'

'No, I'm just saying . . .'

'We can but try,' Norma said firmly, taking the lead and leaving the door swinging behind her.

'Lights, girls!' Agnes's voice rang out as the dinnertime changeover took place. 'Look lively, Brenda. Norma, you have two callers backed up on your board. Take them quickly, please.'

Miss Mouse she may have been, with early grey showing at the temples of her mid-brown hair, wearing a pin-tucked blouse and a grey skirt that reached her calves. But like Ruth, she was a stickler for the rules and made sure that the girls took the lights promptly and were accurate, efficient and courteous at all times.

'Slave driver!' Millicent said under her breath as she pushed cords into sockets. 'Hello, Liverpool. How can I help? Calling Manchester – I have a new ticket on Liverpool 3201.'

'Sometimes I wonder why I carry on doing that job,' Norma complained to Douglas as they cycled on the Common after work.

He'd met her as promised and they'd decided to

make the most of a beautiful evening by spending it outdoors. A quick stop-off at his lodgings to collect the tandem saw them free of the town by half past six, planning to buy a fish and chip supper from Pennington's once they'd had their fill of fresh air.

Douglas lent a sympathetic ear. 'Why, what's up?'

'I've been run off my feet – well, not run exactly, because I'm sitting down all day. But you know what I mean. Anyway, we were one short today and I never stopped.'

'How's that?' Determined not to press Norma over the question of getting engaged, the moment he saw her emerging from the exchange he'd felt his resolution waver. *Marry me*, he wanted to say over and over until she gave in and said yes. *Marry me. Marry me!*

'Molly Scaife has been suspended and Agnes wasn't prepared to put Cynthia at her switchboard until she's finished her training.' Norma pedalled off her frustration and by the time they reached the pavilion she was in full flow. 'I know Cynthia was disappointed, but Agnes does everything by the book. She won't let anyone near the switchboards until they've passed their Full Efficiency Test. Now then, Douglas, humour me. I need to ask you a question in confidence and I want a proper answer.'

'Fire away.'

'It's to do with your work. Does the name Sidney Hall mean anything to you?'

Immediately he grew more alert. 'Why do you want to know?'

'The girls and I have come across him a few times lately and Molly overheard something over the phone that we didn't like the sound of.'

'What kind of something?' He looked over his shoulder with a slight frown, waiting for Norma's reply.

'He was forcing a girl we know to do something that she didn't want to do.'

'What, exactly?'

'To attend what he called a soirée, but beyond that we're not sure. According to Molly, he was making her cry and we'd already decided we don't like the look of the chap – Millicent especially.'

Douglas put on the brakes and stopped the bike on the brow of the hill. 'I must admit, she's spot on in this case.'

'So you do know him?'

'Sidney Hall is the son of Sir Edmund Hall – of Kenworth and Hall's Steel Manufacturing Company. Sir Edmund's Sheffield factory has made him a millionaire twice over, according to what you read in the papers.'

This fitted with Sidney's expensively tailored clothes and man-about-town air, but Norma still couldn't work out how he'd ended up in this narrow neck of the woods. 'So how do you know the son?'

'He fell out with the old man a few years back and has been drifting ever since, mixing with the wrong

144

sort of company, always with a girl on his arm – a different one every few weeks or so. Lately he's drifted in our direction, so to speak.'

'And does he have a job?'

Looking out towards the Crag, a jutting silhouette against the setting sun, Douglas hesitated over how to put things in a way that wouldn't shock Norma. 'Not one that's above board, shall we say.'

'How do you know all this?' Appetite whetted, she got off the bike then tugged at him to follow suit.

He laid the bike by the side of the path. 'Some of it is common knowledge.'

'And the rest?'

'Is an educated guess,' he admitted. 'We get reports about what Sidney gets up to from time to time, usually involving one of these girls he's seen with, but there's never any proof.'

Norma took a few tentative steps off the track into the heather, glimpsing a dark, decadent world she knew little about. The word 'soirée' rattled around her head, conjuring up images of cut-glass decanters and smoke-filled rooms, slim women in white satin and chiffon gowns, bedecked with ostrich feathers and gardenias, fat men in dark dinner jackets with cigars clenched between their teeth. 'These girls,' she began in a faint voice, 'what happens to them?'

'Some of them – not all – eventually end up in the station.'

'The *police* station? What for? No – there's no need

to spell it out. I understand.' Satin and chiffon gowns soon wore out, flowers faded and such girls, reputations ruined, were reduced to walking the streets.

'As often as not Sidney Hall is named as the person who first set them on the rocky road. It's a racket where there's always money to be made – finding the right girl and introducing her to, shall we say, rich acquaintances.'

'Stop,' she said and let out a long sigh, hands to her cheeks, her heart fluttering.

Douglas put an arm around her shoulder and gently guided her back towards the bike. 'I'll bet you wish you hadn't asked.'

'No,' she countered quickly. 'I'm glad I did. But listen, Douglas – would this phone conversation I've told you about act as evidence against Sidney Hall?'

He considered the question then quickly dismissed it. 'Not by itself, no.'

'Why not?'

'Not unless there's been mention of money changing hands for a start. And we'd need to know exactly what's been going on.'

'From Clare Bell?'

'If that's the girl you're worried about – yes.'

'Then I'll find out,' Norma decided, ready to do battle again as she picked up the bike and sat astride it, waiting for Douglas to join her.

They turned the bike around and set off back the way they'd come, stomachs rumbling and ready for supper. 'Don't let the others – Millicent et cetera – lead you into any trouble over this,' he warned as he steered around the pavilion and they were treated to a panoramic view of the town below – a patchwork of terraced streets, the snaking canal bordered by tall mill chimneys.

'I won't,' she promised.

'I know what you girls are like once you get a bee in your bonnet.'

'Don't worry. We'll be careful.' *Just wait until I tell Millicent*, Norma thought, sheltering behind Douglas's broad back to stop her hair from blowing into her eyes. *She was right about Sidney Hall all along.*

CHAPTER EIGHT

The next morning as she hurried across City Square, Millicent caught sight of Cynthia alighting from the Hadley bus. The conductor lent her a gallant hand to step down from the platform and the way he did it made Millicent take a closer look. It was Wilf Evans, no less.

'I saw that!' she cried as Cynthia joined her on the steps into the exchange.

'What?' A flustered Cynthia avoided her gaze.

'You and Wilf.' Millicent cocked her head to one side. 'My, you're a sly one and no mistake.'

'I'm . . . we're not . . . !' Cynthia's feeble protests fell on deaf ears.

'Yes, you are. There's no use huffing and puffing, you went along to that dance together and the two of you have clicked in spite of what I said.'

Cynthia felt her cheeks burn as she tried to defend herself against Millicent's teasing. 'He was very nice to me, as a matter of fact.'

Millicent's mouth twitched at the corners. 'Quite the gentleman, eh?'

'Yes, if you must know.'

'"Softly, softly, catchee monkey!"' Millicent winked then whisked Cynthia through the door. 'Or perhaps the leopard *has* changed his spots – who knows?'

There was no time for any more jungle metaphors because Norma was hurrying towards them across the foyer to share all that she'd learned from Douglas the night before. Her colour was high and she grew breathless as she delivered the newly gleaned details about Sidney Hall.

'Oh no, that's too bad!' Cynthia's shock ran deep and she could hardly believe what she was hearing.

'As bad as can be,' Millicent agreed. 'He struck me as too big for his boots the first time I clapped eyes on him in the King's Head. And again, when we saw him with Mrs Parr – too friendly by half.'

'So what are we going to do?' Norma demanded. 'Now we definitely have to step in and help Clare before it's too late.'

'If it isn't already.' Millicent was distracted by the unexpected sight of Molly emerging from the cloakroom with Brenda and she raised her eyebrows in a questioning look.

Norma once more supplied the explanation. 'Molly did join the union to find out about her rights. It's in the rule book – there *was* no written warning so the powers that be have had to let her come back to work.'

'That'll put Ruth's nose out of joint, and no mistake. But never mind that – what about Clare?' Millicent jumped from one subject to another, keeping an eye on the clock and aware that time was running short. She, Norma and Cynthia were due at their switchboards in under a minute. 'How are we going to get her out of Hall's clutches? That's if she even wants us to.'

'Of course she will!' Norma couldn't see how anyone would willingly enter into the seamy world of the so-called soirées, and Cynthia nodded her head in agreement. 'Millicent, you know Clare better than we do. You ought to be the one to tell her what we've found out.'

'We've got those appointments at the salon the day after tomorrow,' Cynthia reminded them.

'That's true,' Millicent realized. 'One of us could collar Clare while the other two get their hair done.'

'But can we afford to wait that long?' Norma wondered.

'It's not ideal, but there's no point us bursting in unannounced, especially if Mrs Parr is there.' With fellow switchboard operators criss-crossing the marble floor of the foyer and people running upstairs to the general office with folders and files, Millicent cut the discussion short. 'At least it gives us a bit of time to work out what we're going to say.'

'I'm worried about her, though,' Norma said as

they made their way to the switchboards. She sat in her swivel chair and put on her headset, took the lights and prepared to begin work, but she found it hard to shut her mind to the danger that Clare was in. She remembered with a shiver some lurid recent headlines in the *News of the World* about the so-called Jack the Strangler, who, it seemed, had murdered three Soho prostitutes within the space of six months, the latest just last month. Then there was the white slavery that she'd read about in the *Express* – where pimps brought in girls from France and Holland and earned hundreds of pounds a month. So, despite Douglas's concerns for her un-sullied mind, Norma had all too clear a picture of how a defenceless girl like Clare might be preyed upon and used by dozens of men before being thrown into the gutter and left to fend for herself in whatever way she could.

I don't think I'm overdoing it, she told herself in the short gaps between lights. *That girl needs our help and the sooner the better.*

Throughout that day and the next, Ruth Ridley was in the worst of moods. She patrolled up and down the aisle, refusing urgents and picking up on every small fault – fingernails that were too long, elbows that jutted out, words that were missing 'h's at the beginning and 'g's at the end.

'Did you see how she's been ignoring me the entire time?' Molly spent the dinner break on Friday complaining to anyone who would listen. She was in the cloakroom applying bright red lipstick and re-setting the pins that held her hair up in a French roll. 'She's acting as if I'm not there.'

'Count yourself lucky,' Norma told her. 'If she's pulled me up once, she's done it a dozen times.'

Cynthia too had found herself the butt of the supe's bad temper when she'd failed to identify the red lamp glowing on an unmanned console in one corner of the room.

'Miss Ambler, may I refer you to your basic instruction manual, page seven, where you will find that this is the automatic speaking clock and the "golden voice" of Miss Jane Cain, accurate to one tenth of a second.'

'I see. Thank you, Miss Ridley.'

'Instead of thanking me, you must read your manual. The speaking clock service started earlier this year in the London Holborn exchange and is soon to be introduced as standard at exchanges across the country.'

Cynthia had been made to feel a complete dunce in front of everyone and had retreated into her shell. The incident made her incapable of plucking up the courage later that afternoon to join Millicent in informing the sour-faced supervisor that she would miss the Health and Beauty class that evening.

'A prior commitment?' Ruth echoed Millicent's words as Cynthia, Millicent and Norma waited behind her in the queue for coats and hats. 'I see. At this rate, you'll have missed too many classes for me to include you in this year's team for the national display in the Albert Hall.'

Millicent gave a careless, please-yourself shrug, took her coat from the hook, grinned at Cynthia and hurried off.

'What about you, Norma?' Ruth quizzed the next in line. 'Or do you have prior commitments too?'

'I'll be there,' Norma promised. Douglas had been collared for a late shift, so it was either Health and Beauty for her or darning with Ethel and Ivy.

Managing to make herself invisible, Cynthia held back until everyone else had gone, then she took a brush to her hair in readiness for her meeting with Wilf. When at last she crossed the foyer and left the building, she ran into Sam Bower on the pavement outside his barber shop.

In his brusque way Sam thrust a leather satchel into her arms. 'I've been told to give you this.'

Cynthia recognized the scuffed brown bag as her Uncle William's. 'What for?'

'Bert says you have to collect the rent money.'

Pursing her lips, she tried to push the bag back towards Sam. 'Why can't Bert do it?'

'The lad's poorly with the chickenpox,' came the reply. 'It's doing the rounds. His face looked a right mess so I told him to go home early in case he upset my customers. He said I'd have to get you to do his job for him this week.'

'But I can't – I'm meeting someone.' Cynthia knew

that her protest would fall on deaf ears and she felt close to tears as she watched Sam retreat into his shop. Seconds later, Wilf came around the corner, hands in pockets and whistling cheerily.

'What's up?' he asked when he saw her glum expression.

'I can't come out with you after all.' She showed him the satchel. 'Bert's got the chickenpox so I have to collect Uncle William's rent money.'

'You do, do you?' In an instant he came up with a solution. 'I know – let's do it together. What do you say?'

'Honestly?' Her heart lifted and she gave him a grateful smile.

'Cross my heart.' Wilf took the satchel and hung it from his shoulder. 'I'm the first to admit, it's not a patch on sitting with you in the back row of the Victory, but we'll soon get it done between us. Then we can catch the bus out to Hadley, drop the money off at your uncle's and afterwards we can do whatever you like with the rest of our evening.'

'You're sure you don't mind?'

'For you, Cynthia – anything!' he declared.

Laughing and dodging the traffic, they dawdled hand in hand across the square, past the cenotaph, up by the central library on to Ghyll Road and from there on to Ada Street. By the time they reached the cramped quarters of Heaton Yard, Millicent had already set off to meet Harold for their prearranged walk to Brimstone Rock.

*

'I'm sorry I'm late.' Harold's apology to Millicent was rushed and his face looked strained. 'I couldn't leave work until Mr Oldroyd had gone. It wouldn't have looked right.'

They had arranged to meet at the pavilion on Overcliffe Common, which had given Millicent just enough time to get home and change into the comfortable outfit she wore for her weekend rambles – a long navy blue skirt teamed with a pale blue blouse and matching headscarf wrapped turban-style around her head. During her walk up the hill out of town, long wisps of dark hair had escaped and they blew across her face as she accepted Harold's quick kiss on the cheek. 'I've been sitting twiddling my thumbs for ages,' she complained.

'I said I was sorry, didn't I?'

Mindful of the letter she'd almost sent, she overcame the urge to take him to task by breathing in deeply and setting off along the track that led across the moors. Her innermost feelings were at war – the old tenderness for Harold in conflict with a growing sense of unease. A yearning that ran slap-bang into a wall of guilt.

'Where are you running off to?' he said, hurrying to keep pace and snatching at her hand to slow her down.

'We'd better get a move on if we want to get all the way there and back before dark.' The tug of his hand irritated her and she pulled hers away, her face set in the direction of the distant crag as she continued a quick march along the path.

'Mr Oldroyd asked me to go through the order books for June and July,' Harold said gloomily. 'It didn't take long.'

'Meaning, you don't have many orders?'

'No. Who wants to buy woollen cloth during the summer months?'

'Plenty of people, if they think far enough ahead.'

'Those that do can't afford it,' he explained. 'Or else they've gone further afield to where they can buy the cloth more cheaply. We've cut back to the bone to get costs down but we're still losing orders hand over fist.'

It was unusual for Harold to talk about his work and it made Millicent slow down and listen more sympathetically.

'We've already laid off as many as we can. We'd cut back on wages if the unions would let us, but they're threatening to go on strike as it is.'

'That's awkward,' she acknowledged. 'But they won't cut off their noses to spite their faces, will they? I mean, it's the same for everyone these days – look at the number of collieries they're having to close, for a start. If the weavers at Oldroyd's think they can walk out of one job straight into another, they've got another think coming.'

'That's why we've got a stalemate.' Worn down by worry, Harold had come to his open-air assignation with Millicent with the intent of escaping from his everyday cares, but somehow he failed to turn the conversation around. 'The fact is if we don't improve our order book, Mr Oldroyd might have to shut up shop.'

'You mean, close for good? Surely not?'

'I'm only saying "might".' The possibility kept Harold awake at night and when he did eventually drop off, his dreams were haunted by pictures of cavernous spinning and weaving sheds – no workers at row after row of clanking, grinding machines, no furnaces in the cobbled yard blasting fire underneath boilers to create steam for the engines to turn. Only acres of grey, ghostly silence.

It was Millicent's turn to take Harold's hand and draw him close. 'It won't happen,' she said stoutly. 'If Oldroyd's is forced to close, then so would Kingsley's and Calvert's and all the rest. The whole town would wither and die.'

He stopped her and turned her towards him. 'I'm warning you it might,' he insisted, looking directly into her eyes. 'What then? Would you still want to know me – a man without a job or a house to his name?'

Her eyes narrowed and she took a sharp intake of breath. 'That's not why I took up with you, and you know it. It has nothing to do with those things – how could you think it did?'

'Then what was it?' He pressed for an answer by keeping one arm tightly around her waist.

She couldn't find one that she could put into

words, however long he held on to her, here on the open moor, with a breeze tugging at her skirt and the sun sinking slowly in a cloudless sky. There had been a spark between them once, when she'd been young and naive and Harold had seemed so suave. But those days were so far in the past that they no longer seemed real.

'You see,' he said, letting her go at last. He turned away and took a half-smoked cigarette from his breast pocket, struck a match and lit it. 'You've forgotten what drew you to me in the first place.'

'I haven't . . . It's . . . Harold, we've known each other a long time.' The words caught in her throat and came out slowly and awkwardly.

Inhaling, he turned back towards her, tilting his head to aim the smoke away from her. 'I'm like a bad habit that's hard to break, eh?'

She frowned at him, bewildered by a feeling that something had set cold and hard in the soft, loving part of her. 'That must be it,' she agreed, abruptly setting off back the way they'd come.

Nothing was definite. Millicent and Harold had parted at the tram shelter on Overcliffe Road without arranging another meeting but leaving the door open for when either of them wanted to get in touch.

'You know where to find me,' she'd told him.

'Likewise,' he'd replied. 'I'm sorry I've been down in the mouth lately. I've got a lot on my plate.'

'I know. I do understand.' She didn't want to finish

on this note – to be making an ending just at the point where Harold's whole world might collapse.

'I'll be in touch,' he'd promised as a tram rattled towards them.

She'd stayed inside the shelter as he'd got on and she'd waited until it was out of sight. Then she'd walked home and gone straight to bed, still trying to pin down the answer to his question – why had she taken up with Harold in the first place?

'A penny for them?' Next day, Norma leaned over from her switchboard to speak to Millicent. Saturday was a slack morning at the exchange, with offices closed for the weekend and many private subscribers out at the shops.

'Sorry?' Millicent slid her headset back from her ears.

'Never mind. You looked as if you were miles away, that's all.'

'I only wish I was.' The morning had dragged and the weekend ahead held out little promise of excitement of any kind.

Guessing that Harold was the reason behind Millicent's sad face, Norma changed the subject. 'It won't be long before we can talk to Clare and set her straight,' she reminded her. 'That's your job for this afternoon, remember.'

Millicent nodded then caught sight of Cynthia hunched over one of her training manuals inside the supes' office, looking up as Agnes entered the room. Cynthia asked a question and Agnes supplied the answer by pointing to the booklet in front of her. 'Poor lamb,' Millicent commented. 'She spends her whole life trying to please, does that one.'

'Who – Cynthia?'

Millicent nodded. 'She's like Clare in that respect. Neither of them has much notion of how to stand up for herself, especially where men are concerned.'

'But you're not comparing Wilf Evans with Sidney Hall, I hope?'

'Who can guess what Wilf's up to these days? All I know is that it's a good job we're keeping an eye out for Cynthia, because no one else will.'

'Says the woman of the world!' Norma wasn't so sure that their new recruit was as helpless as Millicent supposed. She saw ambition in Cynthia and a determination to succeed, which was not the same as falling over backwards in a desire to please.

Inside the office, Cynthia soaked up Agnes's advice about how to deal with irate customers whose conversations had been broken into by other subscribers who shared their party line. 'You must explain politely that the line is busy and that we're working hard to improve our service. Apologize then helpfully suggest that they try to avoid peaktime calls in future.'

Cynthia nodded and made mental notes. With only a few minutes to go before the end of her shift, she began to look ahead to her appointment at the hairdresser's, wondering what Millicent would say

160

to Clare while she and Norma got their hair done. *Fingers crossed*, she thought as one o'clock arrived and she joined the others on their way out of the building.

The glare of the sun hit them as they stepped down on to the pavement and walked the few yards down the street. Sam Bower's sun blind was rolled down and there were customers queuing to get into the busy barber's shop. Further along, they heard the ring of a shop bell and saw Mrs Parr emerge from her salon with Sidney Hall hard on her heels.

'Wouldn't you just know it?' Norma said as she watched the duo get into Sidney's car and drive off. 'That man hangs around like a bad smell.'

'Yes, but it's good that they've both gone out.' Cynthia realized that this gave Millicent a clear run for her talk with Clare.

However, when they went through the door, they found no sign of the receptionist. Instead, Barbara was at the desk checking the diary for the afternoon's appointments. The small, blonde hairdresser welcomed them with a cherry-lipped smile and offered Millicent a seat close to the window. Then she took Cynthia and Norma further into the salon where she sat them down in front of large mirrors and Margaret joined her to drape nylon capes around their customers' shoulders.

Cynthia kept an eye on a nearby trolley laden with metal curlers and perm lotion, shampoos and scissors, next to an electrical contraption on a metal stand shaped like a beehive that went over your head to dry your hair. It was all new to her and she quaked a little under Margaret's critical gaze. Her earlier nerve failed. 'Just a trim for me, please.'

The hairdresser took up her scissors. 'How much shall I take off – an inch, two inches?'

'Two inches, please,' she answered daringly.

'With a fringe or without?'

'I'll keep it without.' Cynthia steered away from this too-drastic option.

'And would you like a side parting to the left or the right?' Less smiley than Barbara, the tall stylist assessed the task ahead of her.

'To before the left, please.'

'But no permanent wave?'

'No, ta.'

'No, you're right. Your hair has a natural curl and it's nice and thick. I think we could take a little more off the length, though – perhaps level with your chin.'

Sitting next to her, Norma smiled at Cynthia then gave confident instructions to chatty Barbara. 'A short, smart bob, please. And no perm for me either.' She heard the bell ring and looked in the mirror to see Clare come in carrying a batch of new magazines. *Now, Millicent, here's your chance!* she thought.

Millicent stood up and intercepted Clare as she made her way to her desk. 'Hello, I was hoping I'd catch you,' she began warmly.

'Hello, Millicent.' Clare seemed wary of the friendly

greeting. 'What's up? Ruth Ridley isn't after me about leaving the Health and Beauty class, is she?'

'Ruth? No. She's given you up as a lost cause. I wanted to talk to you about something else entirely.'

As Barbara and Margaret combed and snipped away, Norma and Cynthia stared into the mirror, keeping their eyes glued on Millicent and Clare's reflection. Underneath their capes, both had their fingers firmly crossed.

Clare sidestepped Millicent to go behind her desk and spread the magazines across the high counter. Glossy, made-up faces smiled out at them from the front covers of *Woman's Own* and *Vogue*.

'It's about Sidney Hall,' Millicent said with none of her usual flippancy.

Clare placed both hands on the counter to steady herself. 'What about him?'

'I . . . we've heard a few things we thought you should know.'

'Not now, Millicent. I'm busy.'

'Just listen – all right? Normally I'd be the first to say it wasn't any of my business—'

'That's right. It isn't.' With a flushed, stubborn look, Clare pretended to concentrate on the appointments diary.

'Hear me out. I'll come straight to the point, Clare – what do you really know about Sidney and what he gets up to?'

'Leave me alone.' When Clare looked up, her mouth was puckered in angry defiance and her face

163

had turned pale. 'You hear me, Millicent – mind your own business!'

Even from a distance, Norma and Cynthia could tell that Millicent was getting nowhere. Then, as soon as Barbara cottoned on to the fact there was an argument going on, she excused herself, put down her scissors and hurried across to the reception desk.

'Mrs Parr wanted me to pass on a message,' she told Clare, speaking slowly and studiously ignoring Millicent. 'She says that Vincent will pick you up tonight at seven o'clock.'

Clare's eyelids flickered and she leaned more heavily on the counter. 'Seven?' she repeated in a whisper. 'Right you are.'

Vincent? Who's that, when he's at home? Millicent thought.

Her message delivered, Barbara went back to work, snipping away with surgical precision at Norma's bob.

Millicent watched Clare's face. The stubborn anger had vanished and now fear took its place. 'What is it? What's wrong?'

'Nothing. Leave me alone.' Stepping back, Clare bumped into her stool and almost overbalanced. The stool wobbled then fell backwards against a coat stand that Millicent grabbed just in time and set back upright. Meanwhile, Clare rushed across the salon, through a door and out of sight.

What now? Millicent wondered. For a few seconds

she hesitated but then the distress she'd witnessed on Clare's face brought her to a decision and she quickly followed her through the door, up some narrow, uncarpeted stairs on to a dark landing with three doors leading off it. She looked and listened, floorboards creaking as she went along the landing, hearing no other sound until she came to the far end. Then she heard a woman crying behind the closed door and knocked on it. There was no answer so she took a deep breath, turned the knob and walked in.

CHAPTER NINE

Clare lay face down on a narrow bed in the far corner of the room. There was a washbasin in the opposite corner and some basic furniture – a wooden chair at an old-fashioned washstand and a two-bar electric fire set in the grate. There was a wireless on a shelf in the alcove on one side of the chimney breast alongside several pairs of shoes and in the other a green chenille curtain screened what Millicent supposed was a clothes rail.

'I'm sorry, Clare,' she began above the noise of the traffic filtering in through the open window. 'The last thing I wanted to do was to upset you.'

There was no response but the crying had stopped and Clare lay perfectly still.

'You know me – always rushing in where angels fear to tread. But I'm only trying to help.'

Slowly Clare turned on to her back then sat up and straightened the pink satin eiderdown beneath her. 'You're not,' she muttered.

'Not what?'

'Helping. If word gets back to Mrs Parr, I'll be in serious trouble.'

'For being upset?'

Clare sighed and nodded. 'I ought to go back down.'

'Where's the rush? The other girls will cover for you while you give your face a wash.' As Clare showed no sign of standing up, Millicent eased the conversation forward, at the same time taking in more details about the room. She noticed that the washstand acted as a kind of dressing table, with an unframed mirror propped against the wall and a row of bottles and jars containing perfumes, powder, lipstick and cleansing creams lined up carefully. Strings of glass beads and cultured pearls were hung from the back of the chair and a small, white cardboard box full of brooches and rings stood open on the window sill.

'What are you looking at?' Clare demanded, standing up and coming between Millicent and the washstand. Her cream linen dress was badly creased and her smooth hair ruffled.

'Nothing.' There was perfume and costume jewellery but no family photographs, no personal touches. Millicent guessed that the dress rail behind the curtain was crammed with up-to-date clothes. 'I'm not looking at anything.'

Clare seized the box of jewellery and thrust it at Millicent. 'Presents, if you must know! All from the man whose name you mentioned.' She went across the room and pulled back the green curtain. 'Dresses, too.' She took a rose-pink satin one trimmed with matching chiffon from the rail and held it against her slim figure. 'Aren't you jealous, Millicent? I'll bet Harold Buckley doesn't buy you anything like this.'

Millicent frowned and took a step backwards.

'Now you don't feel so clever, do you?' There was a note of triumph in Clare's voice as she slid the pink dress back on to the rail.

'How did you know about me and Harold?'

'I saw you two in the King's Head, remember? As a matter of fact, I know him from when I worked as a loom cleaner, straight after I left school. He was far too friendly with me, if you know what I mean. Then he gave me the sack when I refused to play his game.'

Millicent took the blow then feebly attempted to cover her tracks. 'He's a friend of the family, that's all.'

'What family, pray? You only had your father when we were at school, I seem to remember.'

'Yes, and a fat lot of good he was.' A drinker and a dead loss, unable to cope after Millicent's mother had deserted them when Millicent was eight. She never spoke about her miserable childhood, but that was why she'd had to develop a tough shell and grow up fast, to look after herself and make her own way.

'Exactly. We were in the same boat as schoolgirls and we're in the same boat now.' Clare gave Millicent a challenging look.

168

Millicent shook her head. 'I don't think so. Oh, some things are similar, I admit. We both have secrets for a start. And we both have to fend for ourselves. But I feel as if I've had more practice.'

'You don't know that,' Clare objected. 'You're only guessing.'

'Well then, put it this way – at least I *look* as if I can take care of myself.'

'Whereas I don't?'

The gloves were off and Millicent spoke openly. 'It's what I was saying to Norma and Cynthia – you're too perfect-looking for your own good and yet you go around in a sort of dream. You must have men swarming around you and unless you're on your guard, it would be easy for you to drift into something that you couldn't get out of.' She gestured towards the dresses and the jewellery.

'That's where you're wrong.' Clare's voice faltered and she shook her head. 'Sidney buys me these presents to show me how much he cares. It's what every woman dreams of.'

'And he takes you out in his car and shows you off to all his friends, does he? You've been to Sheffield and met his family?'

'No, but I'm sure I will soon. When he's ready.'

'He won't ever be ready.' Millicent shook her head. 'Don't you see?'

'He will,' Clare insisted. But the fact that Sidney had never once mentioned his family struck home, although she'd never admit it. 'And yes, he does take me out in the evenings and I do meet his friends, so there!'

'Is that where you're going tonight – to one of these "soirées" that Sidney holds?' Millicent knew that she was pushing Clare close to the edge again – she could see it in her eyes, which were shot through with fresh panic. 'Whereabouts is it – in town or out in the country? What will you wear? Will it be the pink dress or the white one hanging next to it?'

'The pink, I expect.' Though she tried her best to hold her head high, fear clawed at Clare's chest and made her breathless. The gathering was in fact out of town with people she didn't know. Sidney himself was unable to come and collect her. That was why she hadn't wanted to go.

'And who's Vincent?' Millicent asked quietly.

That was it – she'd pushed an inch too far and, without answering Millicent's question, Clare fell wordlessly down the chasm, spiralling out of reach.

Norma, Cynthia and Millicent had the rest of the weekend to mull over Clare's predicament. After the hairdresser's they'd spent half an hour talking it through in the Lyons' café then gone their separate ways.

Maybe Millicent's wrong, Cynthia thought during her bus ride home. Rich men did fall in love with poor girls and marry them, and not just in fairy tales – especially girls as beautiful as Clare. Perhaps Sidney Hall is just taking his time, going slowly, paving the way towards a proper introduction of Clare into his family circle. Meanwhile, he was showering her with gifts because he truly loved her.

'Are you sure we're on the right track?' Norma meanwhile asked Millicent on the long walk out of town along the towpath, carrying their hats so as not to flatten their newly styled hair. Wispy clouds drifted across the late-afternoon sky and were reflected in the dark brown water of the canal. 'We're not making two and two add up to five?'

'I'm sure,' Millicent insisted. Rusting tin cans and old newspapers littered the cinder path. A bare-headed man in waistcoat and shirtsleeves stood on the deck of a stationary barge, smoking a pipe and staring at them through a cloud of pungent smoke as they walked briskly by. 'All that silk and satin, the perfume and make-up he makes her wear. It proves Sidney is trying to turn Clare into something she isn't.'

'Don't you think a lot of men do that?'

'Douglas doesn't,' Millicent pointed out.

'No, he likes me the way I am.'

'That's my point.' Millicent went back to considering what more they could do to help Clare.

'Douglas is different to most men,' Norma insisted. 'And before you ask – no, I haven't given him his answer yet. And yes, I do know he won't wait for ever.'

Millicent grimaced then moved on. 'Anyway, you didn't see the look in Clare's eyes when I mentioned tonight's soirée, as if she was teetering on the edge of a cliff.' The memory sent a shiver down her spine. 'Up till that point, I hoped I was on the way to making her see sense. It was just the one little question about Vincent that pushed her over the edge.'

'I know. We heard the sobs.' Norma recalled how raised voices from the room upstairs had made Barbara put down her scissors and rush up to calm Clare down and usher Millicent back into the salon. Then there'd been silence from upstairs and hardly a word spoken as Margaret had finished with Cynthia then started on Millicent's haircut.

'Clare has been doing her level best to keep the blindfold on,' Millicent said as they climbed some steps from the towpath up on to Canal Road, to be confronted by delivery boys on bikes weaving through traffic, sturdy dray horses pulling a beer wagon, cars tooting their horns, a brown and yellow tram laden with shoppers on the way home from town. 'She's been telling herself that Sidney's intentions are honourable, flying in the face of evidence to the contrary. We all know that there's none so blind . . . But tonight is when she'll finally have to face up to the facts – I'm sure of it.'

Norma thought again of the lurid stories in the newspapers then let out a quiet groan. 'We've missed our chance, haven't we?'

Millicent nodded. 'It looks like it. But at least we can say we tried.'

They came to Ghyll Road and the parting of

ways – Norma up Albion Lane and Millicent on to Heaton Yard, each counting their blessings in comparison with Clare.

For the rest of the weekend they basked in the calm waters of normality – Millicent striding out with her rambling group on the Sunday, Norma taking her mother to chapel then making a picnic tea for her and Douglas before the two of them cycled out to Brimstone Rock.

Cynthia, meanwhile, found little time to sit down and study since Uncle William's demands came thick and fast. There was a pile of ironing to catch up on. After dinner on Sunday, he made her take up the carpets to hang them over the washing line and beat every speck of dust out of them before her mother came for tea.

'I saw you gallivanting off with that Evans chap on Friday night, and don't think I didn't.' William gave a suggestive curl of his lip as he watched her beat the last of the carpets. 'No slacking now, Missy. There's still silver to polish and floors to mop.' He stomped back into the house with his stout walking stick and lumbered down the hallway.

On and on, relentlessly, with just enough time for Cynthia to spare a thought every now and then for whatever might be going on between Clare Bell and Sidney Hall.

There were compliments on the Monday morning from Molly and Brenda when Cynthia went in to work.

'Who's got a swanky new haircut?' Brenda winked at her as she took up position at her switchboard.

'Very sophisticated,' Molly agreed.

'No talking. Take the lights!' Ruth cried.

'Where did you get it done?'

'At Sylvia's,' Cynthia whispered, routes and rates booklets tucked under her arm.

'Take the lights, girls. Come along, please!'

Molly sat down next to Millicent. 'We still need a shilling from you for the gramophone, remember? Everyone else has paid up.'

'You can have it next pay day,' Millicent promised.

'Lights, please!'

And so the week began in a flurry of flashing lights and the connecting of cords, voices on the line, operators listening on headsets and enunciating carefully into speaking horns, supes patrolling the aisle.

As usual, Cynthia thrived on the fast pace but the build-up to another midweek test put a strain on her nerves and she made sure she studied well past midnight on the Tuesday evening.

'Good luck,' Wilf told her as she stepped off his bus at the stop on George Street on Wednesday morning. He gave her hand a squeeze.

'Ta – I'll need it.'

'A brainbox like you will breeze through, don't you worry. I'll wait for you by the cenotaph after work,' he promised. 'Then you can tell me how you got on.'

Cynthia's head buzzed with facts and her heart

raced as she entered the exchange. The part of the test to do with the history of the telephone would be straightforward enough, and likewise the technical aspects of the Strowger system for storage and re-directing of information. But it was routes and rates that would really test her knowledge – there was so much to learn.

'Good luck!' Norma and Millicent called in unison as she walked down the aisle towards the supes' office.

'The poor thing looks as if she's getting ready to walk the plank,' Norma murmured.

'Don't forget about the new 999 Emergency system,' Millicent called after her. 'It won't reach this exchange for a good while, but we're still expected to know about it. That's the sort of thing they'll throw in to trip you up.'

Beset by nerves, Cynthia disappeared into the office.

'Hello, London.' Millicent took her first call of the day and efficiently connected the long-distance caller to a local number.

'Hello, caller. I'm afraid the line you require is busy. Please try again later.' Norma had flicked a rear key to no avail. Her board went dead for a while and she glanced at Cynthia in the office, head bowed, scribbling down answers for all she was worth. Another light went on and Norma grew alert as she recognized the number as the one belonging to Sylvia's Salon. 'Hello, caller. Go ahead, please.'

'This is Mrs Parr. I wish to speak to Mr Hall on 351, please.'

'Certainly, Mrs Parr. Please hold the line.' Norma sat bolt upright at her board as she connected cords and opened the line. Once more she glanced down the aisle to see Ruth enter the office to supervise Cynthia's test and she decided it was safe to leave her headset in place and listen in.

'Hello, Sidney. This is Phyllis. I haven't interrupted your breakfast, I hope.'

'Not at all. I was going to call you later, in any case.'

'I'm sure you can guess why I'm ringing.'

'Yes – to find out how our new arrangement went on Saturday.' There was a pause and the chink of a china cup against a saucer. 'The goods proved satisfactory, by all accounts.'

Norma took a sharp intake of breath and kept on listening.

'Excellent. There was some difficulty at this end, according to Barbara and Margaret. But it was all cleared up by the time Vincent arrived.'

There was another pause and the sound of a door closing in the background. This seemed to Norma to provide Sidney with an opportunity to speak more openly. 'It still needed a little persuasion on my part, but after I'd had the necessary words with her, Clare went out and made quite an impact, you can be sure.'

'As expected. She is exceptional, after all.'

For a while, the cool, suave tone of the overheard conversation confused Norma and it was only the introduction of Clare's name that convinced her that Mrs Parr and Sidney were discussing a person and not an object.

'So much so that we now have a number of customers who wish to secure her services,' he went on callously.

'Excellent again.'

Norma shut her eyes and held her breath, as if this would block out what she was hearing. It meant that she didn't notice Ruth leave the office to resume her patrol.

'Our next client has put in a request for this Friday evening – no name, of course, but needless to say a highly respectable person. Vincent will do the honours, as before, and see that the goods are delivered.'

Norma's mouth felt dry. Her eyes were still closed and her earphones were clamped to her head when she felt someone bump into the back of her chair. The force of the collision swung her round to face Millicent and she pushed her headset back from her ears.

'Sorry.' Millicent made a great show of apologizing while rolling her eyes in the direction of the approaching supe. 'Clumsy me!'

Ruth marched towards them, demanding an explanation. 'Millicent, why have you left your switchboard without permission?'

'I needed an urgent and there was no one to ask. I'm sorry – I couldn't wait.' She rushed off as if desperate before the supervisor could stop her.

Norma heaved a sigh of relief. It had been a close call. Another few seconds and Ruth would have caught her red handed. As it was, she had to wait on tenterhooks without listening in again until the supervision lamp came up to show that the call between Sidney and Mrs Parr had ended.

For the rest of the morning, time dragged. Cynthia finished her test and handed in her answers then sat in with Brenda for a final period of observation before she was given a switchboard of her own.

'Miss Ridley says that if I pass my written test, they'll put me to work properly,' she informed Millicent and Norma when she joined them in the restroom for their dinner break. 'I can hardly wait.'

They received the good news quietly and Cynthia picked up a tension in the air. Millicent stood with her back to the window, her face in shadow, and Norma sat on a chair in the corner while Molly and two other women pored over a list of gramophones for sale in the music shop next to the library in the centre of town.

'Do you two fancy a breath of air?' Norma spoke deliberately then stood up and shepherded Cynthia and Millicent out across the foyer into the street.

'What's up?' Millicent asked.

Norma swallowed hard. She wanted to spare Cynthia's feelings but on the other hand she couldn't contain herself any longer. 'I'm afraid there's bad news about Clare and Sidney Hall. Mrs Parr put in a call to him this morning.'

'And you listened in?' This in itself was shock enough for Cynthia, who quaked inwardly at the risk Norma had taken.

Norma nodded. 'I'm afraid it's what you thought, Millicent – the soirée, the reason for Clare being made to attend.'

'Oh, didn't we just know it?' Lost for words, Millicent walked a little way down the street then back again. 'Was it the first time? What exactly did they say?'

Norma remembered the conversation almost word for word. 'Sidney said that it took a little persuasion but that Clare made a big impact. He said it was a new arrangement – so, yes, we can suppose it had never happened before.'

'If only she'd listened to me.' Millicent hated to think what lurked behind that innocent word, 'persuasion'. She tried not to picture it too closely – Clare in her pink satin and chiffon gown being bullied by the salon owner then driven off by the man called Vincent, Sidney greeting her and introducing her to the eager, assembled company, Clare's horror as she saw where events were leading. Had she tried to flee at the last minute and had he prevented her by force or with yet more lies? An arm around her waist, a whisper in her ear – 'You know that I love you, my dear, and that I wouldn't put you in any

179

danger. Just do this one small thing for me. What harm can it do?'

Millicent shivered while Cynthia backed off from hearing more. She thought she understood what was being said but couldn't be sure because there was little that she'd seen or read in her sheltered life that gave her a clear picture of the seedy world being conjured up by Millicent and Norma.

'To think – Clare is probably there in the salon right this minute, still reeling with shock.' Norma restrained an urge to rush next-door-but-one and rescue Sidney Hall's latest victim.

'Or else she's come to her senses, packed her bags and left.' Millicent didn't hold out much hope of this, however. 'Mrs Parr – of all people!'

'She's definitely part of it.' Norma was in no doubt. 'I had the feeling that she's the organizer and that Clare isn't the only one.'

'Maybe Barbara and Margaret are involved as well.' It seemed likely that the two attractive, well-groomed hairdressers who lodged in the other rooms above the salon were part of the same set-up – more experienced than Clare, obviously, and firmly tied into their seemingly respectable employer's secret business dealings.

'I've never felt so helpless.' Norma's declaration echoed Millicent and Cynthia's feelings. 'We ought to be able to do something to stop this.'

'Report Sidney Hall to the police?' Cynthia wondered.

Norma shook her head. 'Douglas says they wouldn't be able to arrest him.'

'No – where's the evidence, for a start?' Millicent agreed. 'And besides – what he's doing may not be against the law.'

'Whereas, I think what Clare has done *could* get her sent to prison, or at least fined.' Norma resolved to check her facts with Douglas.

'And what you've done could get you the sack,' Millicent reminded her. 'How many times have Ruth and Agnes caught you eavesdropping so far this year?'

'Twice,' Norma admitted. All the girls did it in idle moments – it was nothing out of the ordinary. Millicent herself was on her final spoken warning before it went to the written stage.

'What about Mrs Parr?' In Cynthia's mind it was clear that she was as bad as Sidney Hall. 'Can't we tell the police about her?'

'Hmm, that's true.' Millicent gave a quick nod. 'If we're right about the part she plays, they could charge her with keeping a brothel – I'm sorry, Cynthia, it has to be out in the open.'

'As we said before – we need some evidence.' Norma racked her brains for a way forward. She remembered that Douglas had already warned her against playing detective. He would probably hear her out a second time then say, 'Leave it to us,' and then the whole thing would get lost in a pile of paperwork. Clare would still be trapped.

'There's nothing for it,' she decided. 'We'll have to keep our eyes and ears open. In future, whenever we take calls from the salon to Sidney Hall, we'll write down what we hear. Sooner or later, we'll pick up something that will convince the police to make an arrest.'

CHAPTER TEN

Cynthia sat on a wrought-iron bench next to the cenotaph waiting for Wilf to show up. She was sure he'd said he'd meet her here straight after work but so far there was no sign of him and the weather was turning nasty. Dark clouds loomed over the town hall on the far side of City Square and she felt the first drops of cold rain on her hands and face.

She stood up and walked fretfully around the cenotaph, trying to pick Wilf out of the crowd. At last she spotted him, still in his uniform, leaning into a taxi that was parked close to the kerb and talking to the driver. After a short while he gave a thumbs-up to the taxi driver and hurried towards her.

'Come on, we can get a lift home if we're quick,' he told her.

'In a taxi?'

'Yes, but don't worry – we won't have to pay. Alf Middlemiss is a pal of mine. Come on!'

Letting Wilf grab her hand, she felt herself being led towards the waiting car.

'It's about to chuck it down – quick, get in,' he urged before making hasty introductions and holding open the door.

The driver gave a pleasant nod then edged away from the kerb.

'Ta, Alf – this saves us from getting soaked.' Wilf settled beside Cynthia on the back seat.

'Yes, your luck was in – I was on my way out to Hadley to pick up a fare.'

'Anyone we know?' Wilf kept the conversation going while making it plain to Cynthia that he had eyes only for her. He took her hand and clasped it between his, staring at her and drinking in her rapidly changing expressions.

'The Oldroyd girl. I have to pick her up at six.' Alf concentrated on the road, noting to himself that Wilf hadn't taken too long to recover after Adelaide Williams had broken off their engagement. In fact, things were looking pretty cosy, there on the back seat.

'How did you get on in your test?' Wilf asked Cynthia, freeing her hand then sliding his arm around her shoulder.

'Not too bad, I hope.'

'That means you've passed with flying colours, if I know you.'

'Fingers crossed.'

'When will they let you know?'

'Miss Ridley will mark my work tonight. I should find out first thing tomorrow.'

'Champion. Then on Friday we can go out and paint the town red.'

'Steady on, Wilf,' Alf chipped in as he manoeuvred his way along Canal Road, jammed with rush-hour traffic. 'Cynthia can't go counting her chickens before they're hatched.'

Although she could only see Alf's back view, Cynthia liked the look and sound of Wilf's taxi-driver pal. He was about forty, stockily built, with broad shoulders and red patches of skin on his neck and forearm where the sun had caught him unawares. He seemed to be the sort who never got flustered.

'Well then, if you don't pass, we'll go out and drown our sorrows. How about that?'

Cynthia laughed. 'I hope it won't come to that.'

'Hey-up, Alf – the sun's come back out!' Wilf leaned in even closer. 'Oh no, it's just Cynthia's smile. It's bright enough to light up any rainy day.'

'Blimey, Wilf – where did you dig up that old chestnut?' Alf demanded as he took a short cut and steered the taxi up a steep back road. 'You're not going to let him get away with that, are you, love?'

'No. Wilf – behave.' Cynthia felt the day's worries dissolve into more smiles and laughter. 'I'm not sure yet if I can come out on Friday evening. I'll have to ask.'

'That's right – keep him hanging on,' was the driver's contribution.

'Ta very much, Alf.' Wilf pretended to take offence.

'If she wants your advice, she'll ask for it. Anyway, I don't mind how long I have to wait – it'll be worth it.'

'I mean it, Wilf – behave!' Sliding free of his embrace, Cynthia sat up straight with her hands on her lap. It was a new experience for her to be flattered and flirted with and it took some getting used to. She wondered how Millicent and Norma would deal with Wilf's flowery compliments and was relieved that Alf was there to keep things under control.

Wilf held up his hands in surrender. 'See! I'm a good boy.'

'Aye, for five minutes,' Alf growled as they reached the moor-top road and splashed along through a heavy downpour. Wind drove the rain hard against the windscreen and the wipers whined as they swished back and forth. 'I hope this lot doesn't last long,' he complained. 'I have to get Miriam Oldroyd to the railway station in time to catch the seven o'clock train to Whitehaven. I've heard she's being sent to stay at her aunty's house in the Lake District until all the fuss dies down.'

'What fuss?' Wilf asked, dropping the play-acting and tuning into Alf's more serious tone.

'Haven't you heard? Mr Oldroyd has to make a final decision by the end of the week – everyone's on tenterhooks, waiting to hear whether or not he'll be forced to close the mill.'

'The whole bang lot? Blimey.'

'Spinning and weaving – all of it. It looks like

they've reached the point of no return. That means there's seventy-five more jobs on the line.'

The news silenced Wilf. It wouldn't stop with Oldroyd's, he realized. The closure of one mill would be like a pebble thrown into water – there would be ripples up and down the canal side, a disastrous knock-on effect.

So they came to Hadley in a more subdued mood, the rain thankfully easing as Alf dropped Wilf and Cynthia at the fork in the road before carrying on and making a right turn at the far end of the village, past the lodge into the North Park estate.

'I'll walk you home,' Wilf offered.

'There's no need, honestly.' Cynthia knew that if her uncle saw them together, she'd be in for another dose of his sarcasm, or worse.

'I will, though,' he insisted. He was on best behaviour as they drew near to Moor View, advising her not to lose any sleep over her test results. They stopped under a horse chestnut tree, laden with white blossom, out of sight of the house. 'And I hope I haven't upset you,' he checked.

'Upset me – how?'

'By acting the clown in front of Alf – I do that sometimes. But it doesn't mean I'm not serious about you. I hope you know that.'

She hesitated before she replied then she gave way to an impulse to put her arms around his neck. 'I didn't mind,' she said.

He leaned in and his lips brushed hers. 'Good,' he

murmured, his hands on her hips, leaning back to take in her glowing cheeks and the damp strands of hair stuck to them. He pushed them back with his fingertips.

They kissed again, to the sound of raindrops pattering through the broad green leaves overhead. Their wet lips touched softly and they were reluctant to part.

'I will see you on Friday, won't I?' Wilf's breath was warm against her ear.

Cynthia nodded then broke free. 'You will,' she promised before she hurried home.

'Where is it?' William raged as Cynthia walked into the house. He was in the front room, his face apoplectic, yanking open drawers and thrusting books and framed photographs from tables and shelves. 'I can hear you creeping around out there in the corridor. I'm asking you, Missy – where's my cash box?'

She drew a deep breath at the sound of books thudding to the floor then walked fearfully into the room. 'I haven't seen it, Uncle.'

'My cash box!' he roared. 'I keep it here in the bureau. It's vanished.'

'Wait – let me look.' She went straight to the drawer where the box was kept and saw that it was indeed gone. 'Are you sure it was here? You didn't leave it somewhere else?'

'Where else would I put it? This is where it belongs – here, in this drawer.' Shoving Cynthia to one side, he made another frenzied search. 'The key is still here – look, in the secret compartment.' Using too much strength for the concealed miniature drawer, he pulled it right out and flung it to one side. 'See – here's the key, but no cash box!' he spluttered.

Cynthia's heart was in her mouth as she guessed what was coming. Still, she made an attempt to reason with him. 'When did you last see it?'

'Friday – that's when. Rent day.' He turned on her and thrust his face into hers. She saw the raised veins in his temple and the sweat trickling down. 'You stood there and watched me put the money in.'

She nodded. She'd been in a hurry to hand over the satchel and go out again to meet Wilf, but William had made her wait while he'd counted the coins.

'I locked it up and put it back where it belongs – you saw me with your own eyes. I haven't clapped eyes on it since.'

'Nor me,' she insisted. 'Do you know how much is in it?'

'Thirteen pounds, seven shillings and sixpence. I counted every last penny and wrote it down here, ready to take to the bank.' Sliding a red notebook from the bureau, he opened it and stabbed his finger at a list of figures and a total written in pencil. 'And where's it gone, I'd like to know.'

Cynthia's hands shook as she bent down to pick up a broken photo frame and a few scattered books. 'I have no idea. Let me tidy up here then we'll search again. I'll start in the kitchen.'

189

'Where's the use? Thirteen pounds, seven shillings and sixpence – gone. Stolen. And we both know who took it.'

She shook her head and held her breath, longing for the storm to pass.

He pointed his finger at her. She looked up at him in fear and trembling.

'Who else but you knows where I keep it? You'll say Bert – he's seen me take it out of the drawer and put the rent money in. But the lad is in bed poorly. That leaves you, Missy. You and nobody else.'

'I'd have thought she'd be more pleased,' Norma said to Millicent, glancing towards Cynthia who was operating the switchboard nearest to the door. 'In fact, I expected her to be thrilled to bits.'

To no one's surprise, Cynthia had learned first thing on Thursday morning that she'd passed her efficiency test with flying colours and Ruth had set her straight to work. She'd accepted her result with a relieved smile and made light of the congratulations of the other girls.

'I put it down to beginner's nerves,' Millicent commented. 'Give her a few days to settle in and get used to the hurly-burly.'

'Still, she doesn't seem herself. It makes me wonder how your young bus-conductor pal is treating her – is it on or off?'

'On, as far as I know.' As they worked on towards clocking-off time, Millicent connected cords robotically and let her mind drift. *On or off? On or off?* But the question that went round inside her head was not about Cynthia and Wilf but about herself and Harold. 'Hello, Birmingham, I have a new ticket.' *Where do I stand with him? What should I do?* 'Go ahead, caller.' *I know what is the best way forward, but do I have the strength?* 'Hello, Mrs Lawson. Hold the line, please.'

'Millicent?' Seizing a spare moment, Norma leaned sideways and poked her arm. She got no response so poked again and waited for Millicent to slide back her headset. 'Didn't you hear me? I asked you if you were planning to meet up with you-know-who in the near future.'

'Yes,' she decided all at once, the answer coming to her like a flash of lightning in a stormy sky. *This has to stop once and for all.* 'My plan is to see Harold today – straight after work.'

It was the detail that Clare had let slip about Harold getting her the sack from Oldroyd's mill all those years earlier that preyed most on Millicent's mind. True, it must have happened well before she and Harold had got together, but it stuck with her and showed him in a new, bad light. *He's been doing this for years*, she realized, *making a beeline for the best-looking girls and carrying on behind Doris's back.*

So after work she said her hurried goodbyes to Norma and Cynthia then set out on foot towards Brewery Road. *How old would Freddie have been back then?* she wondered. *Probably two or three at the most, with Derek already on the way. But it hadn't stopped Harold from flirting and carrying on and, worse, shoving Clare out on to the scrap heap when he didn't get what he wanted.*

As Millicent walked, her anger built. She grew hot and took off her linen jacket, striding out in short-sleeved blouse and navy blue skirt, heels clicking on the pavement and dark hair lifted by the breeze.

This is definitely the last straw, she decided. *I'm wasting my time with Harold Buckley and the sooner I end it the better.*

She arrived outside Thornley's Brewery and paused. Oldroyd's was the towering, three-storeyed building next door and she saw that the last few mill workers were drifting out from under the entrance arch on to the street, dispersing silently in different directions, their heads down and shoulders sagging. The sight alarmed her and she took time to collect her thoughts. Then she looked up at the tall mill chimney and saw no smoke. There was no sound from the steam-powered engines in the yard set back from the street. So she walked on with mounting apprehension, peering in through the door of the huge carding shed at the sea of raw fleeces ready for combing into slivers on the circular machines. The long, floor-to-ceiling windows cast bright rays across dark wooden floors and dust motes played in the early-evening light.

On she went with faltering steps, past the deserted

spinning shed and through the arch to the main office where she found Harold sitting alone at his desk.

He glanced up but stayed where he was, sagging forward as if the stuffing had gone out of him, his eyes hollow. His jacket was hanging from the back of his chair, his shirtsleeves were rolled up and his waistcoat hung open. A lock of dark hair fell over his forehead.

'Is it all right for me to come in?' she asked.

Still he didn't move. 'What do you want, Millicent?'

'Is it safe? Will anybody see us?'

He sighed and shook his head. 'Come in and close the door.'

Doing as he said, Millicent noted several cigarette stubs and a half-smoked cigar in the ashtray on the desk next to a pile of closed ledger books. The air smelled of tobacco. But it was Harold's face that demanded her attention – pale and shadowed by a day's stubble, with a look of defeat in his eyes. She pointed to the cigar. 'Mr Oldroyd has been here?'

'He left half an hour ago.'

'And?'

'He's closed us down. No ifs and buts this time.'

'For good?' Shock ran through her and her voice was hardly a whisper.

'That's right. He made me gather everyone into the canteen then he got up on his hind legs and made a speech – how nobody wants fine worsted cloth any more and he couldn't bear the cost of bringing in new machinery to make the cheaper stuff that people do want these days. He'd done what he could and he was very sorry.'

'And that was it?'

'That was the gist of it.' Harold let his head sink on to his chest.

'How did people take it? Did they offer to take a cut in wages if it meant the mill could keep going?' She pictured the empty look on Harold's face multiplied many times over on the faces of combers and doffers, burlers and menders – men and women whose lives had collapsed in an instant.

'They didn't get the chance. They were told to pack up and leave then and there – no argument.'

'It's not right,' Millicent protested. 'How are they meant to manage? They all have mouths to feed and rent to pay.'

Harold looked up and fixed his dead eyes on hers. 'No need to waste your breath spouting what I already know.'

'I'm sorry. It makes me angry, that's all.'

He stood up and unhooked his jacket from the chair. 'This has been coming for a long time – there wasn't a man or a woman here who didn't expect it.'

'But still . . .'

'Now there'll be a queue half a mile long outside the Public Assistance office, me included.'

'Oh, Harold.' She couldn't bear his despair, like a visible weight on his shoulders, but she knew better than to offer meaningless words of comfort.

He put on his jacket and spoke in a flat, weary voice. 'Why did you come, Millicent? Was it to tell me we couldn't go on meeting any more?'

She looked away, at the black typewriter on the shelf, the grey metal filing cupboards – anywhere except Harold's face.

'It was, wasn't it? Well, what's stopping you? After all, there's nothing like kicking a man when he's down.'

'What will you do?' she murmured.

'Go out and celebrate my freedom with a couple of pints, I expect.' He spoke mockingly as he came out from behind the desk and reached for his hat from the stand near the door. 'No more working at the mill with slaves, as John Milton said, eh? Oh yes, I know my schoolboy poetry.'

'Harold, don't . . .'

'Don't what?'

'Don't give in. You'll find another job if you look hard enough.'

'And a house to go with it? And enough money to keep my family in the style to which they've become accustomed?'

His bitterness made her step quickly out of his way. 'I'm very sorry. Truly.'

'That makes two of us, Millicent.' He gave her a look that squeezed her heart and made her take another step back. When he reached the door he turned to her one last time. 'Now if you don't mind, I have to go home and tell my wife.'

*

'I know, I know – I was called out to Moor View yesterday morning.' Douglas spoke soothingly to Norma as they sat at the kitchen table in Albion Lane, attempting a jigsaw left out by Ethel for them to complete. For once they had the house to themselves because Ethel, Ivy and Hetty were all out at a beetle drive being held in the meeting room next to the Methodist chapel on Chapel Street. It had given Norma a chance to tell Douglas all about Cynthia's predicament at home.

'The old man is accusing *her*, of all people!' Norma was incensed on Cynthia's behalf. 'Imagine that! Cynthia Ambler is the last person in the world to steal a penny from anyone, let alone her own uncle. And you should have seen her, Douglas. We were in the cloakroom collecting our coats and she broke down in tears. I eventually winkled it out of her – William Brooks has mislaid his money box and he's turned around and laid the blame on her.'

'I know,' Douglas repeated. To see Norma so upset knocked him off balance too. 'He telephoned the station and the sarge sent me up to the house to take down the details and have a poke around.'

'He actually telephoned the police!' Norma stood up and paced the room. 'If you ask me, the silly old so-and-so has forgotten where he's put it, that's all. I bet there was no sign of a break-in, was there?'

Douglas shook his head. 'That's why he says it must have been Cynthia – an inside job.'

'And what did you think?'

'I think if it was her – calm down and listen – she knew where the key to the money box was kept and she'd have used it to open the box. But the box was gone and the key was still in its secret drawer.'

'You see!' Vindicated, Norma sat back down. 'Did you put that in your report?'

'I wrote everything down, including the fact that the nephew, Bert Brooks, was in on where the old man keeps his money.' Douglas moved his chair nearer to Norma to slot a piece of the jigsaw puzzle into place. 'Between you and me, I don't think Cynthia has any need to worry. There's no evidence to incriminate her and once old man Brooks has had time to calm down, the whole thing will get forgotten.'

'I'm not so sure.' Norma was still uneasy. 'He sounds like a vindictive type. He works her like a slave and never lets her forget that he's the one who keeps a roof over her head. Poor girl – she has to ask his permission every time she steps out of the door.'

'You're too soft hearted.' Douglas reached across to fit in pieces of a hay wagon in the rural Constable scene they were working on. 'Cynthia has to learn to stand up for herself – you can't do it for her.'

'But I want to help my friends – it's only natural. Millicent's the same way. Which reminds me, we're wondering about the background of the woman who's just opened that new hairdresser's on George Street – Mrs Parr is her name – Phyllis Parr.'

'What about her?' Douglas's tone became more

guarded, as it did whenever Norma pressed him too hard to talk about his work.

'You tell me,' Norma countered. 'Could she be linked with Sidney Hall, for instance?'

'Steady on, Sherlock.'

'I'm serious, Douglas. Making a joke of it won't throw me off the scent.'

'No, I can see that.' It was his turn to stand up and take a turn around the cramped kitchen. He'd come here tonight with high hopes of them spending a quiet time together, talking over their future, and yet here they were, touching on some none-too-savoury aspects of his job. 'You're like a dog with a bone.'

'Ta very much.' She wrinkled her nose as she followed his progress around the room. 'So, what is it about Phyllis Parr that's set you on edge?'

'Norma, I wish you'd mind your own business.'

'Come on – you can tell me one little thing about her, at least.' She got up and joined him by the window where she put her arms around his waist and looked up winningly.

'She came here last year from Lancashire – there, that's it.' Unable to resist her wheedling, Douglas kissed her upturned cheek.

'And I'm right, aren't I? She's in cahoots with Sidney Hall. There's something shady about the two of them, isn't there? They make introductions and they get paid for their services.'

'Nothing that we can put our finger on – like I

said.' They were talking about procurement – an offence under an 1885 amendment to an even older Vagrancy Act, but it was notoriously hard to prove.

Douglas didn't deny it outright and Norma felt that she'd got the confirmation she needed. 'And there are the two of them, Phyllis Parr and Sidney Hall, putting on airs, acting as if they're the bee's knees.'

'Can't we talk about something else?' he pleaded, holding her close and planting more light kisses. 'Can't we talk about us?'

She smiled up at him a touch too brightly. 'We're all right, aren't we?'

'We are,' he murmured. 'But I'm still waiting for my answer.'

A cloud passed over her face and she rested her head on his chest. A short yes was all he needed from her. *Yes, I will marry you.* It would make everything right for him in an instant.

'Well?' he urged.

Norma took a deep breath and eased herself out of his arms. 'I'm sorry, Douglas – I still can't give you one – not yet. Give me a bit more time to think.'

'How long then?'

'Another month, until my birthday,' she begged. 'I'll be twenty-two on the seventeenth of July. I know it's hard but can you please wait until then?'

CHAPTER ELEVEN

Clare's hands shook as she took a dress from the rail. She slid it from its hanger and held it against her, viewing the effect in the mirror.

The long gown was emerald green and cut on the bias – especially made for her by Muriel Beanland at Jubilee Dressmakers so that the fit was perfect and the finish immaculate – a garment that any young woman would be thrilled to own. But Clare saw that her face was pale, her eyes lifeless, so she laid the dress on the bed and sat at the washstand that served as her dressing table to apply rouge and lipstick and to define her long lashes and dark eyebrows with a slick of Vaseline. Finally she dabbed her nose and chin with her scented powder puff.

Still shaking, she got to her feet and began to dress, slipping the silky gown over her white, lace-edged petticoat and feeling it slide with a soft swish over her slim hips. She brushed her hair and added the final touches – a scarlet silk gardenia worn as a corsage and a matching ribbon around her wrist, its ends fluttering as she reached up to pat her flyaway hair into place.

There was a tap at the door. 'Clare, are you ready?' Barbara asked. 'Vincent is here.'

Clare jumped at the sound of her voice. 'Nearly,' she replied shakily as she studied her reflection once more. It was strange how much her appearance still mattered, she thought, even after Millicent's warnings about Sidney and her own silently held suspicions had turned out to be true. She'd found it out the hard way, the Saturday before. Vincent had collected her from the salon and driven her through town to a large house on Westgate Road, set back behind laurel hedges and flanked by a coach house to one side and a formal garden to the other. Sidney had been there to greet her, smiling and murmuring compliments to her, which she had tried to believe were sincere. The entrance was grand, with a pillared portico and elaborate stained glass. There had been a doorman to let them in and inside a waiter flitting from room to room with a salver laden with cut crystal glasses and a decanter. Sidney had stroked her arm, then led her into a large reception room where the atmosphere was smoky, the smell pungent from cigars clenched between the teeth of half a dozen other guests – all men.

That was the first thing Clare had registered once she grew used to the luxurious surroundings – the absence of women. Straight away she had felt a stab of panic in her chest. She'd caught the waiter's half-closed eye and spotted contempt there before he'd looked quickly away. She'd held on tight to Sidney's arm.

He'd made introductions but she'd failed to take in the names of any of the men – the first with pock-marked skin and a bushy grey moustache, the next clean shaven. Two were tall and upright and might have been brothers, another old and stooped. Another was fat and lumbering. All assessed her openly from head to toe.

Sidney had unfurled her fingers from his arm and gone to fetch a glass of what he said was whisky. To quell her panic she'd taken a sip. It had burned her throat but the fear hadn't diminished. She'd taken another sip and then another.

After that, the memories were hazy. At some point, Sidney must have left her side. The old, stooping man had taken her hand, patted it and spoken kindly, she remembered. Perhaps she was safe after all. But soon he'd led her out of the room and up some wide stairs with portraits hanging on the wall to their right and a carved banister to the left, overlooking the stairwell. The sight of the black-and-white mosaic tiles on the ground floor below had made her feel more dizzy still as they went along a landing with doors leading off.

'No.' She'd protested feebly as the old man opened a door into a bedroom with an old-fashioned four-poster bed. She'd pulled away. Her head had been spinning. Nothing was clear. But Clare was certain she'd struggled. She must have done, because she did remember Sidney running upstairs to calm her and offer her another drink, smiling as he did so. A treacherous smile, a whisper, a firm grip around her upper arm that had bruised her flesh, she discovered later. An open door, crimson velvet curtains, a bed with a quilted counterpane, the old man taking off his jacket, the sound of the door closing behind her.

So now, almost a week later, she knew.

She stared at her reflection and saw the green satin shimmer in the glare of the electric light, heard Barbara calling for her to get a move on because Vincent was waiting for them and it was time. There was dread in her heart, a dead look in her eyes.

'Hurry up,' Barbara urged from outside the door.

It mattered to Clare that she still looked her best in spite of what she knew would happen. It made no sense to care that her hair was in place and her cheeks rouged, that her dress was uncreased and that the black velvet wrap was the right thing to wear with it. After all, no one would really care.

She turned and opened the door. Barbara too was in evening dress, with a white feather boa slung across her bare shoulders and her fair hair crimped and hanging seductively over one eye.

'You took your time,' she complained, turning and hurrying along the landing. 'It doesn't do to keep people waiting, you know.'

As if we're embarking on an ordinary evening out. Clare breathed in deeply and followed Barbara down the stairs. *As if this is what every girl does, every day of the week, year in, year out.*

I could say no. The thought was fleeting and had gone by the time they crossed the salon floor and stepped out on to the street. The taxi was there, its back door hanging open. A man in a grey tweed cap sat in the driving seat, looking straight ahead.

'Get in then,' Barbara urged as Clare hesitated on the pavement.

She bundled her in and closed the door. Vincent glanced in his rear-view mirror. As soon as Clare and Barbara were settled, he pulled away from the kerb.

'Thank heavens it's not raining,' Barbara said. 'I hate to look as if I've been dragged through a hedge backwards, don't you, Clare?' Though there was no answer, she glanced idly to right and left at the pedestrians they passed and prattled on. 'If there's one thing worse than getting there late, it's arriving looking like a scarecrow, don't you think?'

'Now then – what's up?' Leonard Andrews found Cynthia standing on the doorstep at Moor View. He'd come to collect his money for the gardening work that he and his son had carried out earlier that week and he could tell by her face that all was not well.

Though worried, Cynthia did her best to respond. 'Nothing's up,' she replied as she made a weak attempt to return his smile. It was a downright lie. Her uncle's fury over the missing money hadn't

TheWorks.co.uk

What will you discover?

The Works Stores Ltd B46 1AL
Inverness GC(757) 01463220818
VAT Reg No: 135597879

SALE   757 1 244668 18/09/2020 11:26
You were served by IONA B

Qty Description	Amount
1 A Ration Book Wedding	2.00
1 The Bobby Girls Secret	2.00
1 The Telephone Girls	2.00
Total	6.00

Savings
3 for £5   -1.00
        Today you have saved   -1.00
            Total To Pay   5.00
Cash   £5.00

VAT INCLUDED IN ABOVE TOTAL AMOUNT

RATE Z   0.00%   0.00 OF   5.00
*** *** *** *** *** *** *** *** *** ***
You could have earned 25 points with a
Together Rewards card. Forgotten your
card? Bring your Together card and
this receipt within 90 days to collect
these points.
*** *** *** *** *** *** *** *** *** ***

Thank you for shopping at The Works

abated and he'd refused permission for her to go out and meet Wilf, as planned.

'You stay right where you are, Missy,' he'd ordered as she'd cooked his tea of scrambled eggs on toast. 'I've asked your mother to get the bus out here and I want you to be here when she arrives.'

'Then I'd hate to see your face when something really is the matter.' Giving her a curious look, Leonard went on to explain his mission. 'It's a shilling this week as usual, but I can come back tomorrow if you like.'

'Yes, that'd be better.' Cynthia had already seen the 65 bus turn the corner into the village and expected to see her mother walk up the garden path at any moment. 'I'll be sure to let Uncle William know what he owes you.'

With a cheerful goodbye, Leonard went away, crossing paths with Beryl who arrived at the house with an expression that matched Cynthia's own.

'What's this about?' she demanded as Cynthia let her in, forgetting to close the door behind her. 'Why have I been dragged all the way out here on a Friday night?'

'I'm not sure.' Cynthia took her mother's coat and hat then led her into the living room where William was ensconced in his chesterfield by the window. He gestured for them both to sit on the hard chairs set out facing him.

'You took your time,' he grumbled to Beryl.

'I came on the first bus I could manage. Ellis is

poorly again. I had to cook his tea and make sure he ate it before I left the house.'

William made a 'pah' sound and tapped the floor with his walking stick. 'He'd blow over in a puff of wind, would that one. Anyway, now that you're here, I have something to say that you're not going to like.'

This is about the money, Cynthia thought with growing dread. She shifted uneasily on her chair.

'I've been robbed,' William announced with a thump of his stick that startled Beryl. 'Two days ago.'

'Goodness gracious!' Beryl came out with the strongest expression she could muster. Her lips formed an 'O' as she sucked in air and glanced nervously at Cynthia.

'Thirteen pounds, seven shillings and sixpence,' he enunciated. 'All safely locked away, waiting for me to take it to the bank.'

'You don't say,' Beryl tutted and commiserated, while Cynthia waited for the next blow to fall. 'Did you tell the police?'

'Yes, but a fat lot of good that did.' William was enjoying Cynthia's obvious misery. He drew out the story, throwing in as much detail as possible before he reached the climax. 'They sent a young constable out here – still wet behind the ears, if you ask me. Went through everything and made notes in his notebook, had the cheek to ask me if I was sure I hadn't mislaid the money myself. I gave him a rocket for that, I can tell you.'

'But have you any idea who took it?' Beryl's voice

quavered as she looked from her brother to her daughter then back again. 'It's an awful lot of money, William. Who could have done that?'

'Who do you think?' he retorted, narrowing his eyes and resting both hands on his stick as he leaned forward in his chair.

Fear darted into Beryl's eyes and her eyelids flickered. 'Perhaps someone passing the house spotted that the front door was open – a tramp, maybe? They're always lurking in bus shelters and so on at this time of year.'

'Pah!' William popped his lips and let out the same scornful sound. 'If you ask me, it was someone a bit closer to home.'

'Bert then?' Beryl's words faded to a whisper. 'He collects the rent money now, doesn't he? He'd know where you keep your cash box.'

'Ah yes, you'd like to blame your nephew, wouldn't you? If I didn't know better, I'd say that a little bird has flown your way and whispered fibs in your ear.' He looked accusingly at Cynthia as he spoke then back at his sister. 'That would be Missy's sneaky kind of trick.'

'Cynthia hasn't . . . she didn't . . .' Beryl's resistance collapsed and she fell despairingly silent.

'Now listen to me,' he commanded, switching his glare back to Cynthia. 'There's only one thief around here and we all know who it is.'

'Uncle William!' Cynthia's indignant protest fell on deaf ears.

The accusation jerked Beryl back to life. 'Oh no,

Cynthia would never do such a thing. I've brought her up better than that, I hope.'

'Then how does she explain her fancy new togs – the dress and so on? Where did she get the money to pay for all that?'

'If you mean the dress I wore to the Institute dance, I borrowed that from Millicent Jones, my friend at work. She was kind enough to lend it to me.' Something had crystallized in Cynthia's heart and made her unafraid. She sat upright and spoke calmly, even though her mother gave a small gasp and shook her head. 'Anyway, that was before the money went missing.'

'Dancing and prancing about, running around with all and sundry – oh yes, Beryl – you brought her up nicely.'

'What is it, William? What have you suddenly got against Cynthia?' Beryl couldn't understand what was happening or why. All she knew was that her life's hopes seemed to be draining away in front of her eyes. 'Hasn't she always done her best for you? Haven't we all?'

Cynthia stood up and walked across the room. She couldn't bear the pleading tone in her mother's voice or the control that her uncle had over them. 'It's all right, Mum,' she said quietly. 'I didn't take the money, but if I'm not believed, I certainly won't stay here to be insulted.'

'Cynthia!' Distraught, Beryl got up too. 'Don't go. I'm sure we can sort this out. William, did you hear what she said? She's not the thief. It was someone else.'

'Oh yes, Beryl – carry on shifting the blame.' The last to stand, William advanced towards Cynthia and grabbed her by the wrist, raising his voice to a spitting snarl. 'I'll wring the truth out of you, young lady, like it or not.'

'Steady on – no you don't!' Wilf was suddenly in the room, bold as anything. He'd waited for Cynthia at the fork in the road and when she hadn't turned up, he'd suspected something was wrong. He'd ventured to the doorstep of Moor View to investigate and heard raised voices through the open door. So he'd marched straight in, a knight in shining armour, following the sound of the argument. 'You let go of her, you hear.'

Cynthia made a sobbing sound and wrenched herself free. She rubbed her sore wrist where William's fingers had grasped her. Beryl subsided into horrified silence.

'Oh, so you're ganging up on me now!' William swung his stick towards Wilf, who easily dodged out of reach. 'It was a plan, was it? The two of you, plotting to steal my hard-earned money. Yes, I see.'

Wilf resisted the temptation to laugh. If it wasn't so serious, it would be funny. 'No one's stealing anything,' he countered. 'Not me and definitely not Cynthia. She's honest as the day.' He turned to Beryl. 'I'm Wilf Evans, by the way. You must be Cynthia's mother.'

Wilf's casual manner stole the old man's thunder and left him stranded in the middle of his living-room carpet, squirming and helpless, like a fat trout in a fisherman's net. There was only one way forward now. 'Get out!' he stormed at Cynthia. 'Right now, this minute.'

'William, you can't,' Beryl gasped.

'I can and I will. Pack your bags, Missy, and never let me set eyes on you again.'

Cynthia stared at him. She saw with an outsider's eye that his fury was ridiculous and somewhere, not far beneath the surface, she was sure he knew it too. It was this humiliating knowledge that made him bluster and threaten.

'No, William – what will you do if Cynthia goes? How will you manage?' Beside herself, Beryl pleaded for him to change his mind.

The old man sagged and leaned on his stick, breathing heavily as the repercussions of his actions hit home. Then he pulled himself upright. 'I'll manage,' he insisted. 'Pipe down, Beryl. And you, young fellow-me-lad – you're trespassing. I'll set the police on to you if you don't watch out.'

Wilf nodded slowly and warily. 'Just so long as you don't lay another finger on her,' he said, looking towards Cynthia.

'Don't worry, I can cope.' Cynthia stepped in between them and placed a hand on Wilf's arm. 'I'm quite safe,' she murmured. 'You can wait at the gate for me, if you like.'

Another nod from Wilf saw him step backwards out of the room, leaving a weeping Beryl and a stick-thumping William.

'That's how it is, is it?' William's bitter grumbling broke the silence that followed Wilf's departure. 'Stop snivelling, Beryl. Do something useful. Go upstairs and help the girl pack her things. That's the reason I got you out here in the first place.'

'There's no need, Mum. I don't need help,' Cynthia said, aware that she had little enough to gather together. 'Why not wait outside with Wilf?'

Beryl, white faced and breathless, pressed her lips together and closed her eyes. She opened them and for the first time in decades she found the strength to stand up to her brother. 'You're a hard and spiteful creature,' she told him plainly. 'I've known that deep down, ever since we were little and you bullied me and Gilbert at every end and turn. So, more fool me for trying to help you in your old age.'

He returned the gaze, head tilted to one side as if considering a knotty problem, aware that Cynthia had already gone upstairs to her room. 'You did nothing, Beryl. You washed your hands of the girl as soon as ever you could. Then you let her do all the work for you – you know you did. And now I've landed her back on your plate, like it or not.'

211

CHAPTER TWELVE

On the last Sunday in June, Millicent sat in the pavilion on the Common with Cynthia and Norma. 'I don't know which is worse, Cynthia – to grow up and have no mother to keep an eye on you or to have one as useless as yours.'

'Millicent!' Norma remonstrated while Cynthia cleared her throat in embarrassment. 'You can't say that.'

'I just did.' For the last two weeks Millicent had listened to Cynthia's tales of woe – firstly, how she'd been wrongly accused and sent packing by her uncle and then how she'd been blamed for it by her own mother. 'I don't know how you stick it back there with them on Raglan Road,' she commiserated. 'If I were you, they wouldn't see me for dust.'

'Let's talk about something more cheerful,' Norma insisted. 'It's a nice, sunny afternoon. Why don't we walk out to Brimstone Rock?'

'No, it's all right – I haven't taken offence,' Cynthia

insisted. 'Millicent means well, and she's right – I am finding it hard to settle in back at home.'

'You see – she wants to get things off her chest.' Millicent prepared for a longer chat by taking off her straw hat and letting her hair fall loose around her shoulders. 'Fire away, Cynthia.'

'Dad is just Dad,' Cynthia said with a sigh. 'He hardly says a word, just sits in his corner and stares into space.'

'So it's your mother mainly?'

Cynthia nodded. 'She makes out that everything is my fault, even though I've sworn, hand on heart, that I didn't steal Uncle William's money. She starts on at me the minute I get home from work – why didn't you think to lock the bureau and keep the money safe? Why didn't you take it to the bank yourself?'

'Which is all water under the bridge,' Norma pointed out. 'What's done is done.'

Cynthia was silent for a while, picturing her father's vacant face and hearing her mother's bleating voice, with the slow tick of the mantel clock in the background measuring out the minutes before it was time to go to bed. 'I've done my level best to get back into Mum's good books,' she said after a while. 'I've offered to pay my share of the rent and help her with the cooking and washing, and so on, but it doesn't make any difference – she still makes me feel as if I'm letting her down.'

'I've always said you go too far out of your way to

please people,' Millicent commented. 'Me, on the other hand – I've learned you have to look out for yourself and not bother what others think.'

'Listen to the three of us.' Norma's frown showed that she was determined to shake them out of their sombre moods. 'Anyone would think we had the weight of the world on our shoulders.'

'It's all right for some,' Millicent argued. 'You've got two sisters at home to chip in with the rent and a mother who isn't having a go at you all the time.'

'True.' Norma knew she must count her blessings. For her, life at home might be humdrum but there was no nastiness. Yes, she decided – she would take her present lot over what Cynthia and Millicent were going through any day.

'*And* you have poor Douglas waiting in the wings, ready to marry you,' Millicent added.

'Here we go!' Norma jumped up, blocked her ears and left the pavilion to walk a little way along the cinder path. Her pale blue cotton skirt fluttered in the breeze and she had to hold her hat in place as she went.

'Oh dear me, I seem to have touched a sore spot,' Millicent said with a wink. 'Anyway, Cynthia, I do understand what it is to be let down by your nearest and dearest. After all, my mum left home when I was little.'

The confession created an awkward pause before Cynthia took the plunge. 'What do you remember about her?'

214

'Her scent.' Millicent's reply was swift and telling. 'She dabbed eau de cologne behind her ears whenever she went out, even if it was only to the shops. And her hair – it was the same colour as mine – our crowning glory, you might say. And if you're wondering where Dad is now and why I don't mention him – well, that's a story that I'll save until another time.' Millicent gave a wry smile as she pulled Cynthia up from the bench. 'Come along, we'd better catch up with Norma and say sorry.'

So they ran after her and linked arms, while Millicent tried to make amends.

'I didn't mean it – Douglas is a very lucky man.'

'La-la! I'm not listening.'

'It won't do him any harm to wait for your answer.'

'La-la-la!'

'In fact, it'll do him good. And we're jealous, aren't we, Cynthia? There aren't many tall, dark and handsome men like him around. We only wish there were. Oops, sorry, Cynthia, I forgot – you have one of your own.'

Cynthia laughed. 'Wilf isn't dark.'

'No, that's right. He's a fair-haired, blue-eyed boy. Is he behaving himself, by the way?'

'He is.' She smiled enigmatically. Not only had Wilf appeared at Moor View and stuck up for her at exactly the right moment, but he'd also promised to keep his ear to the ground in Hadley to see if he could pick up any clues as to who might have nipped into the house and stolen the money. And Cynthia

215

had seen him four times since then, twice to go to the pictures, once to walk hand in hand by the canal and once to have a drink in the Green Cross.

'He's not taking liberties?'

'No.' *No! I kiss him, he kisses me. Each time we part, I put my arms around his neck and draw him close. He holds me tight. Nothing is said but everything feels right.*

'What about Harold?' Norma asked Millicent, since it seemed this was the time for heart-to-hearts. 'Have you seen him since Oldroyd's closed down?'

Millicent shook her head and broke free. 'No and I haven't heard anything either.'

Norma caught her by the arm and spoke confidentially. 'Well, I have.'

'You have?' Millicent had a sinking feeling that she couldn't disguise.

'I overheard Ruth telling Agnes that he's still looking for work. Ruth is friendly with Doris.'

'Yes, yes – I know.' Millicent bit her lip to stop it from trembling. Suddenly her mood plummeted and she teetered on the brink of that dark hole that she'd always feared – the one where there was no man in her life, no flattery, no promises, no shared future to look forward to. She felt as she had all those years ago, when her mother had walked out of the door, leaving coat hangers dangling in an empty wardrobe and the lingering scent of eau de cologne.

'He's trying his hardest, apparently, but there's nothing out there. Or if there is, he joins the end of a very long queue.'

Millicent shook her head and sighed.

'I thought you'd want to know.'

'Well, I don't . . . No, that's not right – I do.' She stopped, clasped each of their hands and held on tight. 'What would you do if you were me, you two? Would you try to see Harold?'

The question hung in the air. The tables were turned and the one out of the three who usually had the answers seemed desperate for their advice.

'Do you miss him?' Cynthia murmured. 'Do you love him – really and truly?'

Millicent nodded then turned to Norma, waiting for her answer.

'No, I wouldn't,' Norma said, slow and deliberate. 'Yes, you might think you love him and for all I know, you truly do. But you mustn't go after him, Millicent. Not now – not as things stand.'

They'd each reached a turning point, Millicent realized. She sat at her switchboard next day, mulling over Norma's sensible advice and keeping an eye on Cynthia's board in case she was slow to take a light. She needn't have worried – Cynthia had taken to the work like a duck to water, sitting straight-backed in her swivel chair, placing cords into jacks, listening then speaking with crystal clarity before connecting the caller to the required line.

A fresh start – that's what I need, she told herself when her board was quiet. They were coming up to the end of their shift and Millicent had decided on a proposal she would put to Cynthia before they left the building if she got the chance. To her right, she heard Norma take a call.

'Hello, Mr Hall. Go ahead, please.'

Millicent immediately pricked up her ears.

'Hold the line, please.' Norma flashed a significant glance at Millicent then inserted a cord. 'Hello, Mrs Parr. I have Mr Hall on the line.'

Millicent checked Ruth's whereabouts and saw that she was leaning over Brenda's shoulder to help her with an unusual routes and rates query. She held Norma's attention and rolled her eyes towards the supe, meaning that it was safe to listen in.

Norma kept her headset firmly in place.

'Our newest recruit – I'm beginning to think she's more trouble than she's worth,' Sidney Hall said in his laconic, superior way.

Phyllis Parr came straight back at him. 'I disagree,' she said sharply. 'This is still early days, remember.'

'Yes, but the problem can't be easily solved. She's a sensitive type and her sort always proves more difficult than the Barbaras and Margarets of this world.'

'But she's extraordinary-looking.'

'Yes, I'll grant you that.'

'And remember, some of our clients prefer it if there's a little resistance involved.'

Norma followed the circumspect conversation with bated breath, her stomach churning as she read between the lines. Millicent, meanwhile, continued to keep a lookout for the supe.

Sidney sounded amused. 'I must say, Phyllis, I admire you. You know this business inside out.'

'I should do, I've been at it long enough. So listen to me – there's a definite way to manage this situation but it does involve you making a little more effort.'

'Must I?' Sidney gave a weary sigh. 'Haven't I done my bit already?'

'You have, and very well too.' Phyllis's newly smooth tone was calculated to draw him back in and keep him sweet.

Norma checked with Millicent that the coast was still clear and waited to hear more.

'But you must step in again and ply your charms.'

'Is that so?' There was a pause while Sidney stubbed out his cigarette in an ashtray. 'I suppose I could spare five minutes to speak with her on the telephone.'

'No, that won't do. You must come to the salon in person – to make her see which side her bread is buttered.'

'Very well, if you say so. But when?'

Millicent saw Ruth finish speaking to Brenda. She nudged Norma to warn her that the supe was back on patrol and heading their way. Norma immediately flicked two keys and slipped back her headset. She felt her hands shake with disgust at what she'd heard and hoped that Ruth wouldn't notice.

'Millicent, take your light!' Ruth snapped as she drew near. 'Norma, your supervision light is flashing. Disconnect your cords, please. Molly, pay attention – you have two lights. Cynthia, you have one – chop-chop!'

It had been a busy, tiring day but it was almost at an end. Cynthia took her light then mustered the last of her concentration to recognize the local number and speak to her caller. 'Hello, Mr Oldroyd. Go ahead, please.'

'Hello, operator. Please connect me to White-haven 622.'

Cynthia operated her switchboard. 'Hello, White-haven. I have a new ticket, wanted as soon as possible for Mr Oldroyd.'

'Hold the line, please. Whitehaven 622, I have Mr Oldroyd on the line.'

The connection was made but Cynthia was not as quick as usual to flick up both switches and sit back until the call was finished. Instead, she overheard the start of a hurried conversation.

'Miriam, is that you? This is your father speaking.'

'Daddy, please, *please* can I come home?'

'No, Miriam, not yet. And you must stop pestering Aunt Elizabeth to be allowed to.'

'Why, Daddy?'

'You know why. Everything is up in the air here. Nothing is settled.'

'But I don't care. North Park is my home. It's where I belong.'

Curiosity overcame Cynthia and she couldn't tear herself away. Guiltily she went on eavesdropping.

'For now, yes. But you must prepare yourself for the sale of the house and the estate, just like everyone else,' Joseph Oldroyd warned. 'Think of your poor mother – she doesn't want to leave any more than you do.'

As Cynthia's conscience kicked in and she began to slide back her headset, she heard Miriam start to sob on the Whitehaven end of the line. She sat and considered what she'd just heard, hardly registering the bell that signalled the end of her shift.

'Come on, slow coach.' Millicent prompted her by jogging her elbow. 'I know you love your work, but it's time to pack up for the day.'

'Yes – ta.' Cynthia's head was in a whirl as she followed Millicent and Norma into the cloakroom. Unable to think straight, she concentrated on the fact that with luck she would be able to catch the ten-past-five bus. So, in an obvious hurry, she grabbed her coat and ran off without saying goodbye.

'What's got into her?' Millicent wondered.

'I don't know, but she's probably dashing off to meet Wilf.' Norma had more pressing things on her mind and hurried Millicent out of the building where they were met by the usual sound of heavy traffic and the rush of pedestrians. She talked urgently as they weaved their way through the crowd past Sam Bower's. 'Don't you want to know what Phyllis Parr said to Sidney Hall?' Norma prompted.

Millicent tried to see who was inside the salon as they walked by but found that the blind was down and there was no sign of life. 'I do,' she said, bracing herself. *Whatever it is, it can't be good*, she thought.

'To be frank, I don't know who's worse – him or her.' The information was on the tip of Norma's tongue. 'Now listen to this and tell me what, if anything, we can do.'

Cynthia took the long ride out of town wrapped in her own thoughts. She sat in the front seat on the lower deck and paid her fare to a conductor she'd never seen before – a lad even younger than Wilf, with dirt under his fingernails and a prominent Adam's apple. Staring straight ahead, she blocked out the chatter of other passengers and thought about how best to word her dramatic news when she spoke to Wilf.

The bus rocked along the bumpy, winding road. Should she cushion the blow, she wondered, or should she come straight out with it? Not only had Joseph Oldroyd closed down his mill but now he was forced to sell the North Park estate as well!

The bus reached the brow of a hill then plunged down again, stopping at the end of a farm lane to let the farmer's wife alight. A chained dog barked in the distance, the conductor rang the bell and the bus set off again.

Better to come right out with it, Cynthia decided as they came within sight of Hadley. Wilf would

222

probably bear bad news better than his mother and he would break it to her more gently, for there was no doubt that if the main house was sold, then the lodge would go too. Wilf and his mother would have to look for somewhere else to live.

'Watch your step,' the conductor called as Cynthia stood up on the final bend into Hadley and made her unsteady way to the exit.

As she got off, she came face to face with the last person she wanted to see – her cousin Bert, stepping on to the platform as she got off.

'Look who it isn't,' he said gleefully, holding the rail and hanging wide of the bus as it pulled away, waving derisively with his free hand. He wore the same old ill-fitting jacket, flat cap and an open-necked, collarless shirt. 'If you've come to worm your way back into Uncle William's good books, I'd save your breath.'

'Don't worry – I haven't,' she said, turning her back and walking in the opposite direction, picking up pace through the village and on past the church that was pretty in the sunlight with its square tower and the blue clock on one side showing six o'clock.

The entrance to North Park lay in a dip, past a row of terraced houses where countryside took over again. It was marked by tall stone gateposts that mimicked castle battlements. Cynthia found that the wide wrought-iron gates stood open, allowing a clear view of a splendid house with turrets and arched windows at the end of a curved driveway. Close to the entrance, tucked away on the left-hand side, stood a small, scaled-down version of the big house – the lodge.

Now that she was here, Cynthia felt a knot form in her stomach. What if Wilf wasn't at home and his mother answered the door? She hadn't met Mrs Evans and didn't know how she should introduce herself. *Hello, my name is Cynthia Ambler. I'm walking out with your son.* That sounded too bold, so she experimented with a shorter version: *Hello, I'm Cynthia. Is Wilf in?* Still unsure, she approached the open door and heard voices from inside.

'Wilf, honestly – you're the limit,' a woman taunted.

Cynthia caught a glimpse of the woman's back view framed by an inner doorway. Dressed in blue, she was young and slim, with short, dark hair – definitely not Wilf's mother.

Then she heard Wilf's muffled, teasing reply. 'What are you on about?'

'I'm serious,' the woman insisted. 'I came here because I heard you'd turned over a new leaf.'

Cynthia gasped and stepped back out of sight. Her heart thumped and threatened to break out through her ribs.

'Who told you that?' Wilf laughed.

Light footsteps sounded on a stone floor then the woman spoke again – this time inaudibly.

Wilf laughed again. He said something indistinct about becoming Steady Eddie all of a sudden.

Outside, Cynthia fought for breath. She must leave without being seen, get far away and never come back. Luckily Wilf and the woman were in what must be the kitchen at the back of the house, so her coast was clear.

She fled down the short path then out through the main gates, her heart wrung out, a frown creasing her forehead. She passed the row of terraced cottages then the low pub building, hurrying on and reaching the far end of the village just in time to see the number 65 about to set off from the terminus on its return journey into town.

'Blimey – you again,' the young conductor remarked as Cynthia flagged down the bus at the fork in the road. 'That was a quick visit.'

Without answering, she sank down in the nearest seat. She fumbled to open her purse and pay her fare, her eyes filling with hot tears, her fingers numb.

Studying her more closely, the conductor slotted things into place. 'Wait a minute – you're the lass Wilf Evans meets up with on George Street.'

Cynthia swallowed hard and stared out of the window.

'You're his new girl, aren't you?'

'No,' she replied fiercely, her heart in her mouth. 'Not any more, I'm not.'

In Millicent's house in Heaton Yard, she and Norma had talked themselves to a standstill and they sat by the open window silently watching a couple of boys kick a leather ball against the wall of the outside privy. It was still daylight, but the sun had disappeared behind the houses and the air grew chill.

'Brrr, best close that window,' Norma suggested, slipping her arms into the sleeves of her cardigan.

Millicent had to heave hard at the sash window and pray that the frayed rope didn't snap. 'If I ever get William Brooks to mend this, it'll be a miracle,' she grumbled. 'I've written to him once already and spoken twice to that little squirt who comes to collect the rent.'

'Bert the squirt,' Norma trotted out the rhyme with a rueful smile. Then, more seriously, 'We're stuck, aren't we?'

'Over the mess Clare's got herself into? I hate to say it, but yes, we are.' Millicent couldn't get past the fact that it was all too late. Clare had already refused their help, told them to mind their own business then gone right ahead and taken the fatal step that took her beyond the pale. The words 'fallen woman' stuck inescapably in Millicent's mind, bringing a Dickensian picture of dark, dingy streets, foggy nights, the glare of headlights as a car pulled up to the kerb.

'How could she let herself?' Norma wondered with a small shudder. 'I wouldn't – not for anything.'

'I'm not so sure. It's hard to put yourself in someone else's shoes and we only have a vague idea of how it happened.'

Norma nodded. 'But we do know that Clare fell hook, line and sinker for Sidney Hall's tricks.'

Millicent agreed. 'I don't blame her for that, though. He's a handsome enough chap, with a car and plenty of money. And at the start, I expect he whispered sweet nothings in her ear.'

'But there must have been a point when she began to see that things weren't right.'

'Yes, most likely before we ran into her at Health and Beauty. Remember how red she went when we tried to get her to talk about her young man? And later, when I spotted her in the King's Head, she couldn't bring herself to say hello.'

'If she'd had any sense, she'd have backed out as soon as she realized.'

'But think about it,' Millicent said. 'Clare was living in a fairy-tale world of dresses and fur wraps, nylon stockings and Chanel Number 5. That's hard to give up when you've been living from hand to mouth most of your life. Anyway, there are plenty of so-called respectable women who sell themselves for a lot less.'

'Steady on, Millicent.' *Here we go.* Norma prepared herself for a lecture about the traps that women walked into with their eyes wide open – marriages with men they had no feelings for, for the sake of a wedding ring and simply to escape the label of old maid.

Millicent picked up the signals. 'Don't roll your eyes at me. I'm not going to go on about it.'

'Good. Anyway, we're agreed that Clare has made . . .'

'. . . Her own bed.'

They both grimaced at the seedy picture they'd unintentionally conjured up then went to the window together as they saw Cynthia come down the ginnel into the yard. She looked pale and on the verge of tears as she hurried towards the house.

'What now?' Millicent wondered, flinging open the front door.

'I'll put the kettle on,' Norma decided in a flash.

Cynthia stumbled on the bottom step and Millicent had to lend her a hand into the kitchen where she collapsed in the fireside chair.

'Sit back, take a deep breath,' Millicent ordered while Norma was busy with tea leaves and teapot. 'That's better.'

Cynthia rested her head against the back of the chair, her eyes closed. The journey back from Hadley had taken an age and when she'd stepped off the bus, she'd known she couldn't go home but had to come here to Millicent's for advice. 'It's Wilf,' she whispered.

'Who else?' Millicent drew up a chair.

'What's he done to upset you?' Norma asked. Leaving the tea to brew, she pulled up a second chair then fished in her handbag for a handkerchief. 'Here, have this.'

Millicent realized they had to allow Cynthia time to calm down. She raised an eyebrow and glanced at

Norma. 'Whatever it is, it's plainly a matter of life and death.'

'You were right,' Cynthia whispered at last. 'Wilf's not to be trusted. I wish I'd listened to you and kept my distance right from the start.'

'Whoa! Slow down and tell us what this is about,' Norma interrupted.

'Wilf's broken her heart, that's what.' Millicent was genuinely annoyed with herself for not keeping a better eye on things. After all, she'd suspected that Cynthia was too tender a flower to be left to Wilf's mercies.

'He said such nice things to me,' Cynthia wailed. 'And I believed every word.'

Echoes of what Sidney Hall had done to Clare presented themselves to Norma and she grew more concerned. 'What happened? Has he overstepped the mark?'

Cynthia raised her head, gripped the arms of her chair and drew a deep breath. 'Mr Oldroyd is selling North Park,' she began, seemingly apropos of nothing.

Millicent sat back in her chair with a frown while Norma got up to pour the tea.

'He has to sell everything – the big house, the grounds, the lodge. I listened in at work and heard him tell his daughter.'

'Ah.' Millicent began to piece things together.

'You're lucky Ruth didn't catch you,' Norma observed.

'I wanted Wilf to know straight away so I caught the Hadley bus—'

'Yes, yes – we saw you dash off. What happened when you found him?'

'He was at home with—' Cynthia choked over the words and came to a halt.

'With a woman?' Norma guessed.

Cynthia remembered the stranger's back view – the pale blue dress, the sleek dark hair and white shoes. She nodded without speaking.

Norma guessed again. 'You suppose he was with Adelaide?'

As Cynthia nodded a second time, the tears fell. 'She said she'd heard that he'd turned over a new leaf – that was why she was there, ready to try again.'

'Did she actually say that? That she was ready to try again?' Millicent pressed. This didn't fit in with what she'd most recently heard about Adelaide Williams, which was that she'd upped sticks and gone to live with a cousin in Glasgow.

'Yes – no. Not that she was ready to give it another go. But she did tell him that's why she was there – because he'd turned over a new leaf.'

Cynthia hardly knew what she was saying. She felt dizzy with despair.

'Slow down. What did this woman look like?' Millicent asked, one hand on Cynthia's arm.

'I can't really describe her. I only saw her back view. She was tall, I think.'

'With what colour hair?'

'Dark. Short and dark.' They'd laughed together in the kitchen at North Park Lodge – Wilf and his ex-fiancée.

'Tall and dark,' Millicent repeated, the corners of her mouth starting to twitch. 'Then that definitely can't have been the dreaded Adelaide.'

'Why can't it?' Cynthia sat bolt upright with newly sprung hope, clutching Norma's damp handkerchief.

'Adelaide Williams is under five feet tall for a start. And she has red hair. I mean really red – redder than Brenda's at work.'

'Then who . . . ?'

'Tall and dark, you say.' Millicent mulled it over. 'What was she wearing?'

'A blue dress.'

'Did it have a white collar and cuffs? Could it have been some kind of uniform?'

'I suppose so.' Cynthia nodded, looking in confusion from Millicent to Norma and back again.

'Then I'll bet my life that our mystery woman works as a nurse at King Edward's Hospital.' Millicent couldn't hide the smile that pulled at the corners of her mouth. 'You cuckoo – I'll bet it was Wilf's sister Maude you saw at the lodge!'

CHAPTER THIRTEEN

'Ah, the wonders of a good, strong cup of tea!' Millicent's proclamation made Cynthia and Norma smile.

'Goodness gracious, you sound like Mum,' Norma said. 'A cup of tea with three spoonfuls of sugar is her remedy for all of life's problems.'

Millicent rolled her eyes in horror. 'God forbid! I'm only twenty-five, remember.' Collecting the cups and saucers, she put them in the sink. 'I'm not quite ready to hang up my headset, I'll have you know.'

'Don't worry, I don't see you in carpet slippers and curlers for a long time yet.' Norma bustled Millicent out of the way and began to wash the crockery. 'Once I've done this, I'd better be on my way.'

'Yes, it's getting late.' Still feeling foolish over the error she'd made about Maude Evans, Cynthia too got ready to leave.

Millicent stood by the door watching her. 'Before you go, I have a proposition. It's something I've been meaning to mention for a day or two.'

'Ooh, I'm all ears.' Norma was busy drying her hands as she came between Millicent and Cynthia.

'Not for you, silly. This is an idea I want to put to Cynthia.' Millicent hurried to the door before Cynthia could turn the handle. 'I'll get straight to the point. You're not happy at Raglan Road and I have an empty attic room here.'

Cynthia's mind raced ahead and her eyes lit up.

'It's not much to write home about, and it's far from ideal that everyone on the yard has to share an outside toilet, but I wonder if you'd like to move in with me?'

Cynthia gasped and nodded.

Millicent set off up the stairs, taking them two at a time. 'Hold your horses. Don't say yes before you've had a look.'

'Go on!' Norma encouraged Cynthia to follow. She saw straight away that this would definitely be a way to free Cynthia from the shackles of home.

All three went up two flights of rickety stairs to the small, empty room at the top of the house. No more than ten feet square, with bare boards, sloping ceilings and only a small fanlight to let in the light, there was at least a fireplace and a gaslight on the wall.

'We'll have to get you a bed and a mattress.' Now that she looked more closely, Millicent realized there was a lot that needed to be done to make the room habitable. 'We can give the walls a quick lick of paint and I can put up a rail for your clothes.'

'And I'm sure I can get hold of spare sheets and

pillow cases,' Norma promised. 'I know there's a rug tucked away in the cupboard under the stairs at home, too. Between us we'll be able to smarten the place up no end.'

'I don't care. It doesn't matter.' Cynthia would have been happy to move in without any home comforts but then she saw a snag that obviously hadn't occurred to Millicent.

'So you'll say yes?' Millicent prompted.

'If it's up to me – yes. But what will Uncle William say?'

'Ah, my precious landlord.'

'Yes, there is that,' Norma admitted cautiously. 'Are you allowed to share the place with another lodger?'

Millicent raised her eyebrows and spread the palms of her hands upwards. 'Who would tell him, pray?'

'Ah!' Norma laughed. Trust Millicent to see a rule and break it.

'Oh.' Cynthia managed to put to the back of her mind what her uncle would do if he found out. The lure of leaving home and setting up for herself was too strong to resist. If she moved in with Millicent, she would never have to ask permission to go out with Wilf or explain her actions to anyone ever again. She would be free to follow wherever her heart led.

'Well?' Millicent asked.

'Yes please,' Cynthia decided with a broad smile. 'I'd like to move in here just as soon as I can.'

*

The days following saw Cynthia, Millicent and Norma laying dust sheets on the floor and climbing up and down stepladders each evening, paintbrushes in hand. They enlisted Dusty Miller from number 8 to repair some broken skirting board and Chalky White to fetch and carry a small, beer-stained table from the yard at the back of the Green Cross.

'Nobody will miss this,' the barman promised as he carried it up the stairs of number 10. 'We were waiting for the rag and bone man to come and collect it, in any case.'

A bed and mattress were found and thoroughly fumigated on the cobbles outside, and a chair and washstand were provided, courtesy of the friendly dressmakers at Jubilee.

On the Thursday night, the three women stood back to view the fruits of their labours.

'It's a shame about the cracks in the ceiling.' Norma's face was speckled with white paint as she gave the room a final inspection. 'I've done my best to cover them up but they still show.'

'We've all done the best we can.' Millicent closed her paint tin with a satisfied sigh.

'It's champion!' Cynthia insisted that no palace could have pleased her more. 'I can't thank you enough.'

'Likewise.' Millicent acknowledged that Cynthia's offer to help with the rent was more than enough. 'I'll get a new key cut tomorrow then you can move in over the weekend if that suits you.'

*

Before that there was another day at the switchboards and afterwards, for Millicent and Cynthia at least, an hour and a half of Health and Beauty torture at Ruth's hands.

'And stretch, and twist, and relax!' Millicent mimicked the instructions after the Friday-evening class, when she and Cynthia were getting changed. 'Blimey, am I the only one who aches from head to foot?'

'No!' a bunch of exhausted shop girls, housewives and bank clerks chorused. But the complaints were good tempered and soon the invigorated members of the League went their separate ways.

Ruth was on the steps of the Assembly Rooms, checking her wristwatch when Millicent and Cynthia emerged. 'Do you two mind if I walk home with you?' she asked when she noticed them. 'We've just missed the half-eight bus into town.'

'Feel free,' Millicent answered, giving Cynthia a hidden nudge. 'Just so long as you steer clear of anything to do with work.'

'I promise.' Off duty and sportily dressed in pale grey cardigan and slacks, Ruth gave off an altogether more relaxed air. She crossed the road with them on to Overcliffe Common, chatting about the latest royal scandal – notably the report in the *Express* that Wallis Simpson was heading for a divorce.

'Her second,' Ruth reminded them. 'I've got nothing against being divorced – don't get me wrong. How could I? But marrying the wrong man once is one thing. Doing it twice is another matter. What was it that Oscar Wilde said about the difference between misfortune and carelessness?'

As usual Millicent took an unconventional line. 'I say, give the woman a chance. For all we know, Wally may be just what King Edward needs.'

'For what?' Ruth asked sharply. 'For cruising off the Dalmatian coast and listening to American jazz bands?'

'What's wrong with that?' Millicent argued. 'You wouldn't say no to sailing on the royal yacht, would you, Cynthia?'

Ruth turned to Cynthia with a sympathetic smile and a word of advice. 'Don't let Millicent lead you astray, do you hear?'

'You're not the first to warn me about that.' Cynthia smiled back. 'Anyway, far from leading me off the straight and narrow, Millicent has taken me under her wing and I'm grateful.'

'Was she behind your visit to Sylvia's Salon?' Ruth wanted to know. She'd noticed a big change in their young recruit in the few weeks since she'd started work, not least the new haircut that framed her heart-shaped face and accentuated her high cheekbones. There was no doubt about it – Cynthia was growing up in leaps and bounds.

'As a matter of fact, yes.' The change of style had drawn compliments from Wilf and criticism from Cynthia's mother – a true measure of the improvement if ever there was one.

'Is Clare Bell still working there?' Ruth enquired,

stepping to one side as two girls on roller skates sped up behind them, followed by a smaller girl on a tricycle.

'Yes – why?' Millicent asked, aware that Ruth was intent on steering the conversation in a particular direction.

'Nothing. I was just wondering. I was sorry when she stopped coming to classes, that's all.'

'We all were,' Cynthia said.

'It was a real chance for her to make new friends and keep that figure of hers in shape.'

Ruth's heavy-handed concentration on Clare bothered Millicent but it was proving difficult to bring her to the point. 'She has a lot on her plate, what with her new job at the salon.'

'I expect she has.'

'Clare is in charge of answering the telephone and making appointments, keeping them up to date with the latest magazines, and so on. And she must look her best at all times.'

'As must we all,' Ruth said primly. They were nearing the top of Ada Street – the point where they would split off. They stopped and there was a pause before she spoke again. 'Millicent, were you friendly with Clare when you were at school?'

'At Lowtown Juniors – yes. That's to say, I knew her but not very well. She didn't join in much. In fact, I doubt that she had many true friends.'

Ruth cast a sideways glance at Cynthia. 'No one to take *her* under their wing – then or now?'

'No. What are you getting at?'

Ruth frowned, afraid to upset Cynthia by her plain speaking but deciding to plough ahead anyway. 'I'm wondering – would Clare listen to advice from you about Phyllis Parr?'

Millicent and Cynthia glanced at each other in surprise.

'Why?' Millicent asked, sharp as a tack. 'What have you heard?'

'I feel duty bound to tell you that Phyllis is not what she seems,' Ruth confided. 'I've known of her for a long time. We lived not far from each other in Lancashire where, not to put too fine a point on it, she was prosecuted for keeping a brothel.'

Ruth's frankness took Millicent aback but she quickly regained her presence of mind and was careful not to incriminate herself or Norma for listening in at work. 'It's not the first time we've heard about Mrs Parr's murky goings-on,' she assured Ruth. 'Norma's beau, Douglas Greenwood, is a policeman. He knows about her and her links with Sidney Hall – you know who I mean?'

Ruth nodded. 'I've heard of him. And I didn't like what I heard.'

'We did try to warn Clare, but she wouldn't listen.'

'And now it's too late?' Ruth considered for a while then gave a tight-lipped nod. 'It's a sorry state of affairs. I'd have expected better of Clare.'

'It's easy for us to think that,' Millicent reminded her. 'But I'm a firm believer that we shouldn't judge.'

'It's hard not to.' Ruth's opinion was tied up with her own history but Millicent and Cynthia didn't need to know the details: that she'd divorced her husband, Arthur Ridley, after discovering that he'd been a regular frequenter of premises in Bolton run by Phyllis Parr and her then-partner, a Dutchman who went by the name of Max Van Buren. 'Girls like Clare come to a crossroads where they get the chance to say no before it's too late. It's just a question of will-power.'

'No,' Millicent insisted with great conviction. 'More often than not they're drawn in and tricked by men who promise them the world and ply them with drink then sell them off to the highest bidder. That's how it happens. And once it's done, there's no way back.'

Ruth breathed in deeply before conceding the argument. 'We agree that it's a nasty business. And I hope you see that I meant well by mentioning it.'

'Yes, ta, we understand.' Millicent said a stiff goodbye then she and Cynthia crossed the road. 'I might have known,' she muttered angrily.

'Known what?'

'That Ruth would hold a low opinion of Clare. You heard what she said. She sees her as weak willed. It's what so-called respectable people the world over think without stopping to put themselves in the victim's shoes.'

Cynthia nodded and tried to work out her own attitude.

'They don't consider, "There but for the grace of God",' Millicent went on.

'I do feel sorry for Clare,' Cynthia admitted. 'I can't bear to think about what's happened to her and what her life will be like from now on.'

If Cynthia had expected tearful protests from her mother over her decision to move into Heaton Yard, she was proved wrong.

In fact, the parting of ways was low key, with Ellis expressing no opinion whatsoever and Beryl trying to force a promise out of Cynthia that she would build bridges with her Uncle William in the near future.

'We know what he's like,' she reminded her. 'He flies off the handle every now and then. Give him time to calm down then pop out there on a visit. Take him a packet of rich tea biscuits and put things right over a cup of tea.'

Cynthia bit her tongue. Being nice to Uncle William was bad enough, but the idea of coming face to face with cocksure Bert and having to listen to him crow made her vow silently to keep well away from Moor View.

She stood, suitcase in hand, and studied her mother's faded looks – the grey, expressionless eyes wrinkled at the corners, the lined forehead and the mouth turned down in perpetual disappointment. 'I won't be far away,' she promised.

'You know where we are,' Beryl said.

Like acquaintances who part without a handshake and have little intention of keeping in touch, they said their lame goodbyes on the Saturday afternoon and Cynthia's heart was sore as she lugged her brown cardboard case up the street, trudging along Ghyll Road and up Ada Street on a grey day that threatened rain. She was still too inexperienced to understand what made her mother so cold and her father an invisible presence in a corner, only seeing things from her own perspective and freeing herself from the bonds of family with every step she took.

Millicent spotted Cynthia carrying her case across the yard and rushed out to greet her. 'There you are!' she exclaimed, taking the heavy case from her and bundling her up the steps into the house. The wireless played American jazz music, the kettle was on and a dressmaker's pattern was laid out on the kitchen table. 'I'll leave your case here at the foot of the stairs. Come in and have a cuppa before you unpack. I'm busy making a blouse for work. You can buy some material and borrow the pattern when I'm finished with it. My machine is yours whenever you want it.'

Millicent's whirlwind energy blew through Cynthia like several gusts of fresh air and by teatime, to the background noise of ragtime music and the whir of Millicent's sewing machine down below, she'd unpacked her belongings and settled into her room. By seven o'clock she was spruced up and ready to go out and meet Wilf.

'Tell him I say he's a lucky man.' Millicent looked

up from her sewing as Cynthia presented herself for inspection, wearing a new primrose-yellow dress, ruched at the waist and covered in small pink rose-buds. 'You're fresh as a daisy.'

'It must be all that stretching and twirling on a Friday night that's doing me good.'

'No – we're all born with it.' Millicent gave a regretful sigh as she compared her situation with Cynthia's. 'But there's no getting back your shine once life rubs it off, I'm sorry to say.'

Life and the way you choose to live it, she realized. *The men you meet and fall in love with along the way, the rules you choose to break.*

Cynthia smiled and was gone, leaving Millicent to reflect on what she now saw as wasted years. She watched her young friend cross the yard and dis-appear down the ginnel.

Running in her eagerness to meet Wilf, Cynthia almost threw herself into his arms when she reached Canal Road and saw him waiting for her outside the Victory. He was leaning against the wall, next to a queue for the ticket office that snaked down the wide steps and along the street.

Embracing her and holding her tight, he lifted her off her feet and spun her round. They overbal-anced and laughed, ignored onlookers and quickly decided to skip the flicks and go for a walk instead.

'There's blue sky.' Wilf pointed to a patch between white clouds. 'Anyway, we can always nip into a pub if it starts to rain.'

So they walked on into town, arms around each other's waists, ignoring a soft drizzle that began to fall until Wilf noticed that Cynthia was getting wet and he took off his jacket to drape it around her shoulders.

'Shall we?' He nodded his head towards the entrance to the King's Head.

'Let's,' she agreed.

They went in and she sat in a booth in the far corner while Wilf ordered their drinks at the bar. She saw herself reflected in one of the etched mirrors – her damp hair curling against her cheeks, Wilf's blazer hanging loose from her shoulders. Despite the smoky atmosphere, she looked alive, as if her whole body was singing with joy, her eyes dancing with pleasure.

'Just what the doctor ordered,' Wilf quipped as he slid a glass of sherry across the table and sat down beside her. 'Is this your favourite tipple?'

'I don't really have one,' she confessed. 'I don't come into pubs much. My mum and dad are strict Methodists.'

'So what did they think about you moving in with Millicent Jones?' *Stick to safe subjects and keep your hands on the table where they can't get up to mischief,* he reminded himself, though Cynthia's beauty knocked the socks off him every time he looked at her.

'They didn't say much. I don't think they really minded – one way or another.' Two sips of the sweet drink had already loosened her tongue. 'We're not one of those families that sticks together through thick and thin – there are no brothers and sisters, just me.'

'I'm the youngest of two. I have a sister called Maude,' he remarked. 'She's a nurse at the King Edward's.'

Though she hadn't planned it, a confession tumbled out. 'I know – I saw her.'

Then there was a rush of whens and wheres, followed by why. 'It's silly, I know. But when I saw Maude in your kitchen at the lodge, I jumped to the wrong conclusion.'

A grin spread across his face. 'You went all the way out there and all the way back again without telling me?'

'Yes, I wanted to let you know about Mr Oldroyd selling the estate. Don't laugh – it's serious.'

'And you thought . . . that is, you imagined . . .'

'The thing is, I couldn't see or hear properly.'

'Maude? Oh, I say!'

'I said, don't laugh.' Cynthia nudged him with her elbow, her face flushed.

The grin grew wider as he dipped his head and looked up from under brows that were several shades darker than his fair, thick hair. 'You know what they say about the green-eyed monster.'

'I wasn't jealous. I was shocked; I didn't know what to think.'

'*Jealous*,' he insisted, moving closer and taking her hand.

'All right then – yes, a little bit.'

'Because you care about me?'

'Yes.'

Wilf gave a quiet noise that sounded like 'hmm' – nothing else.

A new crowd came in through the door – men and women fresh from attempts to contact the spirit world in the nearby church. Upturned glasses had moved jerkily across a board and spelt out names of the dead and now here they were, eager to empty their heads of ghosts.

'Well, I care about you too,' Wilf told Cynthia, taking hold of the lapels of his jacket to draw her near and staring intently at her. 'I think you're the best thing that could happen to a chap like me.'

'You do?'

'I do.' He let go of the jacket and sat back, reaching out for his pint glass without lifting it to his lips. 'Listen, it's true I was in danger of going off the rails before I met you – I'm the first to admit it. I mean, I was saving up to get married until Adelaide upped and left me. Then afterwards, I blew all the money on gee-gees and the dogs. I didn't care – what was the point of anything?'

Cynthia gazed at him without interrupting, aware that he was showing a side of himself that she'd never seen before.

'I wasn't listening to anybody and it soon reached the point where Maude and Mum gave up on me. There were quite a few girls after Adelaide but they didn't mean anything. I just went out at the weekend and drowned my sorrows, reached rock bottom.'

'She broke your heart.'

'No.'

'No?'

'Not really. She hurt my feelings, but that's different.'

'How?'

'It's doesn't run so deep. Looking back, it was mainly my pride that was hurt. Adelaide knew my heart wasn't really in it. I suppose that's why she broke off our engagement.'

'I see. Really – I do.'

'Cynthia, I want to be honest with you.' Wilf took her hand. Her face in the flickering gaslight was wonderful – smooth and pale, with soft lips and clear, kind eyes that seemed to delve deep below the surface. 'I want to do the right thing so as not to make you bolt.'

She smiled and gave his hand a reassuring squeeze. 'I'm not a horse, you know.'

'No, but you might run away if I put a foot wrong. I feel that and it makes me nervous.'

'Don't be,' she whispered. The soft light was reflected in the copper tabletop – dozens of circular metal dimples glowed yellow. There was a hum of noise in the background.

'I don't have a way with words,' he confessed, 'but I feel this is something special.'

'Good – because I feel the same way.'

'*You're* special.' He spoke what he felt without looking forward or back. This was love, pure and simple.

Her smile wound its way around his heart and he let it. He would be good to Cynthia and not hurt her – it was a vow he made to himself in the warm silence between them. She could trust him and he would not let her down.

CHAPTER FOURTEEN

It was coming up to Friday the seventeenth of July –
Norma's birthday. Douglas needed an answer. *Yes or
no. Yes or no.* To Norma, life sometimes seemed as
random as the child's game of pulling petals from a
daisy, though she altered the words in her own mind
to – 'I love him, I love him not.' *Of course I love
Douglas*, she told herself. *I just don't want to set a date.*

'Tell him yes and put him out of his misery,' was
Millicent's oft-repeated advice. Just recently she
seemed to be surrounded by canoodling couples –
first Douglas and Norma with eyes only for each
other, and now Wilf and Cynthia, who had done
nothing to hide their rapture when he'd come calling the previous afternoon. After half an hour of
watching them bill and coo, Millicent had taken herself off for a brisk walk, but her mood had worsened
as she got ready to take the night shift and she'd left
for work soon after tea with a half-serious warning
for Cynthia not to do anything that she wouldn't do.

'That gives us plenty of leeway,' Wilf had said with

a wink, holding the door open for Millicent as she'd swept out.

A night at her switchboard hadn't lifted her spirits and her face was glum when she came out of the building at eight o'clock on Monday morning and crossed paths with Norma. Standing with her in City Square and listening to her doubts, Millicent repeated her mantra. 'Tell him yes, for pity's sake. But make it clear that you're not ready to start a family. Marriage – yes. Kiddies – no. These days there are ways and means to make sure of that.'

Norma pursed her lips. On her walk into work she'd run through her choices for the hundredth time and came to the conclusion that yes, she would marry Douglas but she would ask for a long engagement – a year or two, at least. She explained as much to Millicent as they stood by the cenotaph amidst the din of the morning rush hour.

'I can imagine how that'll go down.' *Not very well*, Millicent thought. It struck her that one of the reasons Norma might be holding back was the common fear, even in this day and age, of what took place in the marriage bed. Or un-marriage bed in her own case. There was still a lot of ignorance about it amongst the women she knew and she felt sure that the topic wasn't much discussed in the Haig household. Now wasn't the time to talk about it, however.

'I'm sorry, you must be worn out,' Norma realized. 'And here's me wittering on.'

'I don't mind,' Millicent assured her. The night shift

had been quiet – just her, Brenda and Molly at the switchboards, with Ruth stalking the central aisle. Responding to disembodied voices on the line had left her feeling jaded and strangely out on a limb, eager to be back in the real world.

'How's Cynthia settling in?' Norma wanted to know.

'Champion, as far as I can tell. Talk of the devil, here she is.'

A smiling Cynthia did a detour to join them at the foot of the tall marble monolith. 'I left you a fresh teacake on the larder shelf,' she told Millicent after a quick round of greetings. 'I nipped out to the bread shop first thing.'

'Ta very much but I'm not hungry.' Millicent gave a weary smile. 'That's the trouble with the night shift – it takes away your appetite.' She left Norma and Cynthia to cross the road and walk into the exchange before carrying on along George Street towards the empty taxi rank. A whole week of nights lay ahead of her and she went head down, hardly noticing her surroundings and almost stepping into the road in front of a black cab that was pulling into the kerb.

The driver blasted his horn and squealed to a halt. Millicent saw him mouth insults from behind his windscreen then the back door of the taxi opened and Clare stepped out.

One jolt replaced another, for Clare's appearance shocked Millicent. Dressed in a dark velvet wrap over a long, green satin gown, the top half of her face was hidden by a thin veil, draped forward over the shallow brim of a dainty, saucer-shaped hat. She wore black gloves and clutched the wrap around her throat, but she couldn't hide the paleness of her complexion, exaggerated by a bright red lipstick and dark shadows under her eyes.

It took a second or two for Millicent to work out why Clare was dressed in evening wear at eight o'clock on a Monday morning. When she did, her stomach lurched then she felt deep embarrassment on Clare's behalf. *Let's hope no one else notices*, she thought, resisting the urge to rush up and exchange greetings.

Without stopping to pay the taxi driver or to wait for a gap in the traffic, Clare crossed the road. She looked neither right nor left as she threaded her way between cars and buses, walking as if in a daze.

Embarrassment doesn't do it justice, Millicent realized as she watched Clare reach the pavement then drift towards the entrance of Sylvia's Salon. *What she's feeling is thick, black shame. The poor girl is in a pit of despair.*

Inside the otherwise empty salon, a recently arrived Phyllis Parr sat on a high stool behind the mahogany appointments desk, one hand resting lightly on the glossy cover of a copy of *Vogue*. Her nails were newly manicured and she wore a yellow silk scarf teamed with a neatly tailored royal blue dress. Her eyes flashed with anger as the shop bell rang and Clare walked in. 'The wanderer returns,' she remarked with a tap of her nails on the magazine.

Clare didn't react.

'I said – the wanderer returns.' Sliding from the stool, Phyllis intercepted Clare on her slow progress across the shiny salon floor. 'I take it from the way you're dressed that you didn't just pop out to buy a newspaper?'

Clare closed her eyes then opened them, clutching her wrap and staring straight through Phyllis towards the door leading to the stairs.

'No, I didn't think so. Therefore we can safely say that you spent the night elsewhere.'

The cool harshness of her boss's voice seemed to draw Clare out of her trance. She blinked again then shaped her red lips into an 'O', as if preparing to speak.

'That wasn't the bargain that was struck beforehand,' Phyllis reminded her sharply.

Clare's lips quivered and her throat made a faint rasping sound.

'It was perfectly plain that payment was made for the evening only. Everyone concerned was clear about that.'

There was a sigh from Clare and her gloved hand dropped to her side, allowing the velvet wrap to fall open. There were three livid marks on the side of her white throat, left by the pressure of a man's fingers.

Phyllis's eyes narrowed. 'I see.'

Clare attempted to walk on but Phyllis still stood in her way.

'Does Sidney know about this?'

Clare gave a faint nod.

'Is there anything else?'

She slid the wrap from her shoulders to reveal a tear in the green satin bodice and more bruises to her shoulder and wrist.

'Is this what happened when you tried to leave at the time we arranged?'

'Yes.' The answer was hardly audible.

'And you say Sidney was there?'

'Yes.' *He watched it happen. He saw everything.*

'Then he and I will have to have words,' Phyllis promised in a voice of steel.

'He . . . I couldn't . . .' *He laughed when I struggled. I couldn't breathe.*

Clare relived the moment. She stood at midnight in a gentleman's billiard room in a large country house. She took hardly any interest in her luxurious surroundings, feeling sick, trying to recover from what had gone before – there on the smooth green baize of the billiard table.

She was in the dimly lit room with Sidney and the small man whose grey brocade waistcoat hung open. He was collarless and wore dark trousers – the man who paid the piper.

'This won't be cheap,' Sidney had said. 'Vincent will have to go away and come back again in the morning – that's double the trouble, twice the expense.'

'It doesn't matter. I'm willing to pay.'

Amounts were haggled over. Clare was ignored. She felt dirty, paid for, used then thrown away. Sick at heart, she made her way towards the door. The two men followed her, stopped her from leaving. Hands pulled her back as she struggled, her dress tore, fingers pressed against her throat. She fainted.

There was darkness then dawn. Light crept into the sky beyond the heavily draped windows. There was no one else in the room.

Outside in the grey first light she found Vincent waiting for her. He drove her through countryside back into town.

'Sidney and I will have words,' Phyllis repeated, her lips scarcely moving. 'This won't do. It won't do at all.'

'Remind me not to volunteer for another week of night shifts ever again.' Two days later, Molly sat at the switchboard next to Millicent. She leaned back in her chair, yawned and stretched. 'It's only Wednesday and I'm already jiggered.'

Millicent agreed. 'It's not worth it for the little bit extra they pay us. And it's no fun trying to sleep during the day with this heatwave going on.' She glanced at the clock and saw that it was only twelve, with eight long hours still ahead of them. On her other side, Brenda took advantage of a lull between calls to give her nails a fresh coat of ruby-red varnish.

'Calling New York 8347, I have Mr Jones on the line.' Molly spoke briskly into her horn and waited for the foreign operator's reply.

Millicent drifted off into a sequence of lazy, disconnected thoughts. Yesterday had seen peak temperatures across the Atlantic as well as here at home – thermometers had shot up to well over a hundred degrees in some places. She still had to put the finishing touches to the blouse she'd begun at the weekend and must remember to call in at Jubilee to buy buttons on her way home. Brenda had better hope that Ruth didn't come out of her office and see her painting her nails. Then a jack lamp for the party line shared by Sylvia's Salon and two other subscribers lit up on her board and she quickly pressed a front key to take the call. 'Go ahead, please.'

'Help me,' a shaky female voice pleaded. 'Please, I need help.'

Millicent leaned forward in her chair. 'Clare?' She wasn't sure because the voice sounded distorted.

'Yes. I need an ambulance.'

'What's happened? Are you all right?'

'It's not for me.' Clare's pleas for help grew desperate. 'What's the number for the hospital?'

Something told Millicent that it was vital to keep Clare on the line so she scribbled three words on her notepad and shoved it under Brenda's nose: *Fetch ambulance – Sylvia's*.

Brenda read the note then quickly called the hospital.

'Clare, listen. It's me – Millicent. We're doing that for you right now. Are you sure you're all right?'

'Send help,' she pleaded. 'He's lying here. I can't wake him.'

'Who is?' Millicent managed to keep her voice calm.

'Sidney.'

'What's wrong with him?'

'He's bleeding. Send for the police.'

'All right.' She wrote a second note for Brenda: *Call Canal Road police station.* 'Clare, don't try to move him. That's very important. Wait for the ambulance. It's on its way.'

'This is the George Street Exchange. Is that King Edward's General?' Brenda asked, scanning Millicent's second note as she talked. 'Please send an ambulance to Sylvia's Salon, number fifty-two George Street, straight away.'

Molly finished with her international call and pushed back her headset, her attention fixed on Millicent and Brenda. Looking up and sensing an emergency, Ruth came out of her office.

'Hello, this is George Street, calling Canal Road.' Flicking more switches, Brenda spoke to the sergeant on night duty. 'We've had a request for help from number fifty-two – Sylvia's Salon. A man is injured and we've called for an ambulance.'

The sergeant responded immediately. 'We're on our way,' he promised.

'Clare, is anyone else with you?' Millicent asked.

'No. I can't stop the blood from pouring out.'

'Is he breathing?'

'I'm not sure. Please help.' There was a long, despairing sigh followed by a low moan.

'Clare, listen to me. Help is on its way. Clare – are you still on the line?'

There was no answer, only a click then silence as a light flashed to signal the abrupt end of the call.

Ruth reached Millicent's station and made a rapid assessment of the situation – almost tangible tension in the air, scribbled notes, three shocked faces and Brenda still on the line, giving directions to the police. 'Clare Bell is in trouble,' Millicent explained. With trembling hands she took off her headset and stood up.

'What kind of trouble?'

'Something very bad. I don't know the details – I asked Clare to explain but she was in too much of a state and then she put the phone down on me.'

'The ambulance and police are on their way,' Brenda reported.

'I could hardly make out what she was saying. It's something to do with Sidney Hall.' Millicent felt sure that every passing second was vital. 'I should go and find out what's going on. But be careful!'

'Yes, go.' With a mounting sense of alarm, Ruth agreed. 'You have my permission. But be careful!'

Millicent nodded and squared her shoulders. *Run*, she told herself. *Otherwise it'll be too late.*

'Run,' Molly urged.

'Rather her than me,' Brenda muttered as they watched Millicent rush away. 'It'll be a good five minutes before the ambulance gets here.'

'If anyone can cope, Millicent can,' Ruth said.

New jack lamps winked, there were calls to be taken. Fighting off a sense of dread, Brenda, Molly and Ruth kept their heads, sat down at the switchboards and took the lights.

The salon door stood open and the lights were on but there was no one inside. Millicent saw that the telephone had been wrenched from its socket and was lying broken on the floor. There were magazines scattered everywhere, their pages streaked with blood.

She called Clare's name and ran to the door leading to the stairs. There was more blood. It was smeared on the walls of the narrow staircase and splashed across the bare wooden treads. Reaching the landing, she saw that the only door that was open was the one at the far end leading into Clare's room. She called again then followed the trail of blood along the length of the landing.

Clare cowered on her haunches next to the washstand, as far from Sidney as she could get, pressing her bloody palms against the wall. He lay on his back, arms flung wide, eyes open, blood staining his white shirt.

'Clare!' Millicent's gaze was riveted on the blood still gushing from a wound in the man's chest, but before long she sprang into action. 'I need a towel – to stop the bleeding. Clare, we have to do something.'

Clare shook her head and trembled violently. She didn't shift from her crouched position so Millicent grabbed the pillow from the bed, knelt down in a pool of dark blood and pressed it hard against Sidney's chest. He stared up at her but couldn't speak.

'The ambulance is coming,' Millicent assured him.

His eyelids flickered shut.

'They're on their way. We'll get you to hospital. You'll be all right.'

He opened his eyes and turned his head to look at Clare.

Blood soaked through the pillow. Millicent pressed harder still.

Unable to meet Sidney's faltering gaze, Clare covered her face with her trembling hand and let out a despairing moan. Her pink satin dress was stained red. She had blood in her hair, on her face – everywhere.

Leaning over Sidney and continuing to press with all her might, Millicent felt his whole body twitch then shudder. His fingers curled and became claw-like. His face was deathly pale. *He's dying*, Millicent thought, still pressing as hard as she could. *I can't save him.*

Then, during what seemed like endless seconds of suspended animation within the room, blue lights flashed along George Street and there was the sound of sirens in the street below. Car doors opened then slammed shut, followed by rapid footsteps across the pavement into the salon, clattering upstairs.

Douglas entered first, followed by his sergeant. They both quickly assessed the scene and assumed rightly that Millicent had only lately arrived. 'Step aside,' Sergeant Stanhope told Millicent.

She stood up and retreated to the corner of the room next to Clare.

Two ambulance men arrived moments later, armed with canvas bags containing blankets and medical equipment. One tried to stem the flow of blood while the other felt for a pulse at Sidney's wrist and neck then shook his head.

Clare whimpered and turned her face to bury it in Millicent's chest. Millicent put her arms around her and held her tight.

A grey blanket was unfolded and placed over Sidney's body. His face was covered. Under orders from Stanhope, Douglas came towards Clare with an extended hand. 'You must come with us,' he said, gently raising her until she stood upright.

She didn't react. Her stare was blank, her face white.

'And we'll need a statement from you too, Miss,' the sergeant told Millicent.

They took Clare from the room, steering her around the body then walking her along the landing.

Millicent watched the ambulance men pack away their equipment. She caught the gleam of a stethoscope inside their bag and breathed in the scent of

261

lily-of-the-valley perfume from a broken bottle at her feet. Her shoes crunched over shattered glass as she moved forward then her toe caught against something metallic and pointed. It was a knife with a long, curved blade – a butcher's knife.

'Don't touch that,' one of the ambulance men warned when he saw her stoop to pick it up. 'That's evidence, that is.'

She gasped and looked out of the window down on to the gaslit pavement where Douglas was guiding Clare into the back of the police car.

'And you're a witness,' the other man told her, snapping his bag shut. 'You'll have to stand up in court and tell the jury exactly what you saw.'

CHAPTER FIFTEEN

That night, after the police had taken Clare away and another young constable had arrived on the scene to guard Sidney's body, Millicent went back to the exchange. She didn't take her place at the switchboard, however.

'I won't hear of it,' Ruth insisted as soon as she saw the state the other woman was in – her eyes dark and dazed, the skirt of her green flowered dress stained with blood. 'We're fetching a taxi to take you straight home.'

Shocked into stupefied silence by what she'd seen, Millicent didn't resist. She stared down at her red hands and shook her head in disbelief.

'Your dress is ruined,' Brenda whispered as she led her into the cloakroom to collect her coat. 'Come along – sit down here until the taxi arrives.'

'I'll go and keep a lookout.' Molly offered to stand and wait at the front entrance.

'No – you get back to your switchboard,' Brenda insisted, well aware that they couldn't both neglect their duties. 'Now, Millicent – is there anyone at home to help you when you get back?'

'Cynthia will be there,' she replied. The word 'home' appeared as a bright beacon on the dark horizon, signalling safe refuge from the events that she'd witnessed.

So when Alf Middlemiss arrived, she allowed Brenda to lead her out through the revolving door and help her into his taxi.

'Where to?' Alf asked, glancing at Millicent in his rear-view mirror and seeing at once that he would get no sense out of her.

Brenda tapped on the driver's window to attract his attention. 'Heaton Yard. She's had a bad shock,' she explained. 'Make sure she gets home safely.'

Alf nodded and drove off along the empty street. He said nothing about the police car parked outside Sylvia's, minding his own business all the way to Ada Street where he stopped by the ginnel leading into Heaton Yard. 'Do you need a hand?' He turned to check how Millicent was.

'No, ta – I'll manage. How much do I owe you?'

'Never mind that. You can pay me next time you see me. You get yourself off home.' Alf got out to open Millicent's door then watched her make her way down the alleyway without pestering her with questions. Whatever had taken place back there at the hairdresser's salon, he felt certain that it would be splashed across the newspapers soon enough.

Millicent took a deep breath and entered the

silent yard. She needed to get inside her house and then collapse and cry, wail and shake and give way to despair – to somehow get the horror of what she'd witnessed out of her head and into the open. But first she must cross the yard one step at a time, turn her key in the lock and disappear inside.

Upstairs in her attic room, Cynthia slept soundly.

Millicent stumbled through the door. She took two or three steps across the kitchen then her legs gave way and she sank to the floor, knocking against a chair as she went down.

Cynthia heard the crash and woke. She sat bolt upright. Her first, terrifying thought was that a burglar had broken in but then she heard a loud, desperate crying so she flung on her dressing gown and ran downstairs.

Millicent was on her knees, head forward, hands covering her face, sobbing as if the world was about to end.

Cynthia ran to her and tried to raise her up. The sight of dried blood on Millicent's hands and clothes told her to expect the worst.

As suddenly as Millicent had allowed her tears to flow, she stopped. She must stand up and pull herself together, not cry like a baby. 'I'm all right,' she protested, pushing Cynthia away. 'Honestly – I'm all right.'

'Here – sit down.' Cynthia righted the chair. 'Sit, Millicent. Are you hurt? Tell me what's happened.'

Millicent swayed then sat down. She heaved air

into her lungs, looking up at Cynthia without being able to speak.

'It's all right. Take your time.' There was a small bottle of brandy on a high shelf in the pantry – Cynthia fetched it, poured a little into a glass and gave it to Millicent. 'Drink this.'

Millicent drank obediently, feeling the trickle of liquid burn her tongue and throat and waiting for it to revive her, which it did after a minute or two.

'Sidney Hall is dead,' she told Cynthia. Speaking the words made her tremble violently again so she swallowed more brandy. 'He was stabbed in the chest and bled to death.'

For a second Cynthia couldn't believe what she was hearing. It didn't make sense – things like this didn't happen so close to home. They belonged in newspaper headlines and on the cinema screen. But Millicent was covered in blood so what she said must be true.

'The police think that Clare stabbed him.' Millicent forced herself to go on. 'They took her to the station. Ruth sent me home.'

'Were you there when it happened?' Cynthia brought her mac from the coat hook by the door and placed it around Millicent's shoulders to stop her shivering. 'Don't answer if you don't want to – the important thing is that you're all right.'

'There was a knife on the floor. I wasn't allowed to touch it. There was blood everywhere.'

'Don't talk,' Cynthia pleaded. Explanations could wait.

But Millicent had to get it out – she must tell Cynthia what she'd seen and relive every detail – the phone call, the sudden silence, the rush to help. The broken telephone. 'Blood everywhere,' she said again. Clare crouching amidst broken perfume bottles and spilt face powder. Sidney still alive, with the fear of death in his eyes. 'He knew it was all up with him,' she whispered to herself.

Throughout it all, Cynthia held Millicent's hand. She made her drink all of the brandy in the glass and let her talk it out – once, twice, three times – all through the night until gentle daylight washed its way into the bleak nightmare that Millicent had lived through. Then she felt calm enough to rinse her face and hands at the kitchen sink where the cold water ran red and she scrubbed with a nailbrush until every trace of blood had vanished.

In the dawn light Cynthia went up to Millicent's room and fetched a clean nightdress and a dressing gown. 'Here – you should get out of those clothes.'

Millicent stood on the rug and took off her stained dress and stockings. Cynthia hid the discarded clothes in the cupboard under the sink until Millicent had decided what to do with them. 'That's good,' she told her once she had changed into her night things. 'Now, how do you feel?'

'Better,' Millicent insisted. A glance at her wristwatch told her that it was time for Cynthia to get ready for work. Normal service should be resumed.

267

'Get a move on or you'll be late,' she urged with an attempt to sound like her usual jaunty self.

Cynthia held back. 'I don't like to leave you.'

'I can manage.' Suddenly Millicent felt weary to the bone. 'My bed is calling me. I could sleep for a week.'

So Cynthia left Millicent in the kitchen and went upstairs again to get changed. When she came back down there was a knock at the door and there stood Douglas in his police uniform, asking to speak to Millicent.

'Come in.' Cynthia stood to one side and spoke to Millicent. 'Shall I hang on for a bit?'

'No, ta. You get off.' Somehow she overcame her exhaustion. 'I knew you'd want to talk to me, but I wasn't expecting you quite so soon,' she told Douglas as Cynthia shut the door behind her.

He stood uncomfortably in the middle of the rug, hands behind his back and rocking to and fro on the balls of his feet. 'I'm coming to the end of my shift but Sergeant Stanhope said it was best to get this bit over and done with.'

'Where's Clare?'

He cleared his throat and avoided looking Millicent in the eye. 'She's clammed up, not saying a word. We're waiting for the doctor to take a look at her.'

'I didn't say "how" – I said "where".'

'She's still down at the station.'

'The poor thing! How long are you going to keep her?'

'I can't go into that.' Douglas shook his head. It felt peculiar to be interviewing Norma's best pal in his work capacity and Millicent's reputation for being too forthright on occasions made him uneasy. 'Look – it's my job to ask you a few questions. Do you feel up to answering them?'

'Of course I do,' she retorted. Her own distress paled in comparison with what Clare must be going through. 'Sit down, Douglas. The sooner we set things straight, the better.'

He took off his helmet and placed it on the table then sat down opposite her. 'Are you ready?'

'Yes. Fire away.' Though Douglas seemed absurdly formal in the way he took his notebook from his top pocket and sat with his pencil poised, she recognized that she must toe the line.

'First off, how long had you been on the premises before we got there?'

'At Sylvia's? Five minutes at the most.'

He wrote down her answer. 'And for what reason?'

'I was working the night shift at the exchange. I was the one who took Clare's call. And before you ask – that would be at five minutes past twelve on the dot. I checked the clock.'

'What did Clare say to you?'

'She asked for help.'

'What sort of help did she need?'

'She sounded very upset. She asked for an ambulance. And then the police.'

'In that order?'

'Yes.'

'And did she say why?'

'She told me that Sidney Hall had been hurt.'

Douglas glanced up from his notebook. 'Did she say how Mr Hall had been hurt or who hurt him?'

'No, not a dicky bird. She said he was bleeding and she couldn't stop it. I said not to try to move him but to wait for the ambulance.'

'And then what?'

'I asked Clare if Sidney was still breathing. She said she didn't know. Then all of a sudden the line went dead. That's when I asked my supe for permission to leave my switchboard and go and find out what was going on.' Millicent watched as, with painstaking accuracy, Douglas wrote down every word in a forward-sloping, cramped hand.

'And what time was it when you reached number fifty-two?'

'I reckon I was there by a quarter past twelve. I went upstairs and found Clare in her bedroom with Sidney Hall.'

'What was she doing?'

'Nothing. She was crouching in a corner, too frightened to do anything. He was lying on the floor, bleeding.' Millicent's voice faltered as she re-imagined the scene.

'Did Clare say anything?'

Millicent shook her head.

'Did Mr Hall?'

'No.'

'All right, Millicent – we're nearly finished. A carving knife has been recovered from the scene of the crime. Did you see it?'

'Yes.'

'Where was it?'

'On the floor, near the washstand – along with Clare's perfume bottles and make-up. Everywhere was a mess.'

'Did you see Clare drop the knife or touch it at any time?'

'No. It was just lying there.' A cold sensation crept up Millicent's spine, making her shiver. The truth was the truth, but so far it didn't seem to be helping Clare as much as she'd hoped.

Douglas concentrated on writing down her answer then, without looking up, he asked his final question. 'Do you know any reason why Clare might want to harm Sidney Hall?'

'No!' Millicent's answer exploded from her lips. Even to her own ears, it lacked conviction. *Of course there are reasons – any fool can see that. You of all people know what Sidney Hall got up to.* But she lied to Douglas and said no, and the look in his eyes made it plain that he didn't believe her.

'Thank you, Millicent.' He sighed and closed his notebook then put it back in his pocket. 'That's all I need to know – for now, at any rate.'

'It's not how it looks,' she tried to tell him. 'Why would Clare ask for the police to come if she was the one who . . . ?' Her voice trailed off and ended in a sharp intake of breath.

'I'm sorry, I can't talk about that.' He'd been sent to interview Millicent and the job was done. Obviously she was being honest for the most part and the other girls in the exchange would be able to verify times and so on. With luck, Millicent herself would be in the clear. 'I'll let myself out,' he told her as he picked up his helmet.

She followed him to the door. 'What will happen now?'

'There'll be a report – a post-mortem. The fingerprint men will get to work.'

'I don't mean that, Douglas. I mean – what will happen to Clare? When will you let her go?'

'That depends.'

'On what?'

'On fingerprints, and so on. And on what Clare tells us when the doctor says that she's well enough to be interviewed.'

Millicent put a hand on his arm. 'Surely . . .' she began.

He shook his head. 'I'm sorry. I can't say any more.'

Standing in the doorway in full view of curious neighbours, she imagined how it might play out as a cut-and-dried case of a mistress who had stabbed her lover to death in a fit of jealous rage. It would appear in all the papers and the woman's beauty would be made much of. There would be a photograph of Clare on the front page, above a smaller one of the victim – Sidney Hall, a member of the Kenworth and Hall's Steel Manufacturing family. A *cause célèbre*, a crime of passion to be pored over, with only one possible outcome at the end of it all.

That evening Norma came with Cynthia to Heaton Yard bearing a message from Ruth. 'She says you're to take the rest of the week off work.'

'What for? That's the last thing I want to do,' Millicent protested. Since Douglas's departure at breakfast time, she'd tried to sleep without success. By midday she'd been up and dressed, pacing the floor and thinking about Clare. 'I'd much rather keep busy.'

'No arguments,' Norma told her. 'You know how Ruth is – what she says goes.'

'She has a point,' Cynthia said. 'It'll take a day or two for you to get over the shock of what you saw.'

'You do look peaky.' Norma sat Millicent down at the table then quizzed her about Douglas's visit. 'How did he act? Was he wearing his stiff upper lip?'

'His on-duty, policeman's face? Yes, as a matter of fact he was.'

Trust Douglas, Norma thought. *He might have been a bit more sympathetic, considering.* 'Have they started to follow up any leads?'

'He wouldn't say, but no – I don't think they have,' Millicent admitted. 'Steel yourselves – the plain fact is, like it or not, Clare is being treated as their main suspect.'

Cynthia gave a cry of dismay. 'Surely not!'

'That was my first thought – that she's not capable of doing it.' Privately, though, Millicent acknowledged that people sometimes acted out of character when faced with desperate situations. Saying so would sound disloyal, so she kept the notion to herself. 'But think how it must look from the outside. As far as we know, Clare was the only one in the building at the time it happened.'

'And it won't be long before Douglas and Sergeant Stanhope find the motive for Clare to have killed Sidney,' Norma realized. 'In fact, they have one already – I gave it to Douglas myself when I passed on my suspicions about Sidney and Mrs Parr.' Her comments hung in the air while Millicent and Cynthia thought them through.

'It's true – they know Sidney did terrible things to her,' Cynthia murmured.

'Me and my big mouth,' Norma muttered.

'I should have made more of the phone being broken.' Millicent sounded irritated with herself. 'Someone pulled the wire out of the socket and smashed it on the floor, but I didn't draw enough attention to it.'

Cynthia saw what she was getting at. 'Yes – why would Clare break the phone when she'd called the exchange to ask for help? It doesn't make sense.'

'Unless someone else was there who we don't know about – someone who didn't want Clare to call an ambulance.'

'Or the police,' Norma added.

'And where would Clare have come across a knife like that? It belongs in a butcher's shop, not in a salon.' This was another detail that had begun to bother Millicent. Say, for instance, Sidney had gone for Clare and she had tried to defend herself – the nearest thing to hand would have been a pair of hairdresser's scissors, not a butcher's knife. 'Let's suppose that the person who pulled the phone cord out of its socket was the one who carried the knife.'

'It couldn't have been Sidney himself, could it?' Norma was perplexed and wanted to cover all possibilities.

Millicent was adamant. 'No. Sidney was already bleeding to death in the upstairs room when she made the call. Clare wasn't even sure that he was still alive.'

'And where were Barbara and Margaret when it happened?' Cynthia wondered.

'We haven't the faintest idea. Or Phyllis Parr, for that matter.'

'Sergeant Stanhope will have to take statements from them,' Norma predicted. 'I'll see if I can winkle anything out of Douglas when I see him tomorrow.'

'Oh, but tomorrow is your special day.' Millicent suddenly remembered that it was Norma's twenty-second birthday.

'Don't remind me.' Norma grimaced. 'Don't wish me a happy birthday. Because it's not going to be.'

'It can be if you let it,' Millicent insisted.

'Not with all this misery surrounding us.' Norma was in any case all too well aware that July the seventeenth was the date she'd set for giving Douglas a final answer. A murder and an engagement were two events that didn't sit happily side by side.

'Try not to let what's gone on at Sylvia's spoil your day,' Millicent advised, wishing in vain that she could follow her own advice. In fact, her nerves were worn down and her spirits lower than she'd ever experienced. 'I mean it, Norma – put on your best bib and tucker, meet up with Douglas and have a nice time.'

For her birthday Norma received a pair of white cotton gloves from Ivy, a hairbrush from Ethel and an embroidered doily from her mother. Though she'd suggested they club together to buy her a recording of Judy's Garland's 'Waltz with a Swing', she accepted the gifts with good grace then went off to work where all of the talk was of Sidney Hall's murder and Clare Bell's arrest.

'Did you notice – the blinds are down at Sylvia's?' Norma said to Agnes during her dinner break. Cynthia was still at her switchboard so she had no one else to talk to.

'I saw Mrs Parr go in there earlier with a policeman,' Agnes reported. 'To inspect the damage, I suppose. It could be a while before she can open up for business again.'

'*She's* the one who should have been taken in for questioning, never mind Clare.' Norma had tried not to take much notice of the morning's headlines but couldn't resist looking at the newspapers spread across the table in the restroom. It was as she'd expected – the journalists had pounced on Clare and the supposed souring of her relations with Sidney Hall. 'A Woman Scorned', said the caption under a grainy photograph of a glamorous-looking Clare on the front page of the *Herald*.

There were gory details in the report about Sidney's slow and painful demise, the size and shape of the weapon used and the trail of blood on the floor of Sylvia's Salon. Much was made of the victim's wealthy family connections and of the prime suspect's poor background, leading to wild suppositions about her motives – hence the caption and the foregone conclusion.

'It shouldn't be allowed,' Norma insisted as she pushed the newspaper out of sight. 'They're saying Clare is guilty even before the case comes to court.'

'It won't matter in the long run what they print in the papers – it's up to the police whether or not they charge her.' Agnes was her usual calm and sensible self. 'And if they do, Clare will be given the legal help she needs. Meanwhile, we just have to sit tight.'

'You're right,' Norma agreed with a faint smile. 'I wish everyone could keep their feet on the ground the way you do, Agnes, instead of getting caught up in all the silly "Woman Scorned" business.'

'People always jump to conclusions.' Looking at her watch, Agnes saw that it was time to go back to work. 'How's Millicent after her ordeal?' she asked as she stood up and straightened out the creases in her skirt. 'Is she managing all right?'

'As well as can be expected, ta.' Norma gave Agnes an appreciative smile.

Agnes returned the smile warmly. 'I suppose she's itching to get back to work, knowing her.'

'She is.' Norma too was on her feet. 'I'll tell her you were asking after her.'

'Do.' Agnes extended her hand and gave Norma's arm a gentle squeeze. 'And by the way, Happy Birthday.'

Norma was touched. She blushed and thanked Agnes again.

'I trust you and your young man are going out tonight to celebrate.'

'Not as far as I know,' Norma said, following Agnes across the foyer into the workroom. 'Douglas is coming to my house for tea. Ethel's promised to bake a cake.'

'How many candles this year?' The supervisor opened the door to a cacophony of voices and an array of panels displaying winking lights, a scene of fingers darting hither and thither to deftly insert jacks into sockets.

'Twenty-two,' Norma replied. Twenty-two candles and a decision to make – the biggest of her life so far.

*

'Cherry madeira with a frosting of icing sugar.' Ethel presented Norma's birthday cake with a flourish. She set it in the middle of the kitchen table and instructed Norma to blow out the candles while Ivy, Hetty and Douglas stood by and watched.

Norma leaned over the cake, drew a deep breath and blew noisily until every flame had flickered and died. 'This is just the job!' she told Ethel. 'It's my favourite kind.'

Gratified, Ethel took the bread knife and sliced into the cake, handing Douglas the biggest piece first. 'Get this down you,' she urged. 'Put a bit of meat on those scarecrow bones.'

'I'm not sure about that,' he demurred with a wink. 'Norma tells me she likes me just the way I am.'

'There's nothing of you.' Ethel stuck to her opinion that he was too thin. 'If you ask me, it's to do with the worry of chasing after criminals, day in, day out.'

'Especially the likes of Clare Bell.' Hetty brushed cake crumbs from her bosom and settled in her fireside chair. 'It can't be good for your nerves – having to tidy up after that messy business. Is it true what they say – that there was blood everywhere?'

'Mother!' Norma failed to stifle her protest, which popped out in spite of a resolution to keep quiet.

'Yes – leave the poor man alone,' Ivy said hastily. 'Norma, why don't you and Douglas go for a walk?'

Norma readily took up the suggestion and soon

279

they were out of the house and walking hand in hand up Albion Lane towards the Common. 'Don't mind Mum,' she told him. 'She's always putting her big foot in it.'

'Don't worry – I get asked about it all the time. Everyone wants to know the details. It's human nature.'

'Not me,' Norma declared as they waited to cross Overcliffe Road. 'But the one thing that does bother me is what's happening to Clare.'

'Right now this minute?'

Norma nodded.

'I'm not sure. They brought in Detective Inspector Davis from Leeds. He's taken over from Sergeant Stanhope now.'

'So where is she?'

'Still at the station. The inspector questioned her but didn't get much out of her, from what I gather.'

'That doesn't surprise me. She'll be like a rabbit caught in a car's headlights. And from what Millicent says, the poor girl wasn't very good at sticking up for herself in the normal run of things, let alone now.'

'Anyway, as I say – it's out of our hands.' An early-evening light fell across the Common as they started down the cinder track towards the pavilion. There were long shadows and a coolness in the air. 'The inspector read the evidence in the sarge's and my reports and decided it was enough to charge her with murder. They'll be taking her off to Armley.'

'To prison!' The news made Norma's blood run cold.

'Do we have to talk about this?' Douglas flicked back a stray lock of hair and went ahead of her into the pavilion where they sat down facing the setting sun. 'Can't we forget about work?'

'Soon,' she promised. 'But first, tell me – has Clare confessed?'

Douglas shrugged. 'All I know is that she's been charged and held on remand. Oh, and it turns out that Sidney Hall has a wife somewhere, and two kiddies – a boy and a girl.'

'Oh!' Norma gasped then fell silent, contemplating the widow's reaction to news of her husband's death. More anguish, more betrayal. And children too.

'The post-mortem report says that he died from a stab wound straight to the heart, with half a dozen other cuts to his hands and arms, where he tried to ward off his attacker.' Anxious to be done with the subject once and for all, Douglas spoke fast. 'All this will go to the magistrates' court on Monday morning.'

'For heaven's sake!' Norma cried. 'How many lives has this man ruined?'

'And he's paid the price for it, hasn't he?' Suddenly Douglas had had enough. He got up and walked away, hands deep in his trouser pockets, on along the path towards Brimstone, feeling angry with Norma for poring over every detail. All right, so it

281

was a bloodthirsty murder and Clare Bell was a local girl, but why couldn't Norma and her pals stand back and let the law take its course? Didn't he and she have more important things to talk about?

'Douglas, come back,' she called after him.

He picked up his pace without turning round.

'Wait for me,' she cried.

On he went, head down, towards the crags – striding out, not looking back. She'd vowed to give him an answer and he'd waited and waited. He'd come to the house today and eaten cake, been polite to Ivy and Ethel and their tactless, busybody mother, but Norma had failed in her promise and caused him more heartache than he'd ever thought possible. Now he feared that the volcano was about to explode. *Damn her, then, and damn all women who played around with a man's feelings.* He strode on, casting a dark shadow over the buttercup-strewn meadow. *She's had her chance*, he thought. *I won't hang around to be made a fool of a minute longer.*

CHAPTER SIXTEEN

'I'm sorry,' Norma said. 'Douglas, please wait. I'm truly sorry.'

'Don't,' he muttered, casting off the hand that she'd placed on his arm when she'd at last caught up with him. 'You don't consider how hard it's been for me, having to wait for an answer, wondering if you love me as much as I love you.'

'Douglas!' The sadness in his eyes stopped her in her tracks and made her heart jolt.

He walked until he reached the first of the large, dark boulders scattered amongst the heather then he stopped and took a deep breath. Layers of pink clouds edged with gold made a pattern like seashore pebbles in a pale blue sky.

She ran again to keep up with him, her throat dry with fear and exertion.

He shut his eyes and leaned against the rock.

'You're right,' she stammered. 'I'm a selfish so-and-so, making you wait this long. I don't mean to be.'

'Then why do it?' Eyes still closed, he felt the rough, cold rock against the back of his head, which thudded with a dull dread. *Here it comes*, he thought, *the answer I never wanted to hear*. 'Spit it out, Norma. Let's get this over and done with.'

He'd walked away from her, cast her off and her heart shuddered again then raced. 'I'm twenty-two years old,' she whispered.

He opened his eyes and frowned, not registering the look of panic in her eyes and unable to work out where this latest remark was leading. He felt a corresponding fear snake its way into his chest. *Get it over with. Make it quick.*

'That's not old, is it? I mean, I'm only just finding my feet – at work, in life. And getting married is such a big step.'

Here it comes. Oh God, this is misery. Douglas wanted the ground to swallow him up, to dissolve into dust and be blown away across the purple heather.

'It's a bigger step for women than it is for men.'

'There you go again,' he pointed out. 'Putting yourself before me.'

'No. That came out wrong.' Norma managed not to wilt in the face of his anger and went on with her explanation. She stood very close to him, talking softly and looking straight into his eyes. 'What I mean is – you men can go on with your jobs and that's good, there's nothing wrong with that. But we women can't – we have to settle down to being housewives.'

284

'Someone has to look after the home,' he said with a shrug. That was how things worked, and had done for centuries, whatever the suffragettes had fought for.

'I know. And I wouldn't mind – I would enjoy making things nice for you . . . for us.'

'But?'

'It might not be enough,' she murmured, turning his face back towards her when he tried to look away then stroking the frown lines that marked his brow. 'That doesn't mean I don't love you, Douglas. I do.'

Love but not marriage, then. How does that work?

'Say something,' she pleaded.

'What do you want me to say?'

'Tell me you love me too.'

'I do. You already know that.'

'Say it without frowning. Kiss me.'

He shook his head and drew away. She kept shifting the ground from under him, saying she loved him but still not giving him an answer. Yet being this near to her soft, smooth skin and lips was too big a temptation so he leaned back in and their lips touched. Her hands came around his neck and the kiss deepened.

Norma was the first to pull away. 'It's not just leaving a job I love in order to stay at home,' she went on haltingly. 'We'd have children, wouldn't we?'

'I hope we would. Yes, for me that's a big part of it.' Fear began to give way to puzzlement. They'd never talked about things like this before. In fact, he'd never even thought about them – he'd just taken them for granted.

'For me too,' she realized. 'Only – not straight away.'

'There's no rush,' he said slowly, putting a hand on her shoulder and finding that she was trembling.

'Maybe not for a few years yet?'

'Oh.' His head dropped and he avoided her gaze.

'Does that bother you?'

He looked up again. 'No – I understand. Eventually, we'd have them, though?'

'All being well – yes.'

Douglas pulled her close. Her whole body shook as he clasped her in his arms. 'Don't be scared.'

'But I am. I liked things the way they were. I wasn't ready for them to change.' As confessions poured from her, she felt tears well up. *Don't be such a cry baby!* she told herself. *Douglas and I can say anything we like to one another. We're in love.*

For a while he held her without saying anything, breathing in her scent and resting his lips against the top of her head. 'It's my fault – I shouldn't have rushed you,' he murmured at last.

'No – it wasn't you who was in the wrong. It wasn't me either.' Calmer now, Norma stepped away and breathed deeply then she held both of his hands and looked steadily into his eyes. 'You're a fine catch, Douglas Greenwood, and I hope you know it.'

'Likewise, Norma Haig. I reckon I've got the pick of the bunch.'

286

She smiled. 'I only wish I hadn't hurt your feelings so badly and that we'd had this talk sooner.'

'You can say that again.'

Norma let go of his hands and turned back towards the pavilion, silhouetted in the dwindling light, its ironwork tracery and pillars dark against the pink clouds. A tram rattled along Overcliffe Road, past a boy pushing a cart laden with firewood. The scene was nothing special but in her new state of certainty and hope it filled her with contentment. She slipped her arm through the crook of Douglas's elbow. 'Ready?' she asked.

'For what?'

She set off across the Common, leaning into him as they walked. *Ready to go home together and make an announcement, to step out into our future and whatever that will hold.* 'To get married,' she said. The engagement ring, the congratulations, the wedding dress, the walk down the aisle – suddenly it all came together in her mind's eye and her heart sang. 'I'm saying yes, Douglas. Yes, yes, yes!'

Saturday was Cynthia's day off so she spent the morning with Millicent, both keeping their minds off serious matters by doing small jobs around the house.

'Would you like me to wash these for you?' Cynthia asked, steeling herself to take Millicent's bloodstained clothes from the cupboard under the sink. She'd already swept the floors and dusted the ornaments on the mantelpiece so now she was ready to rise to this sterner challenge.

Millicent had just come back from setting their empty milk bottles on the top step. It was a dreary, cloudy day, threatening rain, but the yard was alive with activity: the dustcart men had come to empty the ash pit and Walter's daughter Joan had brought out a stepladder to wash the old man's windows, a chore she did with bad grace during her fortnightly visits. Millicent glanced at the bundle of clothes in Cynthia's outstretched arms. 'No,' she said quickly. 'Those can go straight in the dustbin, ta.'

So Cynthia carried them outside and disposed of them, slamming the lid back on the dustbin just as Norma appeared at the end of the ginnel.

'Hello, Cynthia. I was hoping you and Millicent would be in,' Norma said with a smile that would have lit up the greyest of days.

'She's inside. Come on in.' Cynthia led the way back into the house. 'Here's Norma,' she announced.

Recoiling from the glimpse of her bloodstained dress, Millicent had sat down at the kitchen table, hands clasped and eyes closed, but she rallied quickly and offered Norma a cup of tea. 'Strong with two sugars?' she checked as she put the kettle on to boil.

'I've come to share my news,' Norma declared, taking Millicent's place at the table.

Lifting the tea caddy from the shelf, Millicent paused. Cynthia too stopped what she was doing.

'Douglas and I are engaged!'

'You don't say.' Millicent rapped the caddy down on the draining board.

'Oh, Norma,' Cynthia whispered.

'We are,' Norma said, as if she could still hardly believe it. 'It's official – we told Mum, Ivy and Ethel last night and this afternoon we're going shopping for the ring.'

Norma's happiness radiated around the room and broke through the numbness that Millicent had endured for three nights and two days – a feeling of drifting aimlessly without noticing what was going on around her, as if there was a physical barrier between her and the world. Now, though, she felt a surge of pleasure on Norma's behalf. 'About time too,' she said with a smile. 'Let's forget about the tea. This calls for something stronger.'

'Sherry for me, please.' Norma knew that Millicent had half a bottle left over from Christmas.

Cynthia obliged with three small glasses and the bottle.

'A toast,' Millicent said, holding up her glass. 'To Norma.'

'To Norma,' Cynthia echoed. She knew the drink would go straight to her head but she didn't care. She was with friends, celebrating a special occasion, sharing their happiness. 'To married life!'

'Hold your horses,' Norma cried. The sherry trickled warmly across her tongue and down her throat. 'We're engaged but Douglas knows it'll be a while before we tie the knot. I told him and he understands.'

'I wouldn't be too sure about that.' Millicent downed her drink. 'Now that you've said yes, it's a bit like a runaway train – there'll be no stopping it.' It felt good to be back to normal, even if only for a while – relaxing with friends and basking in Norma's good news.

'What kind of ring will it be?' Cynthia wanted to know.

'A ruby, with two diamonds to either side.'

'See.' Millicent turned to Cynthia with a wink. 'She already knows exactly what she wants. You can't tell me she hasn't been lying awake all night thinking about it.'

'Where will you go to buy it?'

'I've seen one like it in Jasper's, next to the Odeon in town.'

'See again,' Millicent laughed. 'The little minx has it all planned out. A ruby with four sparkling diamonds – I only hope Douglas has been saving up.'

'I can't wait to see it on your finger.' Cynthia sighed, imagining a time when perhaps she and Wilf would be in this situation.

Millicent noticed the faraway look in Cynthia's eyes. '"The runaway train goes down the track,"' she crooned quietly. ' "And she blew, blew, blew, blew, blew . . . !"'

'Someone's feeling better,' Norma observed. 'Will you be back to work on Monday?'

'Yes. Wild horses wouldn't stop me.'

With the sherry warming their insides, they chatted on about their fellow telephone girls. 'Brenda says the same as you – she won't rush to do the night shift again in the near future,' Norma told Millicent. 'Molly's different – she needs the extra money.'

'What about you, Cynthia?' Millicent asked. 'Are you still in the supes' good books?'

Norma answered for her. 'Oh yes, Cynthia never puts a foot wrong, bless her.'

'I try not to,' Cynthia added, blushing slightly. In fact, she took pride in the speed with which she made connections and in rarely having to bother her supervisors with a request for an urgent, feeling that she still had a lot to prove. Her pronunciation was improving too – sounding less stilted as the days went by.

'Talking of which.' Millicent swung the conversation towards the topic that loomed large in all their minds. 'I want us to agree to carry on breaking the rules as far as Clare is concerned.'

A small frown creased Cynthia's brow, which she concealed by collecting the empty glasses and taking them to the sink. Meanwhile, Norma eagerly took up the thread.

'That goes without saying. We could even work out a warning signal every time we take a call to and from Mrs Parr.'

'What kind of a signal?' Millicent wanted to know.

'A little cough, perhaps. No, that would be too

291

obvious. I know – why don't I keep a hankie tucked up my sleeve? Then when a call comes through from the salon, I could take it out and pretend to blow my nose. You two could do the same whenever you take a call.'

'Then two of us could distract the supe while the third one listens in?' Though it sounded childish at first hearing, Millicent considered it and thought it might work. 'Sooner or later, Phyllis Parr is bound to talk to someone about what happened to Sidney, then who knows what we could pick up by listening in? What do you think, Cynthia – shall we try it?'

Still standing at the sink with her back turned, Cynthia nodded.

'Starting on Monday, then,' Norma decided. 'At least then we'll carry on trying to help Clare.'

'Which no one else is,' Millicent added.

The mood darkened as Norma repeated Douglas's news about the magistrates' court and the existence of Sidney Hall's wife and children. 'I'd bet my life that Clare didn't know he was married – he certainly didn't behave as if he was, the swine.'

'But try telling the judge that,' Millicent pointed out. 'In any event, it might make things worse – it would allow the prosecution to argue that Clare found out that there was a wife and that was the real reason she attacked him – in a jealous rage.'

'Worse and worse,' Norma agreed, while Cynthia still busied herself at the sink. She felt uneasy about the plan to keep on listening in and she was sure she would lose sleep over it. Yet she could understand why the other two were so keen.

'Cynthia?' Norma cut into her thoughts. 'I said ta-ta, I'll see you at work on Monday.'

'What? Oh yes.' She wiped the last of the glasses and gave Norma a weak smile as Millicent showed her to the door. 'Congratulations, Norma. Ta-ta.'

'And we'll look forward to seeing the ring, don't forget,' Millicent added.

Across the yard, Chalky was setting off for the Green Cross, detained by Walter who stood propped against his doorpost. Two sleek young starlings dropped out of the grey sky and squabbled noisily over a crust.

Norma looked up and felt a spot or two of rain. She would need to call in at home for an umbrella before she went on to Douglas's lodgings. Town would be busy on a Saturday afternoon and she would probably have to queue for a bus. Should she walk there instead, or would it be too wet? Making her plans, she hurried off.

A smell of boiled vegetables permeated the prison. It drifted along the airless landing where Clare was incarcerated. When a warder slid back the hatch in the door to hand her a tray, she shook her head. The hatch closed.

The cell where she was held on remand was bare except for a bed, table, chair and bucket. A coarse grey blanket was neatly folded at the end of the bed.

The pillow had no pillow case. There was a small, high window with an iron grille and there were heavy bolts on the outside of the door. The brick walls were painted shiny green and cream.

She observed her surroundings without reacting. Night and day meant nothing. The electric light stayed on so that the warder could slide back the panel and see what she was doing. There was no need. Clare didn't move from the bed where she sat, staring at the stone floor.

They'd taken away her clothes for evidence and forced her to have a bath before issuing her with a grey prison uniform. Her face was scrubbed clean of make-up and her hair was pinned back behind her ears. It lay flat to her head, accentuating her pallor and the dark shadows beneath her eyes. The bruises on her neck and shoulder showed against the whiteness of her skin.

Late on Saturday afternoon, the bolts slid back, the metal door swung open and a female warder entered the cell. She was spare of frame, with crimped fair hair and thin, arched eyebrows. 'You've to see the doctor,' she informed Clare.

'I don't want to.' All she wanted was to be left alone.

'You have to,' the woman said. 'They want to examine you. Come along.'

She led Clare along the landing, ignoring faces at the hatches and cat-calls from inmates.

'It's her – she's the one that stabbed her chap,'

a woman hissed from a cell halfway along the landing.

More faces appeared.

'Are you sure?'

'It doesn't look like her. I thought she was meant to be a humdinger.'

'It's definitely her.'

Clare and the warder reached the end of the landing and entered a small room with a table and two chairs. There was no window. A bald, plump man wearing steel-rimmed glasses, a navy blue suit and a wedding ring sat at the table and greeted them without looking up from the typewritten form in front of him. 'Sit down, please,' he said to Clare.

She stared straight in front of her without moving.

'Sit down, please,' he repeated.

The warder took her by the elbow and made her sit.

'This won't take long. My name is Dr Wright. I have to examine you for signs of mental illness. That means I need answers to the questions here on this list.'

Clare looked at him without seeing.

'Do you understand?'

She gave no response.

'If you don't cooperate, I will have to write down that you refused to answer.' He spoke as if he'd been through this routine many times before and really didn't care about the outcome. 'In which case, the judge and jury will have to draw their own conclusions.'

The warder at the door stared stonily at the doctor and gave a single shake of her head. 'She's been like this ever since she got here. No one's been able to get a word out of her.'

Wright tapped the point of his pencil against the table. Clare blinked then went on staring into space. 'Take her back to her cell,' he said.

Later that afternoon Millicent opened the door of number 10 to Wilf, who stood like a puppy with his tongue hanging out, so eager was he to take Cynthia out for a surprise spin in Alf Middlemiss's taxi.

'Is she in?' he demanded, brushing past Millicent and investigating every nook and cranny of the spick and span kitchen.

'Well, she's not hiding under the table so there's no point looking there,' Millicent said wryly. 'Anyway, why has Alf lent you his car?'

'He's gone to watch a cricket match so he gave me the keys as a special favour, provided I put a gallon of petrol in the tank. Is she upstairs? Can I go up?'

'No – you stay here.' Millicent went to the bottom of the stairs and called Cynthia's name. 'Make sure you're decent before you come down,' she warned.

'Don't bother on my account,' Wilf added cheekily, loud enough for Cynthia to hear.

She flew down at the sound of his voice and within a minute she had on her hat and coat, ready to leave. 'How do I look?' she checked with Millicent.

'Fresh as a daisy, isn't she, Wilf?'

'And twice as pretty.'

Millicent gave him a warning look. 'Flattery will get you nowhere – didn't they teach you that?'

'Yes, but they were wrong,' he quipped, sidestepping Millicent and seizing Cynthia's hand. 'Come on – let's take a spin over to Beckwith.'

'In the rain?' Peering out through the open door, she saw that it had set in for the afternoon.

'You won't get wet,' he promised, dangling the ignition key in front of her. 'Your carriage awaits!'

So they left Millicent grumbling about being a wallflower as usual and before long they were speeding along Overcliffe Road towards Hadley and the favoured spa town beyond.

'I've got a bit of good news,' Wilf said as they took the moor road. He was wearing a tweed jacket over a Fair Isle pullover and a collarless shirt, with a cap pulled jauntily over his forehead. He talked above the heavy patter of rain on the car roof and the swish and squeak of the windscreen wiper. 'Mr Oldroyd has sold North Park to Antony Norton.'

'Who's he when he's at home?' Nervous that Wilf was driving too fast and taking the bends too wide, Cynthia tried to be blasé.

'*The* Antony Norton – the chap behind the famous

new chain of department stores. You know – "Norton's for top value and service!" You see them springing up everywhere.'

'And why is it good news?' She cringed as a coal lorry chugged towards them and Wilf had to swerve on to the grass verge at the last minute.

'Because,' he said, righting the car and driving smoothly on, 'Norton has bought the whole estate, including the lodge. He's asked Mum to stay on as housekeeper. It means we won't have to move after all.'

'That is good,' she agreed. 'Your mum must be heaving a sigh of relief.'

'We can call in and meet her, if you like. I'm always going on about you so it's time you got to know each other.'

'I'm not sure about driving into Hadley, Wilf.' Cynthia was reluctant as they came to the familiar fork in the road. 'I don't want to run into Uncle William – or Bert, for that matter.'

'Don't worry – we're steering well clear of Moor View.' He signalled and took the road into the village then was taken aback when a figure wearing a cap and a belted raincoat stepped out suddenly from behind a tree. Wilf slammed on the brakes and squealed to a halt. 'What the flaming heck . . . !'

'It's Leonard.' Cynthia recovered from the shock then wound down the window to ask her uncle's odd-job gardener if he was all right.

'Flipping bike.' Leonard jerked his thumb towards

his motorbike, which was propped against the tree. 'The spark plugs got damp and the engine's packed up on me. Sorry – I wasn't looking where I was going.'

He obviously had something on his mind, so Cynthia rested her hand on the steering wheel to prevent Wilf from driving on. 'Can we give you a lift somewhere?' she asked.

Leonard shook his head. 'Flipping kids,' he mumbled. 'I'll wring the little blighter's neck when I catch him.'

'Whose neck?'

'My eldest boy, Len. You drag them up trying to teach them right from wrong, and look what happens.'

'What does happen, Leonard?'

'They let you down, good and proper.' Ignoring the steady drip-drip of raindrops from the chestnut tree above and looking as if he carried the weight of the world on his shoulders, he gave the broken bike a kick. 'I've just come from your Uncle William's house, if you must know,' he told Cynthia. 'I was summoned by that pipsqueak cousin of yours. It turns out that Bert had been keeping his ear to the ground and found out that my Len had started shelling out cash.'

'What do you mean?' Leonard's tale put Cynthia on high alert.

'He bought his pals tickets for the flicks and treated them to fish and chips all round after youth club last night.'

'Len's spending money that he shouldn't have had?' she queried.

Leonard sighed and nodded. 'You know Bert – he cornered Len in the yard behind the Institute and demanded to know how come he was flinging money around . . .'

'It's all right – I know what you're going to say.' Wanting to spare him further humiliation, Cynthia cut him short. 'It was Len who took Uncle William's cash box, wasn't it?'

Another shamefaced nod confirmed it.

She quickly worked out what had happened. 'Len kept his eyes peeled while he helped you with the gardening and managed to spot where the money was kept?'

'Yes. I'll wring his bloody neck,' he repeated. 'Your Bert forced him to empty his pockets right then and there – ten pounds, two and threepence was what Len had left after treating his pals. Then Bert frog-marched him up to Moor View and carpeted him in front of your uncle.'

All too easily, Cynthia pictured a red-faced Uncle William charging the trembling boy with burglary. 'What now? Will the police be brought back in?'

'Who knows?' Leonard was the picture of misery – dripping wet as he gave the bike yet another vengeful kick. 'According to Bert, Len scarpered before your uncle had time to pick up the phone.'

'Perhaps he won't bother this time.' Wilf entered the conversation, leaning across Cynthia to talk to

Leonard. 'Think about it – the old man got most of his cash back, didn't he?'

'You don't know Uncle William,' Cynthia murmured. 'He's not one to let anybody off the hook. What did he say to you, Leonard?'

'For a start, I've to scrape together the rest of the money and pay him back every penny before the end of next week. Then he sacked me from the gardening work – told me not to bother coming back.'

'That hardly seems fair on you. Would you like us to put in a word?' Wilf suggested. 'Or maybe Cynthia could talk him round?'

Leonard shook his head. 'What's done is done. Let the lad face the consequences.'

'We're very sorry.' Cynthia's heart went out to this decent man who endured hardship but never stopped trying to do his best for his family. 'Let's hope things soon settle down.'

'Ta.' Leonard nodded briefly as he tucked his motorbike gauntlets into his belt. 'Just wait until I catch the little bugger,' he muttered, setting off on foot down the main street. 'For all I care, the police can lock him up and throw away the key.'

'He doesn't mean it,' Cynthia whispered. Rain streamed down the windscreen, blurring Leonard's receding figure. The old mine workings and grim slag heaps behind the long row of terraced houses simply added to her sense of pity for a family who had hit rock bottom.

'He does,' Wilf countered as he turned on the

engine and set off slowly down the street. 'And I don't blame him after all the trouble Len's caused.'

'What's done is done.' Cynthia echoed Leonard's words. She held no grudges – after all, if it hadn't been for the robbery and the false accusations that had been flung her way, she would never have left Moor View and now be living in Heaton Yard, building a new life for herself. 'I'm better off with things the way they are. I wouldn't go back – not for all the tea in China.'

CHAPTER SEVENTEEN

What happened to summer? Millicent wondered. She regretted the disappearance of the recent heatwave as she peered out of her bedroom window early next morning and saw heavy rain falling from a dreary grey sky. Reluctantly she decided to skip her usual Sunday-morning ramble.

Bad weather didn't deter Cynthia, however. She was up with the lark, getting dressed in the pale green frock and matching shoes that Millicent had insisted on giving her for good.

'Where are you off to?' Millicent enquired as Cynthia hurried along the landing.

'To meet Wilf at the top of the street. We want to catch the Sally Army band in Linton Park.'

'Take my brolly!' Millicent called down the stairs as she heard Cynthia open the front door. 'It's tipping down.'

'Ta!' Cynthia took the umbrella from its peg on the back of the door. She opened it then rushed down the steps into the yard, held her breath as she went past the open door of the privy then breathed again and waved at Walter as she entered the ginnel.

There goes love's young dream, Millicent thought, watching from her first-floor window. She faced a long day without much to occupy her unless she took a paintbrush and a pot of green paint from the cupboard under the sink to freshen up the kitchen skirting boards. But this meant running the risk of coming across streaks of Sidney Hall's blood left behind in the space where her ruined dress had been tucked away and she baulked at the idea. Instead, she sat at the table and started to flick through the pages of *Woman's Own* for interesting recipes or attractive knitting patterns. However, she skipped the advice page where readers wrote in describing love tangles and romantic dilemmas. *I have enough of that of my own*, she thought with an exasperated smile. Her attention wandered and took her down the well-worn blind alley of her situation with Harold, so that she almost didn't hear the knock at the door until it came a second time – louder and more insistent than before.

'Hold on,' she called as she scraped back her chair and glanced in the small mirror to the side of the sink to check that she was presentable. *Ugh!* she thought. Her face was pale and without make-up, her eyes dull. There was a third knock. 'Coming,' she said.

She opened the door to find Harold standing in the rain.

'Hello, Millicent. Can I come in?'

'Of course. You're soaked. Give me your coat.' Drawing him indoors, she hid her shock. 'Here – I'll hang it up for you. Sit. Good Lord, Harold – you look done in!'

Divested of his outdoor things, it was evident that the worry of losing his job had taken its toll. In stark contrast to the dapper man-about-town of their early days together, his face was thinner and more gloomy than ever, with a grey, two-day stubble shadowing his chin. His hair was uncombed. The whole dishevelled effect aged him so that he looked closer to fifty than forty.

'Tell me what's happened.'

'Calamity, that's what.'

Millicent nodded. 'Oldroyd hasn't changed his mind, then?'

'No. The mill's finished. I'm finished.'

The hurt he was feeling quickly transferred itself to her and she felt her spirits plummet. 'Don't say that, Harold.'

'Why not? It's true. North Park is sold to Antony Norton, the shop owner. The Oldroyds have to pack up and leave by the end of the month. And before you ask, no one in their right mind will step in and buy a clapped-out old woollen mill, not in this day and age.'

She nodded again slowly then sighed. 'So there's no hope. What about you – how long have you got before they turf you out?'

'It's already happened. I'm out on my backside. I handed over the house keys on Friday.'

'Where's Doris?'

'At her sister's. She took the kids with her.'

The finality of it all and his flat despair hit home. She crouched at his side and put an arm around his shoulder. 'Don't give up. This isn't like you, Harold. Something will turn up soon, I'm sure.'

He pulled himself free then stood up and paced the room. 'Oh yes, something will turn up – but you tell me what. Look at me, Millicent. I've been slaving for that sodding man for more than twenty years, ever since I left school. I know every last thing there is to know about combing and carding, spinning and dyeing, weaving and finishing, but what good is that any more? No – I'm washed up – no job, no house, no family.'

Millicent straightened up and watched from a distance. 'You don't mean to say that Doris has gone for good?'

He nodded. 'She couldn't get away from me quick enough once the writing was on the wall. No wage coming in, no roof over her head. You haven't met Doris, but she's not one to rough it. She'll tell everyone that it's Freddie and Derek she's thinking of – swanning off to sunny Saltburn and not letting on that anything bad has happened. But it's not – it's her and her damned pride.'

Millicent leaned on the front window sill for support. A magician conjuring a rabbit out of a top hat couldn't have astounded her more. Was this a trick or was Harold telling her the truth? Had he really separated from his wife at last and come to her without any ties? 'So where does that leave you?' she murmured. 'Where are you living?'

'In town. There's a spare attic room above the King's Head. Stanley Cooper, the landlord there, has promised to let me stay for nothing until I get back on my feet – in return for me mopping down the floors and taking out the used barrels first thing in the morning.' Harold stopped pacing and watched Millicent warily. 'I was thinking – this could work out all right for us in the long run.'

What is he saying? Does he mean that we can build a future together? Her heart skipped a beat. Then straight away, the thought flashed into her mind: *Is that what I really want?*

'Millicent?' He came towards her, one hand outstretched, offering himself to her.

She looked at him – unshaven, gaunt and bowed, a totally different man to the one she'd fallen for, even though she'd known from the start that he was married and would keep her dangling on the end of a piece of string during the good times, having his cake and eating it.

'I'll stay at the King's Head for the time being – that goes without saying. Until we sort ourselves out.'

Picking me up and dropping me whenever he likes, making me second best, always thinking up excuses.

Harold took no account of the fact that Millicent

stayed pressed against the window instead of taking his hand. 'Then, after a decent amount of time – in a month, say, when everyone gets used to the fact that Doris and the kids have upped sticks – I can move in here with you.'

Millicent blinked then swallowed hard. She must find her voice and speak quickly, before Harold ran away with himself. 'I'm not sure—'

'Oh, come on – what's stopping us?' he wheedled, puzzled by the wary look in her eyes. He moved in closer and put his hands around her waist. 'There's room for me here, isn't there?'

She braced her arms against his chest. 'I don't know. I have Cynthia to think about. She's only just moved in.'

'Then she can soon move out again. You know what they say – two's company . . .' *Just like Millicent to put up a show of resistance,* he realized. *But I can soon win her round.*

'Stop – I have to think.' Willing him to perform another magic trick, she looked into his eyes, desperate to rediscover the old feelings of love and desire. Surely they must be there somewhere.

He pulled her to him and kissed her hard on the mouth. She drew back. He kissed her again.

'Stop.'

'What's wrong? This is what you've always wanted – you and me together, with nothing standing in our way.' Putting his hands on her hips, he swung her round then backed her towards the stairs. 'Come on, Millicent. What are you playing at?'

'Nothing. Don't, Harold. Not now.'

He tilted his head and glanced upstairs. 'But this is our chance. There's no one to stop us for once.'

'I don't want to.' In place of the old feeling of mutual longing, she found only desperation.

'What do you mean? This isn't the time to play games,' he said, narrowing his eyes as he tried to decide between two choices – either to force Millicent to come with him up to the bedroom or to carry on talking. He opted for words and self-pity. 'Have you any idea what I'm going through?'

Millicent nodded. 'And I'm sorry for it.' Sympathy ebbed from her even as she spoke the words. 'But you have to let go of me, Harold. Taking me to bed isn't going to solve anything.'

'You've changed your tune!' He pushed her away so strongly that she fell back against the stairs. Immediately regretting it, he helped her back on to her feet. 'I'm sorry. I'm not myself. I don't know what's got into me.'

'I understand, really I do.' Always alert to the irony of a situation, Millicent almost smiled. She'd spent years listening to Harold's laments and empathizing with his predicament and once upon a time she would have rushed into his arms at a time like this. *But not now.* Was it to do with the fact that she only wanted him when she couldn't have him and

309

now that she could, the spell was broken? Yes – that might be part of it, plus the fact that she at last rebelled, for good, against being at his beck and call.

He kept his distance and watched her back away towards the front door. 'So what now?'

'I don't know.' She'd looked for joy and delight and seen darkness. She'd been true to him all through his faithlessness. And now all that was left was pity. 'Yes – actually, I do know. This won't do, Harold. I can't go on.'

He saw her take a breath and draw herself up, like a soldier going into battle. She was tall and beautiful, regarding him with an unflinching gaze. 'We can do what we want,' he said weakly. 'We can go to dances, take a holiday together. Whatever you like.'

'Dances?' she echoed. 'Oh, Harold.' Sadness overwhelmed her, but there were no tears. She opened the door and stood to one side.

'That's it, is it?' Outside in the rain, the cobbles were dark. Green weeds pushed through the cracks. A gutter spluttered and disgorged its contents of blackened leaves and slime.

'Yes.' There was nothing left – no words, and no cure for the way she was feeling. 'I wish you well, Harold.'

'But you don't want to see me again?' Talking had been the wrong choice after all. It always was with Millicent – she was the type who thought too much and thinking had a habit of complicating things. Harold's face set into bitter, frowning lines.

'I wish you well,' she repeated, seeming to read his mind. She saw at last that he didn't care about her – not deep down. The ties binding her to him stretched then snapped. Her heart eased towards a new freedom. 'But this is goodbye.'

'Welcome back,' Ruth told Millicent on her return to work. 'You look well, considering.'

Millicent took the rare compliment without comment and sat down at her switchboard. She and Cynthia had deliberately cut it fine, arriving at the exchange bang on half past eight to avoid being deluged with questions about the Sidney Hall business. As it was, they'd heard passengers on the bus gossiping about it and had seen the thick, black headlines on newspaper billboards – 'Court Date Today for Murder Suspect', 'Brutal Killing – Local Woman Charged', 'Murdered Man's Wife Speaks Out'.

'Will you have to be a witness?' Brenda asked Millicent during their dinner break, blundering in where angels feared to tread. The gramophone had arrived and Brenda had chosen a record, sliding it out of its paper sleeve and placing it on the turntable. There was a crackle as she lowered the needle on to the shiny disc then strains of an American big-band number provided a background to the stilted conversation.

'Don't ask me,' Millicent replied with a shrug.

'She doesn't want to talk about it,' Cynthia explained.

Brenda lit a cigarette then sat down and crossed

her legs. There was a swish of nylon stockings and the scent of eau de cologne was soon replaced by acrid smoke. 'Oh, come on, Millicent – that's not like you. Give us the inside story, why don't you?'

'I'd rather not.'

'I expect it depends on whether or not Clare pleads guilty,' Brenda speculated regardless. 'To be honest, I can't see what she has to say in her own defence, can you? I mean, you were there, Millicent. What did it look like to you?'

'I really can't say.'

Cynthia intervened again. That morning she'd watched how carefully Millicent had got dressed in a summery, peach-coloured two-piece then combed her hair and put on her make-up, as if building a defence between her and the world. 'She doesn't—'

Brenda tutted as she flicked ash into the ashtray. 'Be quiet, Cynthia. I mean, it's plain as the nose on your face – Sidney Hall pushed Clare an inch too far and the poor girl snapped. And you walked in on the result, Millicent. You're a key witness.'

'Let's wait and see,' Millicent said doggedly. 'It might never get that far.'

'Exactly.' Point taken, according to Brenda. 'All Clare has to do is to plead guilty then claim that she was provoked in order to avoid the hangman's noose.' While the others shuddered at this first open mention of the possible fate awaiting Clare, Brenda pursed her lips and directed smoke high in the air. 'What's wrong?' she demanded. 'I'm only calling a

312

spade a spade. Anyway, let's hope it doesn't drag on too long then we can get back to normal and forget all about it.'

Still at her switchboard while Cynthia and Millicent took their dinner breaks, Norma was thrilled by the sparkle of her ring as she placed a rear cord into a corresponding jack. 'Hello, Muriel. Go ahead, please.'

The dressmaker from Jubilee requested a local number and Norma was able to put her straight through.

The ring was beautiful – just what Norma wanted – and the shop assistant at Jasper's had shown her one from the blue velvet tray that was the right size and that Douglas could afford. She'd walked out of the shop with it on her finger.

'Hello, London. I'm afraid that line is busy. Please try later.'

Norma had still been on cloud nine when she reached work that morning, flashing the ring under everyone's nose with an undisguised delight that the others had been happy to share. Only Millicent had seemed less than thrilled for her and Norma hadn't had time to discover why. It occurred to her again as she operated her board that something more than the Clare problem might be worrying her friend so she set her mind on finding out what it was as soon as she got the chance. *I bet it's to do with Harold*, she decided, flicking a switch and speaking into her headset. 'Hello, Mr Utley. Hold the line, please.' *Yes, Harold – that will be it.*

Sure enough, when Norma engineered an urgent from Ruth and made a quick detour into the restroom, she was able to confirm her suspicions.

'Harold and I have parted for good,' Millicent confessed in a whisper while Brenda and Cynthia were busy chatting to others. 'I mean it this time.'

Norma laid a hand on Millicent's shoulder. 'I'm sorry to hear it.'

'I'm not. It was my decision.'

'But still.' The affair had staggered on for a long time, Norma knew. 'Will you stick by it?'

'Yes, I did the right thing.' Millicent shook herself. 'Anyhow, I'm glad I'm back at work and I'm happy about you getting engaged at long last.'

Norma smiled. 'Ta. I have to go. I don't want to push my luck with Ruth.'

'Yes, go – you don't want her coming down on you like a ton of bricks. By the by, you haven't taken any calls from Mrs Parr this morning, have you?'

'Not a peep. How about you?'

'Nothing. Neither has Cynthia. Still, we'll keep our ears open and let's hope it happens soon if we want to be of any use to Clare.'

'I agree.' Norma hurried off. *Perhaps we don't have time to wait for phone calls from Mrs Parr,* she thought as she resumed her seat in the workroom. *Maybe – just maybe – I can come up with a plan of my own.*

*

That afternoon Millicent worked hard to respond quickly to the lamps that flashed constantly on her high back panel. She took calls from housewives wanting to order coal from the local merchant, groceries from Norton's and cinema tickets from the Victory. She opened up lines to London and Paris, politely asking the callers to wait their turn. Late in the day there was a call from a phone box in Leeds city centre that turned out to be a reporter asking for a line to the editor of the *Herald*. She listened in long enough to hear the latest on the Sidney Hall murder investigation – there had been no application for bail, no legal representation for Clare and the magistrate had ordered her to be held on remand. He had referred the case to the Crown Court.

Seated to her right, Norma had been on the alert, watching out for Ruth, who – as luck would have it – was busy in her office. 'What's wrong?' she asked as soon as Millicent removed her headset.

Millicent lost no time in bringing her up to date. 'That makes both me and Douglas witnesses in a murder trial,' she said grimly. 'And it means Clare is facing the death penalty.'

Norma shuddered. 'It doesn't bear thinking about.'

'I know – it's barbaric. They should have stopped hanging years ago – especially for women.' There was no more time to talk because Millicent had to take another light. 'Hello, Mrs Parr,' she said as she recognized the number. Her voice was higher than usual and she took out her handkerchief to attract Cynthia's attention on her left side. Cynthia and Norma's eyes widened. They scanned the room and saw that Ruth had closed a ledger on her desk and was coming out of the office.

Meanwhile, Millicent pressed a rear key and scribbled down a name and number, speaking as she wrote. 'Mr Poole, I have Mrs Parr on the line . . . Go ahead, Mrs Parr.'

Phyllis Parr's voice was interrupted by interference on the line. 'Radio . . . news bulletin . . .'

Drat! Millicent strained to make out more.

The line cleared and a man's voice replied. 'I didn't hear the news. Crown Court, you say?'

'Yes. As far as I can make out, Clare hasn't put up any defence.'

'That's a wonder.' The man didn't sound convinced. In fact, his deep, mumbling voice was edgy and confused.

By contrast, Mrs Parr spoke insistently. 'Listen to me, Vincent. If Clare was going to say exactly what went on, don't you think she would have done it already?'

Vincent! Millicent added this vital name to her scribbled note.

'And the fact that she hasn't is good news. It means no one will believe her if she waits until she goes before a jury. They'll think she's made it up.'

Cynthia and Norma saw Ruth advancing up the aisle towards them, and they knew they had to find a way to distract her.

'. . . no witnesses as to what actually happened . . . murder weapon . . . no fingerprints.' The line broke up again and Millicent struggled to make sense of what she'd heard.

The supe's advance continued and Cynthia coughed loudly. 'Excuse me, Miss Ridley, please could you help me with a new route?'

Millicent caught on at last. With a split second to spare, she slid back her headset then hid the note under a clean sheet of paper.

To further divert Ruth's attention, Norma shot up her hand to request an urgent.

'Twice in one day, Norma?' Ruth glanced at the clock over the doorway. 'Your shift ends in five minutes. Can't you wait?'

'Please, I'm bursting,' Norma begged.

Ruth sensed something odd and frowned. 'Permission refused,' she said snippily. She stared long and hard at Cynthia then at Norma and Millicent, who was at that moment tucking her hankie back into her sleeve.

Norma and Millicent looked back at her blankly. Cynthia blushed. Millicent's supervision lamp flashed to signal the end of the conversation between Phyllis Parr and Vincent Poole.

The three friends couldn't wait for their shift to end. When it did, they rushed to be at the head of the queue for hats and coats then dashed across the foyer, through the revolving doors on to the steps outside.

'Vincent Poole!' Millicent held her piece of paper aloft. 'That's who Mrs Parr was talking to. The mysterious Vincent!'

'The one who picked Clare up and took her to Hall's soirées.' Excited by the development, Norma grabbed the paper and read the number – 612. 'Now all we have to do is find out exactly where he lives.'

'The general office will have his address,' Cynthia reminded them. 'They have a list of all subscribers.'

'Clever girl, you're right!' Millicent thought ahead. 'Do you think you can make up an excuse to go up to the office first thing tomorrow? Say you need to check some routes and rates that you're not certain of, or something like that?'

'Yes – we need to find out how we can get hold of this Vincent Poole.' Norma's eyes darted here and there, as if expecting to pick out the mystery man from amongst the office workers and shop assistants crowding the pavement on their way home.

'I suppose I could do that.' Cynthia's reluctance struck a false note and made Millicent and Norma turn to her with enquiring glances. 'But it might seem a bit suspicious,' she said. 'What if someone catches me looking up the wrong thing?'

'Then all you have to do is play the innocent,' Millicent suggested crossly. 'Say you picked up the subscribers' list by mistake.'

'It must be worth the risk.' Norma was eager to be off. 'Millicent will rehearse your excuses on the way home, won't you, Millicent?'

'Not now – I promised to drop in at Jubilee for a zip I ordered. Muriel Beanland is staying open especially. We'll talk about it later, Cynthia.'

'And Wilf and I are going to the pictures, anyway.'

While Millicent hurried off in one direction and Cynthia set off to meet Wilf, Norma crossed the road and quietly took up position by the cenotaph. From there she had a clear view of the entrance to Sylvia's Salon.

Through the sea of heads she noticed a figure emerging at speed from Sam Bower's barber's shop next door and recognized Cynthia's cousin Bert. Closer to where she stood, there was a row of six black taxis lined up at the rank and she saw Millicent stop for a hasty conversation with Alf Middlemiss. The amiable driver leaned against his idling taxi, which stood at the head of the queue. However, neither of these observations held Norma's attention, determined as she was to follow her new plan and watch for any comings and goings at Sylvia's. For Norma, in amateur sleuth mode, was convinced that here lay a possible solution to the mystery surrounding Sidney Hall's murder.

'I still owe you my fare home from last week,' Millicent told Alf. She dipped into her bag and drew out her purse but was flustered to find that she didn't have any change.

'There's no hurry,' Alf assured her.

'Oh but there is. I hate to owe people money.'

'Well, let's say that one's on me.' From what he'd

319

read in the papers about the events of that night, Millicent had been through a lot. The least Alf could do was to offer her a free ride home.

'No, Alf – honestly.'

'Really it is,' he insisted. He spotted his next fare approaching – an elderly lady in a grey coat and hat, carrying a heavy suitcase. 'Put your purse back in your bag, there's a good girl. Here you are, madam.' Alf opened the passenger door and swiftly took the case then winked at Millicent as he closed the door on his passenger.

'Ta,' she told him. At this rate, Muriel would have given up on her, and Millicent's evening plan of sewing a new zip into her navy blue skirt would be thwarted. 'I'll buy you a drink some time.'

'I'll keep you to that.' With a nod and a grin Alf got behind the wheel and drove off. The taxis behind him crawled forward and another joined the tail of the queue.

Millicent hurried on, not noticing Margaret and Barbara, the two hairdressers from Sylvia's, step out of the last taxi and cross the road without paying the driver.

Bert dashed out of Sam Bower's and cannoned straight into Cynthia.

'You did that on purpose!' she protested. If it hadn't been for catching hold of the nearby lamp-post she would have been pushed off the pavement in front of a motorbike and side-car.

'Stop moaning and listen,' Bert said. 'You're going to want to hear this.'

Cynthia sighed and sulked as she set her hat straight. 'If it's about Len Andrews stealing Uncle William's money, I already know all about it.'

With the wind well and truly taken out of his sails, Bert thrust his hands in his trouser pockets and sulked back. 'How?'

'Leonard told me. He said you had a hand in bringing Len to justice – which means that Len has probably got two black eyes to show for it.'

Bert grunted and insisted on walking beside Cynthia as they progressed along George Street. 'What if he has? The little squirt deserved everything he got.'

'Perhaps he did. Did Uncle William report him to the police?'

Bert shrugged. 'How should I know? I didn't hang around long enough to find out.'

Cynthia's eyes widened and she came to a halt.

'Ah, that got you, didn't it?' The cocky look returned to Bert's blunt, freckled features.

'Stop acting the fool. What are you going on about?'

Bert grinned and took his time to explain. 'I couldn't stand another hour of the old miser ranting and raving. I'd got his money back for him, hadn't I? But did I get a word of thanks? Not on your nelly!'

Cynthia went on staring in astonishment, trying to picture the scene – her uncle in a rage in that musty, gloomy house, waving his walking stick in the air, striking out at whoever was nearest. 'Don't tell me you expected a reward?'

'The more fool me,' Bert grunted. 'But I soon saw how things stood. And I thought to myself, *Right – I've had enough.*'

'You packed up and left Moor View?'

'Yes – he didn't see me for dust,' Bert confirmed. 'No more running around after the old skinflint for me, ta very much. I'll stick to lathering chins from now on.'

Cynthia walked slowly on. 'I can't say I blame you. But who knows about this – does Mum?'

'I don't know and I don't care. All I'm saying is: good riddance.'

'She'll find out sooner or later.' Cynthia grew thoughtful. 'I hope she's not expecting me to go back and do my old job again. I wouldn't put it past her.'

'Well, don't do it.' Bert had had his say and was ready to depart. 'You hear me – you'd be a fool to put your neck in that old noose.'

'I know it.' The past oozed around her ankles like cold mud, dragging her back to the days when she'd skivvied and slaved and had nothing to look forward to. No, if her mother asked her to return to Moor View, she would refuse point-blank.

Watching Bert dive down the alleyway to retrieve his bike, Cynthia spoke out loud to no one in particular. 'I've made a new life for myself. I'd lose everything by going back there.'

*

Over by the cenotaph, Norma saw Margaret and Barbara alight from the taxi – one tall and dark with something of the look of Millicent about her, though less bold, while the other was smaller, more smartly dressed and fair haired.

They seemed to be in a hurry as they made their way through the crowd but had to pause in the salon entrance while Barbara found her key. She looked in her bag then felt in her pockets, giving Norma time to cross the road and approach them. However, cars and cyclists got in her way and the women were already inside the building by the time she arrived.

She could see them through the glass panel in the door and watched them take off their coats without talking, their faces strained, their movements hurried. Barbara's coat caught on a magazine at the edge of the reception counter and the magazine fluttered to the floor. She stooped to pick it up while Margaret made her way across the room then up the stairs.

Norma rapped her knuckles against the glass.

Looking up and clutching the magazine to her chest, Barbara shook her head. 'Sorry – we're closed.'

Norma lip-read the words and knocked again.

Barbara frowned and once more shook her head.

Undeterred, Norma tried the door handle. The door opened but before she could step inside, Barbara ran and put all her weight against it to stop Norma from entering.

'You can't come in,' she declared. 'You'll have to

make an appointment but we're not open again until next week.'

'I'm not here to have my hair done,' Norma said steadily. She assumed that once she'd explained her mission, Barbara would have to let her in. 'I want to find out if either of you has visited Clare in Armley. And if you have, what you've learned from her about the night of the murder.'

Barbara gasped. Keeping her weight against the door, she called for Margaret, who reappeared at the bottom of the stairs. 'We don't have anything to say to you,' she told Norma fiercely. 'Leave us alone.'

Norma pushed hard and created a gap just big enough to slide through. Barbara was caught off balance and it was Margaret who rushed to slam the door after her.

Inside the salon, the three women breathed hard and sought for something to say.

'Look, I didn't mean to barge in.' Norma spoke first, intending to appeal to their better natures. 'I can understand that you're as shocked as anyone by what happened to Sidney Hall and I know you weren't even here at the time. That's not what I want to talk to you about. It's Clare, as I said.'

'What about her?' Barbara gave Margaret a look that said, *Leave this to me*. Though small and slight in stature, she seemed the more in control.

'You live in the same house with her so you know her better than the rest of us. You must surely have visited her.'

'Why must we?'

'I just thought—'

'Don't just *think* anything,' Barbara snapped. 'As a matter of fact, we haven't been near that woman since she went to prison. No one we know has.'

Norma spread her hands palms upwards in a gesture of disbelief. 'You surely don't think . . . ?'

'That she did it, that she killed Sidney?' Barbara circled Norma warily then put the magazine back on the counter, smoothing the glossy cover with slim, tapered fingers. 'I wouldn't put it past her, would you, Margaret? As a matter of fact, we warned them.'

'Who? What about?' As the situation slid rapidly from her control, Norma's questions grew shorter.

'We said from the start Clare wasn't suited. You could see it a mile off. But they wouldn't listen.'

Was Barbara talking about hairdressing? Norma wondered. Or was she referring to a darker trade? There was no telling and Norma lacked the barefaced cheek that Millicent might have had to pose the question directly. 'I – we want to help Clare,' she confessed. 'I thought you would too.'

'You thought wrong.' Barbara went to the door and held it open, giving a clear message that it was high time for Norma to leave. 'And just so that there's no misunderstanding, neither Margaret nor I has ever been friendly with Clare Bell. We had every reason to steer clear of her before this happened and even more so now.'

With each passing second, Norma grew less confident that she could change their minds, but still she tried. 'Now just a minute—'

'You have to leave.' With mounting impatience, Barbara refused to meet her astonished gaze.

'But Clare was the one who rang for the ambulance.' Norma's appeal was to Margaret, who stood by one of the swivel chairs, her hand gripping the armrest. It fell on deaf ears but she pressed on. 'We're certain that someone else was here with her and that person tore the telephone out of its socket.'

'That's a load of old rubbish!' Barbara spat out the words. The expression in her eyes remained steely. 'Go on – get out of here!'

Meanwhile, as if her legs had given way, Margaret sank into the chair and closed her eyes.

'Leave, before I call for the police!'

'Don't worry – I'm going.' Norma took a last, long look around the salon. No trace remained of the violent scene that Millicent had stumbled upon and with Margaret collapsed in the chair and Barbara standing implacably by the door, she recognized that her naive plan had misfired. There was nothing more to be said.

She trembled as she stepped out on to the pavement and heard the door close firmly behind her. Three buses crammed with passengers crawled by, one after another. A newspaper seller called from his stand close to the taxi rank, confirming the outbreak of a civil war in Spain. Criss-crossing the small

326

green square that surrounded the cenotaph, barrow boys wheeled fruit and vegetables from the open-air market behind the town hall, jaded clerks cycled home from bank and office and worn-out nippies from the Lyons' stepped on to trundling trams.

No one gave a sideways glance at Norma standing in the hairdresser's doorway and staring at the tide of humanity that quickly ebbed from the soon-to-be-empty town centre.

CHAPTER EIGHTEEN

Millicent was in time to pick up the new zip from Jubilee after all, so she went ahead with her plan to fill her evening with some light sewing work. Having changed out of her linen two-piece into comfortable blouse and slacks, she sat in the kitchen alcove and concentrated on tacking the zip into place, only stopping when there was a knock at the door.

She first thought Cynthia had forgotten her key, but when she opened it she found an unexpected visitor.

'Douglas.' Norma's fiancé was in uniform. He was wearing bicycle clips and had his helmet tucked under his arm. 'Come in. What brings you here?'

'I've just been talking to Norma,' he said without preliminaries. His face was serious and he took two steps into the kitchen, choosing to remain standing even though Millicent offered him a chair. 'I expect you know that she took it into her head to call in on the two hairdressers at Sylvia's Salon after work today.'

Millicent controlled her surprise and tried to play

down the significance of the event. 'No – that's news to me.'

'So you didn't put her up to it?'

Millicent stiffened. 'Norma has a mind of her own, you know. Anyway, why the long face? I expect she was only trying to find out more about what went on there – and good for her, I say.'

'Yes, you would.' Exasperation burst through Douglas's impassive, on-duty demeanour. 'I explained the situation to Norma and now I'm telling you straight, Millicent – these things have to be left alone.'

'Who says?'

'I do. Don't you see? What Norma did today could have turned nasty.'

'How so?' Millicent didn't agree – where was the harm in Norma talking to Margaret and Barbara? In fact, she wished she'd thought of it herself.

'The danger is that word will get around that Norma's been poking her nose in where it's not wanted. And when certain people hear about it, who knows what might happen?'

'Why? We're all on the same side, aren't we?' Surely all of them – the police, the two hairdressers, along with herself, Norma and Cynthia – were after the truth.

'Oh, come on, Millicent – don't be such a simpleton.' Douglas's talk with Norma during his tea break had left him angry and frustrated. He'd told her in no uncertain terms that she mustn't interfere any more, however sorry she felt for Clare. Norma had left the station close to tears and he'd deflected his anger on to Millicent, whom he took to be the ringleader in this unofficial campaign to prove Clare's innocence. Hers were the wings he must clip, he decided, and that was the reason he was here now, giving her the low-down.

'Things go on in this town that ordinary members of the public never get to hear about.'

'Oh, don't we? Give us some credit, Douglas.'

'No, I mean it. Lads go around in gangs, carrying knives and Lord knows what else – meat hooks, sawn-off shotguns, you name it. They get into fights down dark alleyways,' he went on grimly. 'It doesn't hit the headlines because no one cares about the victim who is usually a work-shy, homeless ne'er-do-well. And the one wielding the knife is a faceless nobody too – not a woman with film-star looks like Clare Bell. There's a nasty, seamy side to life that you and Norma know nothing about – that's what I'm trying to say.'

'Yes, and that's the world Clare got herself involved in, thanks to Phyllis Parr and Sidney Hall.' Douglas's intention was obviously to look out for Norma, but Millicent resented him coming here and having a go at her. 'She was an innocent abroad. The poor girl thought Hall was in love with her until it was too late and she was forced into selling her body for his bene-fit. Imagine what that must have been like. Don't look shocked, Douglas – we know that's what happened.'

'All the more reason for you and Norma to stay out of it. And Cynthia, too.'

'But who will stand up for Clare if we don't? It

won't be you, will it? What have you and your sergeant and your precious detective inspector done except arrest the poor girl and put her in prison?'

As the temperature of the argument rose, Douglas stood his ground. Deep down he'd never really approved of Norma's friendship with Millicent – she was too strident and unconventional for his taste and likely to carry on leading Norma astray. 'I can't discuss police work with you – you know that. But I'm telling you what I told Norma: leave us to do our job.'

'Or else?'

'Or else suffer the consequences.'

'Is this official or unofficial advice?' Millicent countered.

'Both. And it's not advice – it's an order.'

She nodded and gave him a tight-lipped stare.

'Do you hear me?'

'Yes, I hear you.' But it didn't mean she agreed with him. She opened the door for him without dropping her gaze. 'Thank you for coming, PC Greenwood. And now, goodnight.'

The next morning Norma waited anxiously for Millicent and Cynthia on the steps of the exchange. 'Well?' She spotted them as they alighted from the number 65 and hurried to meet them.

Millicent was on her guard. 'Well what?'

'Did Douglas come to see you last night?'

'He certainly did.' Though she wouldn't admit it, the

visit had given her a sleepless night that had ended with her being more determined than ever to follow up any information they could find, warning or no warning.

Norma's expression was pained. 'I begged him not to but he wouldn't listen.'

'It's all right, Norma – it wasn't your fault.'

'So we're not going to fall out over it?' Norma too had tossed and turned all night. She was angry that Douglas had chosen to go over her head and visit Millicent but had to admit to being touched that he was so keen to keep her out of trouble. Moreover, the argument in the police station had made her see for the first time that the demands of his job might sometimes spill over into their private lives.

'Of course we're not going to fall out.' Realizing that Cynthia was still in the dark about recent events, as she'd been too on edge to broach the subject first thing, Millicent quickly ran through last night's visit.

Cynthia looked startled. 'You mean to say the police came to Heaton Yard?'

'Not the police – just Douglas.' For the second time in twenty-four hours Millicent wished that she didn't have to smooth Cynthia's too-easily ruffled feathers. 'Don't worry, we're not in trouble.'

'What, then? Why did he come?'

'Douglas wanted to make sure that we keep our noses clean, that's all. Come on, we'll be late if we don't watch out.' The revolving doors swallowed her, leaving Cynthia and Norma trailing behind. She was first into the cloakroom then first to her switchboard, smiling a touch too brightly at Ruth and finding time for a quick chat with Molly before one of her lamps lit up and she took her first call of the morning.

'Good morning, Norma. Good morning, Cynthia.' Ruth's greeting was accompanied by a glance at the clock. 'Come along, girls, take your lights!'

Their shift was soon underway and fingers darted across switchboards without respite until ten o'clock, when Millicent seized her moment to nudge Cynthia with her elbow. 'Your board is quiet – now's your chance to pop upstairs to the office,' she reminded her.

Cynthia looked round nervously. 'Where's Miss Ridley?'

'In her office. I'll cover for you – if necessary, say you needed to look up an obscure routes and rates to the Shetland Islands.'

'Are you sure?'

'Yes – go!'

So, with sweating palms and a rapidly beating heart, Cynthia pushed her chair away from her switchboard and hurried off along the aisle, out into the foyer then up the wide stairs to the general office where a dozen typewriters clickety-clacked, carriages whirred and tiny bells went ting-ting.

The room was lower-ceilinged, less well lit and less plush than the ultra-modern one below, the desks were close together, with heavily laden bookshelves lining each wall. The girls, too, were less showily dressed in home-knitted jumpers and plain cotton blouses and they glanced up from their typewriters with bored, slightly hostile expressions.

'I've come to look up some routes and rates,' Cynthia explained to Kathryn Verney, the office manageress, who sat closest to the door. Straight away she kicked herself for not being more vague, thus giving herself the time and opportunity to look up what she really wanted.

Kathryn pointed with her pencil to the appropriate shelf then watched Cynthia closely. 'To your left,' she called when she saw her make a detour towards the shelf that housed the folders containing the alphabetical lists of subscribers. 'That's right, keep going. There – routes and rates are straight ahead.'

For a full sixty seconds Cynthia pretended to study one of the booklets. She could see the subscribers' lists, tantalizingly close on a shelf to her right. A glance over her shoulder told her that Kathryn was now busy feeding a fresh sheet of paper into her typewriter. Surely no one would notice if she shuffled along to what she really wanted to look at.

She was on the point of doing it – of edging sideways then reaching out and taking down the fat, buff-coloured folder containing all the names from P to R – when Ruth Ridley's imperious voice rang out.

'Cynthia Ambler, since when did a telephonist leave her switchboard without permission?'

Cynthia froze as her heart leaped into her mouth. She felt the colour drain from her cheeks. All heads were turned towards her.

'I asked you a question and I'm waiting for an answer,' Ruth insisted. She saw Cynthia's shoulders droop and resisted any urge to go easy on her. After all, a basic rule had been blatantly broken. 'Come over here, please.'

Slowly Cynthia threaded her way between the desks towards the door. 'I'm sorry, Miss Ridley. I needed to look up the rates for Lerwick.'

The supervisor frowned and shook her head. 'Follow me.' She marched Cynthia out of the office, down the stairs into the restroom, where she adopted a more sympathetic tone. 'Now listen – I understand your difficulty. Routes and rates can be tricky – especially the less used ones. But you're a clever girl – you know very well that you can't take matters into your own hands.'

'Yes. I'm sorry, Miss Ridley. It won't happen again.'

'I glanced up from my office work to see an empty chair. What was I supposed to conclude – that you were suddenly taken ill or that you'd had a piece of bad news?'

'No. Yes – I see.'

'I thought the worst until I got the truth out of Millicent that there was no emergency after all.'

Cynthia felt truly dreadful and she couldn't bear to look anywhere except at her feet. 'I've let you down. I see that now.'

'You understand that it would be within the rules for me to suspend you for something like this?'

A dart of apprehension shot through Cynthia and she raised her head in alarm.

'Quite within the rules,' Ruth repeated thoughtfully. 'Think about it, Cynthia – what if everyone felt free to up and leave their switchboards at any time? The whole exchange would grind to a halt.'

The fear of suspension brought home to Cynthia just how vital her job was to her. It was what she'd striven for – an achievement that meant everything. 'Please—' she mumbled, her face deathly pale.

Ruth cut her short. 'I *could* suspend you. But I won't.'

'Oh, thank you—'

'Not this time, at any rate.'

'Thank you!' Relief washed through her, leaving her lost for words.

Ruth raised a warning finger. 'I'm putting it down to inexperience. And this is most out of character, I have to say. I don't expect it to happen again.'

'It won't, Miss Ridley.'

'Good. No more blotting of your copy book, you hear?'

Cynthia nodded and looked on uncomprehendingly as Ruth held open the restroom door.

'Come along – back to work!'

Yes, back to her switchboard, shaking from head to foot. Cynthia darted out into the foyer ahead of her supe. Before she knew it, she was taking lights, making connections and moving on.

*

Millicent poured tea into her cup then topped it up with milk. She'd come alone to the Lyons' café during her dinner break to give herself time to think, hoping that a busy place would allow her to fade into the background and not be bothered by anyone from work. Sure enough, no one noticed her as she chose a seat in a dark corner and placed her order.

Things were not going their way, she realized. They'd come up against an unexpected obstacle in the shape of Douglas and she wasn't sure for how long the three of them – herself, Norma and Cynthia – would carry on presenting a united front.

Funny – I never thought we'd fall out over it. She stirred sugar into her tea, oblivious to her surroundings. *But here we are. Cynthia is scared to death of putting another foot wrong. She can hardly be relied on to make herself a cup of tea, let alone find out Vincent Poole's address for us. And Norma seems to have run out of steam as well. I can tell she's more interested in making up with Douglas than helping Clare. Which leaves it up to me, I suppose.*

Her table was tucked away close to the ladies' cloakroom, where there was a lot of coming and going. Millicent kept her elbows in and her gaze cast firmly down.

Not that we've fallen out, exactly. She sincerely hoped that this wouldn't happen. She liked and trusted Norma more than anyone and over the years she'd felt free to share her feelings about Harold and the mess she'd been in. Cynthia was different – younger, of course, and less robust – but Millicent was fond of her as an older sister might be. She sipped her tea but didn't touch the sandwich that she'd ordered. A woman in a dark green coat and straw cloche hat came out of the cloakroom and waited by her table as two other customers squeezed by. Millicent glanced up. 'Margaret?'

The hairdresser saw Millicent and hastily tried to push her way out of the corner, only to find a stout woman with a walking stick blocking her way.

'Margaret, it's me – Millicent Jones.'

'I don't want to talk to you. Leave me alone.' Margaret's face was pained and she spoke between gritted teeth. Her dark hair beneath the hat was dishevelled and she wore no make-up.

Millicent stood up. 'Look, I don't mean to upset you. I'm just saying hello, that's all.'

'Hello.' Still trapped, Margaret mumbled the greeting, looking around the busy café as though to check that she wasn't being observed.

'You seem out of sorts. Would you like to sit down for a minute?' Millicent pulled back a chair. 'Don't worry – I won't bite.'

Against her better judgement but unable to conjure up an excuse, Margaret agreed to join Millicent at her table. 'I don't have very long.'

'Me neither.'

'I'm waiting for someone.'

The buzz of conversation and tinkle of spoons,

cups and saucers obliged Millicent to speak up. 'I'm glad I ran into you, though.'

Margaret flashed her a wary glance. 'Why? You won't winkle anything out of me. Your friend Norma already had a go.'

'Nobody's winkling,' Millicent assured her. A closer study of Margaret revealed a woman under strain. It wasn't only the lack of powder and rouge – it was the cowed slope of her shoulders and a deep suspicion lurking behind her eyes. 'I'm the one in the know about Sidney Hall. After all, I was there.'

Margaret cocked her head to one side and looked at Millicent through half-closed eyes. 'Unluckily for you – yes.'

'You and Barbara, you're well out of it.' Careful to say nothing that might cause upset, Millicent steered the conversation onwards.

Margaret gave a slight nod. 'Luckily Mrs Parr said we could stay at her house until the police had finished. We're back now, though.'

'It must feel strange.'

'It does. But life goes on.'

'For most of us.' Millicent pushed gently for any scrap of useful information. She noted the physical resemblance between them and felt a small shiver as she recognized how easily their roles might have been reversed. She wasn't quite sure what she meant by this, other than there must have been a fork in the road where they'd been faced with a similar choice. Margaret had taken the rocky path leading her into the clutches of Phyllis Parr and Sidney Hall whereas she'd chosen the less risky route into Harold's arms. They'd both led secret lives – that was it.

Margaret used the pause in their conversation to scan the room once more. 'I'm sorry, I have to go.' She stood up suddenly – a move that attracted the attention of a man dressed in a blue pinstriped suit and grey cloth cap who had just come into the café. He made his way straight towards their table.

'Now then, Margaret. I'm sorry I'm late – I got held up.' The man smiled and laid a restraining hand on her shoulder. He turned his attention to Millicent. 'Who have we here? Is this your sister, by any chance?'

Millicent offered her hand. 'No. My name's Millicent – Millicent Jones.'

'Blimey – two peas in a pod.' The smile flickered but was quickly restored as he shook her hand. 'Pleased to meet you, Millicent.'

She waited for him to round off the introductions with his own name. There was something about the voice that she thought she recognized. It was deep and rough and sat oddly with the man's sinewy, dapper appearance, though a closer look showed work-worn hands and dirty nails. His face, too, suggested a hard life – deep wrinkles marked his forehead and the bridge of his nose was flattened and bent out of shape.

He grasped Margaret's hand. 'Come along, love – I haven't got all day.'

Flustered, the hairdresser walked away without her shiny brown handbag and Millicent had to chase after her on to the street.

She tapped Margaret on the shoulder, aware that a waitress was close behind. 'You forgot this.'

Margaret snatched the bag without thanks.

'Yoo-hoo!' The nippy waved a piece of paper at them. 'Who's paying this bill? Is it you, Vincent?'

Vincent! Millicent's eyes widened. Of course – the voice on the telephone, speaking to Phyllis Parr. Vincent Poole on 612.

'Not me, Berta,' he shot back. 'You're not landing this one on me.'

'It's me. I'm paying.' Millicent felt her heart race as she dipped into her purse. She fumbled for the coins, one eye still on Margaret and Vincent who were now disappearing into Marks & Spencer. 'Keep the change.'

She followed them as fast as she could but they'd already vanished amongst the shoppers thronging the shiny aisles and she knew it would take a while to find them again. In any case, she had the distinct feeling that the last thing Vincent Poole wanted to do was to talk to her. Instead, in the few remaining minutes of her dinner break, she chose to double back to the Lyons' and accost Berta, the waitress.

'That man – Vincent . . .' she began.

'What about him?' Berta was too busy to talk. She had three tables to clear, with a dozen customers waiting to be served.

Millicent watched her stack plates, cups and saucers on to a tray. 'Do you know him?'

'Not really.' The tray was heavy and Berta was getting on in years, with grey hair scraped back beneath her starched white cap. 'Mind out – you're in my way.'

Undeterred, Millicent followed her towards the dumbwaiter next to the cloakrooms. 'Do you happen to know where he lives?'

'I haven't got the faintest idea.'

'Where does he work, then?'

'Look,' Berta said as she offloaded the tray then pressed a button to make the crockery disappear down a dark shaft, 'I don't have time for this.'

'I know. I'm sorry. Just tell me where he works – please!'

Berta's sharp elbow dug into Millicent's ribs as she barged past, order pad and pencil at the ready. 'Vincent Poole doesn't work in one place.'

'Why not?'

'What can I get you?' Berta attended to her new pair of customers – two sprightly old ladies laden down with carrier bags. She wrote down an order for a pot of tea and two poached eggs on toast.

'Does he have more than one job?' Millicent demanded as Berta placed the order. 'I'll stop pestering you if you just tell me.'

The waitress batted her away, then, seeing that this wasn't the quickest way to get rid of her, changed her mind. 'Is that a promise?'

'Yes.' Millicent showed how desperate she was for the information by nodding her head until she feared it would fall off.

'Because,' Berta announced with an air of finality, 'Vincent Poole drives a taxi, that's why.'

'At last we're getting somewhere.' After work, Norma had come home with Millicent and Cynthia to Heaton Yard to share in Millicent's excitement and settle her fears that she would have to continue the fight to save Clare all on her own.

'Yes, it explains why Poole was always on hand, night or day, to drive Mrs Parr's girls to these men's homes,' Millicent said. She was buoyed up by her discovery and the next step was already germinating in her mind.

'What kind of man is he?' Cynthia wanted to know. Though she was still shaken by the morning's close shave in the general office, she tried her hardest not to show it by bustling around the kitchen, washing pots and wiping down the draining board.

Millicent tried to sum up her first impressions. 'Not as big and brawny as his voice made me think. Margaret was an inch or two taller than him when they stood side by side. He might have been a boxer at some time – a featherweight or a middleweight. He had that look about him, broken nose and all.'

'And how did he behave?' Norma was curious. 'Did he seem, well, sinister?'

'Not at all. Most people would pass him in the street without a second glance. He wasn't pleasant to Margaret, though – I did spot that.'

'In what way?' Cynthia had finished cleaning and was buttoning up her cardigan and reaching for her hat.

'His tone of voice, the way he took hold of her hand, the way he smiled. Something was missing – I can't put my finger on it.'

'Respect?' Cynthia suggested.

Millicent nodded. 'Out of the mouths of babes,' she remarked to Norma before turning back to Cynthia. 'Are you on your way out?'

'Yes, I'm meeting Wilf, if that's all right.'

'Of course, you go off and enjoy yourself. You're only young once.'

Millicent's dismissive tone made Norma frown.

'What's wrong?' Millicent asked as an embarrassed Cynthia slid away.

'That wasn't very nice. You're not blaming Cynthia for this morning, are you?'

Millicent let out a long sigh. 'No. The truth is, I should have gone up to the office and done my own dirty work, not made her do it for me.'

'So you'll say sorry when she gets back?'

'I will. I'll remember in future that she's not used to the rough and tumble of the big wide world.'

'Good.' Norma walked around the kitchen with her hands clasped behind her back. 'So what do we do now that we've pinned down our man?'

'*We?*' Millicent echoed. 'Aren't you forgetting something?'

'You mean Douglas?'

'Yes. You have to heed his warning. I might not want to follow his orders, but it's different for you. You're wearing his ring.'

'As if I needed reminding.' Norma gave a shrug to acknowledge her difficult position. 'I'm torn, I admit. On the one hand, I don't want to go against Douglas, but on the other I'm not happy about you putting your own head on the block without any back-up.'

'That's all right. I can look after myself,' Millicent assured her, though she was secretly touched by Norma's loyalty. 'I've had plenty of practice. Besides, I've known Clare for far longer than you and Cynthia.'

'But that doesn't mean you have to do it all by yourself. Listen, why don't I have another go at persuading Douglas to investigate, now that we've found out more about Vincent Poole?'

'I don't think he'd listen. He'd see it as me stirring things up again. And he'd be right,' Millicent added with a wink that vanished quickly and left her looking grave. 'I did wonder if Clare would agree to see me.'

'In prison?' It was an avenue they hadn't considered before. 'She'd need to say yes and you'd have to get a visiting order. It might take a while.'

'Is it worth a try?'

345

'I'm not sure. We have to bear in mind that she hasn't said a word so far.'

'Yes and why not? That's what worries me. If it was me, I'd be telling the police every last little detail – how Sidney Hall trapped me and forced me to go with men for money. I'd show them the bruises on my neck and shoulder. I'd be naming Phyllis Parr and telling them where to find Vincent Poole.'

'So why isn't Clare?'

'I have no idea. But I have heard that sometimes a person who's lived through dreadful things is too shocked to speak about it afterwards. It happened to men in the trenches in the war, when they saw comrades blown to smithereens.'

'Yes, I've read about it. We should ask Cynthia – something like that happened to her dad. He came home in one piece but he wasn't the same man ever again. Look at him now – how many years later is it?'

'Coming up to twenty,' Millicent murmured. 'What if the same thing has happened to Clare? All that blood, the knife, the sight of Sidney dying.'

Grim memories of the scene silenced Millicent. Eventually she pulled herself together and aimed for a cheerfulness that was far from sincere. 'Well, one thing is obvious – I'm a bad influence on you and Cynthia and I wouldn't blame you for steering clear of me in future.'

'Don't be silly, Millicent.' Norma, too, struggled for normality. 'We're all in this together.'

'I mean it. You should try to push poor Clare to

346

the back of your mind and concentrate on putting Douglas's mind at rest instead.'

'Easier said than done.'

'But try,' Millicent insisted. 'This is a time for you to be happy. And to keep him happy, too. Otherwise you might regret it.'

Her comments rang true with Norma, who was already swaying in that direction. She glanced at her watch. 'He's coming to my house in half an hour. I'd better be off.'

'Yes, do.' First Cynthia and now Norma – gadding out and about with their young men. Millicent felt the usual pang of envy that she scarcely managed to conceal.

Norma hesitated by the door. 'You won't go putting your big foot in it without us?'

'Who – me?'

'Yes – you.' Norma realized that Millicent had too much time on her hands since she'd sent Harold packing. 'I mean it. Stay in and read a good book or listen to the wireless for a change.'

'Oh yes and I'll buy myself a pair of felt slippers while I'm at it – the type with the fluffy pom-poms on the front.'

They both laughed at the incongruous image. Norma stepped outside into a balmy evening while inside the house Millicent failed to settle to anything and brooded instead about the circumstances surrounding Clare's upcoming trial. Then her thoughts wandered to Harold and how much she missed him.

Dead loss or not, there was a big hole in her life now. And where was he, right this minute? What was he up to? Had he found a new job? If so, would Doris change her mind and bring the boys back from Salt-burn? Then they would all live in a new little house made cosy with rugs, curtains and cushions. Their future would be back on track. The monster, jealousy, roared in Millicent's bruised chest and would not be silenced by wireless or book.

CHAPTER NINETEEN

'Suggest something better to do on a beautiful summer's evening than spend it here with you and I'll say you're a fibber.' Wilf turned on the charm. He felt that Cynthia needed cheering up and had brought her to Linton Park where the formal flowerbeds zinged with reds and yellows, purples and oranges. They'd walked past a bronze statue of the park's Victorian benefactor, Sir Thomas Beeston. The moustachioed philanthropist was perched on a tall plinth, sightless master of all he surveyed. On they went, hand in hand, towards a playground where children soared high on swings and made themselves giddy on roundabouts.

Cynthia gave a small laugh at Wilf's overblown compliment then stopped to take a deep breath. 'Smell those roses.'

No sooner said than he jumped over a low 'Keep off the Grass' sign to pluck a pale pink rose from the nearest bed. He presented it to her with a flourish. 'Go on – take it.'

'What if someone saw you?'

'Who cares?' A perfect bloom for a girl whose skin was softer than rose petals, who made his heart sing whenever he saw her.

A stooped old man straining to push his wife in a cumbersome wheelchair looked askance as they passed. Wilf wrinkled his nose behind the old man's back then pressed the rose into Cynthia's hand. 'It's corny, I know.'

'No – it's lovely. You can carry on being as corny as you like.'

'As long as the park keeper doesn't catch me, eh?' They walked on for a while, past the children's playground and a miniature golf course, towards an ice-cream stall whose shutters were up for the evening. 'We've got time to walk up through the pine woods if you like.'

Cynthia nodded her agreement. The wood fringed the top edge of the park and was a favourite spot for lovers. 'Can I talk to you about something serious?' she asked as they ventured into the murmuring silence of the evergreen trees.

'Fire away.'

'I've upset Millicent,' she confessed. A sense of failure hung over her like a dark cloud and she hoped that Wilf would help her to find a way of making things right.

'And she's been having a go at you?' Wilf knew Millicent of old – lovely enough to look at from a distance but her stem was covered in thorns. Even his sister Maude said so.

'Not really. It just felt a bit awkward when we got home from work tonight.' The straight trunks branched high over their heads and there was a carpet of needles and cones underfoot. 'It was my fault – I made a mess of finding out Vincent Poole's address.'

Mention of the name brought Wilf up short. 'Come again?'

'Vincent Poole – we've found out that he's mixed up with Mrs Parr and Sidney Hall.'

'Is that the same chap who drives a taxi? I know him. Or at least, I've heard Alf Middlemiss mention him once or twice.'

Cynthia grasped his hand tighter. 'Really?'

'Yes. I've gathered Alf's not that keen on him.'

'Do you know why not?'

'No – I haven't asked. Would you like me to find out?'

She nodded eagerly, imagining how pleased Millicent and Norma would be if Wilf were to discover something important. 'We know that he's been using his taxi to fetch and carry girls like Clare—'

'Say no more,' Wilf interrupted. 'We don't want to spoil our evening by thinking about that, do we? Just leave it to me.'

'Thank you, Wilf.' Happy to have shared the problem, she smiled and slipped an arm around his waist.

'You're welcome. Look – a squirrel, there straight ahead!' Together they stood in the quiet shadows watching the small red creature twitch its bushy tail then shoot up the nearest tree trunk – up into the branches, an aerial acrobat of the woods.

'It turns out that Wilf is fond of nature,' Cynthia told Millicent and Norma the next day as they hung up their coats ready for work. 'He knows the names of trees and wild animals.'

'Does he now?' Millicent took up the topic and ran with it. 'How did you find this out, pray?'

Cynthia was in the middle of telling them about their walk in the wood when she picked up the knowing looks flashing between Norma and Millicent. 'It's not what you're thinking!'

'I'm sure it's not.' Millicent was hardly able to keep a straight face. Young men took their girls to the pine woods in Linton Park for one reason only. 'What else does Wilf know about? Is he an expert on the birds and the bees as well?'

'Millicent Jones – you're as bad as my mother.' Cynthia was determined to give as good as she got. 'She was forever going on at me never to trust boys.'

'Quite right too, eh, Norma?'

Norma was distracted by the sight of Ruth coming down the stairs from the general office. 'Atten-shun!' she muttered under her breath.

Millicent and Norma made themselves scarce,

quick march, and were at their switchboards before Ruth could nab them. Cynthia, however, had to stay behind to search for a free coat hook.

'Ah, just the person . . .' Ruth began as Cynthia emerged from the cloakroom. She steered her into the restroom – the scene of yesterday's warning.

Cynthia tried to steel herself against another possible reprimand. She set her shoulders back and made sure that her blouse was neatly tucked into the waistband of her skirt, aware that the supe was studying her closely.

'Kathryn Verney tells me you seemed more interested in our subscribers' lists than in routes and rates during your little expedition upstairs yesterday,' Ruth began slowly. 'I'm wondering why that might have been.'

'I'm sorry, Miss Ridley – I didn't know where anything was kept.'

'So Kathryn and I decided to get out the list of all yesterday's calls. We went through them with a fine-tooth comb and we didn't see any requests for the Lerwick line – not one.'

Cynthia swallowed hard. 'No. I fancied finding out just in case I ever needed it.'

Ruth didn't try to disguise her disappointment at the feebleness of Cynthia's excuse. 'You're not a very good liar, are you? I suppose that was one of the reasons I had high hopes for you when you started – your honesty, some might say your simplicity.'

'It won't happen—'

'I know, I know. But that's beside the point. Sit down, Cynthia. We need to have a proper talk.'

So Cynthia sat opposite Ruth at the low coffee table, taking in the supe's ramrod-straight posture and the spotlessness of her royal blue dress with its white piping and turned-back cuffs.

'Be honest with me. Were you up to something? And if so, what?'

Cynthia did her utmost to withstand the pressure of Ruth's steely gaze, trying to find an answer that didn't implicate Millicent and Norma but which didn't plunge her into deeper trouble. 'It's true,' she said. 'I did want to look up the number of one of our subscribers.'

Ruth frowned and waited expectantly for more.

Cynthia floundered for an excuse that might ring true. 'My Uncle William, out in Hadley . . . My cousin Bert told me that he'd switched from one party line to another. I wanted to find out if it was true.'

Ruth's gaze hardened further.

'I'm sorry.'

'You will be, if I find out that it's not true.' Really, this was going from bad to worse. 'What's got into you, Cynthia? Why are you of all people lying to me?' There was a pause for thought then, 'Oh, wait a minute – is there someone else behind all this nonsense, egging you on?'

'No, Miss Ridley.'

'Of course, that's it. I might have known you

wouldn't get up to no good all by yourself. This is something that Millicent and Norma asked you to do.'

Feeling as though someone had punched her in the stomach, Cynthia rocked forward, unable to frame an answer.

'*Now* it makes sense.' Ruth's triumph rang out of the cramped restroom into the marble foyer. 'Those two sent you upstairs on some trumped-up mission. What was it? If you tell me, it won't be held against you, I promise.'

Cynthia shook her head and tried to catch her breath.

'Very well, let me ask you about another matter. And this time I want you to tell me the truth.' Now that she had Cynthia on the ropes, Ruth went at her hard with a flurry of punches, each one guaranteed to floor her. 'Whose conversation was Millicent listening in to? And don't tell me she wasn't. Did you think I would be fooled by that little trick with the handkerchief? Come on, Cynthia, out with it.'

Cynthia's mouth went dry. She couldn't have spoken even if she'd wanted to. Instead, she looked out through the door as if working out her escape route.

'She was listening in and both you and Norma were covering for her.' Ruth's certainty grew with every passing second. 'Admit it.'

Cynthia's head dropped forward and a small, coughing sound caught in her throat. She risked losing everything if she told on the others – not only her job here at the exchange but her friendship with Millicent and Norma. So she sat and shook her head.

'I'll ask you again – was Millicent Jones listening in to a call? And was Norma Haig a willing accomplice?' Ruth's patience, worn thin by Cynthia's prevarication, finally snapped. Her neck was flushed with anger as she stood up and walked towards the door. 'Very well – you've missed your last chance to save yourself.'

Pushed beyond endurance, Cynthia gasped and willed her legs to work as she ran after Ruth and blurted out her confession. 'All right – yes, they were listening in.'

The supervisor stopped, turned and jerked her head like a bird pecking at its prey – stab, stab with a sharp, hooked beak. 'Aha!'

'But it was to help Clare – Clare Bell. They – *we* – know Clare didn't murder Sidney Hall but the police think she did. And that's not right.'

'Stop.' Ruth's gimlet stare silenced Cynthia. 'Save your breath. There is nothing you can say to defend them. *Nothing*.'

Panic shot through Cynthia as she realized what she'd done. Fixed to the spot, she watched Ruth turn and stalk across the foyer. There was a glimpse of switchboards and the usual cacophony of voices as she swung open the door into the workroom. Then time slowed. Seconds became minutes. The door opened again and Norma and Millicent emerged, white faced.

Cynthia took one step out into the foyer, her lips trembling, her throat constricted.

Norma saw her and gave a tight-lipped stare while Millicent refused even to look in her direction. They went straight to the cloakroom for their hats and coats and Cynthia was still standing in the same spot when they came out.

She watched them leave the exchange – Norma was first out through the glass door, head held high, Millicent following her with her coat over her arm, hat in hand.

The white and grey floor gleamed, the doors swished as they revolved. Norma and Millicent were gone. Cynthia's stomach twisted with fear and regret. *What have I done?* she wondered. The world had turned on its head and she'd been helpless to stop it. Her job, her new home, her friendships with Millicent and Norma floated from her grasp and left her stranded on a sea of cold marble – drifting, rudderless and alone.

'Not sacked – suspended,' Norma told Douglas with a quavering voice. 'It's out of Ruth's hands, thank heavens.'

'But you could still lose your job?' he asked. She'd come straight to his lodgings before he'd set off for a late shift and told him everything – how the three of them had devised a signal to fool the supes while they listened in to Mrs Parr and Vincent Poole but hadn't managed to pull the wool over Ruth Ridley's eyes, and afterwards Ruth had presumably put pressure on Cynthia to make her confess.

Douglas had come to the door dressed in collarless shirt and braces, his chin freshly shaven, and he'd seen straight away that a calamity had happened.

'Yes, I could lose my job,' Norma admitted. 'Ruth's report went upstairs to the general manager's office.' She struggled to stay calm. 'He'll read it then make a decision. Meanwhile, Millicent intends to get in touch with the union.'

'Much good that will do.' Douglas bit his tongue to stop himself from saying, *I told you so*. 'A rule's a rule and it's pretty clear that you broke it.'

Norma hung her head. 'I'm so sorry. We all thought we were acting for the best – not just Millicent, so don't go blaming her.'

Her plaintive voice softened his anger and he wrapped his arms around her and held her close, his chin resting on the top of her head. 'Let's wait and see, shall we?'

She relaxed as she felt the warmth of his body through his cotton shirt. 'My job means a lot to me. And so does my friendship with Cynthia. We'd all been getting on so well – the three of us. Cynthia's such a clever girl, just beginning to make her way in the world.'

'You can't blame her for what she did,' Douglas pointed out. 'She was in a tricky position.'

'Yes, her back was against the wall.' Norma felt a twinge of guilt as she pictured the moment when Cynthia had broken down. 'Come to think of it, I do remember the stricken look on her face when Millicent and I were given our marching orders. Now I expect she's dreading going back to Heaton Yard to face Millicent.'

'Rather her than me.'

Norma breathed deeply. 'I was scared you'd blow your top when you found out.'

'There'd be no point, would there?'

'Even so. If I do get the sack, we'll be short of money. We'll have to save up for a lot longer before we can afford to get married. We have to find a deposit for our rent, and there'll be furniture to buy, not to mention my wedding dress and the brides-maids' dresses.'

'Hush.' Douglas put a finger to her lips to stop her from running on. 'None of it matters. In fact, in a way I'm glad this has happened. At least now you'll have to give up your wild-goose chase.'

'Oh.' Funnily enough, it hadn't occurred to Norma until now that this would be the end of their listening in and picking up clues. 'Yes, perhaps you're right.'

'There's no perhaps about it.' He was already late for work so he reached for his dark blue tunic, put it on and quickly fastened the row of silver buttons. 'From now on, you, Millicent and Cynthia will have to leave the Sidney Hall murder inquiry to us.'

*

359

There were two empty chairs at the row of switchboards and a frosty atmosphere amongst the girls on duty as Ruth patrolled the aisle with redoubled vigilance.

'I hope that sandwich blinking well chokes her,' Molly whispered to Brenda during their dinner break, observing the supe from the far corner of the restroom and speaking under cover of an Irving Berlin song playing on the gramophone.

'Never mind her – Cynthia is the one I could cheerfully strangle.' Brenda sounded as if she meant it. 'She was as much at fault as Norma and Millicent, if not more.'

'How do you work that out?'

'She was the one who set Ruth's alarm bells ringing yesterday when she abandoned her post and trotted off upstairs,' Brenda explained.

Molly sat with her shoes off and her feet on the coffee table, applying a coat of vermilion varnish to her fingernails. 'Yes, but we all know that Ruth has got a soft spot for Miss Goody Two Shoes so she was never going to suspend her along with the other two. What's more, she's had it in for Millicent for a long time.'

Aware that she was being talked about, Ruth packed up the remains of her sandwich then went to the sink to wash her teacup and saucer.

'Good riddance,' Brenda grumbled as Ruth retreated to the cloakroom to comb her hair. 'Are we agreed that we're giving them the cold shoulder from now on?'

Molly blew on her nails to dry the varnish. 'Who – Ruth and Cynthia?'

Brenda sipped noisily from her cup. 'Yes, the pair of them. What do you say?'

'Consider it done.' Molly hated Ruth anyway, ever since her own suspension, and there was no doubt about it – a traitor like Cynthia deserved to be sent to Coventry. 'I'll enjoy making their lives a misery from now on.'

How Cynthia survived the rest of the day she would never know. No one spoke to her or smiled or paid her the least bit of attention. She simply sat and did her job as the minutes ticked by. 'Calling Manchester – I have a new ticket . . . Hello, Mrs Knight. Go ahead, please . . . I'm sorry, caller, the line is busy.' Lights lit up, cords were connected, supervision lamps winked.

She recalled time and again the expressions on Millicent's and Norma's faces when they'd left the building – refusing point-blank to acknowledge her, looking through her as if she were invisible.

Her shift crawled by. Towards the end of the day her hands began to tremble as she faced the fact that it would soon be time to go back to Heaton Yard.

Ruth paused at her switchboard. 'What's the matter, Cynthia – are you ill?'

Cynthia pressed her lips together and nodded. She felt everyone staring at her.

A glance at the clock told Ruth that the shift was due to end in fifteen minutes. 'Then finish early, go home and look after yourself,' she advised. 'And don't come to work tomorrow unless you're feeling better.'

'Thank you, Miss Ridley.' Still trembling and feeling light-headed, Cynthia left the room without looking to left or right but with a gloom-laden certainty that tongues would continue to wag. Feeling that she wasn't up to facing Millicent, she fetched her coat then walked out on to George Street, hardly aware of her surroundings as she took the bus out of town. She passed her Ada Street stop without getting off, waiting until they reached the one closest to Raglan Road.

'Take it easy, love.' The conductor saw her sway as she stood up and lent her a helping hand. 'Are you sure you can manage?'

Cynthia nodded and thanked him as she stepped down on to the pavement. Here she knew every crack and worn kerb, every tarnished door knocker and broken window pane. She reached the house where she'd spent her childhood, mounted the three worn steps and opened the door.

'Cynthia?' Her mother looked up from polishing the brass fender and gave a sharp cry. 'For heaven's sake – you look as if you've seen a ghost.'

'Can I come in?'

Beryl put aside her cleaning rag. 'What's wrong? Why are you here?'

Ellis didn't stir from his fireside chair but stared fixedly at Cynthia.

'I've made a mistake.' Cynthia launched into the explanation she'd rehearsed to herself on the bus journey but she'd hardly begun before her mother broke in.

'Stop. No need to go on.' Beryl recovered from her surprise and spoke as one who had learned long ago to live with life's disappointments, large or small. She wore a faded flowered overall over a brown dress and her hair was hidden beneath a fawn headscarf. 'Let me guess – they've given you the sack.'

'No, Mum. But they've suspended Millicent and Norma, thanks to me. That's why I couldn't go back to Heaton Yard.' Humiliation swamped her and made her sink on to the nearest chair. She saw her father frown and shift position, leaning forward as if to take his pipe from its rest in the hearth then changing his mind.

Beryl soon pieced together the picture that Cynthia presented. 'So you came here to ask for your old room back. What about your suitcase?'

'Still at Millicent's. I'll have to go back for it. I'm sorry. I didn't know what else to do.'

Beryl sighed and shook her head. 'I knew it. I said time and again to your father, you should never have left Hadley – no good would come of it. And I was right.'

Her mother's platitudes weighed heavily on top of what Cynthia had already gone through that day and she couldn't summon the energy to defend herself. Instead, she let Beryl talk herself out.

'You should have stuck with William and never taken that job in the first place. I felt it in my bones. And Bert was standing by, all too willing to step into your shoes. We were fools not to see that coming.'

'Be quiet, Beryl.' Ellis leaned forward again and rattled his empty pipe against the brass fender.

Cynthia shot him an astonished look.

'After all we'd done for William.' Beryl flinched then went on as if she hadn't heard him. 'Of course, it was obvious from the start that Bert would never stick at it, not even for five minutes.'

'Beryl, I said – be quiet.' It was as if Ellis was speaking from a great distance, rousing himself after years of apathy. 'Can't you see – the poor lass is shaking from head to foot.'

This time his wife couldn't ignore him. 'Be quiet yourself,' she retorted. 'I'm talking to Cynthia.'

'Please don't argue.' Cynthia stood between them.

'I mean it, Beryl.' Ellis wouldn't be silenced. 'Cynthia needs us.'

'Dad – it's all right.' She blamed herself for thinking that coming here had been a good idea. 'I don't want you two to fall out. I'll go.'

'Stay,' her father said, his voice growing louder as it shed the rust and dust of two decades of near-silence. 'I can fetch your things from Heaton Yard, all in good time.'

'Stay?' Beryl echoed in a mocking voice. 'Here with us? How can she?'

'I don't want to cause any trouble.' Cynthia found she could hardly breathe because of the mounting tension in the room.

'Your father doesn't know what he's talking about.' Beryl turned her back on them both, taking up the cleaning cloth and going down on her hands and knees to rub vigorously at the fender. 'You can't stay here, Cynthia, and for a very good reason.'

Though she tried to prepare herself, the explanation when it came forced Cynthia to sit back down on the chair.

'We won't be here for much longer.' Her mother's tone had become matter-of-fact and she grew intent on polishing the metal until she could see her face in it. 'And that's because your Uncle William has asked us to go and live with him at Moor View.'

'You can't mean it,' Cynthia said faintly. *What lay behind this decision?* she wondered. Then it dawned on her – it was her mother's sure-fire way of getting where she'd always wanted to be: in her well-off brother's good books once and for all.

'I can and I do,' Beryl insisted. 'He backed down and said sorry over the stolen money so I've agreed to be his live-in housekeeper. Now, Cynthia, if you don't mind – I have to get this place spick and span ready for us to move out on Saturday.'

CHAPTER TWENTY

Millicent was on a mission. There were a number of things that she intended to do with the rest of her day. At the top of her list was a phone call to her union representative which she made from the telephone kiosk at the bottom of Ada Street. The man's name was Herbert Spence and he wrote down the circumstances surrounding her suspension with infuriating slowness – the date, the time, the name of the supervisor, how long Millicent had been employed by the GPO, whether or not there were any previous blemishes on her record.

'And why were you suspended?' he asked at the end of the laborious form-filling.

'For doing the job the police are meant to do in the Sidney Hall murder inquiry.' She landed the unadorned truth in his lap and waited for further questions.

There was a pause then a pedantic objection. 'I can't put that down as a reason.'

She pictured him at his desk – a typical pen-pusher in shirtsleeves and waistcoat, with heavy, horn-rimmed glasses and Brylcreemed hair. 'Why not? It's what happened.'

'But how did that get you suspended?'

'I was listening in to a conversation between two people who the police need to interview. That's my opinion, anyway.'

'Listening in on duty.' The union man wrote down the misdemeanour without comment.

'The point is – I was suspended without any previous written warnings, along with Norma Haig, who was covering up for me. That's not correct procedure.' Seeing that her money was about to run out, Millicent inserted another coin.

The union man was on surer ground here. 'No – under normal circumstances, you're right – suspension without an official written warning breaks the agreement between employer and employee.'

'What do you mean – under normal circumstances? We did what anyone would have done. Besides, the woman the police have gone and arrested is a friend of ours.'

'This Norma Haig – I take it she's a union member? I'll need her details. Name, age, years of employment, et cetera.'

Herbert Spence's plodding manner raised Millicent's hackles and she gave him the information with bad grace, feeding more coins into the slot until there were none left in her purse. Unions were meant to help workers solve this type of dispute, weren't they? But in the event it seemed that red tape tied them up in knots. 'Are you going to help us keep our jobs, or not?' she demanded at last.

'It's not as straightforward as that,' was the cautious reply. 'It involves a serious police matter. That has to be taken into account.'

'So you're *not* going to help us?' Inside the airless telephone box Millicent's patience and money finally ran out. 'Ta very much. At least now we know where we stand.' She slammed down the receiver, pushed open the heavy door then filled her lungs with fresh air. *So much for that.*

She walked back up to Heaton Yard in a black mood and spent the afternoon ruling columns in her notebook, writing down lists of figures and calculating how long her savings would last without a wage coming in. At first she took Cynthia's rent contribution into account then changed her mind. After what had happened today there was no knowing if Cynthia would stay on in Heaton Yard.

She'll be in a state, Millicent predicted. *Such a shame. If only she had kept her mouth shut . . .* She did her sums again. Savings of five pounds and ten shillings. Weekly outgoings of fifteen shillings, including rent, food, electricity and gas. That worked out at just over seven weeks between her and the workhouse. *It won't come to that – I won't let it*, she told herself, thrusting the notebook to the back of a drawer.

Teatime came and went without Cynthia putting

in an appearance. Millicent was still thinking about her as she got changed into an outfit that had been one of Harold's favourites – the purple, halter-necked satin dress. *I do wish I'd stopped to consider Cynthia's feelings a bit more*, she said to herself. *Norma would say that's me all over – rushing headlong into things.* She teamed the satin dress with a white jacket, jet necklace and sling-back shoes. The effect was eye-catching and boosted Millicent's confidence for the risk she was about to take.

But this time I do know what I'm getting myself into, she convinced herself with one last glance in the mirror on her way out. *I've thought it through and this is the best way forward. Yes, I might come up against some unsavoury types, but I'm ready to hold my own.*

Giving herself this pep talk, she left the yard at seven o'clock and caught a bus into town, getting off at the stop next to the Spiritualist church. From there to the King's Head was a two-minute walk.

The pub was quiet, as she'd expected. A smell of stale smoke and beer filled her nostrils. She noticed three men at the bar and a middle-aged man and a younger woman wearing wide black slacks and a revealing, low-cut top at a table close to the door. The huddle of men turned to look at Millicent – initial glances lingered and became admiring stares. One nudged his pal, as if daring him to go over and speak to her. Meanwhile, the man at the table offered his companion a cigarette from a silver case and she took it languidly, along with the proffered light.

'What can I get you?' the landlord asked as Millicent approached the bar.

'I'll have a Dubonnet, please.'

The confident request brought about a nod of recognition. 'Ah, yes – I remember you.' Stanley Cooper poured the drink. 'With lemonade?'

She nodded back then perched on a stool and leaned one elbow on the mahogany bar, catching her reflection in the mirror. The image was reflected several times over in other, angled mirrors around the room. *I know what I'm doing*, she told herself again to settle her nerves.

'I'm afraid you're out of luck,' Stanley remarked through a cloud of smoke. He tipped ash from the end of his cigarette into a glass ashtray – a man-of-the-world gesture accompanied by a knowing smile.

Millicent tilted her head to one side. 'What makes you say that?'

'Come off it – we both know what you're after. Or should I say *who*?' The landlord rolled his eyes upwards as if indicating the private rooms on the second floor.

'You're wrong there.' Her heart skipped a beat at the unspoken reference to Harold but she kept up the devil-may-care pretence. 'That's not why I came.'

'Pull the other one!'

'It's true.' In fact, she was relieved to learn that Harold wasn't here. 'Anyway, just because I've given up on a certain person, there's no rule that says I have to spend my evenings staying in and knitting socks, is there?'

'You've given up on him, have you?' Stanley leaned both elbows on the bar and spoke confidentially. 'I can't say I blame you.'

'And I'll thank you to mind your own business,' Millicent said briskly.

He disappeared behind another cloud of blue smoke then went off to serve a new customer – a woman done up to the nines in high heels, figure-hugging crimson dress and platinum-blonde hair – only coming back once she'd joined the man and woman near the door. 'Don't you even want to know where he is?'

'No. He can be in Timbuktu for all I care.'

'How about somewhere closer to home? Saltburn, for instance.'

Millicent winced but didn't reply.

'I'm serious – that's where Sunny Jim has gone for the day.'

She took a sip from her glass. 'Honestly, I couldn't care less.' She could, though – despite her recent resolve. The news that Harold had chased after Doris meant that before long Millicent's picture of them as a cosily reunited couple would come true. The realization hit her hard and she downed the rest of her drink.

'Never mind, love. There are plenty more fish in the sea.' Stanley spotted a crack in her defences and winked at the customer closest to them. 'A

371

good-looking girl like her won't have any trouble in hooking another one, will she?'

'They'll be queuing up,' the man agreed as he turned to greet a couple of newcomers. 'Now then, let me buy you a pint, lads?'

Millicent looked in the mirror and saw the reflection of Wilf and Alf Middlemiss heading towards the bar. She soon learned from the conversation that two of the three men propping up the bar were taxi-driver pals of Alf. It was as she'd hoped – the King's Head was the pub where they congregated after work.

'Hello, Wilf,' she said as soon as he noticed her.

'Blimey, Millicent. What are you doing here all by yourself?'

His surprise seemed overdone until she saw him weighing her up against the blonde woman in the red dress and the girl in the low-cut top and the reason why they were here struck her all at once. It wasn't only taxi drivers who gathered in this pub, she realized. But she looked steadily at Wilf and held up her empty glass. 'I'd have thought that was obvious.'

'Let me buy you another.' Gallant Alf stepped in and ordered a second Dubonnet. 'How are you, love? I take it you've got over the shock of witnessing what happened at the hairdresser's?'

Millicent fell into small talk with kindly Alf, at the same time keeping an eye on the comings and goings in the room. She learned that he and Wilf had come here to talk through the possibility of Wilf filling in for Alf when the latter wanted to take some time off.

'There's no point my taxi sitting around doing nothing when I'm not working, is there?' he explained. 'Wilf's a good driver, so why not let him have the use of the car to earn a few extra bob?'

'It's easy – all I have to do is apply for a licence,' Wilf explained with his usual bravado.

'That's nice of you, Alf.' She saw the woman in the low-cut top go off with the older man, leaving the woman in the red dress alone at the table. 'It means you'll have to tear yourself away from Cynthia once in a while, though, Wilf.'

He accepted her teasing comment with a cheeky grin. 'Talking of which, can you give Cynthia a message from me? Tell her that Mum's invited her to tea at the lodge on Sunday.'

'I will if I see her.' Millicent gave a casual reply, wishing to avoid having to tell Wilf about the argument but he was too quick on the uptake.

'Why wouldn't you see her? She lives with you, doesn't she?'

'Yes, but we've fallen out over something that happened at work today, that's all.' Still stalling, she saw in the mirror that the very man she'd been hoping to see had at last arrived. 'I expect it'll soon blow over,' she told Wilf with a distracted air.

'Good evening, Vincent.' Stanley greeted his new customer. 'What'll it be?'

'The usual, please.' Vincent Poole took off his cap

and smoothed down his already sleek hair as he approached the bar and said hello to his fellow taxi drivers.

Millicent kept her eye on him through one of the angled mirrors. Her skin tingled with anticipation and she lost interest in the conversation with Wilf.

'Millicent?' he prompted. 'I said – do you happen to know where Cynthia is right now?'

'I'm sorry, I don't – I haven't seen her since this morning.'

'Rightio – I'll see if I can track her down.' Wilf quickly drank up and went, leaving Alf to drift into conversation with the other men at the bar.

Millicent swivelled on her stool and caught Vincent's eye. 'Hello again,' she said with what she hoped was an inviting air.

He shook his head with a momentarily puzzled expression.

'We met yesterday – in the Lyons' café.'

Realization dawned. 'That's right, we did. Millicent, isn't it?' He moved towards her, sliding his glass along the bar. Then he reached into his breast pocket to pull out a packet of cigarettes and offered her one.

'I don't, ta.'

Vincent took one for himself and lit up. 'Twice in two days,' he commented, using his fingertips to pick a shred of tobacco from his glistening tongue. 'I'm in luck.'

She gave a brittle smile and held his gaze, ignoring

the landlord's and Alf's blatant curiosity. 'You certainly are. You wouldn't normally find me out in town on a weekday evening.'

'So why tonight?'

'I'm drowning my sorrows – that's why. And I can assure you, I've got plenty of them.'

Though Vincent wouldn't strike anyone as the sympathetic type, with his spare, lined face and suspicious grey eyes, he drew closer to Millicent. 'I bet you do. Margaret told me that you're the telephone girl from the George Street exchange. I mean – *the* telephone girl.'

She nodded and shaped her answer carefully. 'The one they sent to Sylvia's Salon, worse luck.'

'It can't have been a pretty sight.' His narrowed eyes were fixed intently on her face, as if trying to drill through her skull and read her thoughts.

Millicent shuddered inwardly. 'The worst was over by the time I got there, thank heavens.'

Poole probed further. 'Still – you probably had to hang around until the police arrived, listening to the girl's sob story.'

'Oh no – Clare didn't say a word.' Millicent was desperate to look away but instead used all her willpower to keep on staring back at him. Whatever happened, he mustn't suspect her of ulterior motives. 'What could she have said? It was clear to everyone what had happened – to me, the police, the ambulance men.'

Vincent closed his eyes as he drew long and hard

on his cigarette. Then he gestured towards her glass. 'Is it doing the trick?'

'Drowning my sorrows, you mean?' She sighed and leaned in as if to share more confidences. 'No – I've got a lot on my plate besides that. Take today – my supervisor at work only went and threatened me with the sack.'

'You don't say.' Poole flicked ash on to the floor, to a hard stare from Stanley. 'Another Dubonnet should help take the sting out of that.' Ordering Millicent a third drink and taking her lightly by the elbow, he steered her away from the bar towards a corner booth.

'I could do with something to tide me over while the union sorts it out for me,' she went on. 'The GPO doesn't pay me my wages while I'm suspended.'

'Could you, now?' His expression changed from ingrained suspicion to a new kind of measured interest that took in her mass of glossy dark hair and her generous curves. She was here alone in the notorious King's Head, wasn't she, and surely she must know the score. His mind headed off along a new track. 'What kind of work are you looking for?'

'Oh – you know . . .' Her skin had begun to creep in earnest and she reached for the new drink that Stanley had brought to their table. On his way back to the bar, he had a passing word with Alf Middlemiss who shot her a disappointed glance before turning his back. 'Why? Do you know of anything?'

'I might,' Poole said in the guttural tone that set her nerves further on edge.

'Anything at all,' Millicent insisted with deliberate innuendo, allowing her gaze to rest on the girl in the red dress who had stood up to greet a portly, unsmiling man of around fifty wearing a straw panama hat, an expensive linen suit and a blue silk tie. The man spoke briefly then turned and left. The girl swiftly picked up her handbag and followed.

Poole, too, followed the sequence of events then raised his eyebrows at Millicent. 'Leave it with me,' he grunted, stubbing out his cigarette in the ashtray and putting on his cap, ready to go.

It took everything she had to remain seated and looking up at him with a willing expression. 'How will you let me know? I won't be passing the taxi rank on my way to the exchange while I'm suspended. Shall I arrange to meet you here?'

'Whoa, not so fast.' Her eagerness brought a cold smile to his lips. 'Give me a day or two to have a word with a couple of people I know.'

Her bright expression faltered. 'A day or two?'

Poole nodded. 'There might well be a vacancy for what we have in mind, but I'm only the driver in this business so I need to check with my boss first.' He moved away swiftly without bothering to say goodbye.

Millicent drained her glass. *Have I put on a good enough act?* she wondered. And if she had, was she ready to take the next step, closer still to the centre of the vice ring run by Phyllis Parr? *I am – more than ready!* she told herself, her head swimming so badly that she almost lost her balance when she stood up to leave.

Stanley watched the scene impassively as he dried glasses behind the bar. Alf took a step towards her then changed his mind. Millicent swayed, righted herself and headed for the door.

Outside it was still light and there was a steady stream of people coming down the steps of the Spiritualist church. They flowed across the street towards the bus stop, past the cenotaph and the names of the sons and husbands they yearned to contact – a list carved in white stone – captains, corporals, gunners, in alphabetical order, since death in foreign fields was no respecter of rank.

'What's wrong with her? Why doesn't she speak?' Clifford Denton, the duty defence solicitor stood outside Clare's cell and spoke quietly to Thomas Wright, the prison medical officer.

'Your guess is as good as mine,' came the reply. 'I still haven't managed to get a peep out of her – neither have any of the warders, as far as I know.'

'So is she fit to plead?' The solicitor was mildly intrigued. It wasn't every day that he was assigned a case like this. Or rather, the case was humdrum enough – the stabbing of a husband by a jealous lover, or vice versa – a *crime passionnel*, as the French called it. But the perpetrator here was out of the ordinary – unusually young, for a start, and

378

exceptionally beautiful. He stared at her through the sliding panel in the cell door, realizing straight away that there was capital to be made out of the accused's good looks in front of a jury.

Clare sat on her bed and stared ahead, seemingly unaware that anyone was outside the door. In her hand she held a sheet of paper – a request from Millicent Jones for a visiting order that she hadn't even bothered to read.

'I've found no evidence of mental illness,' Wright said uneasily. He was older than the solicitor, who struck him as over-confident and a touch brash in his broad pinstriped suit and wide blue and yellow tie. 'How can I, since she's refused to answer any of my questions?'

'Let's hope I have better luck.' Denton was prepared to give it a go, at least. He opened up a file and entered the date – Friday 24 July – and the name of the accused – Clare Bell.

'There's bruising to her neck, shoulder and wrist,' Wright observed. 'Fading now, of course, but still visible.'

'Thank you – that might be useful.' Jotting down the information before entering the cell, Denton was struck again by Clare's perfection and by how she had no reaction to him whatsoever. She simply gazed straight ahead without blinking, her skin smooth and pale as marble, her dark eyes unseeing. He introduced himself and waited for her to respond.

She sat perfectly still and unaware.

'Do you know why I'm here?'

Nothing. Not a flicker of her eyelids, not a twitch of the hands resting on her lap. Denton cleared his throat. 'We have to build a defence before the case goes to court. I have to be ready.'

Clare heard a voice speaking into the void that engulfed her but it was distant and had nothing to do with her. It meant nothing. There was a dark blue shape in the room – that was all.

His approach needed to be more direct to shock her back into the here and now, he decided. 'You're charged with murder, Clare. That brings with it a mandatory death sentence unless we can find some mitigating circumstances.'

Words made no sense. Food was brought to the cell and taken away uneaten. She lay down at night but didn't sleep. People in uniforms came and went.

'Do you understand what I'm telling you?' he asked. Perhaps she wasn't ill but mentally retarded. If he spoke more simply he might get through to her. 'The police think you've killed someone – a man named Sidney Hall. There will be a trial. A jury will decide whether or not you're guilty. It's my job to defend you.'

Clare didn't hear. She was falling into blackness and silence.

'Won't you tell me what happened? How did you get those bruises? . . . Clare, can you hear me? I can't do anything for you unless you give me your version of events . . .'

Nothing, and again – nothing.

The bruises were still there to see. Three distinct marks on her neck, the result of strong pressure. In a spirit of desperation, Denton added another note to his almost empty file – *Attempted strangulation? Possible self-defence?*

'It's the best I can do,' he told Wright on his way out. 'Let's hope it helps her escape the noose – that and the fact that she'll have all the men on the jury on her side as soon as they take one look at her.'

'And they talk about justice,' Wright muttered to himself. He was tired after a call-out in the middle of the night and had no idea whether or not Clare Bell was guilty. He would be called as a witness and vouch for her fitness to stand trial. What more could he do in the circumstances?

Friday came at last – almost the end of Cynthia's working week, since she had to work on Saturday morning but had the afternoon off to help her mother and father pack up. She'd stayed with them for two nights at Ellis's insistence but after tonight she had no idea where she would be living.

'Eat humble pie, the way I had to do with William,' Beryl had told her in no uncertain terms. 'Go back to Millicent and tell her you're sorry. If she's as good a friend as you say she is, she'll let bygones be bygones.'

Cynthia wasn't so sure. 'She and Norma could both lose their jobs over this,' she'd reminded her mother.

Her father surprised her again by standing up for her. He'd insisted she hadn't done anything wrong. 'You make sure you stick up for yourself if this Millicent woman has a go at you.'

'Thanks, Dad – I'll try.' She had to face up to the fact that sooner or later she would have to go back to Heaton Yard, if only to collect her things. *Perhaps early Saturday evening*, she'd thought.

The support from Ellis at home had been in stark contrast to her treatment from Molly and Brenda at work, who had not said a word to her since Wednesday. This wasn't so bad when they were all busy at their switchboards, but it was torture during dinner breaks when they'd made a great show of cutting her out of their conversations or else passed catty remarks within earshot.

'Some people don't know the meaning of the word gratitude,' Molly said to Brenda. It was Friday dinner time and she had no intention of letting Cynthia off the hook. There were three other girls in the restroom besides Molly, Brenda, Cynthia and Ruth who observed everything without comment.

'Millicent and Norma have hearts of gold. They were good enough to take a certain someone under their wing and look at the thanks they got.'

Brenda stared at Cynthia then sighed loudly. 'Some people always look after number one and that's a fact.'

Cynthia tried to pretend that she hadn't heard but the hostile stares soon became too much for her and she fled out on to the street, only to run into Bert who was standing in the doorway to the barber's shop.

'Who's sorry now?' was his opening gambit as he leaped out in front of her.

'What do you mean?' Cynthia sounded as weary as she felt. She crossed the street to take a breath of fresh air by the cenotaph, hoping that Bert wouldn't follow.

But he was like a terrier down a hole, goading her with comments about her being turfed out of house and home. 'Who's sorry that she didn't stick it out at Moor View, eh? It would have been a darned sight better than taking a room in Millicent's house – which by the way, Uncle William still doesn't know about.'

'Don't tell him,' Cynthia pleaded. First Molly and Brenda, and now Bert – she really was at the end of her tether.

He laughed. 'Fat chance. The old devil would as soon shoot me as let me anywhere near him. Anyway, it makes no difference, since I hear she's about to give you your marching orders.'

'Who says so?'

'No one. I work things out for myself, ta. Why else would you be back at Aunty Beryl's house?'

'And why don't you mind your own business?' Out of the corner of her eye, Cynthia noticed Phyllis Parr, immaculate as usual in her dove-grey two-piece, get out of a taxi, cross George Street and approach Sylvia's Salon. She unlocked the door then disappeared inside. 'Anyway, Bert – since you know everything about everyone, when is the hairdresser's going to reopen for business?'

'Why – what's it to you?'

Before she had time to answer, she was distracted by the sight of Wilf jumping out of another of the taxis at the rank and hurrying towards her. At last, here was someone who wasn't against her. She waved and ran to meet him.

'Whoa!' he laughed as she flung her arms around his neck. 'Where have you been? I ran into Millicent at the King's Head a couple of nights back and I thought something was up. I was worried about you.'

After leaving the pub two days earlier, Wilf had been doing his best to get in touch with Cynthia. He'd tried first at Heaton Yard but the house had been in darkness. The following day he'd been on an early shift then pressed into doing overtime, so it was only today that he'd had another chance to try to track her down. Still no luck at Millicent's and none of the neighbours seemed to know where Cynthia had gone. 'I've been looking for you all over the place.'

Cynthia gave a garbled account of where she'd been and why. After the stinging experience of being sent to Coventry by her workmates, the relief of sharing her problem flooded through her. 'I didn't mean to get Norma and Millicent into trouble,' she insisted with tears in her eyes.

Wilf sent Bert packing then led Cynthia to a

nearby bench and sat down beside her. 'I'm sure they realize that.'

Cynthia took a deep breath. 'I wouldn't bank on it. And I hate to think what Millicent will say to me if and when I do get up the nerve to fetch my things from Heaton Yard tomorrow evening.'

He frowned. 'I'm on late shift tomorrow, otherwise I'd come with you.' He thought for a while. 'You never know – she might have cooled down by then.'

Cynthia did her best to believe it. 'There's something else I haven't told you,' she confessed. 'Mum and Dad are packing up and going to live with Uncle William.'

'When?'

'Tomorrow.'

'Blimey.' Wilf quickly saw what this might mean and scratched around for a solution. 'I could ask Mum if you can stay with us at the lodge for a while,' he suggested. 'That's if you want me to.'

Laying her head on his shoulder and feeling sorely tempted, she soon decided against it. 'It wouldn't look right, would it? People would talk.'

'Probably.' Though the shrug of his shoulders suggested that he didn't care if they did, he took her point.

'It's good of you, Wilf, but no ta. Let's just hope you're right about Millicent letting me stay on there with her.'

'When I saw her at the pub, she was in a funny mood.' Wilf was thoughtful again. 'She was off-hand

385

with me. And afterwards Alf told me she'd been huddled in a corner with Vincent Poole of all people.'

This piece of news startled Cynthia. 'That can't be right. He's the last person she would want to talk to.'

'I thought so too. But Alf saw it with his own eyes.'

'Then she's up to something.'

'Yes, but what?'

'Goodness only knows.' Cynthia gave Wilf a quick peck on the cheek. 'I have to get going.'

'Me too.' He stood up with her and together they crossed the road. 'I'm with Alf, learning how to be a taxi driver. How about that?'

'That's champion.' She smiled then leaned sideways for another kiss before running up the steps of the exchange.

Fondness almost turned his legs to jelly as he watched her go – quick and slender, her fair hair shining in the sun. 'And by the way, Mum says come to the lodge for tea on Sunday,' he called.

CHAPTER TWENTY-ONE

'It serves you right.' Hetty held to her stubborn, often expressed view that Norma should have followed the rules and not helped Millicent to listen in.

It was Saturday morning and Douglas had called at Albion Lane to join Norma for an expedition to Clifton Street Market. Ivy and Ethel had set off earlier and had arranged to meet them there.

'I'm right, aren't I, Douglas?' Hetty was determined not to let the matter drop. 'She should have left well alone and not got involved with Millicent's harum-scarum plan.'

'Please, Mum – don't go on.' Norma got ready as fast as she could. 'Will it rain?' she asked Douglas as she glanced out of the window at a partly clouded sky. 'Do I need a coat?'

'I don't think so,' he replied. 'Are you quite sure there isn't anything you want from the market, Mrs Haig?'

'No ta, Douglas. Ethel has my list.' Hetty's stern, pinched face melted into a smile. She told all her neighbours that she liked Norma's fiancé very much indeed, thank you. *So polite. Such a nice, respectable young man.*

'Ta-ta, then.' Norma escaped from the house with Douglas close behind. 'You!' she exclaimed as they walked up the street. 'You can wrap my mother round your little finger.'

'What are you on about? I was only oiling the wheels.' He, too, was glad to be out of the stultifying atmosphere of the house, holding hands with Norma and ready to stretch his legs along Overcliffe Road. 'Have you heard anything from your union man yet?' he asked as they reached the Common.

'Not a dicky bird. I called round at Millicent's yesterday. We decided to give him until Monday then we'll make another phone call to see if there are any developments.'

'How was Millicent?' Douglas wondered. The air on the Common was always fresh and he appreciated the long-distance view of Brimstone Rock then layer after misty layer of hills stretching beyond.

'If I'm honest, she wasn't her usual self.' Norma hadn't been able to put her finger on it but had come away with new worries. 'Normally I can say anything I like to Millicent, but yesterday she clammed up over the situation with Cynthia. I tried to talk about Clare as well but all she would say is that Clare's turned down her request to visit and by all accounts still won't give her version of what happened. That bothers me, Douglas.'

'What – Millicent brushing you off or Clare not mounting any defence?' Reluctant as he was to discuss the case, he regretted that Norma was still upset and he felt himself drawn in once more.

'Both. Well, not so much Millicent – she'll come round when she's ready. But have you ever heard of someone in Clare's position not being willing to defend herself?'

'No, I've not come across it before,' he admitted. 'Sergeant Stanhope says to forget about it – we've done our job.'

Norma seized on this scrap of information. 'So you talked to him about the case again? When? What did you say to him?'

'It was after we got the fingerprint chap to examine the knife – he said the handle was wiped clean – no prints. To me that sounded like someone who knew what they were doing, not someone lashing out without thinking – I told the sarge as much.'

'And what did he say?'

'He gave the impression that he still didn't want to rock the boat, but I must admit it bothered me.' As they got deeper into the discussion, Douglas gave freer rein to his feelings. 'I mentioned the broken phone to him as well.'

'And did your expert check that for fingerprints?'

He nodded. 'The same – it was wiped clean, not a trace. Which means that when Clare put the call through to Millicent for the police and ambulance, she must suddenly have had a change of heart and smashed the thing on to the floor *then* wiped it clean . . .'

'Exactly.' Norma was elated by what felt like a breakthrough. 'It doesn't add up. They'll have to think it through properly now, surely?'

'Not unless the sarge points it out to Inspector Davis, I'm afraid. Or unless the inspector reads the fingerprint report and draws his own conclusions – that might make a difference.'

'But it takes so long,' Norma complained. 'In the meantime, Clare is stuck in Armley, shocked rigid by what she saw. Can't *you* do something yourself?'

With the entrance to the market already in view, he frowned and slowed down, weighing up the pros and cons of what Norma was asking. Against it was the risk of irritating the heck out of his superiors then being made to look a fool if Clare Bell eventually came to her senses and confessed. In favour of Norma's request was his growing certainty that she, Millicent and Cynthia were right – there was more to Sidney Hall's death than met the eye.

'Please, Douglas . . .'

'I'll try,' he decided, quickening his pace. 'But let me work out how to play it, Norma. I'll pick my moment then I'll see what I can do.'

It was half past ten on Saturday morning when Millicent answered the door to Vincent Poole.

'Are you busy?' he asked without preliminaries.

It was a common or garden phrase but Poole's

deep voice always carried an aggressive undertone –
an implied challenge. Millicent suspected he used
his voice to make up for his scrawny stature and
similarly his boxer's stance to keep the world at bay.
'Come in,' she told him, glancing around to see who
might be looking and noting Walter at his open
door. She closed hers then waited for her visitor to
speak again.

'I'll come straight to the point,' he said. 'I've done
what I said and had a word with Mrs Parr.'

'Your boss?' Suppressing a shiver, Millicent feigned
surprise. 'And what did she say?'

'She wants to see you.' His answer was delivered
deadpan.

'When?'

'Straight away.'

Her heart fluttered with a sense of impending
danger but she managed to disguise the fear. 'Right
now, this minute?' She spread her hands in a show of
alarm and glanced down at her blouse and slacks.
'Look at me. I'm not dressed for going out.'

'You look all right to me.' It didn't matter how she
looked, he implied. He and his boss already knew
Millicent could doll herself up and pass muster
along with the likes of Margaret and Barbara. 'Get a
move on, will you? Best not keep Mrs Parr waiting.'

The flutter inside her chest strengthened. Until
now she hadn't really believed that Vincent would
follow through their conversation at the King's Head.
She'd half expected him to go away and forget all

about it, but no – here he was, standing in her kitchen without bothering to remove his cap, staring insolently at her and making it clear that he had no time to waste.

Millicent went to the mirror over the sink to run a comb through her hair and put on some lipstick. 'How do we get there – in your taxi?'

Poole was already opening the door. 'Yes. It's parked out on Ada Street.'

She steeled herself. 'Right, I'm ready.'

He led the way past the outhouses, across the cobbles and down the ginnel, making her run to keep up and hardly allowing her time to get into the passenger seat before pulling the car away from the kerb. He didn't say a word as he drove her into town.

Millicent used the silence to breathe deeply in an attempt to steady her nerves. An old Bible story about Daniel entering the lions' den flashed into her mind and refused to be banished back into the realm of Sunday-school sermons. Daniel hadn't gone in willingly, she remembered – he'd been tricked by his enemies and thrown in by the king as a punishment. Angels had saved him from the lions' ravenous jaws – proof to King Darius that the God of Israel was on Daniel's side after all.

It was strange and ridiculous how much of that tale she was able to recall before Poole parked his taxi outside Sylvia's Salon.

'She's inside waiting for you,' he told her, deliberately brushing the back of his hand across her thigh as he leaned across to open her door. He waited for her to protest and when she didn't, he looked at her with undisguised contempt.

Millicent controlled the urge to shudder. This wasn't quite a den with a massive stone rolling across the entrance to trap her inside, but it was not far off. She got out and slammed the car door then crossed the pavement and entered the salon, hearing the ring of the shop bell and the click of the door behind her.

Phyllis Parr was perched on the stool behind the reception desk that Clare had once occupied. The jacket of her grey two-piece hung open to reveal a cream lace blouse and a long string of pearls. 'Well, well,' she said without looking up from her magazine. 'If it isn't our plucky telephone girl.'

'You asked to see me.' Millicent stood by the door, ready for anything. The salon had been redecorated in greys and pinks, with shiny black lino on the floor and modern sinks and silver hairdryers.

Mrs Parr closed her magazine and followed Millicent's gaze around the room. 'I know – it looks different to the last time you saw it. We decided to give everything a quick lick of paint and start all over again. It was worse upstairs in Clare's room. Bed, mattress, rug – everything had to go.'

'I'm not surprised.' Millicent blocked the memory of blood everywhere, the sticky feel of it underfoot, the spreading crimson pool beneath Sidney's body. 'But you'd never be able to tell, not now that you've had it all redone.'

'As I say, you were brave.' Beckoning for Millicent to come closer, Phyllis Parr made an unblinking study of her face. 'If it hadn't been for you, Clare would probably have taken it into her head to run away. But she could hardly do that, once you'd arrived. And so, before we get down to business, let me say a heartfelt thank-you.'

Millicent felt seriously wrong-footed. She'd been expecting Mrs Parr to launch straight into a businesslike speech about what she required of her girls – how they should dress, what they should and should not say to customers, how much they should charge, and so on. But then again, perhaps there was something going on beneath the surface and she was being tested. If so, it was best to say as little as possible and only answer questions that were put to her directly.

Phyllis Parr stepped down from her stool and went to stand in the window with her back turned to Millicent. 'I can only imagine what you must have gone through.'

'I'd rather not talk about it, thanks.'

A frown flitted across Phyllis's face. 'Added to which, Vincent tells me there are problems for you at work?'

'Yes – a few.'

'Have they sacked you?'

'Not yet.'

'But they might?'

'Perhaps.'

394

'What for, may I ask?'

Millicent knew they were on thin ice and she felt it crack beneath her feet. 'For poor timekeeping,' she lied. 'I've clocked on late a few times in the past month.'

'Really?' Mrs Parr glanced over her shoulder at Millicent. 'Do they make you clock on like they do in the mills?'

'There's no actual clocking-on machine, no. But the supes expect to see you at your switchboard on the dot. If not, they issue a warning. Three verbals and a written warning get you suspended.'

'Hmm. Good timekeeping is important in all lines of work, including mine. But I must say I was expecting something far worse than that – failing to charge the right amount for a phone call, making the wrong connection, being rude to subscribers, that sort of thing.' As Phyllis Parr spoke, she came away from the window and began to circle the room, running her finger along surfaces as if looking for dust. 'I've even heard of telephone girls leaving lines open during a call and listening in to private conversations. That can't be true, can it?'

Millicent managed to keep her voice low key and natural sounding. 'It does happen once in a while, I can't deny it. But the supe would be on to that like a shot. All the girls know they would, so most of us wouldn't take the risk.'

Phyllis Parr gave Millicent another hard stare then nodded. 'I'm glad to hear it. In any case, my dear, let's get down to brass tacks, shall we? You're short of money and you don't mind what you do to make ends meet – is that correct?'

'Correct,' Millicent echoed. *Thin, thin ice and dark, cold water underneath.* But it seemed she'd survived.

'So if I send you to entertain a gentleman customer of mine, are you willing and able to do whatever he asks?'

'Yes, I am.' She hoped that this plain, no-nonsense answer gave the impression that she knew the ropes.

'If we were to say this afternoon at four o'clock, would that be all right?'

Millicent gave a start as the shop bell sounded and Margaret walked in carrying a bag in one hand and a brown parcel in the other. The hairdresser took in the scene then stared hard at Millicent. Her eyes flashed what seemed like a warning but she didn't say anything as she crossed the room and went upstairs.

'Four o'clock,' Millicent agreed, her heart pounding so hard she thought it must be audible.

'Wear a decent dress – the type you would wear to a tea dance, considering the time of day. Look your best.' Phyllis Parr reeled off a list of requirements. 'Perfume and make-up, nylons, nice underwear. This customer is particular.'

Margaret's footsteps could be heard mounting the stairs and walking along the landing.

'Are you sure you can see this through?' Mrs Parr needed reassurance. 'Be in no doubt – the first time takes a lot of nerve.'

'I can do it,' Millicent promised. She felt better now that she'd trodden over the ice and reached the far bank. Phyllis Parr had quizzed her then accepted her. *So far, so good.*

'Four o'clock at the King's Head, then. Vincent will pick you up from home at a quarter to. He will drive you there and make all the monetary arrangements for you.'

'What will I be paid and when?' Millicent asked what any woman entering into this dark world would be bound to ask.

'It's complicated. There are different rates for different services, depending on the amount of time required.' Phyllis Parr fobbed her off. She buttoned her jacket and took her gloves from her handbag on the counter, putting them on with slow deliberation, pressing down between each finger in turn. 'Let's just say you'll earn considerably more than your hourly rate at the switchboard. And for now, let's leave it at that.'

Cynthia glanced at the clock above the door. There were five minutes to go before the end of her morning shift, then she would be free to rush off to help her parents with their house move. After that, she would stick to her plan to visit Heaton Yard. Would Millicent be in, she wondered, and how would she behave?

Ruth walked by on her way up to the general office, eagle eyed as ever. 'No daydreaming – take your light,' she barked as she swung out through the door.

Cynthia came to immediately and flicked a front switch. 'Hello, caller. Which number do you require?'

'This is Mrs Parr speaking. I wish to speak to Mr Poole on 612.'

As if a small jolt of electricity had passed through her body, Cynthia sat bolt upright then fumbled to make the connection. A jack lamp lit up. 'Hello, Mr Poole. I have Mrs Parr on the line . . . Go ahead, please.'

Poised to slide back her headset then wait for the supervision lamp to flash, she held her breath.

'Vincent?' Phyllis Parr's voice was harsh and impatient.

'Yes. What is it?'

Driven by an irresistible urge, Cynthia kept her headset in place and prayed that Ruth wouldn't choose this moment to return.

'About the girl, Millicent.'

'What about her?'

'I've arranged for you to pick her up at a quarter to four and take her to the King's Head.'

'All right, if you say so.' Underneath the usual belligerence, Poole sounded dubious.

'Why, what do you think of her?' Phyllis Parr wanted to know.

'She looks the part, I suppose.'

'But . . . ?'

'I don't know – there's something about her. It

strikes me she's not as desperate as most of them. She has more about her, somehow.'

'You're right – in my experience, few people do this unless they really have to. And it's odd that Millicent is already pleading poverty, without waiting to hear if she's lost her job for good.' She made it clear that she shared Vincent's doubts. 'And there's something else – she didn't own up to being squeamish about what she saw here at the salon. That didn't strike me as being quite right.'

Listening in, Cynthia felt a cold, creeping sensation of dread follow on from the first jolt of surprise and she failed to notice what was going on around her.

'So?' Poole prompted. 'What do you want me to do?'

'I want you to pick her up as arranged, but . . . don't take her to the King's Head. Take her somewhere else. I don't need to know where.'

'Fair enough. Then what?'

Cynthia found it hard to breathe. She leaned forward and clutched the edge of her desk with both hands, only to find her headset suddenly wrenched from her head.

'Cynthia Ambler.' Ruth clutched the headset and spoke with cold anger. She gestured for Molly to cover Cynthia's calls. 'Come with me.'

For Cynthia, the world tilted on its axis. One moment she was at her switchboard, the next she was sitting in the supes' office and she had no notion of how she'd got there. She looked through the glass-panelled door at lights flashing on switch-boards then at Ruth speaking to her in words that didn't come together to make sentences.

'Let me down . . . disappointed . . . serious matter.' She shook her head helplessly.

Ruth stared at the silent, confused figure sitting opposite her, her face white, her body trembling. She considered what she saw and her tone softened. 'All right, Cynthia – calm down. What's this about?'

'Millicent.' The word tumbled from Cynthia's lips as she breathed out. 'They . . . I have to . . .' She tried to stand up but didn't have the strength.

Ruth came round, bent over her and patted her hand. 'It's all right. Take some deep breaths. What about Millicent?'

'She doesn't realize . . . They're tricking her.'

'Who's they?' It was impossible to grasp what was going on – only that Cynthia was shocked beyond words and needed to be taken care of. 'Never mind, you can explain later. For now, I'm sending you home.'

'No. You can't. I didn't mean to—'

'I know, I know.' Ruth's thoughts ran ahead. She would pack Cynthia safely off home then find out from Molly the cords that had been connected and thus the two subscribers' names.

'Don't suspend me, please!' Cynthia was so desperate that she clutched Ruth's hand and refused to let go.

'Come along,' Ruth coaxed as she raised her up then led her down the aisle between the switchboards.

400

'We're going to get your hat and coat. Brenda, run outside and find us a taxi.'

Amidst the babble of voices and the winking of red and yellow lights, Cynthia made her exit. Rumours flew the second the door closed behind her – Cynthia was feeling poorly, over-worked, not sleeping because of the Norma and Millicent fiasco, bad time of the month, et cetera.

A taxi arrived at the door of the exchange and Ruth and Brenda got Cynthia settled on the back seat, checking that she had her handbag and everything she needed.

'Number ten, Heaton Yard.' Ruth gave the driver – a man in his fifties with a bald head and a florid complexion – the address written down on Cynthia's file.

'Right you are,' he said, pulling away from the kerb into a slow stream of traffic.

Ruth watched the taxi disappear with folded arms and lips pressed together. 'Don't worry – I'll soon get to the bottom of this,' she promised Brenda as she stalked back up the steps and through the revolving doors.

CHAPTER TWENTY-TWO

To outside observers all seemed normal in Heaton Yard. Walter's daughter Joan washed the windows of number 4 while Dusty Miller planed and shaped a strip of wood to mend his broken window frame. 'I'd wait for ever to get it fixed by our blinking landlord,' he complained to Millicent, who watched from her top step.

She seemed at ease but she hid wildly see-sawing feelings as she reflected on what she'd arranged to do. She was by turns excited and nervous, confident and afraid, and her way of coping after making the arrangement with Phyllis Parr had been to get stuck into the everyday world of washing and mending, cleaning and ironing, in preparation for her after-noon assignation. Now, however, there was nothing left to do except to hold steady and keep to her chosen path.

She was watching Dusty hack out the old, rotten wood from the frame when Cynthia ran down the ginnel. *About time too*, she thought with a little lift to her spirits. She was glad of the distraction. *Now let's see if we can sort things out between us.*

'Thank heavens you're in,' Cynthia gasped as she stumbled past Millicent into the kitchen. She saw a purple dress on a coat hanger suspended from the mantelpiece and the ironing board leaning against the wall. Millicent's white sling-back shoes stood on a sheet of newspaper on the table waiting to be cleaned.

'Come in, why don't you?' Millicent resorted to irony to keep a step ahead in this tricky situation. 'To what do I owe this pleasure? Oh, I forgot – you live here.'

'Millicent.' Cynthia's voice was cracked, her face white as a sheet. 'I've got something to tell you.'

Millicent cut across her, taking quiet pride in how reasonable she was prepared to be. 'Look, there's no need to go on about this suspension business. Let's wait until it's all come out in the wash then we can sit down with Norma and have a heart-to-heart.'

Cynthia, however, was anything but reasonable. 'It's not that. Oh, Millicent, what were you thinking!' The dress, the shoes, the empty packet for nylon stockings on the table – all showed that she intended to go through with what she'd planned.

'I have no idea what you're talking about.' Affecting carelessness, Millicent fetched the bottle of shoe whitener and a cloth from the cupboard under the sink. 'Listen – I've been wanting us to have a talk, only you went to ground before I got the chance. I

403

can't say I'm happy about what went on at work, but I do know that Ruth Ridley can be a right bully. What I'm saying is – Norma and I don't really blame you for doing what you did.'

'Millicent, please . . .'

She unscrewed the cap then poured whitener on to the cloth. 'There's no need for us to fall out over it, is there? We can go on as we were before.'

'Millicent, listen to me.' Finding her voice at last, Cynthia sat down at the table. 'This isn't about work. This is about me listening in to a phone call from Mrs Parr to Vincent Poole.'

'You – listening in?' The idea struck Millicent as so unlikely that she failed at first to take in the rest of Cynthia's sentence. She set the bottle down on the table and stared open-mouthed.

'To Mrs Parr and Vincent Poole,' Cynthia repeated, snatching the cloth from Millicent's hand. 'Listen to me. I heard them talking about you and what you'd agreed to do for them!'

'Ah.' Now Millicent saw what the fuss was about. Cynthia's simple soul was suffering from a severe bout of moral outrage. 'I understand why you'd be shocked, but keep your hair on – I'm only testing out the ground. I won't actually go through with it.'

'No, you don't understand. It's what they said about you. I heard them agreeing that you looked the part but they said something wasn't quite right.'

Millicent faltered and for a second she let fear come roaring in. 'What do you mean?'

'They're on to you, Millicent.'

'How can they be?'

'I don't know how. But I do know that Vincent isn't going to take you to the King's Head this afternoon.'

'Where then?'

Cynthia let out an exasperated sigh. 'I can't tell you that. Ruth caught me listening in before I could find out.'

'But it doesn't mean to say they're on to me.' Millicent quickly overcame her fear. 'Perhaps the customer has changed his plans and wants to meet me somewhere else. Yes – that's probably it.'

'It's not. I know it's not. Anyway, why are you doing this in the first place, stepping into Clare's shoes and running the risk of . . . ?'

'Ending up like her?' Millicent supplied the conclusion to Cynthia's unfinished sentence. 'Don't you see? I want to get to the heart of what went on the night Sidney Hall was murdered.'

'By becoming one of them, you mean?'

'By *pretending* to be,' Millicent insisted. 'Sooner rather than later they'll let down their guard then I'm bound to pick up a clue that will prove that Clare is in the clear.'

Cynthia groaned. 'People say I'm the simpleton. But take a look at yourself. The risk, Millicent – think about it!'

'I already have.' It was true and now she grew determined to convince Cynthia. 'This is the way I look at it. I was the one who saw Clare in that room with Sidney Hall, not you or anybody else. Her face, her eyes – it was as if the life had drained out of them. I've never seen anything like it and I hope I never will again. The knife was on the floor and there was blood everywhere. And in all that mayhem I knew one thing – no, *two* things – for a fact.'

'That Clare was innocent?' Cynthia guessed.

'Yes, and that someone else had been in that room with her and Hall.'

'How?'

'I sensed it, as if that person was still there. I couldn't have been more certain. But a feeling like that doesn't wash with the police. They need proof. So Clare is locked up in a prison cell and whoever did this has walked away scot-free.'

'I see that – I do,' Cynthia said quietly.

'Besides, what have I got left to lose, really and truly?' Millicent was on the brink of owning up to something she'd never put into words before. 'I'm not talking about the job – I can sort out that side of things soon enough.' She placed her right hand flat across her chest and looked deep into Cynthia's eyes. 'It's the big hole I feel, here in my heart.'

'Harold?' Cynthia knew in a flash what Millicent meant.

'Yes, Harold. When I ended things with him I tried my best not to show how I felt because I didn't want anyone to feel sorry for me. But inside I went to pieces.' Her long-time lover, for all his faults and failings, and for all the secrets and pretences surrounding their affair, had been the glue that had held her life together. 'I loved him but I knew it had to end.'

'I know it must hurt, but you'll get over it – you will.' People did. She, Cynthia, had got over the huge hurdle of having a selfish mother and a father ruined by the war. She'd survived a loveless childhood and the endless drip-drip of her uncle's demands, had broken free and struck out on her own, so she returned the intensity of Millicent's gaze with one of her own.

'Eventually, I suppose.' Millicent reached out across the table and took Cynthia's hand. 'But right now my heart aches. Don't you see that helping Clare is my way of mending that and making a fresh start?'

Slowly Cynthia nodded. She did understand, but the dangers involved were still breathtaking.

'I've already found out how Phyllis Parr runs her business. No money passes between the girls and the customers – it's Vincent Poole who deals with that side. He's the go-between who takes the payment then hands over the lion's share to Phyllis. The girl gets paid further down the line.'

Cynthia felt her flesh crawl as Millicent talked. 'Isn't that enough proof to get them both arrested?' she broke in.

'For living off immoral earnings – yes. But it's not going to make them come clean about what happened to Sidney Hall. That's why I have to keep my ear to the ground until I pick up a clue that will seal things once and for all.'

'And meanwhile you play along.' Cynthia shuddered as she imagined the moment when Poole would take Millicent off in his taxi. She made one last appeal. 'There are two things that could happen later today – either you're right about Vincent Poole driving you to meet the customer at a new venue . . .'

'Somewhere more private,' Millicent agreed.

'Or else I'm right about Mrs Parr and Poole having something more sinister in mind.'

Millicent shook her head. 'Stop worrying. You know me – I'm more than a match for Phyllis Parr. As for Vincent Poole, I reckon I can pull the wool over his eyes for a while longer.'

There was no hope of winning the argument, Cynthia realized. She abruptly changed tack as Millicent retrieved the cloth and went back to the business of whitening her sandals. 'Have you told Norma about this?'

'No – she's the same as you. She'd try to stop me.'

'For good reason.' Cynthia calculated that there was probably time for her to nip to Albion Lane and bring Norma back to Heaton Yard to make a last-ditch attempt to talk sense into Millicent.

She jumped up and made for the door. 'Stay here, Millicent. Don't go anywhere.'

She was gone without another word. The door

banged. Millicent felt a heavy silence settle into the room so she turned on the wireless. 'My old man said follow the van . . .' An old music-hall song played as she sat down at the table and dabbed whitener on to her shoes, taking care to cover them evenly and bring them up like new.

It was a call from Phyllis Parr on 768 to Vincent Poole on 612 that had upset Cynthia so badly. Ruth found this out from Molly straight after she'd put Cynthia into the taxi.

'Did you carry on listening in, by any chance?' she quizzed, hovering behind Molly's chair.

'Hah!' Once bitten, twice shy, Molly refused to walk into the trap that had been so obviously set. 'You won't get me a second time,' she told the supe.

So Ruth waited impatiently for Agnes to arrive. She was already in the foyer during the change-over to the afternoon shift, tapping her foot and counting the seconds.

'Blimey – someone's eager to be off,' Agnes commented as she came on duty.

Ruth didn't waste time by replying. She barged past the short queue waiting to go out through the revolving doors then took one look at the street crowded with shoppers. There were more queues at the bus stops and every passing tram was full to bursting so she set off on foot to Albion Lane, pausing only to glance through the window of Sylvia's as she hurried by. There was no sign of life in the refurbished salon.

409

On she went, out along Canal Road, past the police station, the Victory Picture House and the corporation baths, cutting up some narrow, worn steps on to Ghyll Road. At the Green Cross she turned left on to Albion Lane and rapped loudly on the door of number 7.

Ivy opened it and was confronted by a small, trim, well-turned-out woman in a white toque hat and a pale yellow poplin coat. 'Yes?'

'Is Norma in, please?' As Ruth tried to peer into the kitchen, Ivy edged forward on to the step and closed the door behind her.

'Who wants to know?'

'I'm Ruth Ridley.'

Recognizing the name, Ivy planted herself firmly between her sister's nemesis and the door. 'She won't want to talk to you, not unless you're here to tell her she can have her job back.'

'It's urgent. Please tell her I'm here.'

The door opened again and this time it was Ethel who emerged. She'd been listening through the letterbox and had decided to enter the fray. 'You've got a cheek,' she told Ruth. 'But you're wasting your time – Norma isn't here.'

'Why, where is she?'

'Don't ask me. We saw her and Douglas at Clifton Street Market but we came home ahead of them.'

This was enough for Ruth to back down and be on her way up the hill. Ivy tutted at Ethel for giving too much away. 'Trust you,' she grumbled.

'Who is it?' Hetty called querulously from inside the house. 'If it's the insurance man asking for his money, tell him to come back next week.'

Walking swiftly, Ruth calculated the route that Norma was most likely to take and before long she was up on Overcliffe Road, hoping all the time to run into Norma and Douglas, but she arrived at the entrance to the covered market without success.

It's like looking for a needle in a haystack, she thought with mounting frustration. *Maybe I'll wait until Monday and sort it out then.* But no – she needed to have a word with Norma sooner than that. So she went into the cavernous building with its soaring cast-iron work and made her way down the rows of colourful stalls where traders called out prices for fruit, vegetables and meat – still without any luck.

It's no good – I've missed her, she decided, retracing her steps out on to Overcliffe Road, straight on to a tram, which carried her back the way she'd come. She got off at the stop at the end of Westgate Road then nipped down an alleyway back on to Albion Lane, where she saw Norma and Douglas coming out of the pub at the bottom of the street.

'At last – there you are!' Ruth ran to intercept them before they disappeared inside number 7.

Norma saw her and frowned. 'What do you want?'

'This won't take a minute. I've had to send Cynthia home early today. She overheard something on the line that sent her into a tail spin.'

'What do you mean, "overheard"?' If Ruth had

411

come all this way to gloat about catching Cynthia out, Norma didn't want to know. 'Never mind – I know you'll only be happy once you've got all three of us suspended.'

Ruth shook her head. 'You don't understand. I'm trying to help.'

Norma's eyes opened wide with astonishment. She was ready to brush Ruth off and carry on into the house but Douglas put a hand on her arm.

'Wait. Let's hear what she has to say.'

'The truth is, I couldn't get any sense out of Cynthia so I've come to you to find out if you know exactly what Millicent has got herself mixed up in.'

The suspicious frown remained on Norma's face. 'I've no idea what you're talking about. Anyway, I haven't seen much of Millicent lately.'

'It's to do with Phyllis Parr and her vice girls,' Ruth explained as calmly and plainly as she could. 'From what I can make out, Millicent is involved way out of her depth.'

'No – Millicent wouldn't . . .' Norma's sentence tailed off and she turned to Douglas in alarm.

'I don't know much more than that – only that "they", meaning Mrs Parr and Vincent Poole, have tricked Millicent in some way and that's what sent Cynthia frantic.' Ruth directed the rest of her explanation towards Norma's fiancé. 'As a matter of fact, I'm glad you're here. We need to get the police involved as soon as possible.'

'Hold your horses – I'm off duty until Monday.'

Though intrigued by what Ruth was telling them, Douglas kept to the official line. 'It's probably best for you to go down to the station.'

'No – Millicent Jones has got mixed up with a dangerous woman. I want you to step in before it's too late.'

'How dangerous?' Norma suddenly remembered rumours surrounding Ruth's married life in Manchester. 'You came across Phyllis Parr before you moved here, didn't you? What haven't you told us about her?'

Ruth closed her eyes to give herself the time and courage to confront an uncomfortable truth. 'I don't like to talk about it,' she admitted. 'My husband as-was got mixed up with her. It wasn't a happy time.'

This was news to Douglas. 'So you can't have been too pleased when she moved into the premises down the road on George Street?'

'That's putting it mildly. But I thought it would be best for me to keep quiet. I didn't want people raking through my past – my divorce from Arthur Ridley, especially. Let sleeping dogs lie – that was my motto.'

'But you've changed your mind?'

'Yes, now that I know for certain Phyllis Parr is carrying on the way she always has.' The weeds of the past had a way of pushing up through pavement cracks into the present, however hard Ruth tried to stamp on them. 'She used to be in cahoots with a

Dutch man called Van Buren before they locked him up.'

'What for?' Douglas asked.

'For forcible detainment of the girls they used in their vice ring. He and Mrs Parr made a lot of money between them – a total of a hundred and ten pounds in one month alone, according to Arthur. And he knew the ins and outs of it, believe me.'

Douglas took this in without comment, though he glanced at Norma to see if she was giving him a told-you-so look.

'In any case, somehow Phyllis Parr managed to get off without a prison sentence,' Ruth went on. 'Then she high-tailed it over here and teamed up with Sidney Hall.'

Norma saw how painful this must be for Ruth. 'What's it called when someone makes money like that?' she asked Douglas in an undertone.

'Procurement. It comes under the old Vagrancy Act, but it needs a witness to stand up in court and swear that's what happens. The girls don't want to do it for obvious reasons, neither do the married men who visit these brothels, and nor do their wives, for that matter.'

'That was true in my case,' Ruth admitted as she put her hand up to her flushed cheek. 'I felt too ashamed.'

'So these so-called madams usually get away with it.' As Douglas had tried to explain to Norma before, the crime was notoriously hard to bring before a judge, but if Ruth proved willing to come forward, he thought there was a good chance in this case. 'What exactly do you want me to do?'

'Go down to George Street and arrest Phyllis Parr,' Ruth told him, her eyes flashing with renewed determination. 'Do it now, before Millicent rushes into something she'll regret for the rest of her life.'

Ivy opened the door to number 7 for a second time that afternoon. 'Yes?' she asked Cynthia, who stood with scared-rabbit eyes, shoulders raised and clutching her handbag close to her chest.

'Norma – is she in?'

'You must be Cynthia Ambler.' Ivy recognized her immediately from Norma's descriptions – golden haired, pure and pretty as a picture. 'No, Norma isn't back yet. I'm expecting her any time. Can I give her a message?'

'No. I need to speak to her. Do you know where she is?'

'For heaven's sake.' Ethel sailed up behind Ivy in fine grumbling fettle. 'Why is our Norma in such high demand all of a sudden?'

Minutes were ticking by and Cynthia was getting nowhere. 'Are you sure you don't know where I can find her?'

'You heard what Ivy said,' Ethel said impatiently. 'She's not in. Now scram.'

'No – wait.' Ivy stepped in to prevent Ethel shutting the door in Cynthia's face. From the girl's expression she saw that the situation was urgent. 'Try the Green Cross,' she suggested. 'Norma's out and about with Douglas. They sometimes call in there on a Saturday afternoon.'

'Ta, I'll take a look.' Cynthia was off down the street before the words were out of Ivy's mouth. It was five past three – hardly enough time to find Norma and haul her back to Heaton Yard before Millicent was due to leave the house. Even then – even if they made it back in time – Cynthia wasn't sure that Norma would be able to talk Millicent out of going off with Vincent Poole. *But it's my only hope*, she thought as she squeezed past Dusty Miller and Walter Blackburn who lounged at the entrance to the pub. As she scanned the crowded room, she felt a hand on her shoulder and turned to find Wilf looking quizzically at her.

'Cynthia – what's up? Are you all right?'

She grasped his hand. 'No, Wilf – I'm not.' The reason why she was here tumbled from her. 'So you see I have to find Norma. Can you help me?'

He nodded quickly then led the way past darts and dominoes players to the bar.

'I'm looking for Norma Haig,' Cynthia told Chalky White above the hubbub. 'Is she around?'

'Not any more,' he replied, looking from Cynthia to Wilf then back again as he steadily wiped the top of the bar.

'You're sure?' She hoped against hope that the barman was wrong.

Chalky nodded apologetically. It was a shame to see disappointment flood Cynthia's lovely features but it couldn't be helped. 'Sorry, love – your friend *was* here with her fiancé, large as life. You've missed them by a few minutes at most.'

CHAPTER TWENTY-THREE

Millicent stood by the window watching out for Vincent Poole and working through the events that were about to unfold.

He would arrive and she would act coolly, as if being driven to meet a customer was an everyday thing for her. She could even imply that it wasn't her first time, that this was something she did whenever she was finding it hard to make ends meet. In this way she would settle any doubts that Poole and Phyllis Parr might have harboured.

Then she and Poole would get into his taxi and they would continue to chat. She would speak admiringly of how cleverly Mrs Parr managed her undercover business behind the salon's respectable front. And wasn't it a credit to her that Barbara and Margaret had both stuck with her during recent times. She would find ways to praise him, too – how lucky it was that Phyllis Parr had him to call on at any time of day or night. He was a man who could be trusted not to give anything away.

In her experience of men in general and of Harold in particular, Millicent had grown convinced that they all succumbed to flattery in the end. Poole would be no exception. She would pin her hopes on gaining his trust during the taxi ride. Hopefully he would let things slip – small details at first then more significant ones, such as the names of customers, the recruitment of the girls, maybe even the problems that Sidney Hall had experienced with Clare Bell in the days leading up to his death.

She glanced at the clock on the mantelpiece – only five minutes to go. The yard was unusually empty of activity this sunny Saturday afternoon. Walter wasn't on his doorstep – he must have gone down to the Green Cross for a pint. There were no children playing football or hopscotch, no women gossiping from their top steps.

Poole took her by surprise by arriving three minutes early. He paused at the end of the ginnel to light a cigarette, taking his time before setting off in the direction of Millicent's house. His double-breasted jacket was buttoned, the shoulders wide and padded, the waist nipped in. He wore a stiff collar and dark blue tie that looked oddly formal alongside his workman's cap.

Don't rush out to meet him, don't look as if you've been on tenterhooks. Millicent forced herself to wait for the knock on the door.

He didn't speak when she opened it and didn't step inside.

She put on her white jacket and picked up her handbag, went out and locked her door. They walked together across the cobbles.

'Ta very much. This is a real lifesaver,' she said breathlessly, getting into the taxi that stood waiting at the end of the alley. 'Without this offer of work I'd have had to tighten my belt and miss out on the good things in life.'

Poole looked straight ahead and didn't comment.

'Am I glad I had those chats with you and Mrs Parr. Now *there's* a woman who has her head screwed on.'

They came to a slow flow of traffic on Ghyll Road. He took a side road from there down on to Canal Road.

No need to worry after all, Millicent thought. *Cynthia was wrong – we're heading into town as planned.* 'I take it we're meeting a regular customer?' she mentioned to Poole.

There was no reaction, no comment. He finished his cigarette then wound down his window to throw the glowing butt into the gutter. She noticed that he was wearing leather gloves for driving and that his flattened nose gave him a boyish profile though his real age must have been close to forty. The gloves bothered her for some reason, as did his impenetrable silence. It sank in gradually that her plan was coming unstuck.

He drove slowly past familiar landmarks – the picture palace and the swimming baths on the left-hand side of the road, the police station and the scrap metal yard on the right.

'What happens when you drop me off at the King's Head?' She thought up questions that would force an answer from him. 'Do you come in with me or do I go in by myself?'

He glanced sideways, his expression unreadable as he went on refusing to speak.

Her uneasiness grew. 'I hear you're an old hand at this – that's the reason why I want to run through the routine with you.'

He shrugged and carried on driving until they ground to a halt in traffic outside the Odeon in the town centre. It forced Poole to take another back route down the side of Merton and Groves department store until they came up against a second jam at the end of George Street. Once more Millicent drew comfort from the fact that the King's Head was still their likely destination – this in spite of the fact that she'd failed to get a single word out of him.

Poole's right hand tapped the steering wheel – the only sign of impatience. He checked the traffic in each direction. Two buses pulled away from the stop outside the exchange building, leaving a clear view of the row of shops next to it. She saw that a police car was parked outside Sam Bower's barber's shop.

Hemmed in by cars and motorbikes, trams and horses and carts, Poole also noticed the police car and suddenly gripped the steering wheel. A boy rode his bike on to the kerb to squeeze past the police constable standing beside the car, weaving between curious bystanders.

Time slowed. Millicent looked from Poole's gloved hands on the steering wheel to his expressionless face and from there she followed the direction of his gaze. She spotted two more policemen leading Margaret and Barbara out of Sylvia's Salon, straight into their waiting car.

'Wait!' She gave a strangled cry as Poole swore and swerved out of the line of traffic down a side street behind Marks & Spencer. 'What are the police doing there?'

Tyres squealed and the taxi rocked violently as Poole put his foot on the accelerator and took the corner at speed. As he spun the wheel in the opposite direction, they lurched again, narrowly missing a row of bins before turning into a courtyard behind the Spiritualist church where Poole finally slammed on the brakes and stopped.

'Get out,' he yelled at Millicent, jumping out of the car and running round the back to wrench open her door before she had time to come to her senses. He dragged her out of the taxi into the shaded yard, surrounded on three sides by high walls topped with shards of glass set into concrete. Then he held her arm with an iron grip and forced her back on to the street.

She struggled. 'Let go of me. Where are we going? I said, let go!'

'Shut your mouth. Walk if you know what's good for you.' He propelled her across the pavement towards the cenotaph, his face set in cruelly determined lines.

Surprised by his strength, Millicent tried but failed to pull away. They were attracting attention – people glanced in their direction but didn't step in to break up what must have looked to them like a lovers' tiff. He forced her to walk on past the taxi rank and across George Street towards the hairdresser's.

'Stop. This wasn't my doing!'

Poole ignored her. He was fuelled by an explosive fury as he kept tight hold of her and leaned his shoulder against the door. When it refused to open, he took a step back, raised his foot and kicked hard at the lock, which broke and the door swung open. Millicent fell on to her knees as he thrust her inside.

The salon was empty now. There was no sign of the police and so Poole's risky decision to come here in search of Phyllis Parr had paid off. However, there was no sign of her either. Poole came alongside Millicent, who was still on her knees on the floor. With his face devoid of human feeling, he took aim then landed a vicious kick in her ribs.

She collapsed forward, gasping for breath but too shocked to feel pain.

'What did you tell them?' Now his teeth were bared and his fists clenched.

She clutched her ribs and rolled sideways. 'Nothing. It wasn't me.'

'Liar!' His second kick failed to meet its target so he lunged and pushed her on to her back. Then he knelt astride her and took hold of her by the shoulders. 'Liar. Bitch. Liar, liar!' The words burst from him, each one accompanied by a savage slam of her body against the floor.

Her breath came in short gasps. She managed to resist by bringing her knees up and arching her back so that she threw him off balance. There was a split second when he was thrown backwards, allowing her to roll free, but not enough time for her to stand up and make for the door. He was up before her, grabbing her wrist with both hands and dragging her dead weight towards the stairs at the back of the shop.

'Listen to me,' Millicent pleaded as her body slammed against the bottom steps. 'I had nothing to do with this!'

Poole raised her to her feet then shoved from behind, forcing her up the narrow staircase and blocking her attempts to escape. When they reached the landing he pressed her against the wall, one hand squeezing her throat.

'Tut-tut – bad idea,' he chastized as he applied more pressure. 'Phoning the police – very bad. Stupid.' Anger burned in his eyes.

'It wasn't me.' The murderous look scared her more than the physical violence – so much so that she went limp and would have sagged to the floor if Poole hadn't taken her weight and dragged her along the landing towards Clare's room.

'Let's take a look in here,' he suggested as he kicked open the door. He held her against him, an

424

arm hooked around her throat. 'No – no one here. I might have known Phyllis wouldn't hang around long enough to get herself arrested.'

It was now that Millicent felt pain shoot through her bruised ribs and shoulders. She was locked in his grip and her throat throbbed as she fought for breath. She had no strength to resist being flung against the washstand in the far corner of the room where she dropped to the floor.

Watching from the doorway, Poole took off his right glove then reached into the inside pocket of his jacket to draw out a small metal object with a row of four rings through which he slowly slid his fingers. 'It serves me right for getting mixed up with a bunch of women in the first place.'

Millicent pulled herself upright, her eyes fixed on the brass knuckles. She shook her head then pressed herself hard against the wall.

'What are the chances of Margaret and Barbara keeping their traps shut, eh?' He flexed his fingers inside the rings and tilted his head to one side as if working out the odds. 'You're right – pretty slim. Meanwhile, the lady in charge makes her getaway, leaving me to clear up the mess.'

Millicent drew a ragged breath and clutched at her ribs.

'Not so chatty now, are we?' He held up his fists as he moved one step towards her. 'Just so you know – we were on to you, so it was a waste of time getting dressed up.'

Millicent shook her head. She felt sick and was shaking all over, but still she hoped to talk her way out. 'You're wrong. I didn't call the police. Why would I?'

'Because you and your pals have been poking your noses in for a while now – that's why.' He feinted then ducked and stepped sideways – a boxer's sequence of moves. 'I warned Phyllis from the start – I don't like the look of the tall one with dark hair.'

'Yes and I listened to your advice, didn't I?' Phyllis Parr's voice rang out as she came up the stairs then trod quietly along the landing into the room.

Millicent gasped and took a step towards her in mute appeal until Poole aimed an uppercut at her chin and forced her to retreat. His fist missed her by an inch.

Phyllis took in the situation. 'You were right, Vincent. It's a good thing we kept our wits about us. But you're wrong in one respect. It wasn't Millicent who listened in to our conversation and called the police.'

'How do you know?' With his gaze fixed on Millicent, Poole moved within arm's length, fists raised, the brass knuckles glinting in the low sunlight.

'She's been suspended from work, remember?'

He jabbed at Millicent and feinted again. 'So what?'

'So there will be others from the exchange to deal with once you've finished here.'

Poole's gaze didn't deviate. 'What makes you think you can carry on dishing out the orders, Phyllis?'

'Because that's the way it's always been.' She circled around the back of Poole until she came within his sight line. 'Come along, Vincent, let's not waste time. We've already agreed on how to keep this one quiet.'

Poole's face darkened. 'That was before we had coppers swarming all over the place.'

'All the more reason to put our original plan into action.' She came closer. 'But not here. We don't want a repeat of the Sidney situation.'

'You mean, *you* don't want it. You're expecting me to do all this in broad daylight, drive her out to Devil's Leap and push her over the edge?'

Poole's resentment broke through in a sharp jab in Phyllis's direction.

Millicent groaned as Poole's fist almost made contact with its target. Phyllis Parr's eyes widened and she gasped.

He put his fists up in front of his face again, shifting position to bring both women within range. 'No, Phyllis – I've had a bellyful of taking orders from you.'

She stood her ground and kept her composure. 'Vincent, listen to me. You can easily keep her here for a few hours. Tie her up and use a gag if necessary. Wait until after it gets dark before you move her.'

As the pair described how she would meet her end at the remote beauty spot, Millicent held her breath. She cowered in the corner, aware that the smallest movement from her would be enough to make him explode into violence once more.

'Sidney was the same,' he muttered. 'Do this, do that. Jump through this hoop then that.'

'This isn't the time for us to fall out, Vincent.' Still Phyllis showed no sign of being intimidated. 'You must stick with the plan.'

Millicent cringed. Couldn't she see that Poole was teetering on the edge? The brutal gangsters' weapon could break jaws, crush ribs, smash through skulls if used with enough force.

Tiny muscles in his cheeks twitched. 'Nothing changes – Lord and Lady Muck dish out the orders while I do the dirty work.'

'I'm only reminding you of what we agreed—'

'Well, don't.' He cut her off with another flick of his fist. 'You hear that, Millicent? Phyllis is sticking to the plan to push you over the cliff so she won't have to redecorate all over again.'

Millicent shuddered as he crouched forward and crept towards her then lowered his voice to a whisper. 'You can't trust them, you know.'

She shrank away but he grabbed her arm and jerked her back.

'The trouble is – they're the ones holding the purse strings. And I'll let you in on something else – they don't always pay up when they should.'

'Please, don't!' Millicent felt his breath on her cheek. His lips were against her ear.

'Take Sidney, for instance. The rotten bugger

owed me five bob for ferrying Clare Bell around. I ask you – five measly shillings.'

She tried to put her hands to her ears in a futile attempt to block out the rest of his cold-blooded account.

'I put it to him nicely – pay me what you owe me. But he refused point-blank. He gave me no choice. Ask Clare – she was there.'

Millicent groaned again and put her hand over her mouth, catching sight of Phyllis Parr's angry face as she finally realized that Poole had spun out of control.

'Vincent – enough!' she commanded.

Poole turned on her with renewed fury. He lashed out and punched her on the side of the head. One blow – the sound of metal against bone. She staggered then fell senseless on to the bare boards.

Horrified, Millicent tried to stand up but her legs refused to carry her. She had to crawl across the floor towards them. 'Stop. Stop!'

There were noises in the salon below – shouts and the sound of footsteps rushing upstairs.

Phyllis was slumped on the floor, eyes closed, her necklace broken and pearls scattered everywhere. Poole had his fist raised for a second blow.

Millicent reached him and wrapped both arms around his legs, using all her remaining strength to drag him down. He toppled and fell on top of his victim, taking Millicent with him.

For a second she was able to use her weight to hold

him down. But then he was writhing free, swearing, lashing out with his fists, when Douglas rushed in, bent over him and locked one arm behind his back. He pinned him down with his knee.

Wilf and Norma were there too, crouching beside Phyllis Parr while downstairs in the salon, a woman spoke into the phone. 'Agnes, this is Cynthia Ambler. Send the police and an ambulance to Sylvia's Salon on George Street. Hurry!'

CHAPTER TWENTY-FOUR

There was comfort in familiar objects – the clock on the mantelpiece, the green and orange rug that covered the cracked linoleum, her sewing machine in the corner of the room. And relief at hearing friends' voices. Millicent sat at her kitchen table, glad that Norma and Cynthia were still with her in the house.

'It goes to show – whatever else you say about Ruth Ridley, her heart is in the right place.' Norma had told the others about the supe's efforts earlier that afternoon to have Mrs Parr arrested. 'No one asked her to do it, but once she'd sent Cynthia home, she pulled out all the stops.'

'Is it true that she'll testify in court?' Cynthia asked as she came into the room. She'd been upstairs and put on her blue and white daisy frock, glad of the chance to get her hands on a change of clothes at last. She'd come back down in time to hear Norma telling Millicent about the supe's part in the recent arrests.

'She promised Douglas she would take the stand.' Norma kept a wary eye on Millicent. She must be feeling bruised and sore, never mind reeling from the shock she'd suffered. Norma wouldn't blame her if she were to duck out of coming down to the Green Cross for a quiet celebration.

'Yes, but will Ruth take back the complaints she filed against us?' Millicent wondered, tapping her fingernails against her teacup. She was gradually coming round and was relieved to see that Cynthia was treating the place like her own again. 'I mean – are we still suspended or not?' she asked Norma.

Her friend cocked her head to one side. 'I don't know. I reckon we should turn up at the exchange on Monday and see what happens.'

'Shall we?' Millicent smiled at Norma's cheek. 'They can't sack us now, can they? Not now we've got the proof that Clare is innocent.'

'Yes, we did it.' Cynthia sat down at the table opposite Millicent. 'Or rather – *you* did it.'

'We did it between us,' Millicent insisted. 'No arguments – it was a team effort.'

They sat for a while in silence, taking in the full implications of what they'd managed to do – three friends working together on Clare's behalf.

'I'm just glad you're all right,' Cynthia assured Millicent at last. 'I was worried sick when I couldn't talk sense into you, then afterwards trying to find Norma to see if she could stop you.'

432

'Which is harder than trying to stop an express train,' Norma interjected.

Cynthia agreed. 'It was only when I ran into Wilf that I calmed down a bit.'

'Enough to listen to him and go straight down to the police station,' Norma explained. 'That's where they ran into me and Douglas. We all left for George Street together.'

'You are all right, aren't you?' Cynthia shuddered to think what Poole might have done to Millicent if he hadn't been prevented.

'You heard what the ambulance man said – he gave me the all-clear.' Millicent would keep going until she dropped rather than admit even to herself how terrified she'd been.

'At least you're better off than Mrs Parr. They think Poole has cracked her skull, not to mention knocking out a few teeth when she landed.' Norma realized she didn't feel an ounce of sympathy for the woman. 'If I say I'm glad, does that make me a hard-hearted so-and-so?'

'Not in the least. Anyway, it's all thanks to you two that I didn't end up like her, or worse.' Millicent reached across the table and squeezed their hands.

'No more rushing headlong?' Norma squeezed back.

'Not for a while at least,' Millicent promised with a wry grin.

'We mean it.' Cynthia refused to let go of her hand.

'On one condition – no, two.' Millicent turned first

to Cynthia. 'Number one – you stay on as my lodger at least until Christmas.'

'Agreed.' Cynthia held on tight and grinned.

'Number two.' Millicent looked at Norma. 'You don't let being engaged get in the way of nights out with Cynthia and me.'

Norma laughed. 'As if I would.'

Millicent began a list. 'Friday nights at Health and Beauty for a start.'

'Count me in.'

'Me too,' Cynthia agreed.

'A visit to the flicks at least once a month.'

'Agreed.' Two voices spoke as one.

'Sunday-morning rambles up the Dales.'

'Only if it's fine.'

'Only if Wilf can come too.'

'No men allowed,' Millicent told Cynthia firmly. 'Oh and by the way, I have to admit that Wilf Evans is turning out miles better than I expected.'

Norma broke the circle of hands by standing up and whooping. 'Stop the press. Millicent Jones admits she was wrong!'

'I'm not saying he's perfect,' Millicent pointed out. She winced as Cynthia helped her into her jacket. 'Ouch. Tell him there has to be a big improvement before he gets full marks from me.'

'Tell him yourself.' Cynthia led the way out of the house. 'He and Douglas are already at the bar, ordering drinks.'

Norma linked arms with Millicent and followed

Cynthia down the street. 'You won't ever give Wilf full marks if I know you.'

'Never,' Millicent agreed, walking stiffly but with her head held high. 'Ten out of ten is impossible as far as all men are concerned.'

July eased into August. Newspapers reported charges against Phyllis Parr for keeping a brothel and against Vincent Poole for the murder of Sidney Hall. A sense of anticlimax set in – a taxi driver and a brothel keeper were mundane fodder compared to the bewitchingly lovely Clare Bell. The same applied to hairdressers Margaret Allen and Barbara Mason, originally from Bolton, who already had five convictions for prostitution between them.

'They don't talk about the injustice of locking Clare up in the first place,' Millicent pointed out as she turned the pages of the *Herald* until she came to reports about the Olympic Games in Berlin. Jesse Owens, the wonderful American runner, had won another gold medal, much to Herr Hitler's disgust.

She sat during her dinner break with Norma and Cynthia in the restroom at the George Street exchange. It was as they'd hoped – the complaints against them had been dropped overnight and they were all happily back in the swing of their switch-board routine.

'Or the fact that she had to spend a week in hospital after they let her out.' Norma had followed Clare's progress with interest. 'Douglas says it was a slow job, finding new lodgings for her, getting her to eat and sleep normally again. She had to have daily sessions with a psychiatrist to help get things off her chest.'

'Does anybody know what's happened to her since she left hospital?' Cynthia wondered.

'I do.' Ruth Ridley's surprise announcement came from a corner of the room where she sat quietly doing a crossword. 'At least, I know a little bit.'

Norma, Cynthia and Millicent turned expectantly as the supe put down her magazine.

'Well? Don't keep us in suspense.' Norma spoke for all three.

Ruth dropped her air of mystery. 'She's come to live with me, for a start.'

'You don't say!' Norma exclaimed.

'Yes, I do say. Someone had to keep an eye on her, didn't they? And I had an attic room going spare. It seemed like the right thing to do.'

'It is,' Millicent quickly agreed. After all, Ruth had more reasons than most to hate Phyllis Parr so that her stepping in to help Clare escape from her clutches seemed perfectly fitting.

'The other thing I know is that Clare has applied for a new job.'

'Where?'

'How do you know?'

'What job?'

'Here, at the exchange,' Ruth replied. 'The general office received an application form. She'll come for an interview next Monday.' She revelled in their surprise as she stood up and headed towards the door. 'What's wrong, girls? Don't stand there with your mouths open. It's quite clear that, given the right training, Clare Bell will make an excellent telephone girl.'

'But . . .' Cynthia chased after her. 'Who's leaving?'

'Yes. Where's the vacancy?' Norma insisted on finding out. 'Is it Molly?'

'No, not Molly.'

'Brenda?'

'No.' Ruth swung the door closed behind her, leaving only Cynthia, Millicent and Norma in the room.

'Who then?' Cynthia turned to Millicent, whose expression was an unexpected mixture of secrecy and excitement. 'Not you!' she exclaimed with a stab of alarm.

Millicent burst out laughing. 'The thought of leaving did cross my mind.' In fact, she'd come across a newspaper advert for a job in York that had caught her fancy, and another at the new exchange in Holborn. She'd been tempted – a fresh start in pastures new. But the lure of the big city had quickly faded and she'd settled for something closer to home.

'No, not me,' she confessed. 'Agnes is the one who's leaving to start a new job in Leeds and I'm promoted to take her place. That leaves the switchboard vacancy that Clare is aiming to fill.'

Cynthia's jaw dropped another inch. 'You're stepping into Miss Mouse's shoes?'

'Here in George Street,' Millicent confirmed. She buttoned her jacket and straightened her skirt. 'I'm single and fancy free, aren't I? What's to stop me from climbing up the work ladder when I get the chance?'

'You're a dark horse, Millicent Jones.' Norma closed Cynthia's mouth for her by lightly tipping her under the chin then she turned and thrust her face close to Millicent's. 'Are you honestly and truly moving up to supe?'

'I am!' she declared merrily as she shepherded Norma and Cynthia out into the foyer. Sunshine flooded across the marble floor. 'So come on, girls – it's time to take the lights. Chop-chop!'

The Mill Girls of Albion Lane

Jenny Holmes

In Yorkshire, 1931, times are
hard for the Briggs family.
Eldest daughter Lily works her
fingers to the bone at Calvert
Mill to look after her parents
and siblings. Her father is
haunted by the war, her mother
is worn out, and her sisters rely
on her to be the strong one.

Recently Lily's childhood friend,
Harry, seems intent on securing
her affections, with dances at
the Assembly Rooms, trips to the pictures
and gentlemanly romance. But as Harry and Lily
become closer, a run of misfortune brings trouble
knocking for them and for Lily's family.

Lily knows she can rely on her friends and the community
at the mill to rally together and support her – but will Lily
always have to put others' happiness before her own?

The Shop Girls of Chapel Street

Jenny Holmes

Violet Wheeler is down on her luck. Turfed out of her house after a family tragedy and with no other family to turn to, she has to rely on the goodwill of the local community to help her out.

Working at the Chapel Street drapers, amongst the spools of ribbon, skeins of silk and latest thirties fashions, Violet is given a chance to get back on her feet – and an unexpected chance to find love.
It's only when a forgotten piece of jewellery with a mysterious engraving surfaces that Violet starts to wonder if there is more to her family past than she knows, and her future begins to look uncertain . . .

Violet becomes desperate for answers about her family but it could threaten the stable life she's been building.

Can Violet find a happy ending against all odds?

The Midwives of Raglan Road

Jenny Holmes

September, 1936. Newly trained midwife Hazel Price returns to the Yorkshire streets of her childhood, only to find that her modern methods and 'stuck-up' ways bring her into conflict with her family and other formidable residents of Raglan Road.

Determined Hazel battles on, assisting with home deliveries and supporting the local GP. The days are long and hard but Hazel brings knowledge and compassion to the work she loves.

Then tragedy strikes and accusations fly on Raglan Road. Will Hazel's reputation survive? And what of John Moxon, the man she is beginning to fall for – whose side will he take in the war between the old ways and the new?

Jenny Holmes' brilliantly warm and nostalgic new saga is:

The Land Girls at Christmas

'Calling All Women!'

It's 1941 and as the Second World War rages on, girls from all over the country are signing up to the Women's Land Army. Renowned for their camaraderie and spirit, it is these brave women who step in to tirelessly take on the gruelling farm work left behind by the men consigned to fight.

When Yorkshire girl Una – a town girl through and through – joins the cause, she wonders how she'll adapt to country life. Luckily she's quickly taken under the wings of more experienced Land Girls Brenda and Grace. Together they brave the cold outdoors, but as Christmas draws ever near, the girls' resolve is tested as scandals and secrets are revealed, lovers are torn apart, and even patriotic loyalties are called into question . . .

With only a week to go before the festivities a crisis strikes, one which could spell disaster for their community. Can the Land Girls rise above these challenges to ensure that even in the bleakness of wartime, the magic of Christmas remains?

Available for pre-order now. Coming out in paperback and ebook in November 2017.